**Praise for the novels of
#1 *New York Times* bestselling author
Debbie Macomber**

"A sweet holiday treat from Macomber has become an annual staple for many readers."
—*RT Book Reviews*

"A fast, frothy fantasy for those looking to add some romance to their holidays."
—*Publishers Weekly* on *The Snow Bride*

"Macomber paints a vivid picture in this delightful romantic comedy. You'll often find yourself laughing out loud."
—*RT Book Reviews* on *The Snow Bride*

"[*When Christmas Comes*] is a sweetly satisfying, gently humorous story that celebrates the joy and love of the holiday season."
—*Booklist*

"Macomber is a master storyteller."
—*Times Record News*

"Debbie Macomber tells women's stories in a way no one else does."
—*BookPage*

Dear Friend,

It's Christmas again! A time for family and friends. A time for gratitude. Time to focus on—and celebrate—the things that really matter.

I hope to add to your enjoyment of the season with these two Christmas stories. Both are romantic comedies set in Alaska, the state known as "the last frontier."

I visited Alaska some years ago, when I was researching my Midnight Sons novels about a fictional town called Hard Luck. Back then, my husband, Wayne, and I had the opportunity to explore the tundra; at one point we flew over the Arctic Circle in a four-passenger bush plane. It was an experience I'll never forget. I sat crammed in that tiny plane, holding the US mail in my lap as we landed in a tundra community with a population of less than twenty.

Mail-Order Bride is an early traditional romance I wrote about twenty-five years ago (and have since refreshed). It's a romantic comedy that will, I hope, bring a smile to your face.

The Snow Bride, first published in 2003, is another Christmas-in-Alaska story about a mail-order bride (or I guess an email-order bride). But it evolves in a completely different way. The groom's not the man our heroine expects and—well, I won't tell you any more than that!

My goal with these stories is to make you laugh and revel in the festive, happy feeling of the season.

Wishing you a wonderful Christmas!

Debbie Macomber

PS: I love hearing from readers. You can reach me at www.debbiemacomber.com or on Facebook.

DEBBIE MACOMBER

Christmas in Alaska

MIRA®

Recycling programs
for this product may
not exist in your area.

ISBN-13: 978-0-7783-1913-9

Christmas in Alaska

Copyright © 2016 by Harlequin Books S.A.

The publisher acknowledges the copyright holder of the
individual works as follows:

Mail-Order Bride
Copyright © 1987 by Debbie Macomber

The Snow Bride
Copyright © 2003 by Debbie Macomber

For questions and comments about the quality of this book, please contact us at
CustomerService@Harlequin.com.

www.MIRABooks.com

Printed in U.S.A.

Midnight Sons
VOLUME 1
  (*Brides for Brothers* and
  The Marriage Risk)
VOLUME 2
  (*Daddy's Little Helper* and
  Because of the Baby)
VOLUME 3
  (*Falling for Him,
  Ending in Marriage* and
  Midnight Sons and Daughters)

This Matter of Marriage
Montana
Thursdays at Eight
Between Friends
Changing Habits
Married in Seattle
  (*First Comes Marriage* and
  Wanted: Perfect Partner)
Right Next Door
  (*Father's Day* and
  The Courtship of Carol Sommars)
Wyoming Brides
  (*Denim and Diamonds* and
  The Wyoming Kid)
Fairy Tale Weddings
  (*Cindy and the Prince* and
  Some Kind of Wonderful)
The Man You'll Marry
  (*The First Man You Meet* and
  The Man You'll Marry)
Orchard Valley Grooms
  (*Valerie* and *Stephanie*)
Orchard Valley Brides
  (*Norah* and *Lone Star Lovin'*)
The Sooner the Better
An Engagement in Seattle
  (*Groom Wanted* and
  Bride Wanted)
Out of the Rain
  (*Marriage Wanted* and
  Laughter in the Rain)
Learning to Love
  (*Sugar and Spice* and
  Love by Degree)

You…Again
  (*Baby Blessed* and
  Yesterday Once More)
The Unexpected Husband
  (*Jury of His Peers* and
  Any Sunday)
Three Brides, No Groom
Love in Plain Sight
  (*Love 'n' Marriage* and
  Almost an Angel)
I Left My Heart
  (*A Friend or Two* and
  No Competition)
Marriage Between Friends
  (*White Lace and Promises* and
  Friends—And Then Some)
A Man's Heart
  (*The Way to a Man's Heart*
  and *Hasty Wedding*)
North to Alaska
  (*That Wintry Feeling* and
  Borrowed Dreams)
On a Clear Day
  (*Starlight* and
  Promise Me Forever)
To Love and Protect
  (*Shadow Chasing* and
  For All My Tomorrows)
Home in Seattle
  (*The Playboy and the Widow*
  and *Fallen Angel*)
Together Again
  (*The Trouble with Caasi* and
  Reflections of Yesterday)
The Reluctant Groom
  (*All Things Considered*
  and *Almost Paradise*)
A Real Prince
  (*The Bachelor Prince*
  and *Yesterday's Hero*)
Private Paradise
  (in *That Summer Place*)

*Debbie Macomber's
  Cedar Cove Cookbook*
*Debbie Macomber's
  Christmas Cookbook*

CONTENTS

MAIL-ORDER BRIDE

In memory of Ron Cowden and
for his son, Max,
beloved New Zealand friends

Prologue

"I'm so worried about dear Caroline," Ethel Myers murmured thoughtfully, sipping tea from a dainty porcelain cup. Her fingers clutched a delicate lace-trimmed handkerchief and when a droplet of moisture formed in the corner of her eye, she dabbed it gently. "Sister, I do believe the brew is stronger today."

"Yes," Mabel admitted. "But remember what Father said about the brew enhancing one's ability to solve problems."

"And we must do something to help Caroline."

Mabel shook her head sadly. "Perhaps if you and I had married suitable gentlemen all those years ago…"

"Oh, yes, then maybe we'd know how to help that sweet, sweet child." Ethel's faded blue eyes brightened momentarily. "You do remember that George Guettermann once asked for my hand."

"As I recall, Mother was quite impressed with him."

Ethel's shoulders sagged. "But Father was suspicious from the first."

Mabel sighed heavily. "Mr. Guettermann did cut such a dashing figure."

A wistful expression marked Ethel's fragile features. "If only he hadn't already been married."

"The scoundrel!"

"We must learn to forgive him, Sister."

Mabel nodded and lifted the steaming pot of brew. "I was thinking of Caroline's young man. Another cup, Sister?"

"Oh dear, should we?" Ethel's hand flew to her mouth to smother a loud hiccup, and she had the good grace to look embarrassed.

"We *must* find a way to help her."

"Yes," Ethel agreed as Mabel filled her cup to the bright gold rim. "Poor, poor Caroline."

"There was something in his eyes."

"George?"

"No, Sister. Caroline's young man."

"Indeed, there was something about his eyes." Ethel took another sip and lightly patted her chest at the strength of their father's special recipe. "Sister, the brew…"

"We must think!"

"Oh, yes. Think. What can we do for dear Caroline?"

"If only her mother were alive."

"Or grandmother."

"Grandmother?"

"Her great-great-grandmother, perhaps. *She* would know what to do." Ethel smiled. "Do you recall how she frowned on courting? Said it simply wasn't necessary."

"Grandmother would. Asa Myers brought her to Seattle with the other mail-order brides. She and Grandfather knew each other less than twenty-four hours before they were married."

"A courtship wasn't necessary and they were so happy."

"Very happy and very compatible."

"With seven children, they must have agreed quite nicely," Ethel said and giggled delightedly.

"It's such a shame marriages aren't arranged these days," Mabel said, taking another long sip of tea.

"If only we could find Caroline a husband."

"But, Sister…" Mabel was doubtful. For over fifty years they'd been unable to find husbands of their own. So how could they expect to come up with one for their beloved niece?

Ethel's hand shook as she lowered the cup to its saucer. "Sister, Sister! I do believe I have the solution." Her voice quavered with excitement as she reached for the morning paper.

"Yes?"

"Our own Caroline will be a mail-order bride."

Mabel frowned. "But things like that aren't done in this day and age."

Ethel fumbled with the paper until she located the classified section. She folded back the unwieldy page and pointed to the personal column. "Here, read this."

Mabel read the ad aloud, her voice trembling. "Wanted—Wife for thirty-two-year-old Alaskan male. Send picture. Transportation provided." The advertisement included the name Paul Trevor and a box number.

"But Sister, do we dare?"

"We must. Caroline is desperately unhappy."

"And she did have the opportunity to select a husband of her own."

"She chose poorly. The beast left her standing at the altar."

"The scoundrel!"

"We mustn't tell her, of course."

"Oh, no, we can't let her know. Our Caroline would object strenuously."

"Sister, I do believe the brew has helped."

"Indeed! Some more?"

Ethel raised her cup and her older sister automatically refilled it. A smile of satisfaction lifted the edges of her mouth. "Father's recipe was most beneficial."

"It always is, Sister."

"Oh, yes. Yes, indeed."

One

Caroline Myers waited at a Starbucks in the Seattle-Tacoma airport, accompanied by her great-aunts. She could hardly believe she would soon depart the state of Washington for unknown adventures in Alaska.

"Do you have everything, dear?" Mabel asked her for the third time.

"Aunt Ethel, Aunt Mabel, please—I can't allow you to do this."

"Nonsense," Ethel said briskly. "This vacation is our gift to you."

"But Alaska in October?"

"It's lovely, dear heart. I promise."

"Yes, lovely," Ethel agreed, trying to hide a smile. "And we have the nicest surprise waiting for you."

Caroline stared suspiciously at her great-aunts. Something that could only be mischief danced in their sparkling blue eyes. At seventy-nine and eighty, they were her only living relatives in Seattle, and she loved them dearly. Despite their age, she'd always called them simply *aunt*.

"But this trip is too much," she said.

"Nonsense."

"Hurry, dear. Go and check in or you'll miss your plane."

"One question."

Ethel and Mabel exchanged fleeting glances. "Yes?"

"Why the blood tests? I didn't know anything like that was necessary for travel within the United States."

Mabel paused to clear her throat, casting her eyes wildly about the terminal. "It's a new law."

"A gubernatorial decision, I... I believe," Ethel stammered.

"It's such a pity," Mabel said, changing the subject. "We wanted to give you a thermos with Father's special tea to sustain you during the flight, but all these rules..." She shook her head.

"It's probably just as well," Caroline said, doing her utmost to swallow a chuckle. She'd been eighteen when she'd first discovered the potency of her great-grandfather's special recipe.

"We put some sandwiches in that bag, though." Ethel pointed at the duffel the aunts had packed for her. "Plus tea for when you land. And a little something extra."

Caroline smiled her thanks, feeling a bit foolish about dragging food, not to mention the "tea," all the way to Alaska. She wondered if the duffel with its special wares would survive the baggage handlers.

"Do write. And call," Mabel said anxiously.

"Of course. I'll send postcards." Caroline kissed both aunts on the cheek and hugged them gently. Ethel sniffled, and Mabel cast her a look of sisterly displeasure. Caroline grinned. Her two great-aunts had been a constant delight all her life. They were charming,

loving and thoroughly enchanting. They'd done everything they could to cheer her after Larry's defection. The sudden memory of the man she'd loved with such intensity produced a fresh wave of pain that threatened to wash away the pleasure of this moment.

Ethel sniffled again. "We shall miss you dreadfully," she announced, glaring at her sister.

Caroline threw back her head and laughed aloud. "I'm only going to be gone a week." Ethel's and Mabel's eyes avoided hers and Caroline wondered what little game they were playing.

"But a week seems so long."

"You have your ticket?" Mabel asked hurriedly.

"Right here." Caroline patted the side of her purse.

"Remember, a nice young man will be meeting you in Fairbanks."

Caroline nodded. Her aunts had gone over the details of this vacation a minimum of fifty times. "And he's taking me to—"

"Gold River," the great-aunts chimed in, bobbing their heads in unison.

"There I'll be met by—"

"Paul Trevor." Ethel and Mabel shared a silly grin.

"Right, Paul Trevor." Caroline studied her aunts surreptitiously. If she didn't know better, she'd think they had something up their sleeves. For days, the two of them had been acting like giddy teenagers, whispering and giggling. Caroline had objected to this vacation from the first; Alaska in early October wasn't exactly her first choice. She wouldn't have argued nearly as much had they suggested Hawaii, but her aunts had been so insistent on Alaska that Caroline had finally agreed. This was their gift to her in an effort to heal a

broken heart, and she wasn't about to ruin it by being stubborn. She couldn't bear to inform them that it would take a whole lot more than a trip north for her heart to mend.

Caroline hugged her aunts and secured her purse strap over her shoulder, then got up to join the line at the airline counter.

"Do be happy, dear," Ethel said tearfully, pressing her frilly lace handkerchief under her nose.

Mabel's voice seemed strained as she echoed her sister's words and clasped Caroline's free hand. "Happiness, child. Much, much happiness."

Shaking her head at their strange behavior, Caroline checked in, went through Security and dropped off her bags. She got to the departure lounge without much time to spare. Ten minutes later, she entered the long, narrow jetway that led to the Boeing 767. The flight attendant directed her to the business section and, again, Caroline had to wonder how her aunts could possibly afford this trip.

Ethel and Mabel left the airport pleased with themselves yet already missing their beloved niece.

"It's fate, Sister," Mabel said softly.

"Oh, indeed. Paul Trevor chose her over all those other women."

"He sounds like such a good man."

"And so handsome."

"Only he wrote that he has a beard now. Does Caroline like men with beards?"

Ethel shrugged. "I really couldn't say."

"She'll grow to love him."

"Oh, yes. Given time, she'll be very happy with Paul."

"Perhaps she'll be as compatible with him as Grandmother was with Grandfather."

"Seven children. Oh, Sister!" Ethel brought her gloved hands to her rosy cheeks.

Doubts vanished and the two exchanged a brilliant smile.

"We did our best for her," Mabel said happily. "Her mother would've been proud."

"Her great-great-grandmother, too," Ethel said, and as they giggled with pure delight, several onlookers cast curious glances in their direction.

Caroline slept for most of the night flight to Fairbanks. She was exhausted from a hectic week at work. As a nurse for Dr. Kenneth James, an internist, she often put in long days. Dr. James gave her the week off without complaint and then, on Friday afternoon, shook her hand and wished her much happiness. Now that she thought about it, Caroline found his words puzzling. Vacations were about fun. Happiness came from having a satisfactory relationship. Like hers and Larry's… His name drifted into her mind with such ease that Caroline shook her head in an effort to dismiss it.

Straightening in her seat, she opened her eyes. The cabin lights were dimmed, and the only other passenger in business class was asleep. The two attendants were drinking coffee, but when one of them noticed that Caroline was awake, she immediately approached her.

"You missed the meal. Would you care for something to eat now?"

Caroline shook her head. "No, thanks."

The tall brunette responded with a smile and a slight nod and returned to her coffee. Caroline watched as she walked away. Maybe this flight attendant was the type of woman her ex-fiancé should marry, she mused. She'd known from the beginning how completely dissimilar Larry's and her tastes were. Larry liked late, late nights and breakfast in bed, while she was a morning person, eager to begin each new day. Caroline enjoyed the outdoor life—hiking, camping, boating. Larry's idea of roughing it was doing without valet service. She liked cornflakes with chocolate syrup poured over the top and spaghetti for breakfast. Larry preferred formal dinners with nothing more exotic than meat and potatoes. And those were just the superficial differences between them. But they'd loved each other enough to believe they could compromise. *She* had loved *him,* Caroline corrected herself. At the last minute, Larry had buckled under his doubts and had sent his witless brother to contact her an hour before the wedding ceremony. Once again, humiliation engulfed her.

For the first week, Caroline had hidden from the world. Her two beloved aunts had hovered over her constantly, insisting that she eat and sleep, taking her temperature in case she developed what they called the ague. Caroline assumed it must be some kind of fever and allowed them to fret over her. At the time, it would've taken more energy to assure them she was fine than to submit to their tender ministrations.

A month passed and Caroline gradually worked her way out of the heavy depression that had hung over her like a thundercloud. She smiled and laughed, but suspected that her aunts were unconvinced. Every time she was with them, they stuck a thermometer under

her tongue and shook their gray heads with worried frowns.

Larry called her only once to stammer his regrets and to apologize repeatedly. If she hadn't been so much in love with him, she might've been able to accept that he'd probably done them both a favor. Now there were whole hours when she didn't think about him, or hunger for information about him, or long to be held in his arms. Still, the thought of him with another woman was almost more than Caroline could tolerate. In time, however, she would learn to accept that as well.

The disaster with Larry had taught her that she possessed a far stronger constitution than she'd ever believed. She'd been able to hold her head high and return to work a week after the aborted wedding. It hadn't been easy, but she'd done it with a calm maturity that impressed even her. She was going to come out of this a much wiser, more discerning woman. Someday there'd be a man who would love her enough to appreciate her sometimes unconventional ways. When they fell in love, she'd think about marriage again. But not for a long time, Caroline decided—not for a very long time.

As the plane descended into Fairbanks, Caroline gathered her jacket and her purse, preparing to disembark. It was still dark, but dawn was starting to streak the sky. Just as her aunts had promised, there was someone waiting for her at the airport. She had no sooner walked off the plane than a middle-aged man with bushy eyebrows and a walrus mustache held up a piece of cardboard with her name printed across it in bold letters.

"Hello, I'm Caroline Myers," she told him, shifting her purse from one hand to the other.

"Welcome to Alaska," he said with a wide grin and offered his hand. "Name's John Morrison."

Caroline shook it. She liked him immediately. "Thank you, John."

The man continued to stare at her and rubbed the side of his square jaw. Slowly, he shook his head and a sly grin raised the edges of his mouth. "Paul did all right for himself," he mumbled.

"Pardon?"

"Ah, nothing," John responded, shaking his head again. "I'm just surprised is all. I didn't expect him to come up with anyone half as attractive as you. I don't suppose you have a friend?"

Caroline hadn't the faintest idea what this burly bush pilot was getting at, or why he'd be curious about her friends. Surely he'd flown more than one woman into the Alaskan interior. She was like any other tourist visiting Alaska for a one-week stay. She planned to get plenty of rest and relaxation on the direct orders of her aunts. In addition, she hoped to take invigorating walks and explore the magic of the tundra. Her aunts had mentioned Paul Trevor's name on several occasions and Caroline assumed they'd hired him as her guide. She wouldn't mind having someone show her the countryside. There was so much to see and do, and Caroline was ready for it all.

Once John had collected her suitcase, plus the duffel bag her aunts had so determinedly packed, he escorted Caroline to the single-engine Cessna and helped her climb aboard.

"Won't be long now," he said, placing the earphones over his head and flipping several switches. As he zipped up his fur-lined coat, he glanced in her direc-

tion with a frown. Then the control tower issued instructions and John turned his attention to the radio. Once on the runway, the plane accelerated and was soon aiming for the dawn sky in a burst of power that had Caroline clenching her hands. She was accustomed to flying, but not in anything quite this small. In comparison to the wide-bodied jet, this Cessna seemed tiny and fragile.

"You might want to look in some of those boxes back there." He jerked his head toward the large pile of sacks and cardboard boxes resting next to her suitcase at the rear of the plane.

"Uh, what should I be looking for?"

"A coat. It's going to get damn cold up here. That little jacket's never gonna be warm enough."

"Okay." Caroline unfastened the seat belt and turned around to bend over the back of her seat. She sorted through the sacks and found a variety of long underwear and flannel shirts.

"Paul's right about you needing this. I hope the boots fit. I got the best available."

"Boots?"

"Lady, trust me. You're going to need them."

"I imagine they were expensive." She had her credit cards with her, but if Paul Trevor expected her to pick up the tab on a complete winter wardrobe, then he had another think coming.

Caroline pulled out a thick coat, but it was so bulky that she placed it over her knees. She took off her jacket and slipped her arms into a cozy flannel shirt. She'd put on the coat when they landed.

"What did you bring with you?" John asked, eyeing the duffel bag at Caroline's feet.

She rolled her eyes. "My aunts sent along some food."

John chuckled.

Now that she'd mentioned it, Caroline discovered she was hungry. It'd been hours since she'd last eaten, and her stomach growled as she opened the bag to find half a dozen thick sandwiches and—the promised thermos. There was also a brightly wrapped gift. Somewhat surprised, Caroline removed the package and tore off the bright paper and ribbon. The sheer negligee with the neckline and sleeves trimmed in faux fur baffled her even more.

John saw her blink and laughed loudly. "I see they included something to keep your neck warm."

Caroline found his humor less than amusing and stuffed the gown back inside the bag. She'd never thought of her aunts as senile, but their recent behavior gave her cause to wonder.

She shared a turkey sandwich with John and listened as he spoke at length about Alaska. His love for this last frontier was apparent in every sentence. His comments included a vivid description of the tundra and its varied wildlife.

"I have a feeling you're going to like it here."

"Well, I like what little I've seen," Caroline said. She'd expected the land to be barren and harsh. It was, but there was a majestic beauty about it that made Caroline catch her breath.

"That's Denali over there," John told her. "She's the highest peak in North America."

"I thought McKinley was."

"Folks around here prefer to call her Denali."

"What's that?" Caroline pointed to the thin silver

ribbon that stretched across the rugged countryside below.

"The Yukon River. She flows over two thousand miles from northwest Canada to the Bering Sea."

"Wow."

"Anything you'd like to know about Paul?"

"Paul Trevor? Not really. Is there anything I *should* know?" Like her aunts, John seemed to bring up the other man's name at every opportunity.

He gave another merry chuckle. "Guess you'll be finding out about him soon enough."

"Right." She eyed him curiously. She was anxious to get a look at this man who insisted she have all this costly gear.

"He's a quiet guy. Hope you don't mind that."

"I usually chatter enough for two. I think we'll get along fine. Besides, I don't plan on being here that long."

John frowned. "I doubt you'll ever get Paul to leave Alaska."

Caroline was offended by the brusque tone. "I don't have any intention of trying."

The amusement faded from John's rugged face as he checked the instruments on the front panel. "You aren't afraid of flying, are you?"

She hadn't thought about it much until now. "Afraid? Why should I be afraid?"

"Looks like we may be headed into a storm. Nothing to worry about, but this could be a real roller-coaster for a while."

"I'll be fine." The sudden chill in the cabin caused Caroline to reach for the thermos. "My aunts make a mean cup of tea. Interested?"

"No, thanks." He focused on the gauges. Caroline refastened her seat belt, fingers trembling.

The first cup of spiked tea brought a rush of warmth to her chilled arms, and when the plane pitched and heaved, she carefully refilled the plastic cup and gulped down a second. "Hey, this is fun," she said with a tiny laugh twenty minutes later. If the truth be known, she was frightened out of her wits, but she put on a brave front and held on to her drink with both hands. Her aunts' tea was courage in a cup.

By the time John announced that they were within a half hour of Gold River, Caroline felt as warm as toast. As they made their descent, she peeked out the window at the uneven row of houses. A blanket of snow covered the ground and curling rings of smoke rose from a dozen chimneys.

"It's not much of a town, is it?" she murmured.

"Around three hundred. Mostly Athabascans— they're Indians who were once nomadic, following caribou and other game. When the white settlers arrived, they established permanent villages. Nowadays, they mostly hunt and fish. Once we get a bit closer you'll see a string of caribou hides drying in the sun."

"How...interesting." Caroline had no idea how else to respond.

"What does Paul do?" she asked a few minutes later.

John gave her a curious stare. "Don't you know? He works for the oil company. Keeps tabs on the pump station for the pipeline."

She brushed aside the blond curl that fell over her face. "I thought he was a guide of some sort."

As the Cessna circled the village, Caroline saw people scurrying out of the houses. Several raised their

arms high above their heads and waved. "They see us," she said.

"They've probably spent days preparing for your arrival."

"How thoughtful." The village must only entertain a handful of tourists a year, she figured, and residents obviously went to a great deal of trouble to make sure that those who did come felt welcome. Caroline rubbed her eyes. The whole world seemed to be whirling. The people and houses blurred together and she shook her head, hoping to regain her bearings. The thermos was empty; Caroline realized she was more than a little intoxicated.

A glance at the darkening clouds produced a loud grumble from John. "Doesn't look like I'm going to be able to stick around for the reception."

"I'm sorry." John was probably a local hero. This welcoming party was likely as much in his honor as hers. It appeared that the entire village was outside now, with everyone pointing toward the sky and waving enthusiastically. "I don't see a runway."

"There isn't one."

"But…"

"There's enough of a clearing to make a decent landing. I've come down in a lot worse conditions."

Caroline's nails cut into her palm. She didn't find his words all that reassuring. Why her aunts would choose such a remote village for her vacation was beyond her. This whole trip was turning into much more of an adventure than she'd ever dreamed—or wanted.

As the plane descended, she closed her eyes until she felt the wheels bounce on the uneven ground. She was jostled, jolted and jarred, but otherwise unscathed.

Once they came to a complete stop, Caroline could breathe again.

The single engine continued to purr as John unhooked his seat belt. "Go ahead and climb out. I'll hand you the gear."

Using her shoulder to push open the airplane door, Caroline nearly fell to the snow, despite her effort to climb down gracefully. A gust of wind sobered her instantly. "It's cold!"

"Yeah, but Paul will warm you," John shouted over the engine's noise. He tossed out her suitcase and a large variety of boxes and sacks. "Good luck to you. I have a feeling you're the best thing to happen to Paul in a long time."

"Thanks." She stood in the middle of the supplies and blinked twice. "Aren't you coming with me?"

"Can't. I've got to get out of here before this storm hits." He shut the door and a minute later was taxiing away.

With a sense of disbelief, Caroline watched him leave. Already she could see several snowmobiles and a team of dogs pulling a large sled racing toward her. She waved on the off chance they couldn't see her. Again the earth seemed to shift beneath her feet, and she rubbed her eyes in an effort to maintain her balance. Good grief, just how much of that tea had she drunk?

By the time the first dogsled arrived, she'd mustered a smile. "Hello," she greeted, raising her hand, praying no one would guess she was more than a little tipsy.

"Welcome."

The man, who must be Paul Trevor, walked toward her and handed her a small bouquet of flowers. He was tall and dark, and from what she could see of his

bearded face, reasonably attractive. Untamed curls fell with rakish disregard across a wide, intelligent brow. His eyes, as blue as her own, gazed at her critically. She'd taken to John Morrison immediately, but Caroline wasn't sure she'd like this man. John had spoken of him with respect, and it was obvious that he was considered a leader among the villagers. But his intensity unnerved her. Caroline wasn't about to let him intimidate her; however, now wasn't the time to say much of anything. Not when her tongue refused to cooperate with her brain.

"Thank you." Caroline closed her eyes as she smelled the flowers, expecting the sweet scent of spring, only to have her nose tickled by the prickly needles. She gave a startled gasp and her eyes flew open.

"They've been dried."

"Oh." She felt like a fool. There weren't any flowers in Alaska this time of year. "Of course—they must be."

"Everything's ready if you are."

"Sure." Caroline assumed he was speaking of the welcoming reception.

The large group of people quickly loaded her suitcase and the other boxes onto several sleds. Caroline took a step toward Paul and nearly stumbled. Again the ground pitched under her feet. She recognized it as the potency of the tea and not an earthquake, but for a moment she was confused. "I'm sorry," she murmured. "I seem to be a bit unsteady."

Paul guided her to the dogsled. "It might be better if you sat." He pulled back a heavy blanket and helped her into the sled. A huge husky, clearly the lead dog, turned his head to examine her and Caroline grinned sheepishly. "I don't weigh much," she told him and gig-

gled. Then she groaned. She was beginning to sound like her aunts.

The trip into Gold River took only minutes. Paul helped her out of the sled and led her into the long narrow building in the center of the village. Candles flickered all around the room. Tables filled with a variety of dishes lined the walls. A priest, Russian Orthodox, Caroline guessed, wore a long gold robe. He smiled at her warmly and stepped forward to greet her, taking her hand in his.

"Welcome to Gold River. I'm Father Nabokov."

"I'm pleased to meet you, Father." Caroline prayed that he didn't smell her aunts' brew on her breath.

"Are you hungry?" Paul had shed his thick coat and she removed hers, passing it to him. The force of his personality was revealed in his stance. On meeting him, Caroline understood why both John and her two aunts had found occasion to mention Paul. His personality was strong, but there was a gentleness as well, a tenderness he preferred to disguise with the sense of remoteness she'd noticed earlier.

"Hungry? No...not really," she replied tentatively, realizing that she was staring at him. Paul didn't seem to mind. For that matter, he appeared to be sizing her up as well, and judging by the lazy, sensual smile that moved from his mouth to his eyes, he seemed to like what he saw.

If only Caroline could have cleared her mind, she felt she might've been able to strike up a witty conversation, but her thoughts were preoccupied with the murmuring around her. It looked as though the entire village was crammed inside the meeting hall. Someone was playing music, but it wasn't on an instrument Car-

oline recognized. A fiddle player joined the first man and the festive mood spread until everyone was laughing and singing. Several helped themselves to plates and heaped food on them from the serving dishes.

"Perhaps it would be best if we started things now," Father Nabokov suggested. "It doesn't look like we'll be able to hold things up much longer."

"Do you mind?" Paul glanced at Caroline.

"Not in the least. Why wait?" Nearly everyone was eating and drinking as it was, and she could see no reason to delay the party. Someone brought her a glass of champagne and Caroline drank it down in one big swallow. The room was warm and she was so thirsty. The hardest part was keeping her eyes open; her lids felt exceptionally heavy and, without much effort, she could have crawled into bed and slept for a month.

Paul raised his hand and the music stopped, followed by instant silence. The townspeople shuffled forward, forming a large circle around Paul, Caroline and the priest.

Caroline smiled and closed her eyes, awaiting the announcement that was obviously forthcoming. She felt so relaxed. These wonderful, wonderful people were holding some kind of ceremony to welcome her. If only she could stay awake...

Father Nabokov began speaking in a soft, reverent voice. The smell of incense filled the air. She made an honest effort to listen, but the priest's words were low and monotonous. The others in the room seemed to give heed to his message, whatever it was, and Caroline glanced around, smiling now and then.

"Caroline?" Paul's voice cut into her musings.

"Hmm." She realized the meeting hall was quiet,

each face regarding her expectantly as though waiting for a response. Paul slipped an arm around her waist, pulling her closer to his side.

"Would you like him to repeat the question?" Paul asked, studying her with a thoughtful frown.

"Yes, please," Caroline said quietly. If she knew what these people expected of her, then maybe she could reply. "What did he say?"

"He's asking if you'll honor and cherish me."

Two

"Honor and cherish?" Caroline repeated, stunned. This reception was more than she could grasp. How she wished she hadn't had quite so much of her aunts' brew. Obviously this little get-together in her honor was some kind of elaborate charade—one in which Caroline had no intention of participating.

The circle of faces stared anxiously, growing more and more distressed at the length of time it took her to respond to the question.

"Caroline?" Even Paul's gruff voice revealed his uneasiness.

Caroline opened her mouth to tell them that if they were going to play silly tricks on her, she didn't want anything to do with this party. She looked at Paul and blinked. "I thought you were supposed to be my guide." Apparently folks took the guiding business seriously in these parts.

Father Nabokov smiled gently. "He will guide you throughout your life, my child."

A clatter rose from the crowd as several people started arguing loudly. Father Nabokov raised his arms

above his head and waved. "Miss Myers." He paused to wipe his brow with a clean kerchief that magically appeared from inside his huge sleeve. "This is an important decision. Would you like me to ask the question again?"

Paul's intense blue eyes cleared as his gaze pinned hers, demanding that she answer the priest.

An older man, an Athabascan who was apparently a good friend of Paul's, interceded. "You can't back down now—you already agreed."

"I did?" What had her aunts gotten her into? The other guests continued to glare at her and Caroline felt unsettled by the resentment she saw in their eyes. "Could I have something cold to drink?"

"It's a bit unusual," Father Nabokov said, frowning. For the second time, he reached for the kerchief and rubbed it over his forehead.

"Walter," Paul called to the older man, who immediately stepped forward.

A minute later, he approached them with a glass of champagne, which Paul handed to Caroline. She hurriedly emptied it and sighed audibly as the bubbles tickled the back of her throat. She returned her glass to the man Paul had called Walter and smiled. "This is excellent champagne."

Walter nodded abruptly and glanced in Paul's direction. "Paul wanted the best for you."

Feeling uneasy, Caroline noted the censure in the old man's voice. "What was it you wanted me to say again?"

Paul's posture stiffened as he expelled an impatient sigh. "*Yes* would suffice."

"All right then," she agreed in an attempt to be as

amicable as possible. Everyone had gone to so much trouble on her behalf, cooking and planning this reception for her arrival. She hated to disappoint them, although she wondered if all tourists were graced with this kind of party—the priest, the champagne, not to mention the presence of the entire village. Her adorable aunts had sent her to the one place in the world where she'd be welcomed with an ardor befitting royalty.

"You do?" Father Nabokov looked greatly relieved.

"Sure," she concurred brightly, shrugging her shoulders. "Why not?"

"Indeed." The priest grinned, then turned to Paul. His eyes glowed as he gazed upon them both. Caroline felt Paul slide his arm around her once again, but she didn't object. She attempted to give the priest her full attention, but the room was so warm.... She fanned her face and with some difficulty kept a stiff smile on her lips.

Paul took her hand and slipped a simple gold band on her ring finger. It looked like a friendship ring and Caroline thought it a lovely gesture.

"I now pronounce you husband and wife," Father Nabokov proclaimed solemnly. He raised his right hand, blessing them both. "You may kiss the bride."

Wife! Kiss the bride! Caroline was completely shocked. She tried to smile, but couldn't. "What's he talking about?" she muttered.

Paul didn't answer. Instead, he turned her in his arms and his eyes narrowed longingly on her mouth. Before she could voice her questions and uncertainties, he lowered his head. Caroline's heart thundered nervously and she placed her hands on his chest, gazing up at his bearded face. Surely he could tell how

confused she was. A wedding ceremony! She must be dreaming. That was it—this was all a dream. Paul's blue eyes softened. Gradually, as though in slow motion, his mouth settled warmly over hers. His touch was firm and experienced, moist and gentle—ever so gentle. *Nice dream,* Caroline mused, *very nice, very real.* She hadn't expected a man of his size to be so tender.

Enjoy it, girl, she thought, kissing him back. Dreams ended far too quickly. The world began to spin, so she slipped her arms around Paul's neck to help maintain her balance. Bringing her body closer to his was all the encouragement he needed. His hands slid over her hips, pressing her body invitingly against his own. Caroline surrendered willingly to the sensual upheaval. Ever since Larry had left her at the altar, she'd been dying to be held in a man's arms, dying to be kissed as if there was no moment but this one.

Father Nabokov cleared his throat, but Caroline paid no heed to the priest's disapproval. She might have had her doubts about Paul, but she had to admit he was one great kisser. Breathless, they broke apart, still staring at each other, lost in the wonder of their overwhelming response.

Paul draped his wrists over Caroline's shoulders. A slightly cynical smile touched his mouth. "For a minute there, I didn't think you were going through with it."

"Is this a dream?" Caroline asked.

Paul gave her a funny look. "No."

She laughed. "Of course you'd say that."

His eyes were as blue as anything Caroline had ever seen and she felt as though she was drowning in their depths. She managed a tremulous smile, her mouth still

on fire from his kiss. Involuntarily, she moistened her lips and watched as his eyes darkened.

"Let's get out of here," he growled. Without another word, he hauled Caroline into his arms and stalked toward the door.

Caroline gasped at the unexpectedness of the action, but the villagers went crazy, resuming their dancing and singing. "Where...where are we going?"

"The cabin."

"Oh."

By now his lengthy strides had carried him halfway across the floor. The guests cleared a path and Walter stood ready, grinning boyishly as he opened the large wooden doors. Walter chuckled as Paul moved past him. "Don't be so impatient. You've waited this long."

Paul said something under his breath that Caroline couldn't understand and continued walking.

"How far is the cabin?" she asked.

"Too far," Paul said with a throaty chuckle. Her response to his kiss had jolted him. He'd thought he should progress to their lovemaking with less urgency—court her, let her become acquainted with him first. Yet the moment her mouth had opened to his, he'd realized there wasn't any reason to wait.

Leaning back in his arms, Caroline sighed wistfully. "Why is it dark?"

"It's October, love."

"Love?" she repeated, and sudden tears sprang to her eyes. She hadn't expected to be anyone's love—not after Larry—not for a very long time.

Paul went still. He could deal with anything but tears. "What's wrong?"

"Nothing," she murmured, sniffling. She should

know not to drink champagne—especially after her aunts' special tea. Champagne always led to tears.

"Tell me." He smoothed the hair from her temple and softly kissed her there.

If he hadn't been so gentle, Caroline could have fought the unwelcome emotion. As she felt hot tears sear a path down her flushed face, she bit the corner of her bottom lip. "He left me," she whispered.

"Who?"

"Larry." She turned abruptly, wrapping her arms around Paul's neck, and sobbed into his shoulder. She wouldn't have believed she had any more tears, but her aunts' tea and the champagne had weakened her resolve to put Larry from her mind.

"You loved him?"

She nodded. "Sometimes I wonder if I'll ever stop."

The words stabbed his heart with the brutality of an ice pick. He'd known, or at least he should have known, that a woman like Caroline Myers wouldn't have agreed to marry him and live in the Alaskan wilderness without a good reason. Her letter had been so brief, so polite, unlike the others who'd tried to impress him with their wit and entice him with the promise of sexual fulfillment.

To his utter amazement, the response to his brief advertisement had been overwhelming. Dozens of letters had poured in that first week, but he hadn't bothered to read any once he'd opened Caroline's. Her picture had stopped him cold. The wheat-blond hair, the blue eyes that had spoken to him as clearly as the words of her letter. She was honest and forthright, sensual and provocative, mature and trusting. Her picture told him that, and it was confirmed by her letter. The next day

he'd sent her the airplane ticket and for the past two weeks had waited in eager anticipation.

"In time, you'll learn not to love Larry," he said, kissing her temple again.

With her arms around his neck, Caroline nestled her head against his chest. "I don't know why I told you about Larry. I don't want to think about him anymore. I really don't, but he's there in my thoughts every minute."

"I'll chase him away," Paul teased.

"But how?"

"I'll find a way."

Silently they approached a log cabin and Caroline smiled at how quaint it looked with a huge set of moose antlers above the wooden door. A stepladder leaned to the right of the only window and there was a woodpile that reached up to the eaves beside it. An oblong, galvanized steel tub hung to the left of the door, along with a pair of snowshoes.

"It's so homey. You must love it here," Caroline said as she saw the soft light in the lone window.

"I do."

"I'm sure I'll like it." She sighed deeply. She wasn't dreaming, after all—or at least not anymore.

Paul bent awkwardly to turn the door handle. The warmth that greeted them immediately made Caroline feel that this tiny cabin was the perfect place for her vacation. "It's adorable," she said, looking around.

Without question, the cabin was small—so compact that the living area and kitchen were one room. Bookcases stood beside a large potbelly stove, and a kitchen counter lined the opposite wall. A doorway led

to another room that Caroline assumed would be her bedroom. Everything was spotlessly clean.

Reluctantly, Paul released her from his arms. Her feet touched the floor and she stepped back. She barely knew the man, yet she'd spilled her deepest secrets to him as though he was a lifelong friend. "Are...are you staying?"

"Would it embarrass you?"

She blinked twice. Once again they were having a conversation she didn't quite comprehend. It had to be the alcohol. Caroline shook her head to clear her muddled thoughts. "If you don't mind, I'd like to go to bed."

One side of Paul's mouth edged upward. "I was hoping you'd suggest that. Would you feel more comfortable if I left?"

"Perhaps that would be best. I have lots of questions for you, but I'm too sleepy now. We'll talk in the morning, okay?" She took a step toward the doorway and her peripheral vision picked up the sight of the silky nightgown that had been a gift from her aunts. It was spread out across the large brass bed.

"I'll give you some time alone then," Paul said, heading for the door.

It closed after him and Caroline stood in the middle of the cabin, puzzled by the events of the day. She'd traveled thousands of miles and participated in some strange Alaskan ceremony. For a while she'd thought she was dreaming, but now realized she definitely wasn't. That meant she'd actually kissed a man whose name she hardly knew and then wept in his arms.

Moving into the single bedroom, undressing as she went, Caroline paused to admire the thick, brightly colored handmade quilt. The small lamp on the table illu-

minated the room and Caroline recognized her clothes hanging in an open closet beside those belonging to a man. She assumed they were Paul's. He was a gentleman, letting her use his cabin for the week and going somewhere else to sleep without complaint.

Caroline had a hazy memory of the word *wife* and wondered what *that* craziness was all about; she'd figure it out in the morning. She might even be married. A giggle escaped her as she sat on the edge of the bed. Married! Wouldn't Larry love that. Well, if she was, Paul would understand that there'd been a mistake. Her initial impression of him had been wrong. He'd intimidated her at first, but he was gentle and considerate. She'd witnessed that quality in him more than once in the past hour.

Her clothes fell to the floor as she stripped. With complete disregard, she kicked them under the bed. She'd pick them up in the morning, since she was too tired to do it now.

The sheer gown slid over her outstretched arms and down her body. The faux fur tickled her calves and Caroline smiled, recalling John's comment about how it would keep her warm. Alaskan men obviously had a sense of humor, although she hadn't been too amused at the time.

The gown *did* look like part of a wedding trousseau. Wedding? Married? She couldn't be… When she woke, they'd straighten everything out.

The bed looked soft and warm, and Caroline crawled between the sheets. Her head was cushioned by a feather pillow and her last thought before she flipped off the lamp was of the mountain she'd seen

from the plane—Denali. Somehow its magnificence comforted her and lured her into sleep.

Outside, Paul paced in front of the cabin, glancing at his watch every twenty seconds. He was cold and impatient. With the music from the reception echoing around him, he refused to return to the meeting hall. Caroline had wanted some time to prepare herself and he'd reluctantly granted her that, but he wasn't pleased. Eventually she'd learn to be less shy; there wouldn't be room for modesty when winter arrived.

Once he was sure she'd had as much time as any woman would possibly require, Paul went back into the cabin. The bedroom light was off and he could see the outline of her figure in the bed. His bed. Waiting for him. He recalled the way her body had felt against his. With vivid clarity he remembered how she'd looked at him, her blue eyes huge, when she'd suggested going to bed. Then she'd asked him if she was dreaming. The woman was drunk—drunk on her wedding night. From the day he'd received her letter, Paul had decided to wait for the rewards of marriage. Yes, he'd wait until she was ready. But, oh boy—that kiss. For a moment he'd thought she was as eager as he. He wanted their lovemaking to be slow and easy, but hadn't anticipated her effect on him. The restraint he needed not to rush to her side made him feel weak. The taste of her lips lingered on his own and left him craving more. He took a deep breath and leaned against the counter.

Hoping to gain some perspective, Paul took down the bottle of Jack Daniel's from the cupboard and poured a stiff drink. He had to think things through. He suspected she didn't believe their marriage was real, yet she had to know he'd brought her all this way for

exactly that purpose. During the wedding she'd looked so confused and unsure. As her husband, he expected to claim his marital rights—only he preferred to wait until she was sober. He wanted a wife and had made that evident in his letter. This was to be a real marriage in every way, and she'd come to him on his terms. Yet he couldn't help feeling nervous.

He sat at the table and gulped down the drink, hoping to feel its numbing effect—fast. But if anything, imagining Caroline in his bed, dressed in that see-through silk gown, had the *opposite* effect on him. He'd hoped to cool his passion with sound reasoning and good whiskey, but had ended up fanning the flames.

Standing, Paul took his empty glass to the sink and saw that his hands were trembling. He felt like a coiled spring, tense, ready. Oh, yes, he was ready.

He moved into the bedroom and undressed in the dark, taking time to fold each piece of clothing and set it on the dresser. For a moment he toyed with the idea of sleeping at Walter Thundercloud's place, but quickly rejected the thought. He'd be the laughingstock of the entire community if he spent the night anywhere but with Caroline.

She was asleep, he realized from the evenness of her breathing. He was grateful for that. Much as he wanted her, he felt certain *she* wasn't ready and he needed to respect that.

The mattress dipped as he carefully slid in beside her. She sighed once and automatically rolled into his arms, nestling her head against his chest. Paul's eyes widened with the force of his resolve.

She stroked her fingertips over his lean ribs. He swallowed convulsively against the sweet torture of her

touch and strengthened his self-possession by gently removing her hands. He wished she could appreciate what he was giving up....

"Love," he whispered in her ear. "Roll onto your side, okay?"

"Hmm?" Caroline was having the sweetest dream. And this time, she felt sure it really *was* a dream.

"I know you'd prefer to wait." Paul found it ironic that he was telling her this; she'd come so willingly into his arms.

"Wait?"

"Never mind," he whispered. "Just go back to sleep." Unable to resist, he kissed her forehead and shifted away from her.

Unexpectedly, the comforting, irresistible warmth beside her moved and Caroline edged closer to it. With a sigh of longing, she buried her face in the hollow of his neck.

"Caroline, please, this is difficult enough," he whispered, inhaling harshly. She flattened her hand against his abdomen and slowly brushed her lips over his.

With every muscle, Paul struggled for control. Seconds later, he was lost—irrevocably and completely lost. Their kiss was unlike any he'd ever experienced.... But Paul was the one to break contact, twisting so that he lay on his back. His control, such as it was, seemed to be slipping fast; another minute and he wouldn't have been able to stop.

Caroline felt unbearably hot, as if she was sitting directly in front of a fireplace. The thought was so illogical—she was in bed, wasn't she?—that she bolted upright, giggling, and tossed the blankets aside. She fell back onto the pillow and raised her hands above her

head, intertwining her fingers. The ceiling was spinning around and around. In an effort to block out the dizzying sight, she closed her eyes and sought anew the security of the dream.

Again Paul tried to move away from her but Caroline wanted him close. She couldn't understand why he kept leaving her. If he was part of her dream, the least he could do was stick around! She reached for him, locking her arms around his neck, kissing him.

"Caroline, stop it!"

"Why?"

"Because you're drunk," he hissed.

She giggled. "I know." Her fingers roamed over his shoulders. "Please kiss me again. Has anyone ever told you that you're a great kisser?"

"I can't kiss you." *And remain sane,* he added silently.

"But I *want* you to." She sounded like a whiny child and that shocked her. "Oh, never mind, I wouldn't kiss me either." With that she let out a noisy yawn and rested her cheek against his chest. "You have nice skin," she murmured before closing her eyes.

"You do, too," he whispered, and slid his hand down the length of her spine. "Very nice."

"Are you sure you don't want to kiss me?"

Paul groaned. His nobility had limitations, and he wasn't going to be able to hold off much longer if she asked him to kiss her every ten seconds.

"Good night, love," he whispered, hoping his voice had the ring of finality. He kissed the crown of her head and continued to hold her close, almost savoring the sweet torture.

Caroline smiled, content. Just before she gave in

to the irrepressible urge to sleep, she felt his kiss, and prayed that all her dreams would be this real and this exciting.

Snuggling closer to the warm body at her side, Caroline woke slowly. Her first conscious thought was that her head ached. It more than ached; it throbbed with each pulse and every sluggish heartbeat as her memory returned, muddled and confused. She rolled onto her back, holding the sides of her head, and groaned aloud. She was in bed with a man she barely knew. Unfortunately, he appeared to be well acquainted with her. Extremely well acquainted. Her first inclination was to kick him out of the bed. He'd taken advantage of her inebriated state, and she bit back bitter words as a flush of embarrassment burned her cheeks.

Opening her eyes was an impossible task. She couldn't face the man.

"Good morning," the deep male voice purred.

"It…wasn't a dream, was it?" she asked in a tone that was faint and apprehensive.

Paul chuckled. "You mean you honestly don't remember anything?"

"Some." She kept her eyes pinched shut, too mortified to look at him.

"Do you remember the part about us getting married?"

Caroline blinked. "I'm not sure."

"In case you don't, I suppose I should introduce myself. I'm Paul Trevor, your husband."

Three

"Then it *was* real!" Still holding her head, Caroline struggled to a sitting position. Gradually her eyes opened and she glared down at the bearded man beside her.

Paul was lying on his side, watching her with an amused grin. He rose up on his elbow and shook his head. "I can't believe you didn't expect to be married."

She felt as though the heat in her face was enough to keep the cabin warm all winter. "I knew at the time you…you weren't completely a dream." She had to be honest, even at the expense of her stubborn pride.

"We're married, love."

"Stop calling me your love! I am not your love, or any other man's. And we've certainly got to do something about annulling this…this marriage." She winced at the flash of pain that shot through her head.

"If you'd rather I didn't call you love, I won't."

"Call me Caroline or Ms. Myers, anything but your love."

"I *am* your husband."

"Will you stop saying that?"

"I have the paperwork to prove it."

Caroline tucked the blankets under her arms and scowled at him with all the fury she could muster. "Then I challenge you to produce them."

"As you wish." He threw aside the blankets and climbed out of bed, standing only partially clothed before her.

Caroline looked away. "I would really appreciate it if you'd put something on."

"Why?" He sent a questioning glance over his shoulder.

The red flush seeped down to her neck and she swallowed convulsively. "Just do it…. Please."

Chuckling again, Paul withdrew a slip of paper from his shirt pocket. "Here," he said, handing it to her.

Caroline grabbed it and quickly unfolded it, then scanned the contents. The document looked official and her name was signed at the bottom, although she barely recognized the signature as her own. Vaguely she remembered Paul having her sign some papers when they'd entered the meeting hall. She'd been so bemused she'd thought it had to do with registering a guest.

"I signed first," Paul explained, "and gave you the pen."

"Yes…but at the time I assumed it was something all tourists did." It sounded so ridiculous now that she wanted to weep at her own stupidity. "The party yesterday was our wedding reception, wasn't it?"

"Yes."

Caroline shook her head. "I… I thought Gold River got so few tourists that they greeted everyone like that."

"Caroline, you're not making any sense."

"*I'm* not?" she shouted, then winced. "You should look at it from my point of view."

"But you agreed to marry me weeks ago."

"I most certainly did not!"

"I have the letter."

"Now that I'd like to see. I may not have been in full control of my wits yesterday, but I know for a fact I'd never heard of you until…" The words died on her lips. "My aunts—my romantic, idealistic, scheming aunts…they couldn't have. They wouldn't…"

Paul regarded her suspiciously. "What aunts?"

"Mine. Just get the letter and p-please…" she stammered, "please put something on. This is all extremely embarrassing."

Grumbling under his breath, Paul reached for his pants and pulled them on, snapping them at the waist. Next he unfolded his shirt and slipped his arms inside the long sleeves, but he left it unbuttoned. "There. Are you satisfied?"

"Somewhat." Speaking of clothes reminded Caroline of her own skimpy state of dress. When Paul's back was turned, she scurried to the very edge of the mattress in a frantic search for her cords and sweater. She remembered undressing, but she couldn't recall where she'd put her things.

Stretching down as far as possible, Caroline made a wide sweep under the bed and managed to retrieve her sweater. Fearing Paul would be back at any minute, she slid her arms into the bulky sleeves and yanked it over her head. As she shook her hair free of the confining collar, Caroline came eye to eye with Paul.

He stood over her, his grin slightly off center. "Just give me that letter," Caroline demanded.

"Would you like me to read it to you?"

"No." She grabbed for it, but he held it just out of her reach. "I don't appreciate these sophomoric games, Paul Trevor."

"Go ahead and read it for yourself while I fix us something to eat."

"I'm not hungry," she announced sharply, jerking the envelope from his hand. Food was the last thing on her mind.

Humming as though he didn't have a care in the world, Paul left the bedroom while Caroline's eyes narrowed on his back. How dare he act so…so unruffled by this unexpected turn of events.

The instant Paul was out of sight, Caroline tore into the letter. The creases were well worn and with a mild attack of guilt she realized he must have read the neatly typed page repeatedly.

Dear Paul,
My name is Caroline Myers and I'm responding to your advertisement in the *Seattle Post-Intelligencer.* I am seeking a husband to love. My picture is enclosed, but I'm actually more attractive in person. That isn't to say, however, that I'm the least bit vain. I enjoy fishing and hiking and Scrabble and other games of skill. Since I am the last of the Ezra Myers family left in the Northwest, I am interested in having children. I'm a nurse currently employed by Dr. Kenneth James, but can leave my employment on two weeks' notice. I look forward to hearing from you.
Most sincerely,

The evenly shaped letters of her name were penned at the bottom of the page in what Caroline recognized as her aunt Mabel's handwriting.

With sober thoughts, Caroline dressed, then joined Paul in the kitchen. He pulled out a chair and handed her a cup of coffee.

She laid the letter on the table. "I didn't write this."

"I figured that might've been the case."

Her face flushed, she wondered just what had happened after the ceremony. Surely she'd remember something as important as that. "I have these two elderly aunts...." Caroline hedged, not knowing where exactly to start her explanation.

"So I gathered." He pulled out the chair across from her and placed his elbows on the table. "They answered my advertisement?"

"Apparently so."

"How'd they convince you to marry me?"

"That's just it.... They didn't." Caroline dumped a tablespoon of sugar into the coffee and stirred it several times.

"Then why did you go through with it?"

"I...wasn't myself yesterday. I... I didn't fully realize what was happening." She knew how ridiculous that sounded and hurried to explain. "You see, Aunt Mabel and Aunt Ethel—they're really my great-aunts, but I've always called them Aunt—anyway, they told me they were giving me a trip to Alaska."

"Why?"

She wasn't sure how much she wanted to reveal. She understood the reason her two scheming aunts had answered Paul's ad. They'd been worried about her after the breakup with Larry. The question was: How was

she going to untangle herself from this unfortunate set of circumstances? "The purpose for my agreeing to come to Alaska isn't important," she told him stiffly.

"Not too many people visit Alaska on the brink of winter," he said.

She wished he'd stop arguing with her. Keeping her composure under these conditions was difficult enough.

"Was it because of Larry?"

Caroline felt her blood run cold. "They told you about Larry?"

"No, you did."

"I did!" She opened her eyes wide, then quickly lowered them. "Is there anything I didn't tell you?"

"I imagine there's quite a bit." He paused to drink his coffee. "Please go on. I'm curious to hear how you got yourself into this predicament."

"Well, Aunt Mabel and Aunt Ethel insisted I take this trip. I'd never been to Alaska and they kept telling me how beautiful it is. I didn't know how they could afford it, but—"

"They didn't."

"What do you mean?" She held the mug with both hands. This was getting more complicated by the minute.

"I paid for it."

"Terrific," she groaned. She'd need to repay him for that and God only knew what else.

She paused for a sip of coffee and continued her explanation. "Then John Morrison met me in Fairbanks and the ride to Gold River got a bit rugged, so I drank the thermos of tea my aunts sent along."

"Tea?"

"Not regular tea," Caroline corrected. "My aunts have a special brew—their father passed the recipe to them."

"I see." One corner of his lip curved upward as he made an obvious—but futile—effort to contain his smile.

Caroline wasn't fooled. "Would you stop looking amused? We're in one heck of a mess here."

"We are?" He cocked an eyebrow expressively. "We're married, Caroline, and the ceremony is as legal as it gets. We stood before God, with the whole village as witness."

"But you don't honestly expect me to honor those vows.... You can't be that unreasonable."

"We're married."

"It was a mistake!"

"Not as far as I'm concerned."

"I'll have it annulled," she threatened.

His grin was wide and cynical. "After last night?"

Her cheeks flamed even hotter. So something *had* happened. "All right," she said tightly, "we'll get a divorce."

"There will be no divorce."

Caroline placed her mug on the table. "You can't be serious! I have no intention of staying married to you. Good heavens, I don't even *know* you."

"You'll have plenty of time for that later."

"Later? Are you nuts? I'm not staying here a second longer than necessary. There's been a terrible mistake and I want out before something else happens."

"And I say we make the best of the situation."

"Just how do you propose we do that?"

"Stay married."

"You're crazy." She stood up so abruptly that the chair went crashing to the floor. "Let's talk about this in a logical fashion."

"The deed is done." In Paul's opinion, there was nothing to discuss; she was here in his home and they were legally married.

"Deed," Caroline echoed, feeling slightly sick to her stomach. "Then we… I mean, last night, you and I… we…?" Her eyes implored him to tell her what they'd done.

Paul yearned to assure her they'd shared only a few kisses, but the instant he told her that nothing—well, almost nothing—had happened, she'd bolt. "Caroline, listen to me. It's too late for argument."

"Not from my point of view." Her arms were wrapped around her stomach as she paced the floor. "I want out of here and I want out now."

Paul shrugged. "That's unfortunate because you're staying."

"You can't force me!"

His frustration was quickly mounting. "Would you give us a chance? I'll admit we're getting off to a shaky start, but things will work out."

"Work out!" she cried. "I'm married to a man whose face I can't even see."

Paul ran his hand over the neatly trimmed beard. "It's winter and my beard's there to protect my face from the cold. I won't shave until spring."

"I… I don't know you," she said again.

"I wouldn't say that."

"Will you stop bringing up the subject of last night?"

Caroline was surprised by Paul's low chuckle. "*Now* what's so funny?" she asked.

"You're a passionate woman, Mrs. Trevor. If it's this good between us at the beginning, can you imagine how fantastic it'll be when we know each other better?"

"Stop it!" Furious, she stalked across the room and stood in front of the window. A thin layer of snow covered the ground and in the distance Caroline could see the form of a small plane against the blue sky. Her heart rate soared as she contemplated her means of escape. If the plane landed in Gold River, maybe she could sneak out before Paul discovered she was missing.

"Caroline?"

She turned back to him. "Were you so desperate for a wife that you had to advertise? That doesn't say a whole lot about your sterling character."

"There are very few opportunities in Alaska, love. I don't often get into Fairbanks."

"I already asked you not to call me that."

"I apologize."

He didn't look the least bit contrite and his attitude infuriated her further. "Why did you choose *me?* You must've received more than one response."

"I received...several." *Hundreds, if the truth be known.* "I chose you because I liked your eyes."

"Wonderful!" She threw her hands in the air.

"But your aunts were right—you are more attractive in person."

Caroline couldn't believe what she was hearing. Paul Trevor apparently expected her to honor her vows and live here on this chunk of ice. She was growing increasingly frantic. "I...have disgusting habits. Within a week you'll be ready to toss me to the wolves."

"There isn't anything we won't be able to work out."

"Paul, please, look at it from my perspective." Her eyes pleaded with him.

Paul struggled with the effect they had on him. It was difficult to refuse her anything, but the matter of their marriage was something on which he couldn't compromise. "We'll discuss it later," he told her stiffly and turned away. "I've got to get to the station."

"What station?"

"The pump station by the pipeline."

"Oh. John mentioned it." Already her mind was scheming. She'd let him go and pray that the plane circling overhead would land. If it did, she could convince the pilot to get her out of Gold River before Paul even knew she was gone.

"I won't be more than an hour or two."

"All right." She slowly rubbed the palms of her hands together. "And when you get back, I'm sure we'll be able to reach some agreement. I might even be willing to stay."

Paul eyed her suspiciously, not trusting this sudden change of heart. While he shrugged into his coat, he said, "I want your word, Caroline, that you'll remain in the cabin."

"Here? In this cabin?"

"Your word of honor."

Caroline swallowed uncomfortably; she hated lying. Normally she spoke the truth even to her own detriment. "All right," she muttered, childishly crossing her fingers behind her back. "I'll stay here."

"I have your word?"

"Yes." Without flinching, her eyes met his.

"I won't be long." His hand was on the doorknob.

"Take your time." The plane was landing; she could

hear it in the distance. "While you're gone, I'll find my way around the kitchen," she said brightly. "By the time you return, I'll have lunch ready."

Again Paul eyed her doubtfully. She sounded much too eager for him to leave, but he didn't have time to worry now. Giving her a few hours alone was probably for the best. She'd promised to stay and he had no choice but to trust her. He was already an hour late. Walter had said he'd stand in for him, but Paul had refused. The station was his responsibility.

The second the door closed after Paul, Caroline dashed into the bedroom and jerked her clothes off the hangers, stuffing them back inside her suitcase. With a sense of guilt, she left the winter gear that Paul had purchased on her behalf. He'd gone to a great deal of trouble and expense for her, but she couldn't be blamed for that.

A quick check at the door revealed that Paul was nowhere in sight. She breathed a bit easier and walked cautiously outside. Although the day was clear, the cold cut straight through her thin jacket.

A couple of Athabascan women passed Caroline and smiled shyly, their eyes curious. She returned their silent greeting and experienced a twinge of remorse at this regrettable subterfuge. If he'd been more reasonable, she wouldn't have had to do something so drastic.

The plane was taxiing to a stop at the airstrip where she'd been dropped off less than twenty-four hours earlier.

Caroline watched from the center of town as the pilot handed down several plywood crates. A few minutes later, the dogsleds and snowmobiles arrived.

"Hi." She stepped forward, her calm smile concealing her anxiety.

The tall burly man seemed surprised to see her. "Hello."

"I'm Caroline Myers." She extended her hand for him to shake and prayed he wouldn't detect her nervousness.

"Burt Manners. What can I do for you?"

"I need a ride to Fairbanks," she said quickly. "Is there any way you could fly me there?"

"Sorry, lady, I'm headed in the opposite direction."

"Where?" She'd go anyplace as long as it was away from Gold River and Paul.

"Near Circle Hot Springs."

"That's fine. I'll go there first, just so it's understood that you can fly me to Fairbanks afterward."

"Lady, I've already got a full load. Besides, you don't want to travel to Circle Hot Springs. It's no place for a lady this time of year."

"I don't care. Honest."

"There isn't any room." He started to turn away from her.

"There must be *some* space available. You just unloaded those crates. Please." Caroline hated the whiny sound of her voice, but she was desperate. The sooner she escaped, the better.

"Is that the warmest coat you've got?"

He was looking for excuses and Caroline knew it. "No. I've got another coat. Can I come?"

"I don't know...." Still, he hesitated.

"I'll pay you double your normal fee," Caroline said, placing her hand on his forearm. "I *have* to get to Fairbanks."

"Okay, okay." Burt rubbed his neck. "Why do I feel I'm going to regret this?"

Caroline hardly heard him as she made a sharp turn and scurried across the snow toward the cabin. "I'll be right back. Don't leave without me."

She got to the cabin breathless with excitement and relief, and hurried into the bedroom. Taking the coat Paul had purchased for her went against all her instincts, but she'd repay him later, she rationalized, once she was safely back in Seattle. To ease her conscience, she quickly scribbled an IOU and left it on the kitchen table, where he was sure to find it, along with a note apologizing for the lie. Her suitcase stood just inside the doorway. She reached for it with one hand and her purse with the other.

The pilot was waiting for her when she returned and she climbed aboard, feeling jubilant. Getting away from Paul had been much easier than she'd expected. Of course he could follow her, but that was doubtful unless he had a plane, and she didn't see a hangar anywhere.

As Burt had explained, the seating was cramped.

He talked little on the short trip, which suited Caroline just fine. She didn't have a whole lot to say herself.

The landing strip at Circle Hot Springs looked even more unreliable than the one at Gold River. Caroline felt her stomach pitch wildly when the Cessna's wheels slammed against the frozen ground, but she managed to conceal her alarm.

They were met by a group of four hunters who unloaded the plane, delivering the gear to a huge hunting lodge. When they'd finished, one of the men brought out a bottle of whiskey and passed it around. The larg-

est hunter, a man called Sam, offered the bottle to Caroline.

"No, thanks," she said shaking her head. "I prefer to drink mine from a glass." Burt had said that Circle Hot Springs wasn't any place for a lady, but she'd assumed he'd been concerned about the climate.

"Hey, guys, we've got a classy dame with us." Sam laughed gruffly and handed her the bottle. "Take a drink," he ordered.

Fear sent chills racing up and down her spine as Caroline looked frantically at Burt. "I said no, thank you."

"Lay off, you guys," Burt called. "She doesn't have to drink if she doesn't want to."

An hour later, Caroline was convinced she'd made a horrible mistake. The men sat around drinking and telling dirty jokes that were followed by smutty songs and laughter. Their conversation, or at least what she could hear of it, was filled with innuendo. The more she ignored them, the more they seemed to focus on her.

While the men were engaged in a discussion about the next day's plans, Caroline crept close to Burt's side, doing everything possible to remove attention from herself.

"You okay?" Burt muttered.

"Fine," she lied. "When do we leave for Fairbanks?"

He gave her an odd look. "Not until tomorrow morning."

"Tomorrow morning? That long?" She gulped. What had she gotten herself into now?

"Hey, lady, you asked for this."

"Right." She'd left the frying pan and landed directly in the hot coals of the fire. "I'll be ready first thing in the morning." Although it was the middle of

the afternoon, the skies were already beginning to darken.

The hunting lodge had a large living room with a mammoth fireplace. The proprietor/guide appeared and introduced himself, then brought out another bottle of whiskey to welcome his latest guests. Caroline refused a drink and inquired politely about renting a room for the night.

"Sorry, honey, we're full up."

His eyes were twinkling and Caroline didn't believe him.

"You can stay with me," Sam offered.

"No, thanks."

"Polite little thing, ain't you?" Sam slipped his arm around her shoulders and squeezed hard. The smell of alcohol on his breath nearly bowled her over. "The boys and me came here for some fun and we're real glad you decided to join us."

"I'm just passing through on my way to Fairbanks," she explained lamely. She cast a pleading glance at Burt, but he was talking to another of the men and didn't notice her. She groaned inwardly when she saw the glass of amber liquid in his hand.

"Like I said, we came into Circle Hot Springs for a little fun," Sam told her, slurring his words. "You knew that when you insisted on flying here, I'll bet." Again he gave her shoulders a rough squeeze.

Caroline felt as if her vocal cords had frozen with fear. As the evening progressed, things went from bad to worse. After the men had eaten, they grew louder and even more boisterous. Burt had started drinking and from the looks he was giving her, Caroline wondered just how much protection he'd be if worse came

to worst. Judging by the way he was staring at her, Caroline realized he wouldn't be much help against the burly men.

Sam polished off his glass of whiskey and rubbed the back of his hand across his mouth. "I don't know about the rest of you yahoos," he shouted, "but I'm game for some entertainment."

"What do you have in mind?"

"Burt brought it for us. Ain't that right, little lady?"

Once again Caroline's eyes pleaded with Burt, but he ignored her silent petition. "I... I didn't say anything like that, but...but I think you should know, I'm not much of a singer."

The men broke into loud guffaws.

"I can dance a little," she offered, hoping to delay any arguments and discover a means of escape. Her heart felt as though it were refusing to cooperate with her lungs. She'd never been so scared in her life.

"Let her dance."

The whiskey bottle was passed from one member of the party to the next as Caroline stood and edged to the front door. If she could break free, she might be able to locate another cabin to spend the night. Someplace warm and safe.

"I'll...need some music." She recognized her mistake when two of the men broke into a melody associated with strippers.

"Dance," Sam called, clapping his hands.

"Sure." Caroline was close to tears of anger and frustration. Swinging her hands at her sides, she did a shuffle she'd learned in tap dance class in the fifth grade.

The men booed.

She sent them a feeble smile and stopped. "I guess I'm not much of a dancer, either."

"Try harder," someone shouted, and they all laughed again.

The log door swung open and a cold north wind caused the roaring fire to flicker. A man entered, his head covered with a hood. He flipped it back and stared at Caroline.

"Paul!" She'd never been so glad to see anyone in her life. She wanted to weep with relief.

"What's going on here?" he said gruffly.

"We're just havin' a little fun," Burt said, lurching to his feet. "Do you know the lady?"

Paul looked directly at Caroline and slowly shook his head. "Nope. Never seen her before in my life."

Four

Caroline stared with utter astonishment as Paul took a seat with the other men, removing his parka and setting it aside. Someone passed him a drink, which he quickly downed. Not once did he glance in her direction.

"Well," he said after a moment, "what's stopping you? Dance."

"Dance?" Caroline repeated.

"Dance!" all the men shouted simultaneously.

"And no more little-girl stuff, either."

Caroline's anger simmered just below the surface. Couldn't Paul see that she was up to her neck in trouble? The least he could do was rescue her. All morning he'd kept saying he was her husband and nothing she could do would change that. Well, good grief, if she'd ever needed a husband it was now. Instead, he appeared to find her predicament humorous. Well, she'd show him!

Heaving a deep sigh, she resumed her soft-shoe shuffle, swinging her arms at her sides. She really did need music and if the men weren't going to provide it, she'd make her own. Perhaps because of the snow

outside, all she could think of was Christmas songs. "Jingle bell, jingle bell, jingle bell rock…" she bellowed out.

The only one she seemed to amuse was Paul, but his laugh could be better described as a snicker. Although Caroline made a point of not looking at him, she could feel the heat of his anger. All right, so she'd lied. And she'd taken the coat. She did intend to pay him for it, plus what he'd spent on her airplane fare.

The men were booing her efforts again.

"I told you, none of that kid stuff," Sam shouted, his voice even more slurred. "You're supposed to *entertain* us."

As much as she hated to reveal her fright, Caroline stopped and she silently begged Paul for help. Again he ignored her.

"Take your clothes off," Sam called out. "That's what we want."

"Paul?" she whispered, and her voice trembled. "Please." When she saw him clench his fists, she knew she'd won.

"All right, guys," he said, agilely rising to his feet. "The game's over. I'd like you to meet my wife."

"Your wife!" In a rush, Burt Manners jumped from his sitting position. "Hey, buddy, I swear I had no idea."

"Wait a minute!" Sam burst out. "You said you didn't know her and—"

"Don't worry about it," Paul cut in.

"She came to me begging to leave Gold River. I told her Circle Hot Springs was no place for a lady, but she insisted."

Paul's mouth thinned. "I know."

"You need me to fly you back to Gold River?" Burt asked eagerly.

"No, thanks, I've got someone waiting."

"You do?" Caroline was so relieved, she felt faint. Another minute of this horrible tension would have been unbearable. The men were looking at her as though she was some cheat who'd swindled them out of an evening's fun and games. And from the way Paul kept avoiding eye contact, she wondered what he'd say once they were alone. She'd gone from the frying pan into the fire and then back to the frying pan.

Burt stepped out of the hunting lodge with them to unload Caroline's suitcase from his plane. With every step, he continued to apologize until Caroline wanted to scream. Paul knew she'd practically begged the other man to take her away from Gold River. He didn't need to hear it over and over again.

"Fact is," Burt said, standing beside his Cessna, his expression uneasy, "I didn't hear you were married. If I'd known she was your wife, I never would've taken her."

Paul offered no excuse for her behavior. He was so silent and so furious that Caroline thought he might explode any minute. Without a word, he escorted her to the waiting plane and helped her inside, every movement that of a perfect gentleman. But she had no doubt whatsoever that he was enraged.

Once aboard the plane, Caroline smiled faintly at the pilot and slipped into her seat. No sooner had she buckled her safety belt than the engines roared to life and the Cessna taxied away.

Paul was quiet for the entire flight. By the time they circled Gold River, Caroline was weak with dread—

and guilt. She'd lied to Paul, stolen from him and embarrassed him in front of his friends. Maybe he'd be so glad to get rid of her that he'd give her the divorce. Maybe this whole fiasco could be annulled. Oh heavens, why wouldn't he tell her what had happened last night? She rubbed her temples, trying to recall the events following her arrival. She remembered him kissing her and how good it felt, but beyond that her memory was a blur.

When the plane approached the runway, Caroline closed her eyes. The sensation of the frozen tundra rising to meet the small aircraft made her dizzy. The Cessna jerked hard once, then again, and for a moment Caroline was sure they were going to crash. A fitting end to her day, she thought gloomily—death. She swallowed a cry of alarm and looked frantically at Paul, who was seated beside her. His face was void of expression, as though such a bumpy landing was nothing out of the ordinary. They eased to a stop, and Caroline sagged against the back of the seat, breathless with relief.

Walter was standing with a team of huskies to meet them. His ageless eyes hardened when he caught a glimpse of Caroline, and his angry glare could have split a rock.

"Could you see that Bill has a hot meal and place to spend the night?" Paul asked his friend, apparently referring to the pilot.

"Sure thing."

Once inside the cabin, Caroline turned her back to the woodstove and waited. Paul walked past her, carrying her suitcase into the bedroom.

Caroline removed her parka and hung it beside

Paul's. The cabin was warm and cozy, some kind of stew was simmering on top of the stove and the enticing smell was enough to make Caroline feel limp. She hadn't eaten all day.

Still, Paul didn't speak and she waited another minute before she broached a conversation.

"Okay, I'm ready," she said when she couldn't stand it any longer.

"Ready for what?"

"For whatever you're going to say or do to me."

"I'm not going to say or do anything."

"Nothing?" Caroline uttered in stunned disbelief.

Paul crossed the tiny kitchen and took two bowls from the cupboard.

"But I lied to you."

His eyes narrowed. "I know."

"And I stole the coat."

He nodded.

"And…" Her voice trembled. "I made a fool out of us both."

Paul lifted the lid of the cast iron kettle, filled each bowl to the top with stew and brought them to the table.

Caroline gripped the back of the kitchen chair. "You must be furious with me."

"I am."

"Then don't you think you should divorce me? I mean—it's obvious I'm not the woman you want. If I were you, I'd be willing to admit I made a bad choice and go from there." She eyed him hopefully.

He sat down, unfolded his napkin and laid it across his lap. "There will be no divorce."

"But I don't *want* to be married! I—"

"The deed is done."

"What deed?" she screamed. If she'd had a wedding night, a *real* wedding night, surely she'd remember it.

"We're legally married," he said calmly, reaching for his spoon. "Now sit down and eat."

"No." Stubbornly, she crossed her arms over her chest.

"Fine. Then don't eat."

Caroline glanced at the steaming bowl of stew. Her mouth began to water and she angrily pulled out the chair. "All right, I'll eat," she murmured, "but I'm doing it under protest." She dipped her spoon into the thick mixture.

"I can tell," Paul said.

When they'd finished, it was Paul who cleared the table and washed the dishes. Wordlessly, Caroline found a dish towel and dried them, replacing the bowls in the overhead cupboard. Her mind was spinning with possible topics of conversation, all of which led to one central issue: their marriage. She prayed she'd find a way of getting him to listen to reason.

An hour after dinner, Paul turned off the lights in the living room and moved into the bedroom. Caroline could either follow him or be left standing alone in the dark. She didn't even consider turning on the lights again.

The instant her gaze fell on the bed, Caroline knew she could delay no longer. "Paul, listen to me—there's been a terrible mistake."

"There was no mistake," he countered, starting to unbutton his shirt.

Briefly, Caroline recalled running her fingers down his chest. She felt the blood drain from her face and turned away in an effort not to look at him. If there

was anything else to remember, she didn't want to do it now. "The mistake wasn't yours, I'll admit that. But you must understand that I didn't know anything about the wedding."

"We've already been through this and no amount of talk is going to change what happened. We're married, and as far as I'm concerned that's how we're going to stay."

"But I don't want to be married," she wailed.

Paul heaved a disgusted sigh. "Would it make any difference if I was your beloved Larry?"

"Yes," she cried, then quickly changed her mind. "No, it wouldn't. Oh hell, I don't know."

"The subject is closed," Paul said forcefully. "We won't discuss it again."

"But we have to."

From behind her, Caroline heard Paul throw back the covers and climb into bed. Slowly, she turned, feeling more unhappy and depressed than at any other time in her life.

"Surely you don't believe I'm going to sleep with you?"

"You're my wife, Caroline."

"But..."

"Why do you insist on arguing? We're married. You're my wife and I want you to sleep in my bed."

"I won't."

"Fine," he grumbled. "Sleep on the floor. When you get cold enough you'll come to bed." With that, he rolled onto his side and flipped off the light, once again leaving Caroline in the dark. She remained where she was for a long moment, indecisive, exhausted, bewildered.

"Paul?"

"Hmm?"

"If I... If I come to bed, will you promise not to touch me?"

Silence. Finally he said, "After the stunt you pulled today, I doubt that I could."

Caroline supposed she should've been relieved, but she wasn't. Slowly, she undressed and climbed under the blankets. She shivered once and curled up tightly. As weary as she was, she'd expected to fall directly into a deep sleep, but she didn't. In fact, a half hour later, she lay wide awake, surprisingly warm and cozy.

"Paul?" she whispered.

"What?"

She bit her bottom lip to hold back the tears. "I'm sorry about today."

"I know."

"Under normal conditions, I would never have done anything so stupid."

"I know that, too."

"Do you know everything?" she snapped.

"No."

"I'm glad to hear it."

Another five minutes passed. "Paul?"

"What is it now?"

"Good night."

"Good night, love." She could hear the relief in his voice and her eyes drifted shut.

The next thing Caroline knew, Paul was leaning over her, gently shaking her awake.

"Caroline, it's morning."

Her eyes flew open in alarm and she brushed the hair from her face. "What time is it?"

"Five o'clock. You'll need to get up and dressed. There's coffee on the dresser for you."

Maybe he'd relented and had accepted the impossibility of their circumstances. She struggled into a sitting position, her eyes finding his. "Up and dressed? Why?" she asked, hoping he'd decided to send her back to Seattle.

"You're coming with me."

"Where?"

"To the pump station."

Her spirits sagged. "But why? I don't know anything about—"

"I can't trust you. So I don't have any choice but to bring you with me."

"I'm not going to run away again. I promise."

"You promised before. Now get up."

"But, Paul, I won't—"

"I don't have time to argue with you. Either you do as I say or I'll take you with me dressed as you are."

Caroline didn't doubt him for a second. "Aye, aye, commander," she said and gave him a mocking salute. Furious, she threw back the sheets and reached for her clothes.

Caroline had never spent a more boring morning in her life. Paul sat her down in a chair and left her to twiddle her thumbs for what seemed like hours. After the first thirty minutes, she toyed with the idea of walking back to the cabin, which she found preferable to sitting in a chair, a punishment more befitting a badly behaved child. However, she quickly discarded that idea. All she needed was to have Paul return to find her gone. If he was furious with her after yesterday, it

would be nothing compared to his anger if she pulled the same trick twice. So, although she was bored senseless, Caroline stayed exactly where she was.

Paul returned and she brightened, pleased to have some human contact. But to her dismay, he walked directly past her to another desk and took out a huge ledger, proceeding to record data.

"Paul?"

"Shh."

She pressed her lips together so hard they hurt.

He lifted his head when he'd finished and looked at her expectantly. "You wanted something?"

"I want to go back to the cabin."

"No."

"After what happened yesterday, you can't believe I'll try to get away again." He returned to his work and refused to look at her, ostensibly studying his ledger. Caroline's blood was close to the boiling point. "What are you going to do? Keep me with you twenty-four hours a day?"

"You gave me no option."

"You *can't* be serious. I'm not going to run away." She pointed to the front door. "There are crazy people out there."

He didn't respond.

"Paul, please, I'll go out of my mind with nothing to do."

"Get a book and read." His response was as uncaring as the arctic wind that howled outside the door.

"Oh, I see," she said in a high-pitched, emotional voice. "This is to be my punishment. Not only are you going to keep me as your prisoner, but I have to suffer your company as well. How long?"

"How long what?" With deliberate care, he set his pen aside.

"How long before you learn to trust me? A week? Ten days? A month?"

"I can't answer that. It depends on you."

She flew to her feet, her fists clenched. "Well then, you'd be wise never to leave me alone, because the minute I get a chance, I'm hightailing it out of here. Somehow or other, I'll find a way to escape. You can't keep a person against his or her will. This is the United States of America and kidnapping is against the law."

"I didn't kidnap you, I married you."

"Well, then, you're the worst possible husband a woman could have. I refuse to be your wife, no matter what some piece of paper says." She waited for him to argue with her and when he didn't, she continued her tirade. "Not only that… You've got to be the most stubborn man I've ever met. Stubborn and unreasonable and…and…chauvinistic to boot!"

Paul nodded. "I know. But given time, you'll learn to love me."

"Never," Caroline vowed. "Not while I live and breathe."

"We'll see."

He sounded so sure of himself, so confident, that she wanted to throttle him. Drained, she sank back into her chair. To her horror, tears filled her eyes and fell hot against her cheeks. She wiped them aside and sniffled loudly to hold back the flood. "Paul," she cried softly. "I just want to go home. Please."

His mouth grew hard and inflexible. "You are home. The sooner you accept that, the better for both of us."

With that, Caroline buried her face in her hands and

wept until there were no tears left. Her eyes burned and her throat ached.

Paul felt the weight of Denali pressing against his back, and prayed he was doing the right thing. He could deal with her harangues, even her feisty anger, but her tears were another matter. They brought all his doubts to the surface. A month—he'd promised himself a month. If things hadn't improved by the end of October, he'd send her back to Seattle. Looking at her now, bent over, weeping as though she hadn't a friend in the world, he felt guilt—and an overwhelming compassion. It would be so easy to love her. She had spunk and character and was more woman than he'd ever dreamed he'd find. He knew in his heart that this really could work, that this marriage could be genuine and happy. He knew because—except for one occasion— his instincts hadn't steered him wrong yet and where there was such intense attraction between a man and a woman, there was a chance for lasting love.

By midafternoon, Caroline had read one adventure novel, written her two maiden aunts a scathing letter, destroyed that, and had drawn several pictures of a distorted Paul with a knife through his heart. She couldn't help it; after eight hours of complete monotony, she felt murderous.

Toward evening, Paul handed Caroline her parka. "Are you ready to go back to the cabin?"

Was she ever! But she had no intention of letting him know that. With a regal tilt of her chin, she reached for her jacket and slipped her arms inside the thick sleeves. She hadn't spoken a word to Paul in hours and he hadn't had the decency to reveal the least bit of concern. Well, she could hold out longer than he

could. By the time she returned to Seattle, he'd be so glad to be rid of her, he'd give her the divorce without even arguing.

More snow had fallen during the day, and although the cabin was only a short distance from the pumping station, they needed snowshoes to trek their way back. It was the first time that Caroline had ever worn them, and she was forced to squelch her natural delight.

Again, dinner had been left on the stove. Tonight it was a roast with onions, potatoes and carrots simmered in the gravy. Caroline wondered who did the cooking, but she refused to ask Paul a thing. And she was hungry; lunch had consisted of a peanut butter sandwich many hours before.

As he had the previous night, Paul placed the silverware on the table and brought their meal from the stove. More than once Caroline felt his gaze on her, but she was determined not to utter a word.

"I must admit," Paul said halfway through their dinner, "that I prefer the silence to your constant badgering."

"Badgering!" Caroline shrieked. "I do not badger. All I want is an end to this despicable marriage."

Paul grinned boyishly. "Has anyone told you how beautiful your eyes are?"

Caroline pressed her lips together and stabbed her meat with unnecessary force. "I wish that was your heart. Oops, my mistake. You don't have one."

Paul laughed outright at that. "But I do, love," he said a few minutes later. "And it belongs to you."

"I don't want it." She struggled to hold back tears of frustration. "Didn't you say you'd received lots of letters in response to your ad? Those women all *wanted*

to be your wife. Let me go, Paul. Please let me go. I'll repay you the money you've already spent. I swear I will."

He shook his head. "I refuse to discuss the matter again." Until the end of the month, he added to himself, hoping that by then there'd be nothing to discuss.

"Yes, Your Majesty," Caroline returned, just barely managing to regain her composure.

Neither one of them ate much after that. Caroline toyed with the food on her plate, but her appetite had vanished, and with it her will to fight.

Standing, she carried her plate to the sink and scraped it clean. Paul brought over his dishes and they worked silently together, cleaning away the dinner mess.

"Paul," she said, after he'd wiped the last dish dry, "do you play Scrabble?" She knew he must; she'd seen the game on his shelf.

"A bit. Why?"

"Could you and I play? To help pass the evening?"

"I suppose."

For the first time in two days, Caroline's smile was natural and real. Her aunts loved Scrabble and had taught it to her as a child. With such expert tutoring, she was practically unbeatable. Her whole world became brighter. "It would be far more interesting, though," she said with a feigned thoughtful look, "if we played for something, don't you think?"

"How do you mean?"

She brought the game down from the shelf and unfolded the board. "Simple. If I win you'd grant me one request, and vice versa."

"And of course you'd ask for a divorce. No way."

"No, not a divorce." She'd work up to that.

"If not a divorce, what would you request?"

"Privacy."

"Privacy?"

"Yes, I want to sleep alone."

Skeptical, he eyed the recliner. "For how long?"

She'd go easy on him. "One night."

"Agreed." He pulled up a chair, twisted it around and straddled it. "And on the off chance I win?" He could see the mischief in her brilliant blue eyes. She clearly expected to beat him.

"Yes?" She regarded him expectantly. "What would you want?"

"A kiss."

"A kiss?"

"And not a peck on the cheek either. I want you to kiss me so well it'll turn me inside out." Not that it would take much, he mused.

Caroline hesitated. "But no more than a kiss, right?"

"No more. Agreed?"

With a saucy grin, she stuck out her hand. "Agreed." They shook on it and Caroline laughed. It felt so good to laugh again; she hated the constant bickering. Besides, this was going to be like taking candy from a baby.

"Let the games begin," Paul said, grinning back at her.

For a moment, it was hard to take her gaze off him. His eyes were smiling and although she couldn't see the rest of his face through the beard, she felt he must be a handsome man. His eyes certainly were appealing. Playfully, she held up her hand and flexed all her fingers.

"You draw first." In gentlemanly fashion, Paul handed her the small velvet bag with the letters of the alphabet.

Caroline inserted her hand and drew out an A. She gave him a triumphant look and set it on her letter holder. "I go first."

"Right."

It wasn't until they were a couple of plays into the game that Caroline recognized Paul's skill. He was going to provide some stiff competition. In fact, their scores remained close throughout the match. Caroline was down to her last five letters when Paul gained a triple word slot, added up his score and beamed her a proud look.

"Paul!" Caroline glanced at the board and gasped, unable to hold back her shock. "That's a four-letter word! A dirty four-letter word!"

"I'm well aware of that, love."

"You can't use that. It…it's indecent."

"It's also in the dictionary. Would you care to challenge me?"

She knew if she did, she'd immediately forfeit the game. "No," she grumbled. "But I consider that word in poor taste."

Paul's response was a soft chuckle. "You can challenge me if you wish."

"What's the score?" Five letters left… If she could use them all, she might be able to pull into the lead.

"Three hundred and twenty to two eighty-eight," Paul informed her gleefully. "Do you concede?"

"Never!"

"I'm afraid you have to. I'm out of letters."

"You won," Caroline said, almost in a daze. She'd

lost only one game of Scrabble since her junior year in high school. She'd played brilliantly, yet Paul had outdone her.

"Yes, love, I won."

For a minute all she could do was stare at the board in shocked disbelief.

"Love? I believe you owe me a kiss."

She should object to his calling her "love," but she was too bemused. "You beat me at Scrabble," she said. "And I'm a good player. Very good."

"I'm fairly well versed in the game myself," Paul said. "There's not much else for Walter and me to do on those long winter nights."

Caroline's eyes narrowed. He'd known all along that he had an excellent chance of winning.

"I believe you owe me a kiss," he said again.

"You cheated," Caroline cried. "You used a four-letter word and—"

"Don't tell me you're a poor sport, too."

As fast as she could, Caroline removed the wooden pieces from the playing board. "You mean in addition to being a liar and a thief."

"I didn't say that," Paul told her soberly.

"Well, you needn't worry, I'll give you what I promised, but I still think it's unfair of you to use that word."

"You'd use it, too, if you had to," Paul said, folding up the game and placing it back on the bookcase.

"I wouldn't!"

"If you were down to four letters and that word placed you on a triple word score and would guarantee you a win, then I don't doubt you'd use it!"

"Well," Caroline hedged, a smile lifting the edges

of her mouth. "I'd be tempted, but I don't think I'd stoop that low."

"Yes, you would. Now pay up, love."

Reluctantly, Caroline stood and rounded the table to his side.

"A kiss that'll turn me inside out," he reminded her.

"I remember," she said ruefully. She stood in front of him and Paul's arm circled her waist, pulling her onto his lap. She offered him a weak smile and set her hands on his shoulders. His palms slid around her back, directing her actions.

She twisted her head to the right, then changed her mind and moved it to the left. Slowly, she bent forward and placed her parted mouth on his. Paul's lips were moist and warm and brushed hers in a slow, sensuous way. Then his kiss grew wilder, and she responded with equal intensity.

They broke apart, panting and drained.

"Oh, Caroline," he breathed against her neck. Their mouths fused again. Although she'd initially had no intention of giving him more than the one kiss, she felt as eager for the second as he was.

Again his mouth nuzzled her neck. "Another game, Caroline, love? Only this time the stakes will be slightly higher."

Five

"Another game of Scrabble?" Caroline repeated, feeling content.

Dream or not, her memory served her well; Paul Trevor was one fantastic kisser. Suddenly her eyes flew open and she jerked herself free from Paul's arms. Mere hours before she'd vowed to freeze him out and here she was, sitting on his lap with her arms around his neck, kissing him with all the fervor in her heart.

"Our Scrabble days are over, Paul Trevor," she said coldly, placing her hand on the table to help maintain her balance. She felt a heated flush in her cheeks.

"You mean you're quitting because I'm a better player than you?" Paul returned with a laugh.

"Better player, my foot!"

The whole situation appeared to amuse him, which only angered Caroline more. She stormed into the bedroom and sat on the end of the bed, sulking. Until she'd met Paul, she'd considered herself an easygoing, fun-loving person. In two days' time he'd managed to change all that. With her arms crossed, she fumed, contemplating a hundred means of making him suffer.

It wasn't until they were in bed, Paul asleep at her side, that Caroline acknowledged the truth—she was more furious with herself than Paul. He'd played an honorable Scrabble game, except for that four-letter word, and had won their wager fair and square. What infuriated her most was her overwhelming response to his kiss. She didn't *want* to feel this way; it was far too difficult to hate him when he was so loving, so gentle, so...exciting.

In the morning, Paul woke her. "Time to get up, sleepyhead," he whispered in her ear.

Caroline's eyes fluttered open. Paul sat on the edge of the bed, smiling down at her. "Coffee's ready," he said.

"Paul," she pleaded, trying to appeal to his better nature. "Do I have to go to the pumping station with you again? It's so boring. I hate it."

"I'm sorry, love."

"I promise I won't pull any tricks."

He stood, shaking his head. "No, Caroline, you're coming with me."

Arguing would do no good, she realized with a frown, and tossed aside the heavy quilts to climb out of bed, grumbling as she did. Paul left her to dress in privacy, for which she was grateful.

Caroline prepared herself for the long, tedious hours. She took a deck of cards, some reading material and a pen and paper.

As he had the day before, Paul joined her at the desk beside hers a couple of hours into the morning. He smiled as he pulled out the ledger.

She waited to be sure she wasn't disturbing him before speaking. "Paul, who does the cooking for you?"

He didn't look up from the ledger as he spoke. "Tanana Eagleclaw. You met her the day you got here."

"There were so many people," she explained feebly.

He grinned, but didn't tease her about her memory lapse.

"Paul." She tried again. "I'm a good cook." That might have been a bit of an exaggeration, she added silently, but anything was better than sitting around this infernal pumping station ten hours a day.

"Hmm." He barely acknowledged her, apparently finding his ledgers more compelling.

"Really, I'm an excellent cook." She was getting desperate now. "I could prepare our meals. In fact, I'd like to do it."

"Tanana does an admirable job."

"Yes, but I want to do it!"

"You can't."

"Why not?"

"Because you're here with me, that's why not."

"Do you mean to tell me you're going to drag me here for the rest of my life?"

Paul sighed expressively. "We're going over the same territory as yesterday. You'll stay with me until I feel I can trust you again."

"Wonderful," she said in a sour voice. She couldn't begin to guess when that might be.

A week passed and each morning a sleepy Caroline traipsed behind Paul to the pumping station and each night she followed him home. No amount of pleading could get him to change his mind. He wanted her where he could see her every minute of every day. But, despite

herself, she took comfort from his presence—even if she'd never admit as much.

The mail was delivered twice a week and a letter was sitting on the table addressed to Mr. and Mrs. Paul Trevor when they arrived back from the station during Caroline's second week in Gold River.

"A letter!" Caroline cried, as excited as a child on Christmas morning. Contact with the outside world. A tie with the past. She hurriedly read the return address. "It's from my aunts."

Paul smiled. "The two schemers?"

Eagerly, Caroline tore open the envelope. "The very ones." She hadn't forgiven them for their underhanded method of getting her to Alaska, but she missed them dreadfully.

"What do they have to say?" Paul coaxed.

"They're asking how I like my surprise. In case you don't know, that's you."

"And?" he prodded with a soft chuckle.

"And what?"

"How do you like me?"

It was Caroline's turn to laugh. "I find you...surprising."

"Typical."

"Aunt Mabel, she's the romantic one, says she feels that we're going to be happy and have...oh my goodness."

"What?"

Color seeped up from Caroline's neck and flushed her cheeks. "She predicts seven children, which is how many my great-great-grandmother had as a mail-order bride."

"I'm willing," Paul informed her with a grin.

"Be quiet, I'm reading. And Aunt Ethel..." She hesitated, her eyes scanning the rest of the page. "It was nothing." With her heart pounding frantically, and hoping to appear nonchalant, she refolded the letter and placed it back inside the envelope.

Paul joined her at the kitchen table. "What did she say?"

Caroline dropped her gaze. "It wasn't important."

"Shall I read the letter myself?"

"No..." she said and hid it behind her back. He could have insisted she hand it over, but didn't, although his cutting gaze reminded her that the letter had been addressed to both of them and he had every right to read it. "She told me that Larry Atkins dropped by when... when he couldn't get hold of me. Aunt Ethel said she took great delight in telling him I'm a married woman now."

"I see," Paul said thoughtfully.

"I'm sure you don't." Caroline braced her hands against the kitchen counter as she fought a bout of self-pity. Her relationship with Larry had been over weeks before she'd come to Alaska. It shouldn't hurt this much now, but it did. Her heart yearned to know why he'd contacted her and how he'd reacted to the news that she was married to Paul. She wanted to inform Larry that it wasn't a real marriage—not the way theirs would have been.

Paul placed his hands on her shoulders. "Caroline, here." He turned her into his arms and held her quietly. It wasn't the embrace of a lover, but that of a caring, loyal friend.

She laid her face against his chest and drew in a

wobbly breath. His hand was in her hair, stroking the back of her head in a soothing, comforting motion.

"Do you still love him?" he asked after a moment.

Caroline had to analyze her feelings. She'd been crazy in love with Larry for months. She missed him, thought about him often, wished him the best. But did she love him?

As she pondered his question, Paul decided that holding Caroline was the closest thing to heaven he'd ever experienced. He'd barely touched her in a week, wanting to give her time to know him. Their relationship was in an awkward stage; he wasn't convinced he could trust her yet. She'd outright told him that the first time he left her alone, she'd run away. Winter was coming on, and for her own safety he couldn't leave her until he was sure she wouldn't try to escape. He ached to hold her and kiss her until he felt he'd go mad. His successful restraint should make him a candidate for sainthood, he thought wryly. He regretted that he hadn't made love to her on their wedding night, and yet he'd never coerce Caroline or any woman, never force himself on her.

From her ramblings that night, Paul knew about Larry. The situation was less than ideal and he'd played the role of patient husband, difficult though that was. She'd been with him nine days, and yet it had aged him a hundred lifetimes to be with her—at meals, at the station, especially in bed—knowing her mind was on another man. A man who'd rejected her, for that matter.

"Caroline," he pressed, needing to know. "Do you still love him?"

"I...yes," she answered truthfully, her voice strained and low. This was difficult. Paul was her husband, in

fact if not in deed, and she couldn't deny either her attraction to him or his kindness to her. She had no desire to be cruel to him. "You don't stop loving people
because they've hurt you," she told him softly, relish-
ing the comfort of his arms. "I'm trying not to love
him.... Does that help?"

Tenderly, Paul kissed the side of her face. "It makes
it easier to accept. I appreciate what it cost you to be
honest."

A polite knock at the door drew them reluctantly
apart. A very pregnant young woman walked in. Her
smile was almost bashful, as though she felt she'd in-
truded on their lovemaking. "Did you need me, Paul?"

"Yes." Paul slipped his arm around Caroline's waist.
"Caroline, this is Tanana Eagleclaw. Tanana, my wife,
Caroline."

"How do you do, Mrs. Trevor?" the girl said formally.

"Fine, thank you, Tanana. And please call me Caroline. When is your baby due?" From the way she
looked, it could've been any day.

"Six weeks." Again the young woman smiled shyly,
obviously pleased about the pregnancy.

Caroline guessed she was in her early twenties.
"You're a very good cook."

"Thank you."

Paul said something to her in her native tongue and
Tanana nodded eagerly, her gaze moving briefly to
Caroline. She left soon afterward.

"What was that all about?" Caroline asked.

"You said you wanted to meet Tanana, so I had her
come over."

"But that wasn't the only reason. What did you say to her?"

"When?"

"Just now." Caroline gave him a bewildered look until she realized he was purposely playing dumb. "Never mind. You obviously don't want me to know, so forget it." She did understand one thing; Tanana's feelings would be hurt if Caroline were to take over the cooking. Perhaps when her baby was born, Caroline could assume the task without causing any loss of pride. If she was still here, of course...

That night, sitting in front of the fireplace, Caroline wrote her aunts a long reply. She told them that in the beginning she was furious with what they'd done, but gradually she'd changed her mind. Paul was a good man, a decent man, she wrote, and in that regard, she told the truth. But she couldn't tell them that she hoped and prayed that, given time, Paul would let her return to Seattle. That kind of information would only upset them, and there was no need to disillusion those two romantics. Nor did she say that if she was going to be a bride, she wanted the opportunity to choose her *own* husband. When Paul sent her back, and Caroline believed he would, there'd be time enough to explain everything. For now, she'd play their game and let them think they'd outsmarted her and that she was a happy, blushing bride. It could do no harm.

That night, Caroline fell into bed, exhausted. Paul joined her a little later, and as she did every night, she pretended to be asleep when he slipped in beside her.

"'Night, love," he whispered.

She didn't respond and a few minutes later drifted into a natural, contented sleep.

A noise woke her. She stirred—discovering that she'd been sleeping with her head on Paul's chest. His arm secured her to him.

"Is it morning yet?" she murmured, closing her eyes again, reluctant to leave the warmth pressing against her.

"In a few minutes."

Paul rose before her every morning to stoke the fire and put on the coffee. Caroline had no idea whether she touched him in her sleep and feared that she'd wake in his arms one morning and embarrass them both.

"Do I do this often?" she asked, a little flustered.

"Not nearly enough," he returned. His hand ran down the length of her spine, stopping at the small of her back. He paused and inhaled sharply.

Caroline realized it was that soft rumble from his throat that had awakened her. Still she didn't move. He felt incredibly good—warm, strong…male.

Five minutes passed, then ten. Caroline knew she had to pull herself away; each minute was more pleasant than the one before.

"I'll make the coffee this morning," she murmured, easing away from him.

Paul stopped her. "There's no rush. Go back to sleep if you'd like."

"To sleep?" She lifted her head enough to search his face. "Aren't you going to the station?"

"I'll be there, but you won't."

Caroline was sure she'd misunderstood him.

"I asked Tanana to spend the day with you," he explained. "She's going to introduce you to the other women in the village."

For a moment, Caroline was too stunned to grasp

what he was saying. "Paul, do you mean it? I don't have to go to the station?" Without thought, she wrapped her arms around his neck and covered his cheeks and forehead with a series of tiny, eager kisses.

Paul's hands found her head and guided her mouth to his for a kiss that was long and hard. Leisurely, her lips moved against his. Without her being certain how it happened, Paul reversed their positions with such ease that she lay on her back, staring up at him. Slowly, as though he couldn't resist her a second longer, he lowered his mouth to hers in a kiss that stirred her, heart and soul. Caroline couldn't possibly have denied herself that kiss. Her hands sought his face, luxuriating in the feel of his beard.

Paul broke off the kiss and, with a sigh that seemed to come from deep inside, buried his face in the hollow of her throat.

Caroline entwined her arms around his neck and released her own sigh of contentment. She was shocked at how right it felt to have Paul hold and kiss her. Her heart raged to a primitive beat and her body throbbed with a simmering passion. She didn't want to feel these things. When she left him, she didn't want to be weighed down with regrets.

He raised his head then, and compelled her gaze to meet his own, but she turned her head. "You're going to be late."

He nodded.

No time clock waited for him, and they both knew it. He eased away from her and sat on the edge of the bed for a moment to regain his strength. Caroline made him weak in ways he didn't understand. She wanted him; he could almost taste her eagerness. And yet, she

had to say *yes* to him with complete certainty. With commitment as well as desire.

Exasperated, he plowed his fingers through his hair. He'd be patient a little longer, but he wasn't going to be able to withstand many more of her kisses. She fascinated him. She'd captured his heart and held it in the palm of her hand with as much concern as she would an unwanted sweet.

Although it was midmorning, Caroline was barely up and dressed when Tanana arrived. Again the young woman knocked politely at the door before stepping inside.

"Morning, Mrs. Trevor," she said shyly. "Caroline…"

"Morning, Tanana. I was just fixing myself some breakfast. Would you like some?"

She shook her head. "You come now, please?"

"Now?"

Tanana nodded.

"There isn't time for breakfast?"

"No time."

Muttering disparaging words under her breath, Caroline removed the skillet from the stove and put the eggs back in the refrigerator while Tanana grabbed Caroline's boots and parka.

"Where are we going?"

"The meeting hall."

"The other women are already there?"

"Yes. Many of them."

Caroline had no idea what they were waiting for, but she was so pleased to be able to talk to another human

being that she wouldn't have cared if they were only going to sit around and drink weak coffee.

As Tanana had promised, there were seven or eight women gathered inside the large hall that served as the heart of the small community. Smiling faces greeted her when they walked in and Tanana led an astonished Caroline to an empty chair that stood in the center of the room—obviously the seat of honor.

She soon recognized that the women were giving a party in her honor, something like a bridal shower. One by one, each woman stepped forward and offered her a gift. Not all the women spoke English, but Tanana acted as their interpreter. The gifts were mostly home-made, displaying such talent and skill that Caroline's breath caught in her throat at their beauty. She received a stunning hand-knit sweater, slippers made from seal-skin, several pieces of intricate scrimshaw with scenes that depicted Indian life in the frozen North, as well as smoked salmon and venison. Caroline watched in wide-eyed wonder as they approached her. When it came to material things, they had so little and she had so much, yet they were lovingly sharing a precious part of their lives. Tears gathered in her eyes and she swallowed down a thickness forming in her throat, not wanting to embarrass these friendly, generous women.

When they'd finished, Caroline stood and went to each one to personally thank her. Later, after they'd served lunch, the women gathered their yarn and started to knit.

"What are they making?" Caroline asked Tanana.

"Sweaters for the tourists."

"Gold River gets that many tourists?"

"Some, but they're mostly for the stores in Fairbanks, Juneau and Anchorage."

"Oh."

"All the women of the village work on the sweaters in wintertime," Tanana continued. "Each day we meet here."

"I knit, too," Caroline said, broaching the subject carefully. She wanted to be part of this community—at least, for as long as she lived here. Although her skill might not have been at the level of these women, she could learn. They'd been so kind to her that she wanted to return their kindness.

"Would you like to join us?" Tanana asked politely.

"Please." A moment later, Caroline was handed a pair of needles, several skeins of thick yarn and, with Tanana to guide her, was set to work.

That night, Caroline was bursting with excitement, so much that she could hardly contain it. When Paul walked in the cabin door, she practically flew across the room.

"Hi," she greeted him. "Did you know about the… party?"

His smiling eyes delved into hers. "Tanana told me about it last week. She said it was time I let you out of bed long enough to meet the village women."

Caroline decided to ignore that comment. "They're wonderful people."

"I know, love." Once he'd removed his parka and hung it in the closet, Caroline grabbed his hand and led him into the bedroom. She'd placed the nonfood items on the quilt for him to examine. He picked up each piece and nodded his pleasure at the village's generosity, praising the skill and beauty of their art. When

he came to the oddly shaped piece of knitting, he regarded it skeptically. "And what's this?"

"Oh, yes, I nearly forgot. The women knit, but I guess you already know that. Anyway, they let me sit and work with them this afternoon. Of course I'm not nearly as good as they are and my poor sweater wouldn't be anywhere near good enough to sell to the tourists." She laughed. "It's funny to think that some tourist might buy a sweater assuming it was knit by a local Athabascan only to discover it was made by a Seattle nurse." She giggled again. "At the end of the afternoon, I think Tanana was afraid of hurting my feelings so I asked if I could do something else with my first effort."

"And what was that?"

"I told them I wanted to knit this sweater for you."

"What did they say to that?"

"Oh, they were pleased, but then they would be, since they probably couldn't sell it." She waltzed out of the bedroom and into the kitchen. "And I made dinner. Tanana looked so tired that I offered. Naturally, she argued with me, but not too strenuously."

"So you had a good day."

"I had a marvelous day!" She turned her back to him to stir the simmering gravy. All afternoon she'd been trying to come up with a way of persuading Paul that she should join the other women on a daily basis. He'd been so unyielding in other matters that she dreaded a confrontation now.

"I suppose you want to go back?"

Caroline whirled around, her heart in her eyes. "Yes. Are you okay with that?"

"I think it's more your decision than mine."

She understood what he was saying, but bit back a ready reply while she took slices of meat from the oven and forked them onto a platter, which she set on the table.

"Unless you trust me again," she said, her eyes holding his, "I know I won't ever be able to prove I'm trustworthy in your eyes."

"Then do as you wish."

Caroline was so pleased that she was hard-pressed not to throw her arms around his neck and kiss him the way she had that morning. It wasn't until after they'd eaten that she realized how much she actually wanted to kiss him, but quickly pushed the thought from her mind.

Later, she found herself humming while washing the dinner dishes, and paused, surprised at herself. She was happy—truly content. She turned to find Paul watching her as he dried their plates and they shared a smile.

Once again they played a heated game of Scrabble, but without any wagers. This time Caroline won.

"You'll note that I didn't use a single dirty word," she told him with a proud snicker.

Paul chuckled and reset the board for a second game.

That next afternoon and for several more that followed, Caroline joined the village women for their daily knitting session. The first few days, the women were shy and didn't say much to her. Gradually they opened up and she became privy to the village gossip. More than one of the women seemed to find something about Caroline amusing. Every time they looked in her direction, they leaned over to the woman next to them and whispered something that made the other smile.

Finally, when Caroline's curiosity got the better of her, she asked Tanana about it.

The young woman blushed. "They say you are a fortunate woman."

"Fortunate? I don't understand."

"Yes, you have Paul for your lover. They are envious that at night he sleeps at your side and holds you in his arms. They say you will have many healthy babies with Paul. He is... I don't know the English word."

"Never mind," Caroline returned, her fingers tightening around the knitting needles. "I know what you mean." Did she ever! So Paul was a virile male who had sampled the delights of the village women before her arrival.

By the time she got back to the cabin, Caroline was so furious that she paced the small enclosure, ready to give her husband a piece of her mind the instant he returned home. She'd never dreamed, hadn't thought he'd ever do anything that low. No wonder he wanted a wife. From the looks the women had been sending her way, they'd probably started fighting over him. Well, they could have him. She was finished with him. Nothing could keep her in Gold River now. She didn't care what it took, she was leaving Paul just as soon as she could.

When the wooden door opened and the howling wind whirled through the cabin, it was only a spring breeze compared to the ice around Caroline's heart.

"Hi," Paul said with a grin, but one look at her contorted, angry features and his smile quickly faded. "What's wrong?"

She didn't wait for him to remove his coat. Her index finger found its mark in the middle of his chest. "You

are despicable. You are lower than a snake. You are…" Words failed her as hot tears blurred her vision. "I can't find the words to tell you how much I despise you!"

Paul didn't look particularly concerned. "Was it something I said, or are you still mad about that four-letter word I used in the Scrabble game?"

Six

"You think you're so clever, don't you?" Caroline flared. Her outrage got the better of her and she picked up a book from the end table and hurled it at him.

With a dexterity few could manage, Paul caught the book and the saltshaker that immediately followed. The amusement fled his eyes. "Caroline, what's gotten into you?"

"You...animal!"

"Tell me what I did."

"You...*beast!*" The pepper shaker whizzed past his ear.

"Caroline!"

"You...you...adulterer!" That might not make complete sense, since he hadn't been married, but it conveyed her disgust.

Stunned, Paul watched as she stormed into the bedroom and viciously slammed the door. For a minute he did nothing but stand with a book and saltshaker in his hand, too bemused to move. Beyond her explosive fury, what shocked Paul most was the hurt he saw in her eyes.

"Adulterer?" he repeated in an astonished whisper.

Inside the room, Caroline sat on the edge of the bed. Stinging tears threatened to run down her face and she rubbed the heels of her hands against her eyes in a futile effort to restrain them. Damn it all, she was falling in love with him—head over heels in love with a man who had neither morals nor conscience. If she didn't love him, then knowing what he'd done wouldn't hurt this much. Caroline cried harder. She didn't *want* to love him. A hiccupping sob ripped through her throat and she buried her face in her hands.

Her crying devastated Paul. He'd planned to wait until her anger had dissipated before trying to reason with her, but he couldn't. Every sob felt like a punch to his abdomen.

"Caroline," he called from the other side of the door. "Can we talk about this?"

Silence.

"Caroline, believe me, I haven't the foggiest idea what you're talking about."

"I'll just bet you don't!"

"I don't." He tried the knob, but she'd locked the door. "As your husband, I demand that you open this door immediately." He felt foolish saying it, but couldn't think of anything else.

She snickered.

"Caroline… Please." When she didn't respond, he rammed his hands in his pants pockets. "Are you angry about our wedding night? Is that it?" Standing directly in front of the door, he muttered, "I can see it isn't going to do any good to try talking to you now. You're in no mood to be reasonable."

With that, the bedroom door opened so unexpectedly that he almost fell through.

Caroline glared at him with renewed animosity. "Do you mean to tell me that…that on the night we were married you…you took advantage of me?"

"Caroline, if you'd listen…"

"O-o-h." Her clenched fists pummeled his chest until her hands felt numb with pain.

"That's enough." Paul caught her wrists and pinned her against the wall. Her shoulders heaved with exertion, and tears streaked her face and brimmed in her wide, blue eyes.

Trembling, she collected herself and drew in a ragged breath. Briefly, she struggled, but Paul's hold tightened. His fierce look held her as effectively as his hands. Caroline met his eyes with open defiance.

"Love." His voice was a hoarse whisper of bewilderment and confusion, his face mere inches from her own. "What is it?"

He spoke with such gentleness that it would be easy to forget what he was and what he'd done. "Let me go," she said, her rage gone now, replaced by a far deeper, more crippling emotion—sorrow.

Paul saw the pain in her eyes and was filled with such perplexity that he reacted instinctively. In an effort to comfort, his mouth sought hers.

His kiss was insistent, demanding, relentless. Almost against her will Caroline parted her lips to meet his. Her eagerness for him grew, an eagerness that rocked her soul. Gradually both she and Paul relaxed, the crucial need abated. He loosened his grip, but continued to hold her wrists. Caroline became aware of

the heavy thud of his heart while her own pulsed with a frantic rhythm.

They breathed in unison. Paul's eyes searched her face as he looked for any clue that would help him understand her irrational behavior. Hot color stained her cheeks, but he didn't know if it was from her anger or her excitement during their kiss. Her lips were moist, and he bent his head to taste their sweetness again. When he finally drew back, he and Caroline were both trembling.

He released her hands and Caroline dropped them to her sides. "I was with the women today," she began, in a voice so fraught with pain that Paul wrapped her securely in his arms. "And they told me…"

"Told you what, Caroline?"

"That…you're a fantastic lover."

He frowned. "Ah," he whispered slowly, then cupped her face with his hands, kissing her briefly. "And you assumed they meant it literally?"

"How else was I supposed to take it?"

"I've been living here for several years now," he began. "I've become friends with many of them and their families. They're, uh, kind enough to favor me with certain attributes they *believe* I possess."

Caroline's gaze met his. "They sounded so…so knowledgeable."

He grinned widely. "Hey, I'm only one man. I couldn't possibly have had that many lovers."

"Have you had…even one?" Her intense gaze locked with his.

"By everything I hold dear, I swear to you that I've never had a single lover in Gold River." Paul had assumed she'd welcome his assurance, but his words pro-

duced the most uncanny response; tears flooded her eyes and streamed down her face. Caroline hugged him fiercely, burying her face in his sweater. Half laughing, half crying, she lifted her head and spread eager kisses mingled with salty tears on his face. Gently Paul held her, wondering if he'd been outside civilization so long he'd lost his ability to understand women. He sighed; perhaps he had.

Their relationship altered after that night. The changes were subtle ones and came about so naturally that Paul could only guess their meaning. The first thing he noticed was that Caroline had placed her suitcase under the bed, as though she'd finally accepted her position in his life and planned to remain. He yearned for her to forget her hope of returning to Seattle.

He knew she spent a lot of time with Tanana and apparently they'd worked out an agreement concerning dinner, since Caroline started cooking all their meals. She'd once told him she was an excellent cook and he learned that she hadn't exaggerated. She was clever, inventive and resourceful. It wasn't every woman who could make dried eggs edible.

Everyone was her friend; even Walter had become her ally. Paul had been in the village six months before the old man had fully accepted him. Walter's acceptance of Caroline was typical of the love she received from all the people of Gold River. The children adored her; Caroline couldn't walk out the door without two or three of them running to her side. One day Paul discovered Caroline in the meeting hall, skipping rope with the sixth-grade girls. Another day he found her involved in a heated soccer game with the junior-high boys.

When an old woman had a toothache, she came to Caroline. A feverish baby was brought to her as well. A little boy with a stomach ache showed up unexpectedly one afternoon. The medical clinic was open once a week when a team from the Public Health Department flew in for appointments, but it was Caroline the villagers came to. At first she used her own personal quantity of painkillers and bandages; then, as a qualified nurse she received access to the clinic's supply. Paul felt absolutely delighted that she could use her training this way.

But now he was so much in love he thought he'd die from wanting her. But to rush into lovemaking now would be foolish. She was so close to recognizing she loved him, and when that day came it would be right and beautiful, although he often wondered how much longer he could hold out. He endured the sweetest torture every morning when he woke to find her in his arms. At night, the agony was far greater; he dreaded her touch and at the same time craved it.

That evening after dinner, Caroline brought out a large package and placed it on the ottoman in front of him.

Paul lowered the two-day-old newspaper and raised questioning eyes to his wife. "What's this?"

"Open it and see." She'd worked so hard on this sweater that if it didn't fit, she'd burst into tears. "I probably should've saved it for Christmas, but…" It was silly to be this nervous. She wanted to please him and the holidays were still six weeks away. Besides, she couldn't think of a better way to tell Paul she loved him.

"But what, love?"

"But I thought you deserved it now." For calming her angry tirades, for being so patient with her, for his gentleness and a hundred other admirable qualities. And because she longed to be his wife in the truest sense of the word.

Carefully, Paul removed the paper and held up the Irish cable-knit sweater. "Caroline, I'm…stunned. It's a fine piece of work."

"If it doesn't fit, I can redo it." She couldn't believe she'd made that offer; the pattern was difficult and complicated. If it hadn't been for Tanana's and the other women's help, she would've given up and unraveled the sweater weeks before.

"I'm sure it'll fit perfectly." To prove his point, he stood and pulled it over his head. "Where did you get the yarn?" he asked, running his hand over the sleeves. The sweater was a lovely shade of winter wheat and far lighter than the material the village women typically used.

"I sent away for it. Mary Finefeather had a catalog."

"How did you pay for it?" She'd never come to him for money, although he would've been more than pleased to give it to her. They had little need for cash in Gold River. The supply store and grocery sent him monthly accounts and his paychecks were automatically deposited in the Fairbanks Savings and Loan.

"I used my credit card."

He nodded and kissed her lightly. "Thank you, love. I'll always treasure it."

Caroline's returning smile was weak, as though she was disappointed by his response. Paul watched her leave and wondered if he'd said something to offend her. He began to doubt that he'd ever understand her.

Hours later, Paul lay at her side. His even breathing convinced Caroline he was sound asleep as she lay on her back wide-eyed, staring at the ceiling. She was now convinced that she was a failure. For two weeks, she'd been trying to tell Paul that she was ready to be his wife in *every* way. How a man could be so completely blind was beyond her. If it hadn't been for a few secret looks of longing she'd intercepted, she would have abandoned her cause. She made excuses to be close to him, to touch him. All the signals she'd been sending him would have stopped a freight train! The sweater had been her ace in the hole and even that had failed. In return, he'd kissed her like an affectionate older brother.

Ah well, there was always tomorrow. Maybe if she wore the nightgown her aunts had given her… She smiled and her eyes drifted shut. She couldn't get any more obvious than that.

The next day was a busy one. The small town was holding an early Thanksgiving feast, and it seemed half of Alaska had been invited. People had been arriving from the outlying areas all morning. Caroline and Tanana were responsible for decorating the meeting hall and the two of them made a comical sight. Caroline wouldn't allow Tanana, who was in an advanced stage of pregnancy, to climb the ladder to hang the crepe-paper streamers, so Caroline wrapped them around her neck and hauled them up herself.

"This isn't fair," Tanana complained. "All I'm doing is holding the ladder for you."

"I'm not going to let you stand on this rickety old

thing," Caroline muttered, stretching as far as her limbs would allow to stick a thumbtack into the beam.

"If Paul ever saw this, he'd be mad."

"He isn't going to know, and you're not going to tell him—right?"

"What will you bribe me with?"

Caroline laughed. "Hush, now, and hand me another streamer." She climbed down a couple of steps and Tanana gave her the next set of bright orange and yellow crepe-paper strips.

When they'd finished, the two women surveyed the hall, proud of their accomplishment. It was astonishing how much a little color added to the festive spirit.

Mary Finefeather, a foster grandmother to many of the village kids, delivered sandwiches to Caroline and Tanana. Typical of the old woman's personality, Mary spoke in choppy one-word sentences.

"Eat," she said with a grin.

"I think that's an order," Caroline commented, and looked at Tanana, who smiled in reply. The younger woman had lost much of her shyness now and Caroline considered her a valued friend.

"What are you getting Paul for Christmas?" Tanana asked, studying Caroline.

"I...don't know. I gave him the sweater last night." She wished she hadn't; with the holidays fast approaching, she had wasted her best gift—seemingly for naught.

"I know what he wants."

"You do?"

Tanana placed her hand on her swollen abdomen and stared at her stomach. "He wants a son."

Caroline nearly swallowed her sandwich whole. "Oh?"

"You'll give him fine sons? And daughters?"

Embarrassed, Caroline looked away. "Someday."

"Soon?"

"I… I don't know." Caroline couldn't very well announce that she and Paul had never made love, at least not that she could remember.

Caroline worked for part of the afternoon, then returned to the cabin, frustrated and tired. She'd slept poorly, and tonight would be another late night. Before she could talk herself out of the idea, she climbed onto the bed and closed her eyes, intending to rest for only a few minutes.

Paul found her there an hour later, barely visible in the soft light of dusk. He paused in the doorway of their bedroom and experienced such a wave of desire that he sucked in a tight breath. Her blouse had ridden up to expose the creamy smooth skin of her midriff. Blood pounded in his head and his feet seemed to move of their own accord, taking him to her side.

His gaze lingered on the smooth slant of her brow and a smile briefly touched his face. She could make a clearer statement with an arch of her eyebrow than some women said in twenty years. Her nose was perfect and her sweet, firm lips were enough to drive a man insane. He thought about the last time they'd kissed and how, for hours afterward, he'd been in a foul mood, barking at Walter and the others until Walter had suggested that Paul do something to cure whatever was ailing him.

Caroline was ailing him. He wanted to touch her, to—

Caroline yawned and rolled over.

Paul jumped away from her as though he'd been caught doing something wrong. His knees felt like slush in a spring thaw. On unsteady feet, he walked over to the dresser.

"Caroline, it's time to get up." He hardly recognized the strained, harsh voice as his own.

Slowly she opened her eyes. She'd been having the most wonderful dream about giving Paul the child Tanana claimed he wanted so badly. One look at her husband, who stood stiffly on the other side of the room, was enough to return her to the cold world of reality. His back was to her.

"Hi," she said, stretching her hands high above her head and yawning loudly.

"Hi," he said gruffly. He didn't dare turn around. If her midriff had been showing before, he could only imagine what he'd glimpse now. He felt himself go weak all over again.

Caroline frowned at his abruptness. "Did you have a good day?"

"Sure." He pulled open the top drawer and took out a clean T-shirt. "You'd better get dressed or we'll be late for the party."

"What time is it?"

"Five."

Caroline's frown deepened. No one was expected before seven. "We've got plenty of time."

No, we don't, Paul wanted to shout. He, for one, was at the end of his rope.

"Paul, what's wrong?"

"Nothing." He slammed the drawer shut with un-

necessary force. "I just happen to think it's time you got out of bed."

"Are you angry because I took a nap?"

"No," he snapped.

She rose to a sitting position and released a long sigh. "Sometimes I don't understand you."

"That makes two of us."

"Will you please turn around? I don't like talking to your back." She made the request softly, confused by his mood. She'd never known Paul to be so short-tempered and illogical.

"If you don't mind, I'm busy."

Caroline blinked. She replayed the conversation with Tanana, and a heaviness settled on her shoulders. She loved Paul and yearned to have his child, but instead of growing together they seemed to be drifting apart. Sudden tears misted her eyes. She'd thought that once she acknowledged she was in love with him everything would be perfect. Instead, it had gotten worse—much worse.

Paul tossed his sweater on the bed. "Good grief, don't tell me you're crying! One day you're hurling saltshakers at me and the next you're weeping because I tell you to hurry and get ready for a party you've been working on all day."

Her eyes widened with determination to hold back the tears. "I'm not crying. That's ridiculous. Why should I be crying?"

He threw up his hands. "Who knows? I've given up trying to understand you."

The party was a grand success. The meeting hall was filled to the rafters with friends and loved ones

from nearby communities. The dinner proved to be delicious and Caroline received rave reviews for her apple pies and decorating efforts. Although she smiled and made all the appropriate responses, she couldn't seem to get into the party mood.

When the tables were cleared and the dancing began, Caroline saw how Paul seemed to dance with every woman in the room but her. Not that Caroline was given much time to notice. One partner after another claimed her hand for a turn around the floor. After an hour, she pleaded exhaustion and sat down, fanning her flushed face with one hand.

To her surprise, Paul joined her, sitting in the chair beside hers. His lips were pinched, his face grim. "I imagine you're pleased to have every man for a hundred miles panting after you."

Caroline's mouth fell open at the unjust accusation. Quickly she composed herself, stiffening her back. "I'm going to forgive you for that remark, Paul Trevor, because you owe me one. But from here on we're even." She stood up and purposely walked away from him. Her eyes clouded by confusion, she nearly stumbled into Walter, and glancing up at him, hurriedly stammered an apology.

"Didn't you promise me this dance?" Walter said.

Still unable to find her tongue, Caroline nodded.

Studying her, the older man guided her onto the dance floor. A waltz was playing and Caroline slipped one arm around his neck and placed her hand in his.

"All right, girl, tell me—what's made you so unhappy?"

Caroline's mouth formed a poor excuse for a smile. "Paul. I don't know how any man can be so stupid."

"He's blinded by his love for you."

"I sincerely doubt that's it." Caroline looked directly into Walter's face. "I have the feeling he's ready to ship me back to Seattle." There'd been a time when she'd prayed for exactly that, but now her heart ached at the mere thought of leaving him.

Standing by the punch bowl, Paul watched her. Caroline could feel his dark gaze on her back. With every passing minute, his eyes grew darker and more angry.

Walter chuckled. "Paul would rather cut off his arm than send you away. Have you told him you love him?"

Caroline's shocked gaze clashed with the man's wise old eyes. "No."

"Then do it, and soon, before he makes an even bigger fool of himself."

When the dance ended, Walter delivered her to Paul's side and quietly left them. Caroline and Paul stood glaring at each other until the music started.

"Shall we?" Caroline asked, glancing toward the crowded floor.

"Why not? You've seen fit to dance with every other male here tonight."

"Paul," she whispered. "Are you jealous?"

He didn't answer her, but she saw that his face was as grim as she'd ever seen it. His hold on her was loose, as if he couldn't bear to touch her.

Caroline swallowed her pride. "There isn't anyone here I'd rather dance with than you."

Still he said nothing. His eyes were focused straight ahead and she didn't see so much as a flicker in his rock-hard features to indicate that he'd heard her or that her words had any effect.

"When I first came to Gold River, I hated it."

If possible, his mouth grew harder, more inflexible.

"But...things changed and I realized I was happy here. There's a wildness to this land. A challenge that makes people strong and wise. I've seen that in you and admired your patience and gentleness."

Momentarily, Paul dropped his eyes and studied her as though he didn't quite trust what she was saying.

Caroline thought her heart would burst with pain when he quickly glanced away.

"You idiot," she said and brought her shoe down hard on the top of his foot.

Paul let out a small yelp of pain.

"I'm trying to tell you I love you, but you can forget it! And while you're at it, you can forget about our son, too!" She broke away and left him holding one leg like a flamingo while he nursed his injured foot.

At the door, Caroline grabbed her boots and parka and stormed out of the meeting hall, too angry for tears, too frustrated to consider what she was doing. She knew only that she had to escape.

"Caroline!"

His frantic call came to her before she reached the cabin door. With heightened resolve, she pretended she hadn't heard him.

"Caroline! Would you wait?"

She ignored his pleading as well. By the time he arrived, she was sitting by the fireplace with a book in front of her face.

"Caroline...what did you just say?" He was breathless, his voice rushed and uneven.

"It was nothing."

"It was everything," he whispered in awe. "*Do* you love me? Caroline, would you please look at me?"

"No."

Paul felt he was going to explode with happiness. "And what was that crazy remark about a son?"

She turned the page of her book and glanced with keen interest at the beginning of the next chapter, although she had no idea what was going on in the story.

Paul fell to his knees at her side and pried the book from her stiff fingers. She refused to meet his eyes.

"Caroline…" He breathed her name with a heart overflowing with expectancy and hope. "Are you telling me you're ready to be my wife?"

"I couldn't have made it any plainer. I've flaunted myself in front of you all week. I gave you the sweater… hoping… Paul Trevor, you're an idiot! For days, I've been throwing myself at you and you…you've been so blind and so stupid."

"You have?" Paul was flabbergasted. "When? Days?"

"Weeks!"

"Weeks?" He *had* been blind, but no longer.

His hands framed her face as he guided her lips to his, kissing her with such hungry intensity it robbed her of breath. Somehow he lifted her from the chair, cradled her in his arms and carried her into their bedroom. He placed her on the mattress and knelt over her, studying her to be sure this wasn't a dream.

Caroline stared into his eyes and twined her arms around his neck, bringing his mouth back to her own. "You idiot," she whispered again.

"Not anymore, love."

Their lips met over and over, as though each kiss was sweeter and more potent than the one before. Holding back nothing, Caroline surrendered to him with

joyful abandon. He explored her face, her neck, her shoulders, charting undiscovered territory with his lips as he helped her undress. Finally they were both free of restricting clothes and Paul kissed her until she responded with a wantonness she didn't know she possessed. They broke apart, winded and panting.

"Caroline," he murmured, his face keen and ardent in the moonlight. "Are you sure?"

"I've never been more sure of anything in my life."

Deeply content, Caroline lay with her cheek against her husband's chest. Her leg stroked his and she sighed her happiness. There was no turning back for them now; they were truly husband and wife, their commitment to each other complete.

Paul's hand smoothed the tumbled hair from her face. "Are you happy, love?"

"Very." Her nails scraped playfully at his chest. "Why didn't you tell me it was this good? If I'd known, I would've demanded my wifely rights." She raised her head to kiss the strong, proud line of his chin. "Tanana and the other women guessed correctly—you *are* a fantastic lover."

Paul opened his mouth to answer her when there was a loud knock on the front door. Caroline gave him a look of dismay; no one would come unless there was trouble.

Paul rolled to his feet, his body alert. He reached for his clothes and threw them on, then hurried to the door.

Caroline dressed in a rush, anxious now. When she entered the living room, she found Paul speaking to Thomas Eagleclaw, Tanana's husband.

"Tanana's gone into labor," Paul explained. "Her mother's with her, but she wants you."

Caroline nodded. "I'll be there in a minute."

Seven

By the time Caroline arrived at Tanana's cabin, her heart was pounding, not with exertion from the long walk, but with excitement and, she admitted, anxiety. Her experience was limited to a sterile hospital delivery room with a doctor, other nurses and all the necessary emergency equipment. None of that existed in Gold River, and Caroline had never felt more inadequate.

Thomas, Tanana's husband, and Paul led the way to their cabin. Tanana lay in the center of a double bed, her face glistening with perspiration, her eyes wide with pain. The young woman held out her hand to Caroline. "Thank you for coming."

"When did the contractions start?" Caroline asked, sitting on the edge of the bed.

Tanana lowered her gaze. "This afternoon."

"Why didn't you tell me?"

"I wasn't sure they meant I was in labor."

Caroline understood. Tanana had mentioned twice that week that she'd been experiencing "twinges" and Caroline had told her those were normal and she needn't worry.

The older woman in the bedroom rose to greet her. Tanana's mother smiled her welcome and returned to her rocking chair, content to let Caroline assume the role of midwife. Caroline went to the kitchen to wash her hands, praying silently that this would be an easy birth, routine in every way.

It wasn't. Hours later, both Caroline and Tanana were drenched in sweat. The girl was terrified. Caroline, although outwardly calm, was equally frightened. Tanana's mother continued to rock, offering an encouraging smile now and then.

"It shouldn't be long now," Caroline said, smoothing the hair from Tanana's brow and wiping her face with a cool washcloth.

Tanana tried to smile, but the effort was too great. "Rest as much as you can between pains," Caroline instructed.

Tanana nodded. She closed her eyes and rolled her head to the side, ruthlessly biting the corner of her lip as another contraction took hold of her body.

"Don't fight it," Caroline said. "Try to breathe through the pain."

Tanana's death grip on Caroline's fingers slackened and Caroline relaxed, too. "You're doing great, Tanana. I'll check you with the next contraction and we'll see how far things have progressed."

Caroline's worst fears were confirmed; the baby was breech. A knot of fear clogged her throat. Didn't this baby realize she didn't have a lot of experience in this area? The least it could do was cooperate! "I'm going to get some fresh water," she told Tanana, and stood to leave the bedside. Tanana's eyes revealed her fear.

"Don't worry," Caroline said with a reassuring smile, "I'll be right back."

In the next room, Paul was playing cards with Thomas, although it was easy to see that neither man's attention was on the game. One look at Caroline's distraught eyes, and Paul moved to her side at the kitchen sink. "What's wrong?"

"The baby is breech. Paul, I'm frightened. This is far more complicated than anything I've ever handled. My training was all in a hospital setting, and I've worked in a doctor's office for two years. You don't get much experience delivering breech babies in an office building."

"Tanana needs you."

"I know." Paul was referring to strength and confidence, but she couldn't offer the poor girl something she didn't have herself.

"If you think it's more than you can cope with, we'll call in a plane and fly her to Fairbanks."

"Yes. Please call." But that would take hours and they both knew it. "In the meantime I'll...do my best."

"I know you will, love." His hands cradled her face and he kissed her, his lips fitting tenderly over hers, lending her his own strength. A whimper from Tanana broke them apart and Caroline hurried back to her friend's side.

The hours sped by, but Caroline was barely aware of their passing. She was busy every minute, talking softly, encouraging Tanana, calling on not only her experience but her instincts. Her friend's fortitude and inner strength impressed her. When the squalling infant was finally released from the young woman's body, unrestrained tears of happiness filled Caroline's eyes.

"You have a son," she said, gently placing the baby on his mother's stomach.

"A son." Tanana's wide smile revealed her overwhelming delight and with a cry of joy, she fell back against the pillow.

A few minutes later, Caroline entered the kitchen, carrying the crying infant in her arms. Her eyes met Paul's as the two men rose slowly to their feet.

"A boy," she said softly.

Thomas let out a hoot of exhilarated happiness and paused to briefly inspect his son before he rushed past Caroline to join his wife.

Paul looked down at the small bundle in her arms. His eyes softened at the wrinkled face and tiny fingers protruding from the blanket. "You must be exhausted," he said, studying Caroline.

Lightly, she shook her head. She'd never experienced such a feeling of bliss in her life. It was as though she'd labored to deliver this child herself and he'd been born of her own body. "He's so beautiful." Unabashed tears rained from her eyes and she kissed the baby's sweet brow.

"Yes, but not as beautiful as you, love," Paul said tenderly, his heart constricting at the sight of a baby in his wife's arms. The day would come when they'd have a child of their own and the thought filled him with happy anticipation.

An hour later, the emergency medical team had been and gone, pronouncing both mother and son in good health. Paul took Caroline back to their cabin. Now that the surge of high spirits had faded, Caroline realized how weary she was. "What time is it?"

"Noon."

"*Noon?* Really?"

Paul led her directly into their bedroom and sat her on the bed, where she fell back on the rumpled sheets and heaved a sigh, closing her eyes. Smiling down at her, Paul removed her shoes.

"Paul?"

"Hmm?" He unzipped her jeans next and slid them down her long legs. A surge of desire shot through him and he forced himself to look at her face and remember how exhausted she was. Given the least amount of encouragement, he would've fallen into bed beside her.

"Tanana told me you wanted a son." Her eyes still closed, she felt lethargic, yet oddly contented.

"A daughter would do as well."

"Soon?"

"Sooner than you think if you don't get under these blankets," he grumbled, covering her with the quilts.

Caroline smiled, feeling warm and secure. "I love you," she murmured dreamily.

Paul stood by the edge of the bed, unsteady. "You love me?" She didn't answer him and he knew she was already asleep. His heart swelled with such joy that he felt like shouting and dancing around the small room. Instead, he bent down and kissed her temple. To stay with her now would be torture and although it was a different kind of agony, Paul left the room and curled up on the recliner, meaning only to rest his eyes.

Caroline found him there several hours later. "Paul," she whispered, shaking his shoulder.

With reluctance, he opened his eyes. When he saw it was Caroline, he grinned tiredly. "Did you sleep?"

"Like a baby. Why are you out here?"

"Because you needed your rest, love." His arm cir-

cled her waist and he brought her into his lap, where he nuzzled her neck. She felt so good in his arms, soft, feminine, his—all his. Larry was in the past now and gone forever.

Paul thought of his life before she'd come to him and wondered how he'd managed all those years without her. She was as much a part of him as his own heart. She was his world, his sun, his stars. All these weeks she'd led him down a rock-strewn trail, but every minute had been worth the wait. She was more than he'd ever dreamed.

Caroline smiled. Her hands directed his mouth to hers and she kissed him hungrily. He didn't need to tell her why he'd slept on the recliner; she knew and she loved him for it.

"Oh, Caroline," he groaned. "Do you realize what you're doing?"

She answered him by unfastening the buttons of his shirt and slipping her fingers inside to stroke his chest. The wild sensations he aroused in her were so exquisite, she wanted to weep.

The sounds of their lovemaking filled the cabin. Whispered phrases of awe followed as Paul removed her blouse.

"Caroline," he moaned. "If we don't stop right now, we're going to end up making love in this chair."

"I don't want to stop...."

In the days afterward, Caroline could hardly believe that they'd waited so long to become lovers when everything was so extraordinarily right between them. Now they seemed to be making up for lost time. His desire for her both delighted and astonished her. They

made love every night and often Paul couldn't seem to wait until their usual bedtime. One evening, in the middle of a Scrabble game, she found him looking at her with a wild gleam in his eye.

"Paul?"

He glanced toward the bedroom and raised his brows in question.

"It's only seven o'clock," she said, laughing.

His expression was almost boyish. "I can wait… I think."

Caroline smiled, stood and walked around the table to take him by the hand. "Well, I can't."

They never finished playing Scrabble that night. Instead they invented new games.

Some days, Paul was barely in the door when he wanted her.

"What's for dinner?" he'd ask.

She'd tell him and catch that look in his eye and automatically turn down the stove. "Don't worry, it can simmer for an hour."

Their dinner simmered and they sizzled. This was the honeymoon they'd never had and Caroline prayed it would last a lifetime.

She yearned to get pregnant, but the first week of December, she discovered sadly that she wasn't.

"If the truth be known," Paul said comfortingly, "I'd rather have you to myself for a while."

Caroline nestled close to his side, her head in the crook of his arm. "It may not be so easy for me. My mother had difficulty getting pregnant."

"Then we'll just have to work at it, love."

Caroline laughed; if they worked any harder, they'd drop from sheer exhaustion. Paul kissed her and held

her close. "I never thought I'd find such happiness," he told her.

"Me neither." He wasn't a man of many words or flowery speeches. Nor did he shower her with expensive gifts. But his actions were far more effective than mere words. He loved her, and every day he did something to let her know how much he cared.

One morning after Paul had gone to work, Caroline realized she'd nearly let all this happiness slip through her fingers. The pain of Larry's rejection had nearly blinded her to Paul's love—and her own feelings. When Larry had left, Caroline had almost died inside. Now she realized how mismatched they were. They'd been friends, and had erroneously assumed their friendship meant they'd also be good lovers. Not until she'd slept with Paul could Caroline acknowledge that marriage to Larry would have been a mistake. Larry had recognized the truth long before she did.

Undoubtedly, he was torturing himself with guilt. Her aunts had mentioned his visit in their first letter and although his name was brought up briefly in subsequent letters, Caroline knew he'd been back to visit her aunts, eager for word of her.

In an effort to ease her friend's mind, Caroline decided to write him a letter. It was the least she could do. He'd feel better and she could tell him herself how happy she was. She wished him the best and was eternally grateful that he'd had the wisdom and courage to keep them both from making a colossal mistake.

Caroline had originally intended her letter to be short, but by the time she was done, she'd written five pages. She told him about Paul and how much she loved her husband and thanked Larry for being her friend.

She added bits and pieces about her life in Alaska and how beautiful the land was. Come summer, Paul had promised to take her hiking and fishing, and she joked with Larry because he got queasy at the sight of a worm. When she'd finished, Caroline read the letter and realized her happiness shone through every word. Larry would have no more doubts.

After stuffing the five pages into an envelope, Caroline carried the letter to the supply store, which also served as the local post office.

"Good afternoon, Harry." She greeted the proprietor with a ready smile.

"Mrs. Trevor," he returned formally. "Nice day, isn't it?"

"It's a beautiful day." She handed him the letter. "It already looks like Christmas." The snow was drifting slowly down, sparkling and pristine.

He nodded. "This all I can do for you?"

Caroline shrugged. "It is unless you can sell me a pizza. I've had the craving for a thick, cheesy pizza all week."

He chuckled and rubbed the side of his jaw. "Sorry. Can't help you there."

"That's what I figured. Oh, well." With a cheery wave, she was gone.

Paul rounded the corner of the supply store just as Caroline disappeared. "Afternoon, Harry. Was that my wife?"

"Yup, you just missed her. She came to mail a letter."

He glanced over at Caroline, but she was too far away for him to shout.

"Thick letter, too, now that I look at it. She might be needing an extra stamp. I'd best weigh it."

Paul nodded, hardly hearing the man. "She's fond of those aunts of hers."

"Her aunt has a funny name then. Larry Atkins."

The name sliced through Paul as effectively as a knife. He attempted to hide his shock and anger from Harry, but wasn't sure he'd succeeded. Without bothering to buy what he'd come for, Paul left and went back to the pumping station. He tried reasoning with himself that it was only a letter, then he recalled all the times Caroline had walked letters over to Harry, preferring to deliver them herself, claiming she needed the exercise.

His anger increased when he remembered how she'd sat at the desk across from his own at the station and vowed to find a means of escaping him. Her voice had been filled with conviction and vengeance. In his foolishness, Paul had believed her feelings had changed. He certainly hadn't expected her to be so deceitful.

"That's ridiculous," Paul said aloud. "No woman is that good an actress."

All the talk of a child. He groaned. She knew his greatest weakness. He sat at his desk and slumped forward, burying his face in his hands. He couldn't condemn her on such flimsy evidence, but he couldn't trust her either. She'd taught him that once—when she'd walked out on him with Burt Manners—but it seemed he was a slow learner.

By the time Paul arrived home that evening, he was, to all appearances, outwardly calm.

Caroline whirled around when he entered the cabin. "Guess what I'm making for dinner." Her smile was brighter than the sun had been all day.

"What's that, love?"

"Pizza."

"Pizza?"

"Well, a close facsimile. I didn't have a round pan so I'm using a square one. And I didn't want to make bread dough, so I'm making do with biscuit batter. And last but not least, we didn't have any sausage so I'm using ground caribou."

"A caribou pizza?"

"How does that sound?"

"Like we'll be eating scrambled eggs later."

"Oh, ye of little faith."

Paul laughed shortly; she didn't know the half of it.

Dinner was only partially successful. To her credit, the caribou pizza wasn't bad. He managed to eat a piece and praised her ingenuity.

"What's for dinner tomorrow night? Moose Tacos?"

She laughed and promised him fried chicken.

While Caroline did the dishes, she watched Paul. He sat in the recliner with the paper resting on his lap as he stared into space. His face was so intent that she wondered what could be troubling him.

"Paul."

He shook himself from his reverie.

"Is something wrong?" she asked.

"No. I was just thinking."

"About what? You looked so pensive."

"Life." His grin was wry.

"Life?"

"It's taken an unexpected turn for us, hasn't it?" He eyed her carefully, hoping to read her heart and recognize the truth. He saw the love and devotion shining from her eyes—and didn't know what to believe.

"Tanana let me watch Carl for her this afternoon," she announced, smiling. "He's growing so fast."

"You love that baby, don't you?"

"As much as if he were our own."

Tenderness wrapped its way around his heart, suffocating his doubts. He loved Caroline more than life itself. If she was playing him for a fool, then he was the happiest idiot alive. He planned to hold on to that contentment, hug it close and treasure every minute she was with him for as long as it lasted. She might dream of her precious Larry, she might even write the bastard, but it was in the curve of his arm that she slept. It was his body that filled hers and gave her pleasure. It was his name she now had and later, God willing, it would be his children she bore.

When they made love that night, it was as if a storm of passion had overtaken them. As if electricity arced between them, the current more powerful than lightning. Each caress became a fire fueled by their love.

Afterward, Caroline lay limp and drowsy in her husband's arms. Her cheeks were bright with the blush of pleasure, her breath uneven. Paul closed his eyes, wondering how he could ever have doubted her. He buried his face in her hair, savoring the fragrance, and held her against him until her breathing grew even and regular.

Caroline wasn't sure what woke her. One minute she was asleep and the next awake. It took her a moment to realize Paul wasn't asleep, either.

"Paul, what's wrong?"

"Not a thing, love."

She slipped her hand over his ribs and kissed his throat. He'd been so quiet this evening and their lovemaking had been a desperate act of passion. Paul

wasn't himself and Caroline wondered what had happened. "I've failed you in some way, haven't I?"

He hesitated. "No, love, I fear I may have failed you."

"Paul, no. I'm happy, truly happy."

"Do you miss Seattle?"

"I miss my aunts," she admitted. "I wish you could meet them. And now and then I think about my friends, but there's nothing for me in Seattle now that I'm with you."

"I love you, Caroline."

She smiled and kissed the side of his mouth. He'd shown her his love in a hundred ways, but he'd never said the words. "I know."

"You're laughing at me, aren't you?" His grip on her tightened, and Caroline jerked away from him with a gasp.

"Paul, what's gotten into you?"

He held himself rigid and didn't speak for an interminable moment. "I told you I loved you and I know you were smiling."

"I...was happy." She lay on her stomach, her hands beneath her.

Another long minute passed. "I'm sorry, love. I didn't mean to frighten you."

She nodded and rolled away from him. Their happiness was shattering right before her eyes and she was powerless to stop it.

"Caroline," he said at last, reaching for her. "I talked to Harry after you were in the store today. I saw the letter you'd written to Larry Atkins."

"It's obvious you didn't read it."

"Why?"

"If you had, your reaction would be altogether different."

"Have you written him in the past?" Paul hated his jealousy. All day he'd been brooding, furious with himself and unreasonable with Caroline. If love did this to a man, he wanted no part of it, and yet he wouldn't, couldn't, give her up.

"This is my first letter to him."

"Why did you feel it was necessary to contact him now?"

"To thank him."

"What?"

"It's true. You mean, *this* is what's been bothering you?"

He didn't answer, ashamed of his behavior.

"Why didn't you ask me earlier? I would've told you all about it. I wrote Larry to let him know he'd done me a gigantic favor by standing me up at the altar."

"You told him that?"

"Not exactly in those words, but basically that's what I said."

"Why didn't you tell me you were writing him?"

Caroline expelled her breath on a nervous sigh. "To be truthful, I didn't think about it. My mistake. Are you always going to be this irrational?"

"When it comes to my wife contacting another guy, I guess I am."

"It isn't the way you're making it sound."

"I have only your word for that."

Caroline fumed, feeling insulted and angry, but rather than argue, she turned her back on him. "Good night, Paul," she grumbled. It wouldn't help matters to talk to him now. In the morning things would be better.

For two days they put the incident behind them. Their happiness was too complete to be destroyed over a silly letter and they each seemed to realize it. On the third day, Paul got home two hours before his usual time.

"You're home early." She looked up from writing Christmas cards, delighted to see her husband.

He sat at the table across from her. "I've got to fly into Fairbanks for a few days."

"Oh, Paul, Fairbanks? I can hardly wait! The first thing I'm going to do is order a real sausage pizza with extra cheese and then I'm going to shop for twelve hours nonstop. You have no idea how much I want to buy Tanana and the baby something special for Christmas. Why didn't you tell me earlier?"

"Because—"

"And you know what else I'm going to do?" She answered her own question before he had the chance, her voice animated and high-pitched. "I'm going to soak in a hot bubble bath and watch television and then I'm—"

"Caroline," he broke in gruffly, his gaze avoiding hers. "This is a business trip. I hadn't planned to bring you along."

Eight

It took a minute for the words to sink in. "You're not taking me with you?" With deliberate patience, Caroline set down the pen and pushed the Christmas cards aside. "Why?"

Paul refused to meet her probing gaze. "I've already explained that it's a business trip."

"That's not the reason and you know it." She'd thought they'd come so far, but the only one who'd moved had been her. She'd walked into his arms and been so blinded by her love she hadn't even seen the chains that bound her.

"I don't know what you're talking about."

"Like hell!"

"I go to Fairbanks every other month or so...."

"Every other month?"

"You can come with me another time."

"I want to go now."

"No!"

"Why not?" She was growing more furious by the moment.

"Because—"

"Because you saw that stupid letter to Larry and you're convinced I've made arrangements to escape. To catch a plane out of Fairbanks."

"Don't be ridiculous." But her accusation was so close to the truth that Paul's heart pounded hard against his ribs.

Caroline's smile was sarcastic. "Since I'm your prisoner, after all, you might as well lock me in a cell."

"You're my wife!"

"I'm the woman who was forced to stay married to you. What we have isn't a marriage!" She saw him open his mouth to contradict her, then close it again. "It takes more than a piece of paper."

"Caroline, you're making too much of this."

"Yes, master," she said, gazing straight ahead, refusing to look at him. "Whatever you say, master." She bent low in a mocking bow, folding her hands in front of her.

"Caroline, stop that."

"Anything you say, master." He wanted a slave? Fine! She'd give him one. She'd speak only when spoken to, accede to his every wish, smother him with servitude.

Her unflagging calmness shocked her. It was as though the sun had come out, revealing all the glaring imperfections of their relationship. She stared at the flaws, saddened and appalled. She'd come to love Paul and Alaska. She'd found happiness with him— only to discover it was badly marred. She was no better off now than she'd been that first week, when he'd turned her into his shadow. The only difference was that she'd grown more comfortable in her cell.

Another thought came to her and she forgot her re-

solve not to speak. "How...how do I know you don't have a lover in Fairbanks?"

Paul stood, pushing back the kitchen chair so suddenly it threatened to topple. "That's crazy! I can't believe you'd even think such a thing!"

"Why? I've lived with you for these past two months, so I'm well aware of your appetite for—"

"The only lover I have is you!" He shouted the words and shoved his hands inside his pants pockets.

"If you can't trust me, there's nothing that says I have to trust you." She didn't think for a minute that Paul did have another woman, but she wanted him to sample a taste of her own frustration. "The fact that you don't want me along speaks for itself. It's obvious you're hiding something from me." She arched her brows speculatively. "Another woman, no doubt."

Paul's mouth was tight. "That thought is unworthy of you."

"What else am I supposed to believe?"

His expression darkened. "I'm leaving for Fairbanks and you're staying here and that's the way it's going to be."

"Yes, master." She bowed in a sweeping, exaggerated manner.

He sighed loudly. "Are we back to that?"

She didn't answer. Instead she walked across the cabin and reached for her parka and boots. "I'm going to see Tanana unless my master demands that I remain here."

"Caroline." He stopped her just before she opened the door, but she didn't turn around and Paul knew she was fighting back tears. He felt himself go weak; he loved her and wished he could take away the pain,

but it was too late to change his plans. "Never mind," he said gruffly.

Caroline left, closing the door behind her.

Paul paced the room, his emotions in conflict. Caroline was right; she'd given him everything—her love, her heart, her trust… And yet, he wasn't satisfied. He wanted more.

The cold wind cut through Caroline's jacket as she trudged the frozen pathway that led to the Eagleclaws' cabin. She needed to get away and think. Paul had hurt her; he'd never guess the extent to which his doubts and his exclusion had pained her sensitive heart.

Tanana answered the knock at her door, looking relieved to discover it was Caroline. The baby cried pitifully in the background.

"Carl cried all night. I'm afraid he's sick."

Caroline didn't bother to take off her parka, but walked directly to the baby's side. Gently, she lifted him from the crib. His little face was red and his legs were drawn up against his stomach.

"He might have colic."

"Colic?"

"Does he cry after each feeding?"

"And before. All he does is cry."

From the young woman's obvious exhaustion, Caroline could believe it. "Then I think you should make an appointment with the medical team for next week."

Tanana agreed with a brief nod.

"Lie down for a while and rest," Caroline said. "I'll hold Carl."

"You spoil him."

Caroline grinned and kissed the top of his small head. "I know, but let me do it, okay?"

"You'll make a good mother for Paul Trevor's sons."

Caroline quickly averted her face so her friend couldn't read her distress. She spent most of the afternoon with Tanana and the baby, leaving only when she was sure Carl would sleep and that his mother had received a few hours' rest.

"Send Thomas if you need me," she said on her way out the door.

Paul met Caroline halfway back to the cabin. His eyes held hers in a long, steady look. "I'll be leaving in a few minutes."

"Does my master wish me to carry his bags to the airstrip?"

"Caroline...don't, please."

Keeping up this charade was hard enough when her heart was breaking. "Carl has colic and poor Tanana's been up with him for two nights." She tried to cover the uncomfortable silence.

Paul's eyes caressed her. "Don't go to the airstrip. There's no need."

She lowered her gaze, already feeling herself weaken.

Walter met them and loaded Paul's suitcase onto the back of his sled. He seemed to realize that Paul and Caroline needed time alone.

"Caroline," Paul began. "You're not a prisoner." He took her in his arms and held her close, shutting his eyes to savor the feel of her against him. Their coats were so thick, holding each other was awkward and he reluctantly dropped his arms.

Caroline swallowed her anger. "When will you be back?"

"In four days, possibly five."

It seemed a lifetime, but she said nothing. His hands caressed her face with such tenderness that Caroline closed her eyes and swayed toward him. When he covered her mouth with his, her lips parted in eager welcome. The kiss was long and thorough, making her all the more aware of the seductive power he held over her senses. Of their own volition, her arms slid upward and around his neck. One kiss and he'd destroyed her resolve. Caroline didn't know whether she was more furious with Paul or with herself.

"Oh, love," he breathed against her lips. "Next time maybe you'll come with me."

Purposefully, she stepped away from him. She was frustrated with herself for being so weak and even more so with Paul for not trusting her. "I'll be happy to go with you if I'm still here."

The shock that contorted Paul's features and narrowed his eyes caused Caroline to suck in her breath. Abruptly he turned away, marching to the airstrip without a word of farewell.

Caroline wondered what had made her say something so stupid. She regretted her sharp tongue, but Paul had hurt her and she wanted him to realize that.

"Damn!" She stamped her foot in the dry snow. If she'd hoped to build a foundation of trust, she'd just crumbled its cornerstone.

Caroline stood where she was until Paul's plane had taxied away and ascended into the gray sky. Only then did she return to the cabin, disillusioned and miserable. She was astonished by how empty the place felt. She remained standing in the middle of the living room for several minutes, hardly able to believe that in the

span of a few hours, her entire world could have been jolted so badly.

That night, Caroline slept fitfully. She was too cold, then too hot. Her pillow was too flat and the mattress sagged on one side. After midnight, she admitted it wasn't the bed or the blankets. The problem was that the space beside her was empty. With a sigh, she turned and stared up at the ceiling, trying to think of ways to repair her marriage.

Paul set his suitcase on the carpeted floor of the Hotel Fairbanks. His room was adequate—a double bed, dresser, television and chair. He stared at the TV set and experienced a twinge of regret. The sensation multiplied when his gaze fell on the bathtub.

Regret hounded him. Not once in all the weeks that Caroline had been in Gold River had she complained about the less-than-ideal living conditions. Yet she'd been denied the simplest of pleasures.

Slowly, Paul removed his parka and tossed it carelessly on the bed, then rubbed his eyes. He was determined to rush this trip so he could get back to Caroline and rebuild what his jealous doubts had destroyed.

After he'd undressed and climbed into the soft bed, Paul lay on his back, arms folded behind his head. It didn't feel right to be here without Caroline. He smiled as he recalled how quickly she'd dropped her self-imposed role of servant; she had too much fire in her to play the part with any conviction.

He thought about her being alone in the cabin, curled up and sleeping in his bed, and experienced such an overwhelming surge of desire that his body tightened and tension knotted his stomach. She often

slept in that thin piece of silk her aunts had given her. Usually it rode up her slim body so that if he reached for her, his hand met warm, soft skin.

Paul inhaled sharply at the memory. Her eagerness for his lovemaking had been a surprise and a delight. She hadn't refused him once, welcoming his ardor with an enthusiasm he hadn't dared expect. He wouldn't leave her again, wouldn't take another trip unless she could join him. He planned on telling her so the minute he returned to Gold River.

Caroline woke early the next morning. As usual it was dark. The hours of daylight were becoming shorter and shorter as they approached the winter solstice. More and more of each day was spent in complete darkness. She contemplated the summer and what it would be like to have the sun shine late at night. Then she wondered if she'd be in Gold River to see it. The thought stunned her. Of course, she'd be in Gold River. This was her home now.

No sooner had she dressed and made breakfast than there was a knock at her door. Walter Thundercloud stood on the other side.

"Good morning, Walter."

He nodded politely, and stepped inside, looking a bit uneasy.

Without asking, she poured him a cup of coffee and set it on the table.

"You okay?" he asked gruffly.

"Of course I am."

"Paul asked me to check on you."

Caroline pulled out a chair and sat across from the old man. Naturally Paul would want to be sure his pris-

oner was in her cell, she told herself wryly. Her hands tightened on the thick mug. "I'm fine. You needn't worry about me."

Walter hesitated. "Paul's been in Gold River for several years now."

Her husband's friend seemed to be leading up to something. She nodded, hoping that was encouragement enough for him to continue.

"When he first came, he had the cabin built for privacy. The oil company had supplied his quarters, but he wanted a larger place—more homey—so he could bring his wife to live with him."

"His wife!" Caroline nearly choked on her coffee.

"Oh, the woman wasn't his wife yet. She'd only promised to be."

"I...see." Paul had been engaged! "What happened?"

"He never told me, but one day he got a letter and after he read it, Paul left the station and got sick drunk. He never mentioned her name again."

Nor had he mentioned the woman to Caroline. The heat of jealous anger blossomed in her cheeks. The night of her arrival, she'd spilled her guts about Larry. Apparently, Paul had gone through a similar experience and hadn't bothered to tell her. Talk about trust!

"For many months, Paul was angry. He worked too hard, not sleeping some nights. He scowled and snapped and drank more than he should."

"He didn't leave Gold River and try to work things out with this woman?"

"No."

Caroline took another sip of her coffee, somehow

not surprised. He had an overabundance of pride, often to his own detriment. "Why are you telling me this?"

"For the first time since Paul moved to Gold River, he smiles every day. He laughs. Before my eyes I've seen him change. He's happy now. These changes began when you came here."

So Walter wanted to reassure her. She smiled softly and stared at her coffee. His words only proved how little she knew of the man who was her husband.

"What made Paul decide to get married now?"

Walter shrugged. "He wants a family."

She nodded. Tanana had told her that, too.

"He loves you," Walter continued. "I don't believe Paul ever thought he'd be fortunate enough to find a woman as good as you. He put the ad in the paper because he was lonely."

"But why did he advertise for a wife? Surely there were women who'd want to marry him. Someone in Fairbanks, maybe?"

Walter added sugar to his coffee, stirring it a long time. "You'll have to ask him that."

Alarm turned her blood cold. "He has a woman in Fairbanks?"

Walter chuckled and shook his head. "He advertised for a bride because he didn't have time to properly date someone and build a relationship by the usual means. I also think he was afraid the same thing would happen to him a second time and she'd change her mind."

No wonder he'd been so insistent that they stay married. "Why is a child so important to Paul?"

"I suppose because he didn't have a family when he was growing up."

This was another shock to Caroline. Paul had spoken

only briefly about his background. He'd been raised somewhere in Texas. As far as she knew, he hadn't contacted his parents about their marriage and now that she considered it, Paul seemed to change the subject whenever she asked about his childhood.

The faded eyes brightened. "I'm not telling you these things to stir up trouble." The old man paused. "I can see that most of what I've said has been a shock. Paul might not appreciate my loose tongue, but I felt you should know that he's gone through some hard times. You've been good for him."

"Our relationship is still on rocky ground."

"I can see that. I was surprised he didn't take you to Fairbanks and when I mentioned it, he nearly bit my head off."

"You were right when you guessed that I love him."

"He feels the same way. He'd move heaven and earth to see that you were happy. He—"

An abrupt knock sounded, drawing their attention to the front door. Thomas Eagleclaw stepped in without waiting for an invitation. His eyes were frightened. "Mrs. Paul, please come."

"What is it?"

"Tanana and the baby are sick."

As Walter and Thomas spoke in low voices, Caroline stood and reached for her coat. Momentarily, her gaze collided with Walter's. The older man pulled on his parka, as well, and followed her to the Eagleclaws' cabin. Even before they arrived at the small log structure, Caroline had a premonition of disaster.

The baby lay in his crib, hardly moving. He stared at her with wide eyes and when Caroline felt his skin,

he was burning up with fever. "How long has he been like this?"

"Apparently Tanana's been ill, too." Walter answered for the young man.

"Why didn't you let me know?" Caroline asked Thomas.

"Tanana probably told him not to. She didn't want to trouble you," Walter whispered, standing at Caroline's side.

"But Carl's very sick."

"Mary Finefeather has a fever," Thomas announced.

"Mary, too?"

Caroline turned to Walter. "I'll do what I can here and meet you at Mary's. We may need to get help."

Walter nodded and left.

Tanana's face felt hot, and the girl whimpered softly when Caroline tried to talk to her.

The young husband stood stiffly by the bedside. "She's much worse this morning."

"Oh, Thomas, I wish you'd come for me," Caroline said, more sharply than she intended.

The young man looked guiltily at the floor.

"How are you feeling?"

He shrugged, still not looking at her.

Caroline pressed the back of her hand to his forehead and shook her head. "Get into bed and I'll be back when I can."

Although she tried to stay calm, her heart was racing. She hurried from the Eagleclaws' to Mary's. Once there, Caroline discovered that the older woman's symptoms were similar to Tanana's and the baby's.

"Walter, contact the Public Health Department and

see if they can fly in some help. I don't know what we've got here, but I don't like the looks of it."

Walter's eyes met hers. "In the winter of 1979 we lost twelve to the fever."

"We're not going to lose anyone this time. Now hurry!"

After his meeting with the oil company engineers, Paul paused on the sidewalk outside the jewelry store to study the diamond rings on display. It'd never occurred to him to ask Caroline if she wanted a diamond. She wore the simple gold band he'd given her and hadn't asked for anything more. Now he wondered if she was disappointed with the simplicity of the ring.

He thought about the gifts he'd already purchased and realized he'd probably need to buy another suitcase to haul them all back to Gold River. He smiled at the thought. He'd bought her everything she'd ever mentioned wanting and, in addition, purchased gifts for Tanana and the baby, knowing Caroline had wanted to get them something special. Paul was trying to make up to her for excluding her from this trip. Never again would he leave her behind. He decided he'd buy her a ring and save it for Christmas. Everything else he'd give her when he got home.

Never had he been more anxious to return to Gold River.

The Public Health Department flew in a doctor and two nurses that same afternoon. The community meeting hall served as a makeshift hospital and the sickest were brought there. Tanana, the baby and Mary Finefeather had been the first to become seriously ill. Oth-

ers soon followed. Within two days, Caroline and the medical staff were tending twenty-five patients. The following day it was thirty, then thirty-five.

"How long has it been since you slept?" Dr. Mather asked Caroline on the third day.

Her smile was weak. "I forget."

"That's what I thought. Go get some rest, and that's an order."

She shook her head. She couldn't leave when so many were sick and more arrived every hour. The other staff members had rested intermittently. "I'm fine."

"If you don't do as I say, you'll be sick next."

"I'm not leaving."

"Stubborn woman." But his eyes spoke of admiration.

Later that day, Walter brought her something to eat and forced her to sit down. "I think I should contact Paul."

"Don't." She placed her hand on his forearm and silently pleaded with him. "He'd only worry."

"He should worry. You're working yourself into an early grave."

"I'm totally healthy."

"You won't be if you go on like this."

Walter gave her one of his looks and Caroline sighed. "All right, we'll compromise. I'll go lie down in a few minutes, but I'll have someone wake me after an hour."

Mary Finefeather died early the next morning. Caroline stood at Dr. Mather's side as he pulled the sheet over the woman's face, relaxed now in death. Tears burned Caroline's eyes, but she dared not let them flow. So many needed her; she had to be strong.

"Are you doing okay?" the doctor asked.

"I think so," Caroline answered in a strangled voice. "What about the baby?" She'd held Carl for most of the night. He was so weak, too weak even to cry. He'd lain limp in her arms, barely moving.

The doctor hesitated. "It doesn't look good. If he lasts through the day, then his chances will improve."

The floor pitched beneath her feet. She'd known it herself, but had been afraid to admit it. "And his mother?"

"She's young and strong. She should make it."

"Anyone else?"

"Two others look serious."

Caroline bit the inside of her cheek and followed him to the next bed.

At the end of the fourth day, his meetings finished and his shopping done, Paul returned to the hotel, packed his bags and checked out. He felt as anxious as a kid awaiting the end of school. He was going home to Gold River, home to Caroline. After a short trip to a pizza parlor, the taxi delivered him to the airport. If Burt Manners was late, Paul swore he'd have his hide.

The pilot was waiting for Paul at the designated area inside the terminal. Burt rose to his feet as Paul approached.

"I've got bad news for you," he said, frowning as he eyed the pizza box.

"What's that?"

"We aren't going to be able to fly into Gold River."

"Why not?" Frustration made Paul tighten his grip around the handle of his bag.

"A white-out."

"Damn!" Paul expelled the word viciously. A white-out was dangerous enough to put the finest, most experienced pilot on edge. Visibility plummeted to zero, and flying was impossible. The condition could last for days.

"There's nothing more you can do." Dr. Mather spoke gently to Caroline and attempted to remove the lifeless four-year-old child from her arms.

"No, please," she whispered, bringing the still body closer to her own. "Let me hold her for a few more minutes. I... I just want to say goodbye."

The doctor stepped aside and waited.

Caroline brushed the hair from the sweet face and kissed the smooth brow, rocking her to and fro, singing the little girl a lullaby she'd never hear. Anna was dead and Caroline was sure Carl was next. Tears rained unchecked down her cheeks. She took a moment to compose herself, then handed the child to the doctor. "I'll tell her mother."

A week after Paul had left Gold River, he returned. Walter was at the airstrip waiting for him when the plane taxied to a standstill. One look at the other man's troubled frown and sad eyes, and Paul knew something was terribly wrong.

"What is it?"

"The fever came. Five are dead."

Fear closed Paul's throat. "Caroline?"

"She's been working for days without sleep. Thank God you're back."

"Take me to her."

By the time Paul reached the meeting hall, his heart

was pounding. Rarely had he moved more quickly. If anything happened to Caroline, he'd blame himself. He'd left her, abandoned her to some unspeakable fate. He stopped in the doorway, appalled at the scene. Stretchers littered the floor, children crying, staff moving from one patient to another.

It took him a moment to find Caroline. She was bent over an old woman, lifting the weary head and helping her sip liquid through a straw. Caroline looked frail, and when she straightened, she staggered and nearly fell backward.

Paul was at her side instantly. She turned and looked at him as though he were a stranger.

"I'm getting you out of here," Paul said, furious that she'd worked herself into this condition and no one had stopped her.

"No, please," she said in a voice so weak it quavered. "I'm fine." With that, she promptly fainted.

Paul caught her before she hit the floor.

Nine

Caroline struggled to open her eyes. The lids felt incredibly heavy. She discovered Paul sleeping awkwardly in a kitchen chair by her bed. She realized he must have brought her home. He was slouched so that his head rested against the back. One arm hugged his ribs and the other hung loosely at his side. Caroline blinked. Paul looked terrible; his clothes were wrinkled, his shirt pulled out from the waistband and half-unbuttoned.

"Paul?" she whispered, having difficulty finding her voice. She forced herself to swallow. When Paul didn't respond, Caroline raised her hand and tugged at his shirttail.

His eyes flew open and he bolted upright. "Caroline? You're awake!" He rose to his feet and shook the unkempt hair from his face, staring down at her. "How do you feel?"

The past week suddenly returned to haunt her. She thought of Mary Finefeather and Anna, the bubbly four-year-old. An overwhelming sadness at the loss of her friends brought stinging tears to her eyes.

"Carl?" She managed to squeeze the name of the baby from her throat.

"He's improving and so is Tanana."

"Good." Caroline closed her eyes because sleep was preferable to the memories.

When she awakened again, Paul was sitting in the chair beside their bed. Only this time his elbows were resting on his knees, his face buried in his hands. She must have made a sound because he slowly lifted his head.

"How long have I been asleep?" she asked.

"Almost twenty-four hours."

She arched her eyebrows in surprise. "Did I catch the fever?"

"The doctor said it was exhaustion." Paul stood and poured a glass of water and supported her so she could sip from it. When she'd finished, he lowered her back to the bed.

Caroline turned her face away so she wouldn't have to watch his expression. "I want to go home."

"Caroline, love, you are home."

Her eyes drifted shut. She hadn't thought it would be easy.

"Caroline, I know you're upset, but you'll feel different later. I promise you will."

Despite her resolve not to cry, tears coursed down her cheeks. "I hate Alaska. I want to go where death doesn't...doesn't come with the dark, where I can hear children laugh and smell flowers again." People had died here—people she'd loved, people she'd come to care about. Friends. Children. Babies. The marriage she'd worked so hard to build wasn't a real one. The only thing that held it together was Paul's indomitable

pride—he wasn't going to let her go after he'd already lost one woman.

"You don't know what you're saying," he told her, discounting her words as he reached for her hand.

"I want to go home. To Seattle."

He released her hand and she heard him stalk to the other side of the room. "I'll fix you something to eat."

Alone now, Caroline pushed back the covers, then carefully sat up. The room spun and teetered, but she gripped the headboard and gradually everything righted itself.

Suddenly she felt terribly hungry. When Paul returned, carrying a tray of tea, toast and scrambled eggs, she didn't even consider refusing it.

He piled her pillows against the headboard and set the tray on her lap. When it looked as though he meant to feed her, Caroline stopped him with a gesture.

"I can do it."

He nodded and sat back in the chair. "Walter said you nearly killed yourself. You wouldn't leave or rest or eat. Why did you push yourself like that, love?" He paused and watched her lift the fork to her mouth in a deliberate movement. "He told me about little Anna dying in your arms."

Caroline chewed slowly, but not by choice; even eating required energy. She didn't want to talk about Anna, the fever or anything else. She didn't answer Paul's questions because she couldn't explain to him something she didn't fully understand herself. In some incomprehensible way, she felt responsible for the people in Gold River. They were her friends, her family, and she'd let them down.

"I can't tell you how bad I feel that I left you here to deal with—"

"Why didn't you mention her?"

Paul gave her an odd look. "Mention who?"

She glared at him. "You *know* who."

"Don't tell me we're going through this again. Should I duck to avoid the salt and pepper shakers?" Mockingly he held up his hands, his eyes twinkling.

For a moment, Caroline was furious enough to hurl something at him, but that required more energy than she had.

"Caroline, love…"

"I'm not your love," she said heatedly.

Paul chuckled. "You can't honestly mean that after the last few weeks."

"Correction," she said bitterly. "I'm not your *first* love."

Paul went still and his eyes narrowed. "All right, what did you find?"

"Find?" Caroline discovered she was shaking. "Find? Do you mean to tell me you've got…memorabilia stored in this cabin from that…that other woman?"

"Caroline, settle down…."

"Oh-h-h." It took all her restraint not to fling a left-over piece of toast at him. He must have noticed the temptation because he quickly took the tray from her lap and returned it to the kitchen.

While he was gone, Caroline lay back down and tried to compose her thoughts. He'd loved another woman so much that it had taken him years to commit himself to a new relationship. Caroline was simply filling some other woman's place in his life. What bothered her most was that he'd never told her about

this previous lover. The more she learned, the more imperative it became to leave.

He entered the bedroom again, his steps hesitant. He'd slipped the tips of his fingers in the back pockets of his jeans. "This isn't the time to talk about Diane. When you're feeling better, I'll tell you everything you want to know."

"Diane," Caroline repeated, vowing to hate every woman with that name. An eerie calm came over her as she raised her eyes to meet Paul's. "This... Diane didn't happen to be blond, blue-eyed and about five-five, did she?"

Paul looked stunned. "You knew her?"

"You idiot, that's me!" She grabbed a pillow and heaved it at him with all her strength. She was so weak it didn't even make it to the end of the bed.

Paul shook his head. "Love, listen, I know what this sounds like."

"Get out!"

"Caroline..."

"I'm sure the doctor told you I should remain calm. The very sight of you boils my blood, so kindly leave before there's cardiovascular damage!"

He advanced toward her and Caroline scrambled to her knees and reached for the glass of water. "You take one more step and you'll be wearing this!"

Exasperated, Paul swore under his breath. "How you could be so utterly unreasonable is beyond me."

"Unreasonable!" She lifted the tumbler and brought back her arm, making the threat more real. That persuaded him to exit the room. Once he'd gone, Caroline curled up in a tight ball, shaking with fury. Not only hadn't he told her about Diane, but he'd chosen

her because she obviously resembled the other woman. He'd told her often enough that as soon as he'd seen her picture, he'd known. Sure he'd known! She was a duplicate of the woman he'd once loved…. And probably still did.

Caroline escaped into a deep, blissful slumber. When she awakened, she felt stronger and, although she was a bit shaky on her feet, she managed to dress and pull the suitcase from beneath the bed. Her hands trembled as she neatly folded and packed each garment.

"What are you doing?" Paul asked from behind her.

Caroline stiffened. "What I should've done weeks ago. Leaving Gold River. Leaving Alaska. Leaving you."

He didn't say anything for a long, tense moment. "I realize things are a bit unsettled between us," he finally muttered, "but we'll work it out."

"Unsettled. You call this *unsettled?* Well, I've got news for you, Paul Trevor. Things are more than just unsettled. I want out. O-U-T. Out!"

"I won't agree to a divorce."

"Fine, we'll stay married if that's what you want. We'll have the ideal marriage—I'll be in Seattle and you can live here. No more arguing. No more disagreements. No more Scrabble." Frantically, she stacked her sweaters in the open suitcase. "Believe me, after this experience I have no desire to involve myself with another man ever again."

"Caroline—"

"I'll tell you one thing I'm grateful for, though," she said, interrupting him. "You taught me a lot about myself. Here I was, playing Clara Barton to an entire town

as if I were some heroine, dispensing medical knowledge and good will. But…but people *died*."

"Caroline—"

"I even fooled myself into thinking you and I could make a go of this marriage. I thought, 'Paul Trevor's a good man. Better than most. Fair. Kind. Tender.' I'll admit the events leading up to our marriage were bizarre to say the least, but I was ready to stick it out and make the best of the situation. Things could've been worse—I could've married Larry." She laughed without amusement.

His hands settled on her shoulders and he attempted to turn her around, but Caroline wouldn't let him. "Please don't touch me." His touch was warm and gentle, and she couldn't resist him. Her eyes filled with tears and Paul swam in and out of her vision as she backed away from him.

"I can't let you go, love," he said softly.

"You don't have any choice."

"Caroline, give it a week. You're distraught now, but in a few days, I promise you'll feel differently."

"No," she sobbed, jerking her head back and forth. "I can't stay another day. Please, I need to get out of here."

"Let me hold you for just a minute."

"No." But she didn't fight him when he reached for her and brought her into the circle of his arms.

"I know, love," he whispered. "I know." He felt his heart catch at the anguish in her tormented expression. She hid her face in his shirt and wept, her shoulders shaking with such force that Paul braced his feet to hold her securely.

"Anna—she died in my arms," she wailed.

"I know, love, I know." His hand smoothed her hair in long, even strokes. Regret cut though him. He'd abandoned her to face the crisis alone, never dreaming anything like this would happen, thinking only of himself. He'd been so selfish. And despite the way she'd disparaged her own efforts, she *had* been a heroine.

When her tears were spent, Caroline raised her head and wiped her face. Paul's shirt bore evidence of her crying and she guiltily tried to rub away the tear stains.

His hand stopped hers and he tenderly brought her palm to his mouth. He kissed it while his eyes held hers. She didn't want him to be so gentle; she wanted to hate him so she could leave and never look back.

"Please don't," she pleaded weakly.

Paul released her hand.

"Caroline," he said seriously. "You can't go."

"Why not? Nothing binds us except a piece of paper." He flinched at her words and she regretted hurting him.

"I love you," he whispered.

Knotting her hands into fists, she raised her chin a fraction. "Did you love Diane, too?"

Paul's face seemed to lose its color.

"Did you?" she cried.

"Yes."

Caroline pressed her advantage. "You let *her* go. You didn't go after her and force her to marry you and live on this frozen chunk of ice. All I'm asking for is the same consideration."

"You don't know—"

"I do. I know everything I need to know about Alaska and Gold River. I know I can't live here anymore. I know I can't look you in the face and feel I'm

your wife and you're my husband. I know I can't bear any more pain. Please, Paul, let me go home." She was weeping again, almost uncontrollably.

Paul advanced a step toward her. "You'll feel better tomorrow," he said again, then turned and left the room.

Caroline slumped on the bed and wept until her eyes burned and there were no more tears. Spent, she fell asleep, only to wake in a dark, shadowless room. Paul had placed a blanket over her shoulders. She sat up and brushed the unruly mass of hair from her face.

Instantly, Paul stood in the doorway. "You're awake."

"Yes, master."

He sighed, but said nothing more.

"I've fixed you something to eat. Would you like to come out here or would you rather I brought it in to you?"

"Whatever my master wishes."

He clenched his fists. "It'll be on the table when you're ready."

"Thank you, master." Her words were spoken in a sarcastic monotone.

Patience, Paul told himself. That was the key. Caroline had been through a traumatic experience that had mentally and physically exhausted her. She needed to know she was loved and that he'd be there to protect her. For the hundredth time, he cursed himself for having left her while he'd gone off to Fairbanks.

He ladled out a bowl of vegetable soup and set it on the table, along with thick slices of sourdough bread. Next he poured her a tall glass of milk.

While he was in the kitchen, Caroline changed

clothes and brushed her teeth and hair. She looked a sight; it was a wonder Paul hadn't leapt at the chance to be rid of her.

Paul glanced up expectantly when she entered the room and pulled out a kitchen chair for her. Caroline sat down, staring at the meal. Although it smelled delicious, she had no appetite.

Her lack of interest must have been obvious because Paul spoke sharply. "Eat, Caroline."

"I… I can't."

"Try."

"I want to go home."

Paul's fists were so tight his fingers ached. *Patience,* he reminded himself—and she'd only been awake a few hours.

He took the chair across from her and watched her as she methodically lifted the spoon to her mouth. "I brought you some things from Fairbanks. Would you like to see them?" he coaxed.

She tried to smile, but all she could think about was Seattle and her two aunts and the life she'd inadvertently left behind. A life of comfort and security she suddenly, desperately, missed. There was too much pain in Gold River. "Will you let me go home if I do?"

He felt a muscle leap in his temple, but didn't respond. He stood, opened the closet door and brought her an armful of packages.

"Go ahead and open them," he said, then changed his mind. "No. You eat, I'll open them for you." From the first package, he produced a bottle of expensive perfume, a brand she'd once mentioned. He smiled at her, anticipating her delight.

Caroline swallowed down her surprise. He could be

so loving and she didn't want him to be. Not now, when all she could think about was leaving him.

"Well?"

"It's very nice. Thank you, master."

Paul had had it. He shot to his feet. "Don't ever call me your master again!"

"Yes."

"I wish you'd stop this silly game."

"Will you let me go home if I do?" Caroline asked and took another spoonful of soup.

Paul ignored the question. From the second package he withdrew a huge teddy bear and was pleased when she paused, the spoon halfway to her mouth.

"For Carl," he explained. "You said you wanted something special for him. I thought we'd save it for Christmas."

She nodded and recalled how close they'd come to losing the baby. Tears filled her eyes.

Paul turned the bear over. "You push this button in the back and Mr. Bear actually talks."

Caroline's nod was nearly imperceptible.

"Would you like to see what I got Tanana?"

"Not now…please." She looked straight ahead, feeling dizzy and weak. Setting the spoon back on the table she closed her eyes. "Would it be all right if I lay down for a minute?"

"Of course." He moved to her side and slipped an arm around her waist as he guided her back to the bedroom. The suitcase was open on the bed. Paul moved it and put it on the floor.

Caroline felt sluggish and tired. "Do I really look like her?"

"Her? You mean Diane?"

Caroline nodded.

"I suppose there's a certain resemblance, but it's superficial."

"Why didn't you tell me about her?"

"It's a long story. Too long and complicated for right now."

"And you think my involvement with Larry *wasn't* long and complicated?"

Paul sighed and closed the lid of her suitcase. "The two aren't comparable."

"Then there's your family…"

Paul went tense. "Who told you about my family?"

"We're married," she said sadly, "and yet you hide your life from me."

"I have no family, Caroline. I was raised in a series of foster homes."

"So you're willing to tell me about your childhood, but not Diane. I think I know why."

Irritated, Paul shook his head, his mouth pinched and white. "I love you."

"Then let me go back to Seattle," she said.

"Please don't ask me that again. Give this—us—a chance."

"Yes, master," she said dully.

Paul groaned and slammed the door.

If Paul thought Caroline would forget her quest to return to Seattle, he was wrong. For two days, she sat in the cabin, listless and lethargic, gazing into space. She never spoke unless spoken to and answered his questions with as few words as possible. She wore her unhappiness like a cloak that smothered her natural exuberance.

He tried to draw her out, tried reasoning with her. Nothing helped. By the time they climbed into bed at night, he was so frustrated with her that any desire for lovemaking was destroyed. He longed to hold her, yearned to feel her body close to his, but each time he reached for her, she froze.

She didn't talk about Seattle again. But her suitcase remained packed and ready, a constant reminder of how eager she was to leave him. He placed it back under the bed once, but she immediately pulled it out and set it by the front door. He didn't move it after that.

Every morning Paul promised himself that Caroline would be better, but nothing seemed to change. He had to find a way to reach her and was quickly running out of ideas.

But today, he vowed, would be different. He had a plan.

After dinner that evening, Paul sat in his recliner, reading the Fairbanks paper. His mind whirled with thoughts of seduction; he missed Caroline; he missed having his warm, loving wife in his arms. It had been nearly two weeks since they'd made love and if anything could shatter the barriers she'd built against him, it was their lovemaking. He smiled, content for the first time in days.

"Caroline."

She turned to him, her eyes blank. "Yes?"

"Dinner was very good tonight."

"Thank you."

"Would you come here a minute, please?"

She walked toward him with small, measured steps, refusing to meet his eyes, and paused directly in front of his chair.

"Sit on my lap."

Caroline hesitated, but did as he requested.

His hand massaged the tense muscles of her back. "Relax," he whispered.

Caroline found it impossible to do so, but said nothing.

"Okay, put your hands on my shoulders."

She did that, too, with a fair amount of reluctance.

"Now kiss me."

Her eyes narrowed as she recognized his game.

"You're so fond of calling me 'master,' I thought you might need a little direction."

She didn't move.

"Just one kiss, love?"

Lightly, she rested her hands on his shoulders and leaned forward.

"Now kiss me...."

Caroline stared at him blankly, then touched her mouth to his.

"No, a *real* kiss."

She brushed her closed mouth over his in the briefest of contacts.

"Come on, Caroline. It'll be Christmas soon, and even a grinch could do better than that."

With the tip of her tongue, she moistened her lips and slanted her head to press her mouth over his. She felt as if this was all a dream, as if it wasn't really happening.

The kiss was routine. Paul wove her hair around his fingers, placing his hand against the back of her head, holding her to him. His warmth seemed to reach her heart and Caroline felt herself soften.

"I've missed your kisses, my love." His eyes held hers. "I've missed everything about you."

Caroline couldn't seem to tear her gaze from his.

"Kiss me again—oh, Caroline, you taste so good."

He tasted wonderful, too. She settled her mouth over his, and with a sigh, she surrendered.

He continued to kiss her with an urgency that quickly became an all-consuming passion. She felt weak, spent. Her arms clung to Paul and when he ran his hand along the inside of her thigh, she squirmed, craving more and more of him. Her fingers shook almost uncontrollably as she pulled the shirttail from his waistband and rubbed her palms over his chest.

"I want you," he whispered.

Somehow those words permeated the fog of desire when the others hadn't. With a soft moan, she lifted her head to stare at him with tear-filled eyes.

"Love?" He reached for her and she moved away as though he held a gun in his hand.

"Paul, I can't live here anymore. It hurts too much. Please don't make me stay."

His face lost all color. He could see it was pointless to reason with her and shook his head in defeat. "Alaska is my home."

"But it isn't mine."

"You'll get over this," he told her.

"I *can't*... I won't. I tried, Paul, I honestly tried."

He was silent for so long that she wondered if he was going to speak again. "I won't come after you, Caroline. I didn't with Diane and I won't with you."

She nodded numbly. "I understand."

He clenched his fists at his sides. "I give up. I won't keep you against your will."

Tears streaked her face and when she spoke, her voice was low and hoarse. "Thank you."

"Shall I arrange for the divorce or would you rather do it yourself?"

Ten

"Oh, Sister," Ethel Myers said with a worried frown, "I don't think the brew will help dear Caroline this time."

"We must deliberate on this, and you know as well as I do that we do it so much better with Father's brew." Mabel Myers carefully poured two steaming cups of the spiked tea and handed one to her younger sister. Soft Christmas music was punctuated by the clinking of china.

"Poor Caroline."

Mabel placed the dainty cup to her lips, paused and sighed. "She sounded so happy in her letters."

"And she tries so hard to hide her unhappiness now."

"Paul Trevor must be a terrible beast to have treated her so—"

"He isn't, Aunt Mabel," Caroline said from the archway of her aunts' parlor. "He's a wonderful man. Good, kind, generous."

Ethel reached for another porcelain cup. "Tea, dear?"

"Not me," Caroline said with a grin, recalling the

last time she'd sampled her great-grandfather's brew. Before she'd known it, she'd ended up married to Paul Trevor—and in his bed.

"If he wasn't a beast, dear, why did you leave him?"

Caroline took a seat on the thick brocade sofa and shrugged. "For the wrong reasons, I suppose."

"The wrong reasons?" Ethel echoed, and the two older women exchanged meaningful glances.

"Then, dear, perhaps you should go back."

Caroline dropped her gaze to her lap. "I can't."

"Can't?" Mabel repeated. "Whyever not?"

"There was another woman…."

"With him?" Ethel sounded shocked. "Why, that's indecent. He *is* a beast."

"He loved a woman named Diane a long time ago," Caroline corrected hurriedly. "He never actually told me about her, but when he gave me the ticket home, he said he didn't go after Diane and he wasn't coming after me."

Mabel put her hand on Caroline's in a comforting gesture. "Do you love him, dear?"

Caroline nodded again. "Very much."

"Then you must go to him."

Her two aunts made it sound so easy. Every day since she got home, Caroline had thought of Paul. He'd been right. Time had healed her, and she'd reconciled herself to the shock of losing her friends to the fever. She'd been distraught; the people who'd died were more than patients. They'd been friends—part of her Alaskan family. Each one had touched her in a special way.

"Go to him?" Caroline repeated. "No, I can't."

"No?" both sisters exclaimed.

"If he loved me enough, he'd come to me. I need

that, although I don't expect anyone else to understand the reasons."

The doorbell chimed and Caroline stood. "That must be Larry. We're going to a movie."

"Have a good time, dear."

"Oh yes, dear, have a good time."

No sooner had the front door closed than Ethel glanced at her sister, her eyes twinkling with mischief. "Shall I get the stationery or will you?"

"Hi." Larry kissed Caroline lightly on the forehead. "At least you've got some color in your face tonight."

"Thank you," she said, and laughed. Leave it to Larry to remind her that she'd been pale and sickly for weeks. "And you're looking handsome, as usual." It frightened her now to think that they'd almost married. Larry would make some woman a wonderful husband, but Caroline wasn't that woman.

"Is there any movie you'd like to see?" he asked.

"You choose." Their tastes were so different that anything she suggested would only be grounds for a lively discussion.

"There's a new musical comedy at the Fifth Avenue. Some kind of Christmas story."

His choice surprised Caroline. He wasn't really interested in musicals, preferring action movies, the more violent the better.

"Is that okay?"

Caroline looked up at him and had to blink back tears. She hadn't cried since she'd returned to Seattle. Tears were useless now. She was home and everything was supposed to be good. Only it wasn't, because Paul wasn't there to share it with her. They might have

begun their marriage at a disadvantage but she'd grown to love him. And she loved his small Alaskan town, more than she would ever have believed. She'd been a fool to leave him and even more of one not to acknowledge her mistake and go back.

"I've said something to upset you?" Larry asked anxiously. "I'm sorry." His kindness only made her weep louder.

"Caroline?"

"Paul liked musicals," she explained, sniffling. "He can't sing, but that didn't stop him from belting out songs at top volume."

"You really liked this guy, didn't you?"

"He was the only man I ever met who could beat me at Scrabble."

"He beat you at Scrabble?" Even Larry sounded impressed. "As far as I can see, you two were meant for each other. Now, when are you going to admit it?"

"Never," she said and an incredible sadness came over her.

Ethel Myers sat in front of the ancient typewriter—no computers for them!—and glanced at her sibling. "Pour me another cup of tea, will you, Sister?"

"Certainly, Sister."

They looked at each other and giggled like schoolgirls.

"Caroline must never know."

"Oh, no. Caroline would definitely not approve."

"Read the letter again, Sister."

Ethel picked up the single sheet of paper and sighed. "My darling Paul," she said in a breathless whisper, as though she were an actress practicing her lines. "I feel

you should know that I find myself with child. Your loving wife, Caroline."

"Excellent. Excellent."

"We'll put it in the mail first thing tomorrow."

"More tea, Sister?"

Ethel giggled and held out her cup. "Indeed."

A few days later, Caroline lay on her bed and finally admitted there was no hope. Paul wasn't coming for her. He'd told her he wouldn't, so it shouldn't be any great shock, but despite that, she'd hoped he would. If he loved her, he would have forsaken his pride and come to Seattle. So much for dreams.

She turned onto her side. Surely he realized she was waiting for him. She needed proof of his love—proof that she was more important to him than Diane had ever been. More important than his pride. She was his wife, his love. He'd told her so countless times.

Caroline sighed and closed her eyes. She missed baby Carl and Tanana and their long talks. She missed the women of the village, missed knitting the "authentic" sweaters for tourists. She missed the dusk at noon and the nonstop snow and even the unrelenting cold.

Most of all she missed Paul. He might have been able to live without her, but she was wilting away for lack of him.

With the realization that Paul's pride would keep him in Alaska came an unpleasant insight; it was up to her to swallow her own pride and go to him.

Within twenty minutes, her luggage was packed. She'd waited long enough; another day was intolerable. She'd go to him. She hated the thought of not being

here to share Christmas with her aunts, but her love for Paul was too strong to give her peace.

"Are you going someplace, dear?" Aunt Mabel asked as Caroline descended the stairs, a suitcase in each hand.

"Alaska."

"Alaska?" Mabel cried, as though Caroline had said outer space.

Immediately Ethel appeared and Mabel cast a stricken gaze toward her sister. "Caroline says she's going to Alaska!"

"But she can't!"

"I can't?" Perplexed, Caroline glanced from one addled face to the other. Only last week they'd suggested she return.

"Oh, dear, this is a problem."

Ethel looked uncomfortable. "Perhaps we should tell her, Sister."

"Perhaps we should."

Caroline knew her lovable and eccentric aunts well enough to figure out that they'd been plotting again. "I think you'd better start at the beginning," she said in a resigned voice.

Ten minutes later, after hearing all the details, Caroline accepted a cup of the special tea. She needed it. "Paul will come," she murmured. If he believed she was pregnant he'd certainly show up.

"He'll come here and then you'll be happy. Isn't that right, dear?"

Her aunts gave her a look of such innocence, she couldn't disillusion them. "Right," Caroline said weakly.

"You were going back to him," Ethel pointed out.

"Yes." But this was different. At least if she returned to Gold River, Paul would have his pride intact. But now, he'd realize he'd been tricked again.

"You're not unhappy, are you, dear?" Mabel asked softly.

"I'm happy," she replied. "Very happy."

Nodding with satisfaction, her aunts brought the teapot back to the kitchen while Caroline remained in the room off the entry that her aunts insisted on calling the parlor. The doorbell gave a musical chime and, still bemused from the tea and her aunts' schemes, Caroline rose to answer it.

The man who stood outside was tall and well-built. Attractive. Caroline glanced up at him expectantly and blinked, finding him vaguely familiar.

"Caroline, I know..."

"Paul?" She widened her eyes and felt her mouth drop open. It was Paul, but without a beard. Good grief, he was handsome! Instinctively, she lifted her hand to his clean-shaven face and ran the tips of her fingers over the lean, square jaw.

"May I come in?"

For a moment, Caroline was too shocked to react. "Oh, of course. I'm sorry." Hurriedly, she stepped aside so he could enter the Victorian house, then led him into the parlor with its beautifully decorated Christmas tree. "Please sit down."

He wore gray slacks, the Irish cable-knit sweater she'd made for him and a thin jacket. Everyone else in Seattle was wearing wool coats and mufflers and claiming it was the coldest winter in fifty years.

"How are you, Caroline?"

She was starving for the sight of him and couldn't

take her eyes off his smooth jaw. "Fine," she said absently. Then she remembered what her aunts had told him and frowned. She'd have to tell him the truth, which would no doubt disappoint him. "How are you?" she asked, stalling for time.

"Fine."

Having forgotten her manners once, Caroline quickly tried to reverse her earlier lack of welcome. "Would you like some tea?"

"Coffee, if you have it." He paused to look at the portraits of her aunts on the mantel and added, "Just plain coffee."

"But you drank your coffee with cream before."

"I meant with cream. It's the other, uh, additions I'm hoping to avoid."

Her bewilderment must have shown in her eyes. "I don't want any of your aunts' brew."

"Oh, of course."

Caroline rushed into the kitchen and brought back a cup of coffee for Paul and a glass of milk for herself. Her aunts joined her and when the three of them entered the room, Paul stood.

"You must be Ethel and Mabel," he said politely.

They nodded in unison.

"He's even more handsome in person, don't you think, Sister?" Mabel trilled.

"Oh, very definitely."

"Caroline," Paul murmured when the two older women showed no signs of leaving the parlor. "Could we go someplace and talk?"

"Oh, do go, dear," Ethel encouraged with a broad grin.

"Someplace *private,*" Mabel whispered, and the

way she said it suggested a hotel room. Even Caroline blushed.

Paul escorted her to the car, a rental, and opened the passenger door for her. She couldn't stop staring at him. He looked so different—compelling, forthright, determined.

Once she was seated, he ran his hand over the side of his face. "I feel naked without it."

"Why…why did you shave?"

He gave her an odd look. "For you."

"Me?"

"You once said you refused to stay married to a man whose face you couldn't see."

Caroline remembered his response, too. He'd told her to get used to his beard because it was nature's protection from the Alaskan winter. He'd adamantly refused to shave then, but he'd done it now because this pretend pregnancy was so important to him. She should be the happiest woman alive, but unexpectedly Caroline felt like crying.

"I said a number of things," she told him, her gaze lowered to her clenched hands in her lap. "Not all of them were true." She dreaded telling him there wasn't any baby. False pretenses and disappointment—this was no way to negotiate a reconciliation. "How's Tanana?" she asked, changing the topic.

"Much better. She misses you and so do the others. Carl's growing every day."

"I…miss them too."

"Do…did you miss me?" he asked starkly.

He sounded so unsure of himself, so confused, that finding the words to tell him what was on her mind was impossible. Instead she nodded vigorously.

"I know I've made some mistakes.... I know I haven't got any business asking you to reconsider the divorce, but I love you, Caroline, and I'll do whatever you want to make things right between us."

"I know," she said miserably.

"If you know that, then why are you acting like my being here is all wrong? It's that Larry guy, isn't it? You've started seeing him again, haven't you?"

"Yes...no. We went to one movie and I cried through the whole thing because I was so miserable without you. Finally Larry told me I should go back to you where I belong."

"He told you that?"

She nodded again.

"Is Alaska the problem, love? Would you rather we lived somewhere else?"

"No," she said quickly. "I love Alaska. It was the fever and the exhaustion and everything else that scared me off. You were right—a week after I got here, I knew Seattle would never be my home again. My home is with you."

"Oh, love, I've been going crazy without you. Nothing's good anymore unless you're there to share it with me." Although it was awkward in the front seat of the car, Paul gathered her in his arms and kissed her with the hunger of long absence. His mouth moved over hers slowly, sensuously, as though he couldn't believe she was in his arms and he was half afraid she'd disappear.

Caroline wrapped her arms around his neck and kissed him back with all the passion of the lonely weeks. Tears dampened her face and she buried her nose in his throat, heaving a sigh. "There's something you should know."

"What's that, love?"

"I… I didn't write the letter."

He went still. "What letter?"

"The one that told you I was pregnant."

Caroline could feel the air crack with electricity. The calm before the storm; the peace before the fury; the stillness before the outrage. She squeezed her eyes shut, waiting.

"You're not pregnant?"

"I swear I didn't know my aunts had written to you. I can only apologize. If you want, I—"

"Love." His index finger under her chin raised her eyes to his. "I didn't receive any letter."

"You… What? No letter?"

"None."

"You mean… Oh, Paul, Paul." She spread kisses over his face. She kissed his eyes, his nose, his forehead, his chin and his mouth…. Again and again, until they were both winded and exhilarated.

"I didn't ever think I'd be thanking the postal service for their biweekly delivery," Paul said and chuckled.

"You love me more than Diane." She said it with wonder, as though even now she wasn't sure it could possibly be true.

"Of course. You're my wife."

"But…"

"Diane was a long time ago."

"But you saved things to remember her by."

"Only her letter. She decided she wasn't the type to live in the wilds of Alaska. She said if I loved her, I'd be willing to give up this craziness and come to her."

"But why keep the letter?"

"To remind me that it takes a special kind of person to appreciate the challenge of Alaska. It's not right for every woman, but it's right for you, Caroline."

"Because *you're* right for me." Her face shone with her love. She was so happy. So very happy…

"I can't promise you there won't be fevers or accidents or that things won't go wrong, but I vow I'll never leave you to face them alone and I'll never doubt you again."

"I promise you the same thing." She felt like singing and dancing and loving this man for the rest of her days. She placed her head on his shoulder and sighed. "Can we go home soon? I miss Gold River. I want to spend Christmas there! With you."

"Yes, love. When would you like to go?"

"Is today too soon? Oh, Paul, I had the most marvelous idea about getting some additional medical training so we could open a permanent clinic."

He chuckled. "I sent for a mail-order bride, not a doctor."

"But I could've done so much more when the fever broke out if I'd had the proper supplies."

Paul's hand slipped under her sweater to caress her skin. "I have a feeling you're going to be too preoccupied for a while to be doing much studying."

"But it's a good idea, isn't it?"

"Yes, love. It is."

"Oh, Paul, thank you for loving me, thank you for coming for me and thank you for playing Scrabble with me."

"No, love," he said seriously. "Thank *you*."

With a happy, excited laugh, she hungrily brought her mouth to his.

"Merry Christmas, Caroline," he whispered a long moment later.

"Merry Christmas, Paul. This is the best Christmas gift I ever got."

"Me, too, love. Me, too."

* * * * *

THE SNOW BRIDE

One

"Alaska, Jen? This is crazy! You have no idea what you're letting yourself in for." Her mother swerved from one lane of the Los Angeles freeway to the next without bothering to glance in her rearview mirror. A car horn blared angrily from somewhere behind them, but Chloe Lyman was unconcerned; she'd never observed the rules of the road any more than she'd lived a conventional life.

Jenna Campbell swallowed a gasp and clung to her purse. When her mother was in this frame of mind, it was far better to agree with her and let her temper take its natural course. "Yes, Mom."

"Don't be so damned agreeable, either."

"Whatever you say, Mom."

"Asking me to drive you to the airport is just adding insult to injury."

"I know, I'm sorry, but—"

"Didn't I tell you to stop agreeing with everything I say?"

"Yes, Mom."

"I can't believe any daughter of mine is so...so

mealymouthed. How on earth could you even think about something as ridiculous as becoming a mail-order bride? Haven't I taught you anything?"

"I didn't say I was *marrying* Dalton—"

"That's another thing. What kind of name is Dalton, anyway? And Alaska… *Alaska?* Have you lost your mind? This is the kind of thing *I'd* do, not you!"

"Mom…"

Chloe Lyman veered sharply across two lanes of traffic, going twenty miles above the speed limit as she did so, and nearly collided with the concrete wall dividing the freeway. "I don't like it."

"Dalton's name?" Jenna asked, purposely obtuse.

Chloe muttered something probably best left to the imagination, then added in a more audible voice, "I don't like anything about this. You find some man on the internet and the next thing I know, you're quitting a job any woman would love. You give up a beautiful apartment. You uproot your entire life and take off for Alaska to marry this character you've never even met."

"I'm an executive assistant, which is a glorified way of saying *secretary,* and I'm only going to Alaska to meet Dalton. I never said anything about marrying him." While that sounded good, Jenna did, in fact, expect to marry Dalton Gray.

Kim Roberts, her best friend, thought this plan of hers was wildly romantic, although she had some qualms. For that matter, so did Jenna. She wasn't stupid or naive, but her desire to escape her mundane, predictable life outweighed her usual caution.

Once Jenna knew Dalton a little better, she sincerely hoped their relationship would evolve into something

permanent. However, she wasn't rushing into marriage, despite what Kim and her mother seemed to think.

"You're the executive assistant to the founder and president of Fulton Industries," her mother needlessly reminded her. "Do you realize how many women would give their eyeteeth to work for a man as rich and handsome as Brad Fulton?"

Jenna didn't want to discuss that. Yes, she had a good job and the pay was fabulous, but as far as she was concerned, it was a dead end. She'd fallen in love with Brad Fulton, but in the six years she'd been working with him, he'd never noticed her except as his assistant. Competent, capable Ms. Campbell. Besides, she had no life. Correction, no dating life. At thirty-one she was unmarried and there wasn't a possibility in sight. Meeting a man on the internet wasn't so unusual these days and it was perfect for someone like her. Jenna was shy, but when she sat in front of a computer screen, she found the confidence to assert her real personality. Dalton thought she was witty and he made her feel good about herself. Yes, this might be risky; however, Jenna didn't care. She was about to have the first real adventure of her life, and adventure was what she craved. Nothing was going to stop her now. Not her mother. Not Kim. No one!

"Say something," Chloe challenged.

"What would you like me to tell you, Mom? That I don't know what I'm doing and that in a few weeks I'll be flying home with a broken heart?" If that was the case, then so be it. At least she would've experienced life and had an escapade or two, which was all she wanted. Jenna had witnessed her mother's approach to marriage, and that certainly hadn't worked. So she

was doing it her own way. Dalton might very well be her only chance. Another year at Fulton Industries and every feminine instinct would shrivel up and die. Brad Fulton's primary interest was his company. Jenna was convinced she could parade around the office naked and it would take him a week to notice.

"You know what they say about the men in Alaska," her mother muttered.

"Yes, Mom, I've heard all the jokes. Alaska—where the odds are good but the goods are odd."

Her mother chuckled. "I hope you pay close attention to that one."

"Alaska," Jenna said, her voice sarcastic, "where the men are men and so are the women."

Her mother giggled again.

"Dalton told me those, Mom. He wants me to be prepared."

"Did he happen to mention what the winters are like in Fairbanks? It's November, Jenna, and they have storms there, blizzards that last for days. You could freeze to death walking from the plane into the terminal. When I think of what could happen, I—"

"You don't need to worry, Mom. Dalton sent me books and it isn't Fairbanks, it's Beesley. I'm flying into Fairbanks, where Dalton's meeting me."

"Did he pay for your airfare?"

"I wouldn't let him do that!" Jenna was surprised her mother would ask such a question. She had more sense than that and more pride too.

"Thank God for small favors."

"I'm not changing my mind, Mom."

"Jenna, oh, Jenna," her mother cried and slowed to twenty-five-miles an hour, which made even more

cars blare their horns, not that her mother was aware of it. "Why couldn't you be like other daughters who cause their mothers grief and heartache from the ages of thirteen to thirty? It makes no sense that a daughter of mine would turn into this model of virtue." Chloe shook her head. "Why did you wait till thirty-one to shock me like this? I'm not used to worrying about you."

"I know, Mom."

"By your age I'd been married and divorced twice. You were twenty before you went out on your first date."

"I was not," Jenna protested, her cheeks heating. "I was eighteen."

"At ten you were more adult than I was."

"One of us had to be."

Her mother sighed, acknowledging the truth.

Jenna didn't understand Chloe's reaction. "I'd think you'd be pleased that I'm doing something exciting."

"But I'm not," her mother wailed. "Oh, Jenna," she sobbed, "what am I going to do without you?"

"Oh, Mom…"

"My divorce from Greg was final last month. You know how I get without a man in my life."

Jenna did know. Husband number five had bit the dust, but considering her mother, it wouldn't be long before she found the next man of her dreams. Dream man number six, no doubt a replica of the previous five. All of whom, Chloe had believed, would rescue her from the drudgery and hardships of life. Without a man she was lost. She preferred them rich and—Jenna hesitated to use the word stupid, but frankly her mother had yet to choose a husband with any common sense,

let alone advanced brain power. If they did happen to have money, it never lasted for more than a few years.

Her mother frowned, shifting her eyes from the road to look at her daughter. "I can't go to Alaska, Jenna, I just can't. You know I have to be around sunshine. I could never take the cold."

"I know, Mom, but I'm not sure if I'll even be living there."

"You're leaving me," she murmured in a hurt little-girl voice. "You're going to marry Doug—"

"Dalton."

"All right, Dalton, and you're going to love Alaska." She said it with such finality that Jenna might as well be wearing a wedding band. Jenna pictured Dalton eagerly waiting for her at the Fairbanks Airport, with a diamond engagement ring in his pocket and a romantic proposal committed to memory. It wasn't a likely scenario, but Jenna figured she was allowed to dream.

This romantic fantasy had originally been intended for her boss, but if Brad hadn't even asked her out in six years, then it simply wasn't happening. Jenna was furious at herself for all that wasted time.

Her mother bit her lower lip. "Why can't I hold on to a man? I should've known better than to marry again. He's a crook."

"Greg isn't a crook, he's just, uh, creative when it comes to employment opportunities."

Her mother snickered and let the comment pass. "You'll phone me the moment you arrive in Fairbanks?" She turned and cast Jenna a pleading glance.

"Of course I will."

"What do you want me to tell Brad Fulton when he calls?"

Jenna stared out the passenger-side window. "Mr. Fulton isn't going to call you, Mom."

Her mother laughed. "Trust me, he'll call. He doesn't realize how valuable you are, otherwise he would never have let you go."

"Ms. Spencer is every bit as good an administrator as I am." In some ways, the middle-aged Gail Spencer was more efficient than Jenna because she wouldn't be tempted to fall in love with her boss.

After a long silence, Chloe murmured, "Just promise me you won't name any of your children after Dalton."

"Mom, you're making too much of this." Nonetheless, Jenna prayed the relationship would fulfill the promise of those countless emails. She'd stumbled across Dalton in a poetry chat room and they'd connected immediately. After two months of chatting daily, of quoting Emily Dickinson and discussing the Shakespearian sonnets, Dalton had wooed her with his own sensitive words. Eventually they'd exchanged snapshots. Jenna had studied Dalton's photograph, memorizing every feature. He stood stiffly by a nondescript building and stared into the camera. It was difficult to tell if he was handsome in the conventional sense because he had a full beard, but his deep blue eyes seemed sharp and intelligent. He wore a wool cap, a red plaid shirt and heavy boots; his arms were crossed over his chest as if to say he wasn't accustomed to having his photo taken. She'd sent him her photograph, too, although he'd insisted looks weren't important. Dalton said what was inside a person was all that counted. He possessed a poet's heart, although Jenna had a hard time equating this with the rough-looking figure in the workingman's clothes.

She sent her picture for practical reasons. He needed to be able to identify her when she stepped off the plane. She, too, stood facing the camera in her work uniform—a gray jacket and straight skirt. She'd worn her hair pulled away from her face, revealing features she'd always considered plain, although Kim called her looks "classic." Her hair was a mousy shade of brown that she detested and usually lightened, but it'd been due for a treatment just then. When Dalton had emailed back that his first look at her photo had stolen his breath—only he'd said it much more poetically— she knew he was the one.

The exit for L.A. International came into view, and her mother slowed. Irritated drivers honked their horns as the road narrowed to a single lane; cars were backed up all the way to the freeway.

"You have a place to stay?"

"Dalton's arranging that."

"You sincerely like this man?" Her mother's voice softened with the question.

"Yes, Mom, very much."

Her mother gave a shaky smile. "You've always been a good judge of character. But, Jenna, I'm going to miss you *so* much."

"I'm going to miss you, too." Unlike her own life, her mother's was never dull. Even now, as she entered her midfifties, Chloe "Moon Flower" Campbell Roper Haggard Sullivan Lyman was an attractive, desirable woman who never lacked for attention from the opposite sex.

Her mother followed the directions to the departure area and angled between two buses and a taxicab jockeying for position. From the way she'd parked,

anyone might assume she intended to drive directly into the airport.

Leaping out of the car, her mother raced around to the passenger side and hugged Jenna hard before she could even unfasten her seat belt. The death grip around her neck made it impossible to climb out. "Mother," she protested.

"You can't go!"

"Mom, we've already been through this."

"I know, I know… I've begged you to loosen up for years and now when you do something crazy, as crazy as I would myself, I don't want you to."

"You have no choice, Mother. I'm leaving." Jenna finally managed to remove Chloe's arms from around her neck and got out of the car.

"For Dalton?" Her mother cringed as she said the name.

"For Dalton." For life and adventure and all the things she'd missed out on, being the responsible one from far too young an age.

Her mother stepped aside as Jenna pulled her large suitcase from the backseat.

They hugged, and Jenna entered the airport. Unable to resist, she turned back for one last look and noticed an airport security guard speaking to her mother. The two appeared to be arguing and the man withdrew a book from his hip pocket and started to write a ticket.

Jenna's first inclination was to race outside and rescue her mother as she had countless times. Instead, she gritted her teeth and forced herself to turn away. Her mother would have to cope without her.

Their lives were about to change. Jenna realized these adjustments were long overdue. For much of her

life—except for brief periods during Chloe's marriages—she'd been the one taking care of her mother. She'd provided emotional support, handled practical details and kept track of their lives. No wonder she was so good at organizing her boss, she often thought.

The first part of her journey was uneventful and relaxing. She had a plane change in Seattle, where she boarded the flight for Fairbanks. She was assigned the window seat. The man sitting beside her had a beard similar to Dalton's. He was also dressed in a similar manner.

"Hello," she said, hoping to make polite conversation as a prelude to asking him a few questions.

He muttered something and stuffed his bag into the overhead compartment, then settled in the seat, taking more than his share of the arm space. She glanced around, hoping she could get another seat, but unfortunately the flight was full.

"Do you live in Alaska?"

He scowled at her and leaned back. Within seconds he was snoring. How rude!

Midway through the flight, she had to get up to use the restroom. He grumbled when he was forced to straighten so she could pass.

"Excuse me," she said as she exited the row.

He complained again when she returned, only louder.

Jenna frowned. Dalton had told her about men like this. They flew down to the lower forty-eight, squandered their money on women and booze, and then returned to Alaska hungover and broke.

Jenna tried to read but her eyes grew heavy; she closed her magazine and felt herself drift off. She'd

been up late, too excited to go to bed, carefully selecting what she'd take with her. Dalton had been wonderful, offering suggestions and assuring her he'd be at the gate when she landed.

The next thing she knew, Jenna was jarred awake. Her head rested on something hard and unyielding, and the man's voice in her ear was— Man's voice? She jerked upright and to her dismay discovered that she'd pressed her head against her companion's shoulder.

"Sorry..." she whispered, too embarrassed to look at him.

"I wasn't complaining."

She stared out the window rather than face him.

"What's the matter? Did your own snoring wake you up?"

Jenna clenched her jaw. "I don't snore." *He* was the one with the problem, not her.

"Believe what you want, but you're right up there with my lumberjack friends."

She did look at him then, giving him a blistering stare. "Are you always so rude or is this strictly for my benefit?"

He grinned, apparently enjoying himself.

"For your information I do not snore."

"Whatever you say." Not bothering to hide his amusement, he crossed his arms.

Just her luck to sit next to this Neanderthal. This *large* Neanderthal.

Then, to Jenna's relief, the pilot announced that the flight was about to land. She reached for her purse and freshened her makeup, all the while conscious of her companion closely studying her. She ignored him as best she could, until the plane landed at the terminal.

As she left the plane, her heart racing with excitement, Jenna reflected that this was the moment she'd been waiting for all these months. At last she'd be meeting Dalton Gray. Dalton—strong and responsible yet sensitive, a rugged man of the outdoors who'd won her heart.

The cold air that blasted her as soon as she stepped into the jetway came as a shock. Dalton had warned her that the temperature often dipped below freezing in November. The cold actually brought tears to her eyes.

The airport's warmth was more than welcome. Walking inside, she looked around, a smile on her lips. Two feet past the secure area, she stopped, and then slowly, guardedly, moved forward. She surveyed the room, searching for Dalton. He'd said he'd be there to meet her. Promised he would. Nothing would keep him away, he'd told her. Gold could be found on his property, oil could spurt from the ground, but he'd be at the airport waiting for her.

Only he wasn't.

Two

Reid Jamison followed the blonde out of the airplane, wryly shaking his head. God save him from uppity women, and that one was about as uppity as a woman got. Uppity and a real Miss Priss.

She stood in the middle of the waiting area, obviously looking for someone. Reid strolled past her, headed for the baggage claim. He had another flight to go before he got home, and he hoped to fly out of Fairbanks before dark. First, however, he needed to collect his luggage and grab something to eat. With the airlines cutting back, one of the first casualties was the meals, not that they'd ever been that spectacular.

Unfortunately, his bag was one of the last to appear and he had to stand around and wait while all the passengers retrieved their suitcases and made a fast escape. His seatmate hung around, too, he noticed, although her bag had been one of the first to arrive. She looked anxiously about, then after a few minutes walked over to the phone. Whoever she called didn't have a lot to say, because she hung up shortly afterward.

The minute he had his bag, Reid hurried over to the cafeteria. The food wasn't great, and it was damned expensive, but he had few options. A couple of sandwiches from the airport restaurant would fill his stomach until he got home.

"How you doin', Reid?" Billy asked when he'd placed the pre-made, pre-wrapped sandwiches on his tray as well as a cup of coffee.

Reid spent enough time at the airport to be on a first-name basis with a number of people. Billy was a good guy, retired from construction, who worked part-time at the airport to make entertainment money. Mostly he blew his wages on poker. Reid had played with him a time or two, and had suggested Billy keep his day job. "Good to be home." Almost home, he amended silently.

"Where you comin' back from this time?" Billy asked.

"Seattle." Reid sipped his coffee. It was hot enough to burn his mouth, but he didn't care. "You wouldn't believe what those Seattle folks are doing to ruin a good cup of coffee."

Billy chuckled and gave Reid his change. "You flyin' out tonight?"

Reid nodded, took his tray and sat down at the table by the window. His Cessna 182 was parked below. It was comforting to think he'd be sleeping in his own bed tonight and not some too-soft mattress in an anonymous hotel room.

He ate the first turkey sandwich without stopping, then started on the second.

His seatmate from the flight came into the cafeteria and scanned the almost empty room. She seemed even

more forlorn than she had before. He watched as she took a tray, walking past all the food on display. Then, as if she hadn't found a single thing to tempt her appetite, she simply poured herself a cup of coffee. She began talking to Billy, and they were engaged in conversation for at least ten minutes.

"Reid, you're flyin' right over Beesley, aren't you?" Billy called across the cafeteria. The two other customers, a pilot and a lumberjack, both grinned.

"Yeah."

"Do you mind givin' the little lady here a lift?"

Now this was downright interesting.

Miss Priss peered over her shoulder. When she saw him, she jerked back and started talking animatedly to Billy. Billy shook his head repeatedly but apparently couldn't get a word in edgewise. It was enough to arouse Reid's curiosity. He couldn't imagine what he'd done that took five minutes to describe, complete with agitated gestures. He couldn't help it; he *had* to find out. He stood and walked over to the cashier just in time to hear Billy tell Miss Priss that Reid worked on the Alaska Pipeline and was a fine, upstanding citizen.

"You going to Beesley?" Reid asked the woman.

She raised her chin an extra notch. "How much will it cost for you to fly me there?"

"He's one of the best bush pilots around, miss," Billy rushed to assure her.

"Cost?" Reid shrugged. "I'm flying that way myself. It's no trouble to land and let you off."

She blinked as if she wasn't sure she should believe him. "You'd do that?"

"Folks in Alaska are neighborly," he said. "We lend a hand when we can."

She offered him a tentative smile, which transformed her features, made her seem softer, somehow. He was struck by what an attractive woman she was. All he'd noticed earlier had been the disapproving look in her eyes every time she happened to glance in his direction.

"You ready to leave now?"

She nodded. "That would be great. I have no idea what happened.... My friend was supposed to be here. I phoned his place, but apparently he's already left."

"Not to worry, I'll get you to Beesley."

"I can't thank you enough." She was all sweetness now, he thought wryly. Women were like that. Sweet as honey when they needed a man, and sour as lemons when they didn't. He'd dated but not much. There weren't any women in Snowbound. No single women, anyway. In fact, Snowbound was a one-woman town, and that one woman happened to be his younger sister. She'd tried to set him up with friends of hers from Fairbanks a few times, but nothing ever came of it.

"Thank you," she said to Billy as she began to follow Reid to his four-seater plane, which was tied down outside.

She half ran behind him. "My name is Jenna Campbell," she said.

"Reid Jamison."

"Thank you so much," she said, hurrying to keep pace with him.

"You aren't in Beesley yet," he said. "You can thank me then."

While he did the preflight check, she prepared to climb inside the plane, but obviously had a problem figuring out how to do it.

He stared at her. "I take it you've never been in one of these before?"

She seemed a bit abashed to admit it. "No, I can't say I have."

"Use the wing," he said. "Climb on that and just scoot on in."

"Oh." She eyed it as though it was impossibly far off the ground, but she did as he suggested. He smiled at the inept way she maneuvered herself into the second seat. He had to give her credit, though, for not complaining.

As soon as he was inside, he put on the headphones and started talking to the tower. He handed her the second pair while he waited for clearance. She placed them over her head and clung to the door, closing her eyes as he roared down the runway for takeoff.

Once they were airborne, he circled the airport and headed north. "You can open your eyes now," he said, speaking into the small microphone.

Her eyes flew open. "Wow, that was incredible."

"It's even prettier when you're actually looking at it."

She smiled, and once again he was impressed by her beauty. He forced himself to turn away.

"How long before we reach Beesley?" she asked.

"About an hour."

"Oh." She couldn't quite conceal her disappointment. "I didn't realize it was that far from civilization. The distance between Fairbanks and Beesley was pretty small on the map."

He laughed. "What's in Beesley?" he asked. "Or should I say *who*?"

"I have a friend there—a man. The one I tried to

call. He was supposed to meet me in Fairbanks but something must've happened. I'm actually kind of worried."

"How well do you know your…friend?"

She frowned. "Well…we've never met—technically, that is—but I feel I know him."

Reid didn't like the sound of this. Dalton Gray lived in Beesley and the man was lower than a swamp-crawling snake. "How long do you intend to stay?" he asked next.

"I… I'm not sure. I hope to find work in Beesley. I can support myself if that's what you're thinking."

"In Beesley?" Reid echoed. "Doing what?"

"I'm an executive assistant, or I was until recently."

He turned to look at her again, and wondered how much she really knew about the tiny Arctic community. "There's no one in Beesley who needs an executive anything."

"I heard otherwise." The prissy expression was back. "My friend assured me I wouldn't have any problem finding employment should I choose to do so."

The bad feeling he'd experienced earlier intensified. "And just who is your friend?"

"His name is Dalton Gray."

"Dalton Gray!" Reid shouted and cursed loudly. He should've suspected something like this. Damn fool that he was, he should've asked her before they departed.

Jenna yanked the headphones off and glared at him. "There is no need to use that kind of language and furthermore, shouting hurts my ears."

Reid muttered an apology, but there was nothing he could do now except fly her back to Fairbanks.

As the Cessna banked sharply to one side, Jenna let out a small cry and grabbed the bar across the top of the door.

"What are you *doing?*" she demanded, replacing the earphones.

"I'm taking you back to Fairbanks."

"You most certainly are not. You said you'd fly me into Beesley and I insist you follow through on your promise."

"By your own admission, you've never even met Dalton," he said. "One day you'll thank me."

"I'm fully capable of making my own decision about a person. Now I must ask you to fly me to Beesley per our agreement."

He couldn't help grinning at her business-speak. Did she think he was a CEO or something? Nonetheless he had his answer ready. "No way, lady."

She narrowed her eyes at him. "Who appointed *you* my guardian?"

Reid ignored her outrage. "You say you met him online?" This was becoming as interesting as it was scary. So Mr. Sleazebag was expanding his horizons, finding new prey through the miracle of modern technology.

She drew herself upright and folded her arms across her chest.

Reid's jaw tightened. This woman couldn't possibly understand what kind of man Dalton Gray was, and he knew he owed her an explanation. "Dalton isn't a man you can trust." That was putting it mildly.

"It seems to me you're the untrustworthy one."

"You don't believe me?"

"Damn straight I don't. Furthermore, I'm flying into

Beesley whether you take me there or not. I'll find someone else."

This woman was starting to rile him. What was it about Dalton that turned sane, sensible women into gibbering idiots?

"If that's what you want, fine. Good luck finding another pilot, though, especially at this time of day." For enough money she could, despite the growing darkness, but most folks felt the same way about Dalton as he did. It was men like Dalton who gave Alaska a bad name.

"Tell me what's wrong with Dalton," she said after a while. "I'm not an unreasonable person, but you can't expect me to take the word of a stranger. Especially a stranger who happens to have a personal vendetta against the man I know in my heart to be decent and honorable."

"Decent and honorable? Dalton? We can't be talking about the same man."

"Yes, Dalton," she snapped. "Dalton Gray."

Chances were there might be another man named Dalton Gray somewhere in the world, but it was considerably less likely that this second man lived in Beesley, Alaska.

"If you won't tell me exactly what you mean, then all I can say is you're a coward."

"A what?" Reid exploded.

"A coward," she said without the least hesitation.

"And you're about to make the biggest mistake of your life."

"It's my life," she reminded him.

Reid shook his head. "I'm telling you here and now that Dalton Gray is bad news. He'll use you and when

he's finished he'll discard you like yesterday's newspaper."

She raised her chin. "That's your opinion."

"No," he corrected. "It's my sister's. And it's the opinion of half a dozen other women I know. Gray is about as slimy as they come. He's a selfish, arrogant creep who takes advantage of women and—"

"I refuse to believe you."

"Would you believe someone else?"

Her certainty seemed to waver. "Possibly."

"So it's just me you don't trust?"

She didn't answer. This woman, this stubborn, idiotic woman, was about to make a first-class fool of herself. Worse, she'd be putting herself in danger. He could prove everything he'd said. Or he could take her to Fairbanks and let her discover this on her own.

Reid made his decision and banked steeply a second time.

"You're turning back?" she asked.

"Yes."

Her eyes revealed her astonishment. "Thank you for seeing this my way."

He didn't comment.

She held herself primly in the seat next to him and ceased conversation, which suited Reid just fine. He'd said everything he intended to.

An hour later, she glanced at her wrist. "I thought you said Beesley was an hour out. We've been in the air almost ninety minutes."

"I know."

She twisted around and looked over her shoulder. "Those lights we passed a while ago, could that be—"

She paused and glared at him accusingly. "That was Beesley, wasn't it?"

"It was."

She gasped. "Where are you taking me?"

"Not to Beesley and not to Dalton Gray, if that's what you're wondering."

"You're—you're kidnapping me!"

"In a manner of speaking, I guess you could say that."

"I'll have you arrested!"

It was difficult to keep from laughing outright. "You could do that, too."

"I will. I plan to prosecute you to the full extent of the law."

"Good for you."

"And to think you said *Dalton* was arrogant."

She sat with her arms folded for the remainder of the flight. He landed in the tundra town of Snowbound and rolled to a stop on the gravel runway. The sense of home was immediate as he gazed out at the small hangar and the dark expanse beyond.

His ungrateful passenger sat there unmoving and unspeaking as he cut the engine. He studied her pursed lips and narrowed eyes—that disapproving look again—while he waited for the engine to wind down. As soon as it was safe, he unlatched the door and climbed out.

"You coming?" he asked.

"Reid!" His name came from somewhere in the night.

"Jim," he called back, recognizing the voice of his brother-in-law and best friend.

"Welcome home." Jim appeared under the single light outside the hangar door.

Leaving Jenna, Reid walked over to his friend and slapped him on the back.

His passenger was out of the plane and scrambling off the wing so fast he did a double-take. But then he'd suspected she would once she saw Jim's uniform.

"Officer! Officer!" she shouted, pointing to Reid. "Arrest this man. He's kidnapped me."

"You kidnapped her?" Jim asked.

Reid nodded. He'd explain later. Jim would understand; he'd had more than one run-in with Dalton Gray himself.

"Jim works for the Parks Department," Reid told her.

"Oh. Where am I?"

"Snowbound," he answered without further explanation. He didn't mention how small it was or that the only woman in town was his sister. Lucy would tell Miss Priss everything she needed to know about Dalton Gray and then some. Once Jenna Campbell learned the truth, she'd thank him, just as he'd predicted earlier.

"Come on," Reid said gruffly, "I haven't got all night."

She made an angry sound, which Reid ignored.

He walked away and left her standing next to the plane.

He noticed with some amusement that it didn't take her long to grab her suitcase and hurry after him.

Three

"I demand to know where you're taking me," Jenna panted, scurrying behind her kidnapper.

"Yeah, Reid, where are you taking her?" the other man asked.

They became involved in a lively discussion, most of which Jenna couldn't hear. What she did manage to discern depressed her. Apparently Reid had thought she could stay with Jim and his wife, Lucy. Lucy, if Jenna understood correctly, was also Reid's sister, but Lucy happened to be away at the moment. Oh, great!

Lugging her heavy suitcase, Jenna did her best to keep up with the two men. But hurrying after them in her pumps, concentrating on not tripping in the dirt, made listening nearly impossible. It was all she could do to keep Reid and his friend in sight.

They passed what some would consider the town's business district. Using the word *town* loosely, of course. There was a store of some sort, a café and then a row of houses. That was it. The entire town consisted of ten buildings without even a car.

Jim went in one direction and Reid turned in the

other, past the small houses, glowing with light, to a scattering of cabins a little way past them. The suburbs of Snowbound, she supposed. Jenna paused, not knowing what to do.

Reid glanced over his shoulder. "Well, come on," he barked.

"Where are we going?" Jenna refused to move another step until she knew what his plans were.

"You'll be staying with me. I don't have any choice."

"I will not!"

"Fine. Park yourself in the street. Frankly, I don't care. I've had a long day and I'm tired."

He'd had a long day? *He* was tired?

Jenna hesitated and looked back to where Reid's friend had gone. Surely someone in this forsaken town would be willing to help her. She was considering her options when Reid turned to face her.

He shrugged in a resigned manner. "Listen, I apologize about this. Bringing you here wasn't the most brilliant idea I've ever had. I intended to have you stay with Lucy, but apparently she's in Fairbanks."

"I'll stay with another woman then."

"You can't—there isn't one."

"Lucy's the only woman in town?"

Reid nodded.

Surely he was joking. "In the *entire* town?"

He nodded again, marched back and took the suitcase out of her hand. "Come on. Everything will look better in the morning."

"Look better for whom?" she cried. This situation was horrible. Inconceivable. Like something out of a bad movie—or a worse dream. Dalton must be frantic worrying about her and she hadn't even contacted

her mother yet. The only person in the entire world who knew where she'd gone was some cafeteria worker named Billy. This was what she got for listening to him. Apparently it was high praise that Reid Jamison didn't cheat at poker. She should've known better than to assume that made him reliable enough to keep his bargain with her.

"Isn't there anywhere else I can stay?" she pleaded. "Any other people?"

"There's Pete," Reid muttered. "He runs the store. He's sixty, but I wouldn't feel good about putting you in his home."

"Why not?"

Reid shook his head. "Just trust me on this one. He's a nice guy, but it's been a while since he spent any time with a woman and, well…you get the picture."

Jenna did.

"I don't know what I was thinking, bringing you here," Reid said as he opened the front door, which apparently wasn't locked. "I should have my head examined." He turned on the lights.

"In my opinion, you weren't thinking at all." Jenna followed him into what had to be the messiest quarters she'd ever seen in her life. Magazines and newspapers littered the furniture and floors. The kitchen was filled with dirty dishes. There appeared to be only one bedroom and through its wide-open door she could see an unmade bed and clothes strewn from one end to the other.

"I wasn't expecting company," Reid said, obviously a bit chagrined. He put down her bag and his.

"So I gathered."

"You can have the bed," he said, gesturing toward the bedroom.

"Is there a lock?" Since there didn't appear to be one on the front door, she sincerely doubted it.

"Lock?" he repeated, then laughed sarcastically. "Don't worry. I have no intention of attacking you."

"You've already kidnapped me, so I don't exactly trust you, Mr. Jamison."

He flopped down on the sofa. "No, I don't suppose you do."

Jenna carried her suitcase into the bedroom and immediately set about creating order. She started by picking up the dirty clothes.

"Do you have a washing machine?" she asked.

Reid had apparently fallen asleep. Her question startled him and he bolted upright. He blinked in her direction. "What?"

"A laundry room?"

"Sorry, the architect forgot that."

"How do you wash your clothes then?"

"Lucy." He said it as though she should've figured it out herself.

"Fine." She dumped the pile in a corner of the living area and returned to the bedroom. Cringing, she peeled back the sheets. Lord only knew how long it'd been since they were last changed.

Back in the main room, she found him sitting upright and snoring. "Sheets," she demanded loudly. "I need clean sheets."

He opened his eyes, which widened as if he were seeing her for the first time. "I only have the one set."

Jenna was afraid of that. "I refuse to sleep on those." She pointed to the room behind her.

"Wait…" He struggled to his feet and walked over to a closet and brought out two sheets so new they were still in the package. "I nearly forgot. Lucy gave these to me last Christmas."

She didn't want to ask if he'd been sleeping in the same sheets all year, figuring it was better not to know.

"Happy now?" he asked.

"Ecstatic."

"Good. Can I go back to sleep?"

"By all means," she said sarcastically. "I'd hate to see you grouchy through lack of sleep."

Her comment earned her a hint of a smile.

"I believe every prisoner is entitled to one phone call and I'd like to make mine."

"Fine, you can call whoever you want as long as it isn't Dalton Gray, but you'll have to wait until morning."

"Why?"

"The only phone is over at Pete's."

"Pete who owns the store?"

"Right."

Oh, yes. Pete who hadn't seen a woman in years.

"*Now* will you go to bed?"

"Gladly." She marched into the bedroom and closed the door. Then, to be on the safe side, she stuck a chair beneath the door handle. It took her ten minutes to make the bed. After she'd stripped off the sheets, she flipped the mattress. This was done with some difficulty, but she managed it on her own and felt a sense of triumph when she succeeded.

"What the hell is going on in there?" Reid shouted from the other side of the door.

"I'm making the bed."

"Sounds like you're tearing down the walls."

It probably had sounded like that because she'd knocked over the lamp on the nightstand and the mattress had hit the wall with a solid thud.

"Go to sleep," she shouted back.

"I'm trying," he replied tersely.

Jenna smoothed a blanket over the mattress to serve as a mattress pad and put on the crisp, fresh-from-the-package sheets. Without a chair on which to lay her clothes, she folded them over the footboard and changed into flannel pajamas.

Jenna didn't expect to sleep well, and was shocked to wake seven hours later. She hadn't stirred once the entire night. As she dressed, she decided to confront Reid and demand that he take her either to Beesley or Fairbanks. If he agreed, she wouldn't press charges against him. If not, she'd be using the one and only phone in Snowbound, Alaska, to call a lawyer. *That* should tell Reid Jamison she was serious. He didn't look like the kind of man who'd take well to life inside a prison.

With a plan of action, she removed the chair and jerked open the door, prepared to confront her kidnapper.

To her dismay she discovered he was nowhere to be found. Nor had he bothered to leave her a note telling her where he was going. The man had some nerve!

However...

It could be that luck was with her. Jenna cheerfully packed her suitcase and left the house. As soon as she stepped outside, she saw two vehicles, both trucks and both parked in front of the café. That seemed like a good place to start.

Jenna walked over to the building and frowned at the display of elk horns above the doorway. The café consisted of five tables and a counter where two older men with thick gray beards sat eating hotcakes.

They turned and stared at her as if she were an alien species. To them, she probably was.

"Good morning," she said politely.

"You must be Jenna," the closer of the two said. He offered her an uncertain smile. "Reid said you'd be stopping by sooner or later."

"Sit down and make yourself at home," the man behind the counter instructed.

"Reid didn't say what a beauty she was," the first man whispered to the second in tones loud enough for her to hear.

"Jake Morgan here," the man behind the counter said. "And these two varmints are Addison Bush and Palmer Gentry."

Both men clambered to their feet and bowed at the waist. "Friends call me Addy," the taller one said.

"Hello, Addy."

"Most everyone just calls me Palmer."

"Palmer." She acknowledged him with a nod.

"Could I get you a cup of coffee?" Jake asked her.

"Please." She sat two stools down from her new-found friends, who continued to stare at her.

"Reid's down at the pump station."

She must have looked confused, because Jake added, "The pump station for the pipeline."

"Oh."

Jake brought her the coffee and she accepted it gratefully. "I'd like to hire someone to fly me to Beesley," she said, smiling at the two men.

Her three admirers put their heads together and immediately started mumbling among themselves.

"We only got two planes here in Snowbound," Addy explained. "Reid has one and Jim has the other."

"Jim left this morning to pick up Lucy," Palmer said.

"Yup. Lucy told him the only way she'd live up here was if Jim took her into Fairbanks every month so she'd be able to do woman things." All three men seemed to consider those things, whatever they were, a deep and incomprehensible mystery.

"Jim and Lucy will be back tomorrow," Addy told her.

So flying out with the other man was no longer an option. "Would it be possible to use the phone?" Jenna asked.

"The only phone here belongs to Pete," Jake replied.

So it was true and not just another lie of Jamison's. "Then I'll talk to Pete," she said, and took one last restorative sip of coffee before slipping off the stool.

"They got phones down at the pump station," Palmer said. "But that's a mile or so from here."

She thought of all the cell and car phones in L.A. that she took for granted. Her mother alone had six or seven phones: one in each car, a personal cell phone and four in the house. That number wasn't unusual among Jenna's friends, either.

All three men accompanied her to the grocery, which was a generous term for this place. Yes, there were shelves with grocery items—a few cans of this and a few cans of that. The shelves were sparsely stocked, to say the least. Under a glass countertop were several pieces of Alaskan art, scrimshaw and beaded

jewelry, along with what appeared to be small chunks of gold.

A man who must be Pete walked out from behind a denim curtain and smiled broadly when he saw her.

"Well, hello, little lady. Let me personally welcome you to Snowbound." He looked her up and down, apparently enjoying the view. Then he reached for her hand and brought it to his lips.

"Pete's something of a ladies' man," Palmer explained from behind her.

"Manners and all," Jake added, whispering close to her ear.

"I understand you have a phone," Jenna said, ignoring the other three men. "I was wondering if I could use it. I have a phone card so I wouldn't be putting any long distances charges on your line."

"I would consider it an honor to be of service." He bent forward and kissed the back of her hand a second time. "But alas, the telephone is no longer in working order."

Jenna wanted to weep with frustration.

"I was afraid of that," Jake said sadly.

"Me, too," Addy and Palmer whispered in tandem.

"You aren't going to be mad, now are you?" Jake asked and retreated a step. "Reid said you get downright testy when you're mad."

"I most certainly do not," she flared angrily. He'd accused her of snoring and now this! "How dare he say such things about me!"

The four men exchanged looks that suggested Reid knew what he was talking about and they'd be well advised to keep their distance.

"Where is Mr. Jamison, anyway?" Jenna demanded.

"Perhaps it'd be best if you took me to him." She wasn't keen on the idea, but he was the one responsible for getting her into this mess, so he *had* to help her.

Her request was met with silence. Finally Pete ventured, "I'm afraid I can't do that, miss."

"Why not?"

"Reid said we shouldn't," Jake murmured.

Palmer agreed. "Said you'd caused him nothing but trouble from the moment he laid eyes on you. He didn't want that trouble following him to work."

Of all the unfair and untruthful statements the man had made, this exceeded everything. "Did he happen to tell you he kidnapped me?"

"Yes, miss."

"He said you came to Alaska to meet Dalton Gray."

"Dalton and I are friends," Jenna explained.

All four men frowned. "You don't want anything to do with Dalton," Pete said. "But if you're looking for a man, a real man, no need to search any farther. I might be sixty but I'm here to tell you I'd make a mighty fine lover."

"I beg your pardon?"

"Just an alternative, miss."

"An alternative that is of no interest to me."

Pete sighed resignedly. "You can't blame a man for trying."

Oh, yes, I can, Jenna thought. But all she said was, "When will Reid be back?"

"Can't say."

"No, can't say," Addy echoed.

"He doesn't keep regular hours?"

"He comes and goes as needed," Jake said importantly.

"Oh." Defeated, Jenna returned to Reid's cabin. There was nothing to do but wait for him and pray that in the light of day he'd be more reasonable.

The hours dragged. Jenna completed the crossword puzzle book she'd bought at the airport in Los Angeles and was halfway through the novel she'd started on the plane when the front door opened.

Reid came into the cabin, glowering when he saw her. What did he expect? It wasn't like she had anywhere else to go.

"I thought, being as fussy as you are, that you'd clean the place up a bit."

Jenna glared at him. What right did he have to assume she'd clean up after him? "I am not your housekeeper."

He held up his hand, warding off her outrage. "My mistake."

"Par for the course as far as you're concerned," she snapped.

Reid looked everywhere but at her.

"I want out of here."

He sighed. "Seems like you've got yourself riled up again."

"You could say that." Standing now, she planted her hands on her hips. "I insist you take me back to Fairbanks." She'd given up hope that he'd deliver her to Beesley.

"Believe me, your highness, I'd like nothing better."

"Good. Then we understand each other."

"Perfectly."

A face appeared in the window; Jenna caught a glimpse of it out of the corner of her eye and gasped.

"What?" Reid demanded.

"There's someone out there, peeking in the window."

Reid marched across the room, threw open the door and bellowed, "Addy... Palmer."

The two men crept around the side of the building, heads bowed, wool caps in hand. "What the hell are you doing listening in on a private conversation?"

"Sorry, Reid," Addy mumbled. "We were just curious."

"Yeah, Reid, we don't get much entertainment and we wanted to be here when you tell her."

"Tell me what?" Jenna asked.

Reid ignored her. "You two scat, and don't let me find you peeking in my windows again, you hear?"

"Yes, Reid."

"Sorry, Reid."

The two disappeared and Reid closed the door. "I apologize for that."

"What are you going to tell me?" she asked again.

"Now, listen," he said, stretching out his arm toward her. "You have every right to be upset, but a man can't be responsible for the weather."

"What the hell are you talking about?"

He shook his head. "If it was up to me, I'd have you back in Fairbanks in nothing flat."

"With an apology?"

He hesitated, then reluctantly nodded. "Okay, with an apology. You're a stubborn, rebellious woman, and if you're set on self-destruction, then it's none of my damn business. I was only trying to save you grief, but I'll admit I was wrong to bring you here."

"Exactly."

"I want you to know I've never done anything like this before."

"I should hope not."

"However," he went on, "it looks like you're going to be stuck here for the next two or three days."

"What?" Jenna exploded.

"There's a bad storm coming in."

Jenna studied him suspiciously. "And how do you know this?"

"There are weather-tracking devices down at the pump station. Now, listen, I don't like this any more than you do. I made a mistake and I apologize, much as it goes against my nature. I shouldn't have brought you to Snowbound. But we'll just have to make the best of it."

"I want to see this weather-tracking device for myself." She grabbed her coat, then flung open the door and stepped out of the cabin. She didn't know where she was going, only that she wasn't taking this man at his word. He'd already tricked her once and she refused to fall victim a second time.

Arms swinging at her sides, she marched in the direction of where she assumed the pump station must be. From her peripheral vision, she noticed Addy and Palmer, following her at a safe distance.

"Jenna!" Reid shouted.

She'd find that pump station if it was the last thing she did.

And it might *be* the last thing, she thought when a large black figure ambled out from between two houses. Jenna strangled a scream and froze.

It was a bear.

A huge black bear, and he was looking directly at her as if he'd just spotted dinner.

Jenna's heart was in her throat. Her mouth moved in a wobbly erratic manner, but no words came out.

The bear stopped and stood on his hind legs and seemed as tall as a California redwood. Jenna was so terrified that she feared she was about to lose consciousness.

"Blackie!" Reid shouted. "Get out of here. Shoo. Shoo." Reid came forward, waving his arms.

The bear thumped down on all fours, shook his massive head, and went casually on his way.

"That's Blackie," Reid said. "He generally doesn't cause a problem. Actually, it's pretty late in the year for him to be around."

Coherent speech remained beyond Jenna's capabilities. A bear had confronted her!

"You're all right, aren't you?" Reid asked, waggling a hand in front of her face.

She tried to move, but the shock and fear had incapacitated her.

Snow began to fall. Not thick flakes, but small icy ones.

"Here's your weather report," Reid said, glancing up at the sky. "Come on. We'd better get back to the cabin." He forged ahead, but came back for her a moment later, taking her elbow and gently steering her toward his cabin.

By the time they arrived, the snow was coming down fast. Having lived in Los Angeles most of her life, Jenna had only seen snow once before, on a vacation to Colorado. It had covered the ground and frosted

the trees, but this was the first time in her life she'd seen it fall.

"It's beautiful," she said, pausing outside the door. She thrust out her hands and let the snow land on her palms.

"Yes, yes..." Reid seemed in a mighty big hurry to get her inside.

"How long did you say the storm would last?" she asked, thinking it would be so beautiful. The snow—not being trapped with Reid Jamison.

Reid hesitated. "Longer than either of us is going to like," he muttered, looking miserable.

Jenna was afraid of that.

Four

Brad Fulton stared at the woman standing in front of his desk and realized with a start that it wasn't his executive assistant. Where the hell was Jenna?

A couple of weeks earlier, before he'd left town to investigate a venture capital project, she'd made some threat about leaving. As he recalled, she'd even gone so far as to hand him a written notice. Not for a moment did Brad believe she'd really do it. He'd instructed Accounting to give her a twenty-percent raise and assumed that was the end of it.

"Where's Ms. Campbell?" he asked.

"Ms. Campbell's last day was Friday, Mr. Fulton."

"Who are you?" This was not the way he'd intended to begin his work week. He was a man accustomed to his comforts. He didn't like change and he liked surprises even less.

"I'm Gail Spencer, Ms. Campbell's replacement." She set a cup of coffee on his desk.

Brad glared at it. "I drink my coffee with cream."

"Sorry, sir, Ms. Campbell told me that, but I guess I

forgot." She removed the coffee, was gone momentarily and returned with a fresh cup, complete with cream.

One look told Brad that she'd put in far more cream than he liked. "Where's my mail?"

"It's on the corner of your desk, sir."

"I prefer it in the center so it's the first thing I see in the morning."

"Sorry, sir, I'll make sure it's there tomorrow."

"It would be appreciated." He forced a smile, trying to reassure her, and waited until she was out of the office before he walked over to his small kitchen area, dumped a third of the coffee in the sink and added black coffee to the cup.

He sat back down at his desk and leafed through his mail.

Jenna had actually gone and done it, after six compatible and productive years as his right hand. It irritated him. No, in fact, it downright perturbed him. He'd given Jenna her start, offered her a position that assistants twenty years her senior would have envied, and *this* was the appreciation he got.

He didn't even know why she'd left. He pressed his buzzer.

"Yes, Mr. Fulton?" Ms. Spencer asked.

"Do you know if Ms. Campbell took another job?"

"I… I'm not sure, sir, but I believe she did."

Now he was more than perturbed. He was furious. The woman he had considered loyal and dedicated had defected to another firm.

"Do you know the name of the company, Ms. Spencer?"

"I'm not sure, Mr. Fulton. I was only with her for

two days before she left. I recall her mentioning something about Dalton."

"Dalton Industries?"

"I really couldn't say, sir."

"Find out what you can about Dalton Industries and get back to me as quickly as possible."

"Right away, sir."

"Ms. Spencer?"

"Yes, sir?"

"Please don't call me sir."

"Yes, sir... I mean yes, Mr. Fulton."

Frowning darkly, Brad released the intercom button. He couldn't imagine what he'd done to warrant Jenna's leaving his employ. He liked her; they worked well together and there was a lot to be said for that. Brad realized he wasn't an easy man to work for. He knew there were times he could be demanding and impatient, but Jenna never got flustered. One of the things he appreciated most about her was that she was a sensible woman. She anticipated his needs and saw to his comforts. Last Christmas he'd had her buy all his Christmas gifts. She'd done a beautiful job. His mother had adored the porcelain figurine Jenna had chosen, and his father was pleasantly surprised by the autographed copy of the latest Tom Clancy techno-thriller. Brad didn't have a clue how she'd managed that.

It was this ability to pull off the impossible that he valued so much. She managed *everything,* and she did it with effortless calm. When Jenna was around, he could trust her to capably handle both his business and personal needs, from gift-buying to arranging for his suits to be cleaned. He depended on her and now she was gone.

Pressing down hard on the intercom button, he asked, "Ms. Spencer, what have you found out?"

"Sir—"

Brad cringed. He only had to tell Jenna something once and she remembered.

"I'm sorry, Mr. Fulton, I can't find any Dalton Industries."

"You're sure it was Dalton?"

"I—I think so, sir. It was just those two days."

The woman apparently couldn't remember from one minute to the next not to call him *sir.* It was highly unlikely she'd recall a conversation held last week. "Who would know?"

"I—I couldn't say. Did she mention anything in her letter of resignation?"

Now the woman was earning her pay. "Good idea. Bring it to me, please."

"Right away—Mr. Sir."

Brad paced the room until she entered his office five minutes later. Her hands were empty.

"I believe it might be somewhere on your desk, Mr. Fulton."

"Ah, yes—never mind, I'll find it."

"Very good." She backed out of the room as if she half expected him to demand something more of her.

As soon as the door closed, Brad tore into the stacks of files and memos piled on his desk. It took him thirty minutes to find Jenna's notice. He scanned it again, and wished he'd read it more carefully the first time.

Dear Mr. Fulton,
I would like to thank you for six wonderful years
as your executive assistant.

It is with regret that I give you my two-weeks' notice. I've decided it's time to move on and seek adventure, which I'm sure I'll find in Beesley, Alaska. Who knows, I might even find a husband, too.

Sincerely,

Jenna Campbell

Alaska? Jenna was going to Alaska? Husband? Jenna wanted a husband? Never once had she said anything to him about marriage. Hell, Brad would marry her himself if it meant she'd continue to work as his assistant. Didn't she know how much he needed her? Clearly not.

"Ms. Spencer," he said, speaking into the intercom.

"Yes, Mr. Fulton?"

"Get me a phone number for Jenna Campbell. She's somewhere in Alaska—try a town called Beesley."

"Right away, sir."

Brad cringed; this sir business put his teeth on edge.

Another ten minutes passed and he was about to lose his patience. His intercom buzzed. "Yes?" he said, pen in hand.

"I'm afraid she didn't leave a forwarding phone number."

"Did you speak to anyone in Alaska?"

"I did. I checked with the only hotel in the town you mentioned, but she didn't check in there. The clerk suggested she might be visiting friends."

"I see. She didn't happen to mention any friends, did she?"

"Not that I can remember. But I may have misunderstood."

Brad wouldn't put it past her.

"I did find her mother's home number if you want that."

"No," he snapped, his blood pressure shooting up twenty points. The woman was to be avoided at all costs. "That won't be necessary."

So Jenna didn't want to be found. Well, there were ways around that. Brad Fulton wasn't a man easily dissuaded; he intended to find her and when he did, he'd make her an offer she couldn't refuse. One way or another, he was getting her back in his office—even if it meant he had to marry her.

Five

"Dammit," Dalton Gray shouted at the Alaska Airlines representative on Monday afternoon. "I've talked with my associate, and Jenna Campbell was on Flight 232, leaving LAX on Sunday morning with a plane change in Seattle. The flight landed in Fairbanks on schedule."

"I'm pleased you were able to confirm that." The woman behind the counter displayed a decided lack of patience, which irritated him further.

"*And* she collected her luggage." He wasn't entirely sure of that, though. The airlines had offered damn little help in locating Jenna.

"Yes." The woman's gaze dropped to the computer screen. "That's the information I have as well."

Dalton did his best to maintain his composure. "Unfortunately, I haven't been able to find any trace of her after she left the baggage claim area." He'd spent almost twenty-four hours searching every hotel in Fairbanks, looking for his internet sweetheart. So far, all his efforts had achieved was more frustration.

"Perhaps you should notify the authorities," the airline representative suggested.

"No, thanks," he muttered as he stepped away from the counter. The "authorities" were the last people he wanted to visit. He'd been so anxious to meet Jenna, he'd arrived at the airport a full day early. With twenty-four hours to kill, he'd stopped for a beer at a local tavern. No need to sit around the airport and wait, Dalton had decided. That was his first mistake.

Sure enough, he'd met up with an old friend and one thing had led to another and before he knew it he was drunk. He might have made it back to the airport in time, but the waitress knew him and, well— what could he say? Dalton was weak when it came to women. He never could refuse a lady. Never had and probably never would.

Only now, his roving eye had caused him to miss Jenna's flight and he didn't have any idea where she was. Walking over to the pay phone, he dialed his office in Beesley.

Larry Forsyth answered. "Beesley Air Service."

"It's Dalton."

"You find your ladyfriend yet?" Larry asked.

"No. She didn't happen to show up there, did she?" He could always hope.

"I haven't seen hide nor hair of her. Just spoke to her the one time. You didn't tell me you had this woman flying in, Dalton. If I'd known, I would've told her you were on your way. She sounded anxious, too—said she was afraid something might've happened to you."

Dalton wanted to groan. He had a live one on the line, and due to his own foolishness he'd let her slip away.

Larry sure hadn't been much help. "The next time

I'm not there and a woman phones for me, tell her where to reach me, okay?"

"You don't want me to do that," Larry told him. "Because you don't want certain women to know where you are—remember?"

Dalton ground his teeth. "You know what I mean!"

"You can't expect me to keep track of all your ladyfriends. Besides, it's your own damn fault for getting drunk."

Luckily he hadn't told Larry about his interlude with Trixie, the waitress. The woman was trouble—not only was she married, but she had a habit of clinging to him, especially when he needed to leave.

"I'll call back in a couple of hours. If Jenna phones again, find out where she is so I can get her."

"You looked outside recently?" Larry asked.

Dalton had been too busy canvassing the airlines and searching for Jenna to care about the weather. "No, why?"

"We got a storm coming in."

"What?" This situation was getting worse by the second.

"You're grounded."

Dalton ran his hand over his face. "How long?"

"Up to three days."

Dalton resisted the urge to stamp his foot. Damn, he didn't have any luck but bad.

"What you need to do," Larry suggested, "is think like a woman."

Dalton frowned. "Think like a woman?"

"Yeah. If you were this Jenna Campbell and you landed in Fairbanks and expected to be met and weren't—what would you do?"

Dalton thought about it. He didn't know. "I've already contacted every hotel in town. She isn't in any of them."

"Does she have friends in the area?"

"She said she didn't." This was helping, though. With so many frustrations getting in the way, he hadn't been thinking straight.

"Well, what else would she do?"

"If you were a woman in this kind of situation, what would *you* do?" Dalton asked.

"I'm not a woman."

"Dammit, Larry, don't get cute with me."

"If I were a woman," his friend said, elevating his voice to a squeaky, irritating pitch, "I'd be really, really upset."

Dalton let that sink in. "Yeah, I bet she's furious all right."

"Then I'd… I'd want to get even," Larry continued in his falsetto.

"Get even?"

"I'd want you to worry."

"I'm worried, I'm worried." Actually Dalton was more angry than worried. He'd already wasted two good days and now it looked like he was stuck in Fairbanks for three more. Normally that wouldn't be so bad, but Trixie's husband was due back this afternoon, if he could make it through the storm. Dalton wouldn't find any solace with her until his next visit, and only if his arrival happened to coincide with her husband's absence.

"How long have you known this new girl?" Larry asked, his voice returning to normal.

Dalton had to mull over the question. He'd been cor-

responding via the internet with five or six women, but he'd chosen Jenna over the others. For some reason, he had an innate ability when it came to attracting the opposite sex. For him, it was all about conquest, about persuading a woman to fall in love with him. After the initial seduction he quickly lost interest.

The internet had been a real boon. The word was out around town, but the internet gave him a whole new field of operation. Women loved to weave unrealistic fantasies around Alaskan men. Dalton did his best to fulfill the role, dramatizing his life and adventures in the bush. They swooned over the fact that he was a pilot. He was equally good at playing the sensitive poetic type; a secondhand edition of *Bartlett's Quotations* had come in mighty handy there. That was the persona Jenna had preferred.

She was the third woman he'd convinced to visit Alaska. The first two had lasted less than a month. By the middle of the second week, Dalton was tired of them, anyway, and eager for them to leave.

"Dalton, you there?" Larry yelled.

"I'm here. I was just thinking about your question. I guess we've been emailing back and forth for three or four months now. Maybe longer."

"Three or four months?" Larry echoed. "But wasn't Megan Knoll with you then?"

"Yeah, and your point is?" Dalton figured Larry was jealous of his ability to attract women. He'd offered to give the other man lessons on the subtle art of seduction, but his business partner showed no talent for it.

"My point is…" Larry hesitated. "Never mind, you wouldn't understand."

Obviously not. "Hell, Larry, where could she be?"

"Is she like all the others?" Larry asked. "Or does this one have a brain?"

Dalton wasn't necessarily interested in that part of a woman's anatomy. "I suppose so, if talking about poetry means you have a brain."

"Could she have hired another pilot to fly her in?"

Dalton expelled his breath. "I thought of that. I've talked to everyone I know and a few I don't. As far as I can tell, she didn't connect with anyone here."

"Then I don't know what to tell you."

"Yeah, think like a woman," Dalton muttered sarcastically.

"Have you called the cops?"

Larry knew damn well he wanted nothing to do with the sheriff's department. He wasn't on friendly terms with Alaska's finest. No, sirree. He'd barely escaped jail time with his most recent scam and had no desire to further his acquaintance with the law.

"What're you going to do next?" Larry asked.

"Hell if I know." Damn fool woman should've stayed in one place. This was what he got for crediting her with common sense.

"You know—"

"What?" Dalton interrupted, anxious.

"Women like to talk," Larry said.

"Yeah." Dalton already knew that.

"Maybe she made friends with someone on the flight, chatting the way they do."

"Good idea, Lar."

"I was just thinking like a woman." The falsetto voice was back.

"I'll check with the airline right now."

"You do that, sweetheart," Larry purred.

Dalton ignored him. "I'll call back in a couple of hours. Maybe by then Jenna will have tried to reach me at the office."

"I won't tell her about us, darlin'."

"Cut it out, Larry." Dalton slammed down the receiver. He wasn't in the mood for jokes. However, Larry had given him a helluva good idea. He should've thought of it himself—Jenna meeting up with someone on the flight. When Dalton wasn't at the airport as planned, Jenna had probably accepted an invitation to stay with this newfound friend of hers. What didn't make sense was no contact since that time.

When he got to the Alaska Airlines counter, there was a long line of people waiting, hoping to escape before the full force of the storm hit. Thankfully he moved forward quickly as he waited his turn to talk to the airline representative. The same woman he'd spoken to twice before.

Her smile faded when she saw it was him. "How can I help you?" she asked.

"It's about my friend."

"Yes, I suspected it was. Have you been able to locate her?"

"Not yet." Dalton leaned closer to the desk. "I think that when I wasn't here to meet her, she went home with someone she met on the flight."

The middle-aged woman's expression didn't change.

"Do you think that might've happened?"

"It's a possibility."

"Yes, well, I'm short on those, so I was wondering if you'd be kind enough to let me see the names of everyone else on the flight."

She shrugged her shoulders ever so slightly. "I'm afraid I can't do that."

"And why not?"

"It's company policy. I can't hand over the passenger manifest simply because someone asked for it."

"But—"

"In these days of high security, you can't honestly expect me to give you sensitive material."

"Sensitive material?" he exploded.

"Perhaps you'd care to speak to my supervisor?"

Now that was more like it. "Yes, I would."

"I don't think it'll do any good," she added as she rang for someone else.

Dalton snorted. "We'll just see about that."

The woman had the nerve to look him full in the eye and say, "Yes, you will."

Six

Jenna had been thrilled at the first appearance of snow. It had seemed truly lovely and had brightened the whole landscape. The day had been overcast and bleak but an inch or two of snow had turned the world a pristine, sparkling white. Christmas was only six weeks away, and it seemed as if she'd stepped inside a holiday greeting card.

However, after several hours of continuous snowfall, she'd lost her fascination with it. It was still snowing, the wind so strong the flakes blew horizontally.

"Staring out the window isn't going to change anything." Reid spoke from behind her.

These were the first words either of them had uttered in ages. She didn't bother to respond.

"You can stand there and mope or we can make the best of this," he added.

"I am not moping." She whirled around to face him and discovered he'd brought out a deck of cards and was playing solitaire.

"I know Blackie frightened you."

Frightened her? It'd taken her pulse hours to re-

cover from her encounter with the bear. "That isn't the half of it."

"You're over it now, aren't you?"

If she lived another hundred years, she would never forget the sight of that humongous bear rearing up on his two hind feet directly in front of her. The gleam in his eyes said she looked good enough to eat, and God help her, she couldn't have moved an inch if he *had* decided to make her his evening meal.

"Blackie's harmless," Reid insisted. "He comes into town to scrounge through the garbage, although I will admit he's generally down for the winter by now."

"I don't find that reassuring."

"This is Alaska, Jenna."

"Okay, fine. This is Alaska. I should've expected to meet a black bear on Main Street. Silly me." For emphasis she slapped her forehead with the palm of her hand.

"There's no need to be sarcastic."

She turned back and resumed staring out the window.

"Do you play cribbage?"

She didn't answer him.

"I was just trying to pass the time, but I can see you're determined to make us both miserable."

"It's what you deserve."

"Trust me, I'd have you out of here in a New York minute if I could. I don't need a woman messing up my life. In fact, I don't need anyone."

Turning back, she did a slow appraisal of his living quarters and then let her hard gaze rest on him. "I can tell."

He was angry now if his narrowed eyes were any

indication. Slowly he rose to his feet. He opened his mouth as though to give her a verbal flaying, but before he could get out a word, there was a loud knock on the front door.

Jenna's gaze flew to the door. Maybe Dalton had found her and come to rescue her from this horrible man.

Reid stomped over to the door and threw it open. His brooding frown dissolved when Addy, Palmer and Pete marched inside. Pete carried a steaming cast-iron kettle.

"We brought you dinner," Addy announced.

"It's Jake's stew," Palmer said.

"Jake thought it might be just the thing to welcome Jenna to Snowbound, seeing that the town's living up to its name."

"How thoughtful." Jenna smiled at the three men. "I'll thank him when I can."

"Jake said there was plenty for four or five people." Addy eyed the pot suggestively.

"We figured you two might welcome company," Palmer said, glancing from Reid to Jenna and then back to Reid again.

A tense silence followed before Reid spoke. "Would you three care to join us?"

"Don't mind if I do," Addy leaped in.

"I suppose I could, since Addy's staying," Palmer said.

Pete shook his head. "I better get back. I only came to see if there was anything you needed from the store before the worst of the storm hits."

Jenna and Reid spoke at the same time.

"It's getting *worse?*" she muttered.

"We're fine," Reid assured the other man.

"How's it going?" she heard Pete ask Reid in a low whisper. The older man gave Reid a knowing poke in the ribs. "You going to score?"

"The only thing Reid is going to score is a black eye if he so much as comes within twenty feet of me." Jenna wanted every man in town to understand that right now. If Reid entertained any notion of a dalliance with her during the snowstorm, then he was in for more trouble than he'd know what to do with.

"I'd rather kiss a rattlesnake than *her*," Reid retaliated, inclining his head in Jenna's direction as if there might be some other female in the vicinity.

Addy laughed and slapped his knee. "I'd like to see you try."

Palmer and Pete laughed heartily. As they'd mentioned earlier, there wasn't much entertainment in town, and they took their laughs where they could get them. Apparently they had a penchant for low comedy.

"So—we going to eat or not?" Addy asked.

"I'm starved." Palmer rubbed his palms together eagerly.

Pete stepped closer to the door. "See ya later."

"Be sure and thank Jake for me," Reid said.

"I will." The door opened and closed, and Pete was gone.

Addy and Palmer headed toward the pot of stew and waited impatiently while Reid washed four bowls and spoons.

Now that she thought about it, Jenna realized she was famished, too. It was dinnertime and she hadn't eaten all day.

Reid placed a ladle in the middle of the table, and

Addy and Palmer both grabbed for it. Elbowing each other, they fought for the top bowl; Addy won and dug into the pot of simmering stew as if it was his last meal.

"Addy, Palmer," Reid barked.

The two older men froze, then glanced toward Reid.

"There's a lady present."

Addy scratched his beard and was about to argue, but changed his mind after Reid sent him a stern look.

"Ladies go first," Palmer said and reluctantly stepped aside.

"You help yourself," Reid instructed Jenna, stretching out his arms to hold back the two old geezers.

"Thank you," Jenna said, reaching for the third bowl.

"Don't be takin' all the meat, either," Addy grumbled.

"Addy," Reid said beneath his breath. "I can uninvite you."

Addy grumbled again, something she couldn't hear. Then he said, "You take as much of that tender meat as you want, Miss Campbell. Just remember, some people got real teeth."

"And some don't," Palmer added.

Jenna ladled a helping of stew into her bowl and picked up a spoon. As soon as she moved away, the two men landed on the stew like vultures on fresh kill.

The old men ate standing up. They kept their faces close to their bowls and slurped up the stew. There were only two chairs at the kitchen table and they'd insisted the lady have one and their host the other. Moments later Addy and Palmer had gulped down their meals.

"Good vittles." Addy nodded and placed his bowl in the sink.

"We hate to eat and run, but we better get home," Palmer said, following his friend.

"Goodbye, Addy, Palmer," Jenna said. "I hope I didn't take more than my fair share of the meat."

"It's all right," Addy told her kindly.

"You gonna stay in town after the storm?" Palmer asked.

"No," but it was Reid who answered instead of Jenna. "I'll have her out of here the first chance I get."

"I have no intention of staying a moment longer than necessary." She cast Reid a look that informed him she was capable of answering questions on her own.

"See ya," Addy said.

Palmer waved politely, put his wool cap back on his head and then the two of them were gone.

When the door banged shut, the ensuing silence seemed deafening.

Jenna finished her stew. Now that her stomach was full, she felt more relaxed, less irritated. She glanced at Reid and he immediately looked away.

"I'll do the dishes," she said, hoping he'd view her offer as a gesture of peace.

"No, I will," Reid snapped. "Far be it from me to ask anything of you."

"Then you do them." She was only trying to help.

"You were the one who made such a fuss about cleaning up earlier, remember? I'll take care of it myself."

"I wouldn't dream of destroying your sense of order." His housekeeping method consisted of accumulating piles of junk in every corner of the cabin.

"Good. That's the way I want it."

"Fine." She crossed her arms.

"Do you always have to have the last word?"

She shrugged.

He snorted.

She coughed.

He laughed.

While he did the dishes, Jenna picked up the deck of cards and shuffled them, then dealt out a game of solitaire. She pretended not to notice when he'd finished and momentarily left the room.

He came back carrying a thick paperback novel. He settled down in front of the fire with every appearance of comfort.

Jenna had read the courtroom drama several months earlier and been enthralled by its twists and turns, marveling at the author's ability to casually weave in elements that would later turn out to be of key importance. She'd read an interview with him recently and would have enjoyed discussing the book with Reid. His mood, however, didn't encourage conversation.

A half hour later, Reid went into the kitchen and she heard the coffeepot start to perk. He returned, standing behind her. She couldn't see him, but she felt his presence.

"Red jack on the black queen," he said.

"I saw that," she muttered, although she hadn't. She moved the cards around.

"Would you like a cup of coffee?"

"Please."

A few moments later, he brought her a mug.

When he set it down on the table next to her, she said, "To answer your earlier question, I do know how to play cribbage. My grandfather taught me—but it's been years since I played so I might be a little rusty."

"Are you saying you'd be willing to play?"

She rolled her eyes. "Yes."

"All right." He opened a drawer and brought out an exquisite hand-carved playing board.

Jenna picked it up and examined it, impressed by the fine workmanship.

"My father made that nearly thirty years ago," Reid told her.

"I don't think I've ever seen a more beautiful one."

An almost-smile flickered, then faded.

He shuffled and they cut for the deal. Reid easily won the first game. They decided to play a second one.

"How long have you lived in Alaska?" she asked as she gathered up her cards.

"Born here."

"In Snowbound?"

"No, Fairbanks."

He certainly wasn't forthcoming with details.

"There's just your sister and you?"

"Yup." They laid down their hands, counted back and forth, and each moved the pegs forward.

"I envy you having a sister," Jenna murmured. As an only child, she'd often dreamed of what it would be like to have a sibling. Her parents' marriage hadn't lasted long. Her father had moved on, remarried and apparently had other children. He'd never kept in touch with Jenna. It had just been Jenna and her mother— between marriages, of course!

"Then you can understand why I feel about Dalton the way I do. He used Lucy. She was young and naive and she fell right into his trap. He's a womanizer of the worst kind—seduce 'em and throw them away."

Jenna counted to ten before she spoke. "I think it

would be best if we didn't discuss Dalton." She'd need to make her own judgments about the man. She would, once she'd met him for herself, but until then she'd go by what she knew of him from their internet relationship.

Reid glared at her, then handed her the deck. "Your deal."

"Okay." She shuffled the cards and dealt. "My mother must be worried sick. I told her I'd phone as soon as I landed."

"I saw you on the phone."

"I've already explained that I was calling the man we decided not to discuss."

"You phoned Dalton before your mother?"

"Why, yes. I was concerned. He said he'd be waiting for me and he wasn't. I didn't know what to think."

"Maybe his not showing up was a clue to the kind of man he is."

Jenna slapped the cards on the table. "We weren't going to discuss Dalton, remember?"

Reid cut the deck with such frenetic movements, it was a wonder the cards didn't go flying in every direction.

Jenna turned over the top card and flung it down. She hated being put in a situation in which she had to defend Dalton, but Reid refused to drop the matter. "Dalton Gray is one of the most intelligent, sensitive men I have ever known."

"He seduced my sister."

"So *you* say." When she had the opportunity, Jenna would speak to Lucy herself.

Reid stood forcefully as if he could no longer sit still. "I thought you didn't want to talk about Dalton."

"I don't. Now please sit down."

He hesitated before lowering himself into his chair. They finished their second game and played a third. Reid won all three. Jenna yawned. She was tired, upset and although she was trying to look on the bright side of her situation, it was difficult.

"I think I'll turn in for the night," she said.

"I will, too."

While Reid put the cribbage board away, Jenna stared out the window. It was still snowing hard and nothing was visible outside except swirling white. The wind howled and moaned with the pounding storm.

She closed the bedroom door, secured it with a chair and undressed. The room was bitterly cold; obviously the generator-run furnace couldn't keep pace with the falling temperature. She figured that once she was covered by the down comforter she'd be warm. Snuggling under it, she turned off the light on the bedstand.

Her mother drifted into her mind, and Jenna wished there was some way to reassure her. Then she remembered that Addy had mentioned a phone at the pump station. Turning on the light again, she climbed out of bed and opened the bedroom door. Reid glanced up from his chair, where he sat reading.

"There's a phone at the pump station?"

He looked at her a moment, then nodded.

"In the morning, I want to phone my mother."

"All right."

He'd surprised her; Jenna had expected him to argue.

"Thank you," she said, turning back to the bedroom.

"Jenna…"

She looked over her shoulder.

"It depends on the severity of the storm."

"I'm going to talk to my mother," she said with determination. Nothing was going to keep her from making that phone call.

"Let's not borrow trouble. I'll do everything within my power to get you there. You have my word on that."

He sounded sincere and she desperately wanted to believe him. "Thank you."

A half smile formed, one of regret. "I apologize for this. It was never my intention to keep you here for more than a few hours."

"I know." She didn't blame him entirely. Well, he'd had no right to kidnap her, but his reasons for doing it were obviously sincere; he'd wanted to protect her from whatever fate had befallen his sister, supposedly at Dalton's hands. Not that Jenna's life was any of his business... And she couldn't blame him for the storm. "I'll see you in the morning."

She started to close the door.

"If you get too cold, you can open the door and let some warm air in. I'm not going to attack you."

She pondered his words and shook her head. "I'll rest easier with it closed."

He grinned and she thought he said, "Me, too" but she wasn't sure.

Surprisingly, Jenna fell into a deep sleep soon after she settled back under the covers. She didn't know how long she slept before being startled awake by a loud booming noise. It sounded like an explosion of some sort or something huge crashing down. The cabin shook with the reverberation.

Bolting upright, she screamed.

It happened a second time, closer, louder. Terrified, Jenna screamed again.

"Jenna! Jenna!"

She heard Reid on the other side of the door, which was secured by the chair. The door rattled and just when she'd managed to find the lamp and turn it on, the door splintered, falling open.

Reid stumbled into the room. "What's wrong?"

She stared at him, hardly able to believe her eyes. He wore long underwear and his hair was disheveled.

"What's wrong?" he repeated.

"Something fell on the cabin!" Surely he'd heard the racket himself.

Reid placed his hands on his hips. "You mean to tell me I broke down my own bedroom door because you're afraid of a little thunder?"

"That was *thunder?*" In the middle of a snowstorm? Jenna had never heard of such a thing.

"And lightning. It occasionally happens in snowstorms."

"I... I didn't know that was possible."

"It happens," he insisted.

Jenna was in no position to argue. "I didn't know what it was." Now she felt like a fool.

Grumbling under his breath, Reid examined his shattered bedroom door.

"Sorry," she whispered. "The thunder woke me out of a sound sleep."

"Your screaming woke *me*. Scared ten years off my life. I didn't know what to think."

"All I can do is apologize."

Reid paused and wiped a hand across his face. "Want a glass of whiskey to settle your nerves? Per-

sonally I could use one." He leaned over and picked up the two pieces of the broken door and set them aside.

Jenna had never been much of a drinking woman, but as Reid had said, there were times a person needed something to settle the nerves.

"I think it might do us both good."

Seven

Reid hurriedly pulled on jeans and a shirt. Next he took two shot glasses from the kitchen cupboard, plus a bottle of his finest single malt Scotch. After the fright Jenna had given him, he needed a stiff drink. He wasn't sure liquor would help, but he needed *something,* and from the look on Jenna's face, so did she. Silently Reid cursed himself for ever having brought her to Snowbound. If he came out of this unscathed, it would be a miracle, he thought grimly. But on the other hand, he refused to deliver her or any woman to Dalton Gray.

He poured them each a finger's worth and carried both glasses into the living room. Jenna sat at one end of the sofa, her feet on the cushion's edge, chin resting on her bent knees. She looked small and shaken. A surge of guilt shot through him. He wanted to apologize again, but restrained himself; there were only so many times he could admit he'd been wrong.

"Thanks," she whispered when he handed her the drink.

Reid sat at the opposite end of the sofa and stared straight ahead. He wasn't good in this kind of situation.

If he'd been able to think of some reassuring words, he would've said them. "Lightning during a snowstorm is rare, but like I told you, it does happen." That was the best he could do. Reid glanced in her direction and saw her squint as she swallowed her first sip of Scotch.

"You do this often?" she asked.

"Drink or hijack women?"

A slight smile played across her lips. "Both."

"You're the first woman I've ever brought here." The last one, too. He'd learned his lesson.

"I don't mean to be disagreeable, but I'm not flattered."

Reid wasn't sure if it was the whiskey or the fight she'd given him, but he found that amusing.

"You're actually quite nice-looking when you smile." Jenna cocked her head to one side and stared at him. "At least I think you are. It's difficult to tell with your beard."

Reid's hand went to his face. His beard was so much a part of him he didn't ever think about it. On the tundra, a beard was protection against the elements, as much protection as his hat or gloves. He explained that.

She took another sip, shuddering dramatically. "You *like* this stuff?" she asked.

"I'm not much of a drinker, and I don't often touch hard liquor," he said. "But there are occasions that call for it."

"Occasions such as having ten years shaved off your life?"

"Exactly."

She stared down at the shot glass as if she had no idea what to say next. Reid spent a great deal of his time alone and readily acknowledged that he wasn't

much of a conversationalist. He found himself puzzled by the fact that he wanted to know more about Jenna. He couldn't understand why a woman who, from all outward appearances, was savvy and intelligent would link up with a rat like Dalton Gray. It didn't make sense. But sure as hell, the moment he mentioned the other man's name, Jenna would leap to Dalton's defense.

"Are you enjoying the novel?"

Reid's gaze fell on the thriller he was currently reading. "Very much."

"I read it a while back. The ending will surprise you."

Reid held up his hand. "Don't tell me."

"I wouldn't dream of ruining it for you, but I definitely predict you're going to be surprised."

"Did you figure it out?" he asked. He didn't mean to be smug, but he'd pegged the killer from the fourth chapter, and all the evidence since that point confirmed his insight. The novel was a courtroom drama in which one attorney's skill was tested against that of another. The case had gone to the jury, and the man being tried was clearly innocent. "Jones did it," Reid said.

"Jones?" Jenna had the audacity to laugh at him. "He's the prosecuting attorney."

"I know who he is. No wonder he's working so hard to convict Adam Johnson."

"Oh, puleeze."

"That's what all the evidence tells me. Why else would Jones be covering his tracks the way he has?"

She shook her head. "To be fair, I thought it was him, too. At first..."

"You mean it isn't?"

She pantomimed zipping her lips closed.

Reid wanted to reach for the book and turn to the last page to prove her wrong, but that would've been childish. Besides, having already read the story, she was in a position to know.

"Look at you," she said, sounding absolutely delighted.

"What?"

"You're trying to figure out who else it might be."

She was right. That was exactly what he'd been doing.

"Tell me about Addy and Palmer," Jenna said.

They were a thorn in his side and—at the same time—two of his greatest friends. "Addy and Palmer both came up to work on the pipeline a hundred years ago, made big money, blew their wad and then stayed in the state. Pretty soon, they were drifting from town to town. They settled here because they knew Jake and he gave them enough work to keep them occupied and out of trouble."

"They seem harmless enough."

Reid nodded. "They are certainly characters."

Jenna laughed softly. "Did you see the look on Addy's face when I scooped up a ladle full of stew? I thought his eyes were going to bug out of his head."

"That was just his way of warning you not to take more than your fair share."

"So I assumed."

"Anybody else you want to know about?"

"Tell me about Jim and Lucy." They were the only married couple in town. She'd seen a few men wandering around before the storm hit. Since then, everyone seemed to have hunkered down to wait it out.

"Well, you already met Jim."

"You wanted me to stay with him and your sister, didn't you?"

Reid shrugged. So much for the best-laid plans. "Yeah, but Lucy was in Fairbanks and now Jim's there, too. What would you like to know about them?"

She looked unsure. "Addy told me Lucy agreed to marry Jim and live here only if she could return to Fairbanks every so often."

"That's true. Lucy says it's because she's the only woman in Snowbound."

A one-woman town. "She must be lonely."

"Nah, Addy and Palmer are company for her—"

"Addy and Palmer," Jenna repeated, sounding incredulous. "They're *men*."

Reid couldn't see why that made any difference. "I'm here, too." She ignored that.

"Lucy must crave female companionship. She's way up here, completely isolated from her friends and everything that's convenient and familiar. I don't know how she does it."

Reid hadn't thought of it that way.

"No wonder she flies into Fairbanks every chance she gets."

"She only goes about once a month. She might fly in more often now that she's pregnant."

"She's *pregnant?*"

"Only a few months. She's got Jim flying in all kinds of equipment for that baby. I had no idea babies needed that much stuff." Actually Reid was thrilled for his sister and her husband.

"I haven't met Lucy yet, but already I admire her," Jenna said solemnly.

Now that he considered it, his sister did deserve a lot of credit. Moving to Snowbound couldn't have been easy for her. Lucy invited him to dinner once a week, but he'd never realized how lonely she must be for female friends.

"She obviously loves Jim very much." Jenna said this with unmistakable awe.

"She does." The conversation was growing a bit uncomfortable for Reid. He didn't understand women, not even his sister. Romance had never played a large role in his life. Most women seemed mysterious and temperamental—as much a mystery to him as the novel he was reading. Still, he *liked* women; he adored Lucy and he had several female friends, including Susan Webster in Fairbanks, whom he met for dinner every once in a while. Even his one semi-serious relationship had ended without pain or suffering on either side.

And Reid had to admit he enjoyed talking to Jenna; when they managed to avoid the subject of Dalton, they were able to find common ground without difficulty.

"Care to play another game of cribbage?" he asked. Now that he was awake, he wasn't the least bit sleepy.

"No, thanks. I think I'll go back to bed."

He didn't let his disappointment show. "I'll put the door in place for you."

She took another sip of the liquor and blinked away tears.

Reid found it difficult not to smile.

"I am sorry about the door," she said carefully as she took her empty glass to the tiny kitchen.

"I was the one who tore it down."

"Yes, I know, but I shouldn't have put a chair under

the doorknob. Other than holding me captive, you seem to be an honorable man."

"Except for that one minor detail."

"Right." But she was smiling when she said it.

The oddest sensation came over him. It was as though Jenna's smile had traveled all the way through his body. He actually *felt* it. He wasn't the most intuitive of men, but he sensed that this smile offered his absolution. A forgiveness of sorts…an understanding.

He didn't want their night to end. He didn't want her to go to bed, to leave him alone with his thoughts—and his yearnings. Unfortunately he couldn't think of any way to stop her.

"Don't bother about the door," Jenna said. "Since it's in two pieces."

She had a point. "I don't suppose it would help much if someone wanted to break in. Not that anyone's going to." He hoped to convey that she was perfectly safe with him.

"'Night, Reid."

He lingered in the doorway with his hands in his pockets. "'Night." As he turned away, he heard the mattress shift and realized she was already back in bed. His bed. He tried not to think about that—her hair spread out on his pillow, his blankets covering her.… Reluctantly he returned to his makeshift bed on the sofa, which was less than comfortable. Lying down, he tucked his hands behind his head and closed his eyes.

Try as he might, he couldn't sleep. He kept thinking about Jenna and the way her smile had affected him. It was a small thing—and yet it wasn't. Maybe he was going soft in the head. He recalled when Jim and his sister had first met. His friend walked around town

wearing a funny grin, and flew into Fairbanks so often people began to wonder how he could still manage his job. Then before Reid understood what was happening, Jim had asked Lucy to be his wife, and his sister was living in Snowbound.

A sleepless hour passed and then he heard Jenna climb out of bed. The mattress squeaked, followed by the sound of her feet shuffling on the floor.

"Jenna?" he called in a loud whisper.

She didn't respond for a moment. "I didn't wake you, did I?"

"No," he said. "I can't get back to sleep."

"Me, neither." She padded into the darkened room. "Don't turn on the lights, all right?"

He frowned. "Why not?"

Again she hesitated. "I don't know… It's more… relaxed with them off."

"Okay." He sat up.

"Do you mind if we talk for a few minutes?"

Mind? Of course he didn't mind. "What do you want to talk about?"

She sat on the corner of the sofa in the same position she'd assumed earlier, feet up, knees bent. "I want to ask you something."

Reid hoped it wouldn't be a personal question; he wasn't good at answering those. "Fire away," he muttered.

She didn't speak immediately, and when she did, her question took him by surprise. "Why do you live up here so isolated from the world?"

"You mean in Alaska or in Snowbound?"

"Snowbound."

That was easy enough. "I work here."

"Monitoring the pump station for the pipeline?"

"Yes." It was a good job and he enjoyed his work.

"What exactly do you do?"

"For eight hours every day, I'm at the station monitoring the flow of crude oil. It might not sound involved, but it actually is."

"Do you have a lot of free time?"

"Some." He didn't elaborate.

"How do you spend it? Doing what?"

Reid paused. She was right; talking in the dark was more relaxed, but even in the anonymity of the night, there were certain subjects that left him uneasy.

"Is that such a difficult question?" she asked, a smile in her voice.

"No, it's just that I never told anyone—none of my family or friends."

"It's a secret?"

"Not exactly, but it's private." He wished he knew how to turn the conversation in a different direction, but verbal maneuvers had never been his forte.

Jenna's voice rose with enthusiasm. "Now I'm fascinated."

"Tell me something about you first."

"Me? No fair. We're discussing you."

"Tell me a secret. Something few people know about you."

"I don't have any secrets," she insisted.

"You do. Everyone has secrets."

"All right." She sighed, and Reid could see she wasn't happy about this. "I bit my nails until I was sixteen."

"Now *that's* shocking."

She slapped playfully at him and managed to graze his elbow.

Reid chuckled. "You really are an innocent, aren't you?"

"It's men," she said, speaking in a whisper. "I don't have what it takes to attract them."

"How do you mean?"

"Oh, I don't know. Look at me—I'm thirty-one and the only successful relationship I've ever had was over the internet. I think there must be something seriously wrong with me."

Oh, boy. Reid was stumbling into territory he had no desire to explore. It did explain why she'd sought out Dalton Gray, though. She was getting desperate and afraid, and a man, especially one she'd met online, must have seemed safe. Little did she know she was about to tangle with a tundra rat.

"I'm like everyone else. I want a husband and family but I just don't know how to attract a man."

"And that's why you're in Alaska."

She didn't confirm or deny the statement. The words fell between them, and then she seemed to gather herself emotionally, reminding him it was his turn. "What's *your* deep, dark secret?"

Reid wasn't ready to drop the matter. "Why, Jenna? I don't understand it. You're a beautiful, desirable woman." It probably wasn't good manners to admit that, especially while they were sitting in the dark, both of them a little tipsy.

"I'd rather not discuss me anymore, okay?"

That was a problem, because Reid wasn't eager to drag his private life into the open, either. "I need another drink."

"Me, too," she said. As he got up to refill their glasses, she added, "Don't think you're going to escape from telling me your secret."

He returned a couple of minutes later and they sat beside each other on the sofa, so close their shoulders touched.

"Does it have to do with being spurned by a woman?" she asked in a low voice. "Or did you commit a crime? Or—"

His nervousness made him laugh. "Not exactly. Okay, here's my secret. You asked me what I do with my free time. Well, I draw. I'm—"

"What?" she demanded, outraged.

"I said I like to draw. Especially landscapes. I—"

"You mean to say being an *artist* is your deep, dark secret?" She set aside her drink and got to her feet. "I should've known you'd pull something like this. I spill my guts, tell you how hopeless I am with men and you—you tell me you like to draw."

Reid stood, too. "Well, I'm sorry, but that really is my biggest secret."

"You're making fun of me."

He caught her by the shoulders. "I'm not. I swear I'm not. I've had a knack since I was a kid, but I never did anything with it and now… I guess I'm not ready to tell anyone because I'm not sure I'm any good, beyond having a…superficial facility, I suppose you could say." He shrugged. "I'm not ready to have my work judged."

He ran his hands over the curve of her shoulders. With all his heart he wanted her to understand he wasn't teasing her. "I draw, Jenna, and that's the honest-to-God truth."

"This is baring your soul?"

"I've never told anyone about it before." He'd fumbled this whole conversation.

"No one else in Snowbound knows? Not even your sister?"

"No one."

"Oh." Her response was the merest whisper.

His fingers relaxed against her shoulders. She felt so small and soft and utterly feminine. His pulse started to react to her nearness—the first sign he was in trouble—but he didn't break away from her. He knew he should drop his hands and back off before he did something they'd both regret. Instead he drew her closer. He refused to listen to common sense, which was ordering him to stop. Ignoring all caution, Reid lowered his mouth to hers.

Jenna leaned into him. A tiny sound came from her just before their lips touched, but for the life of him Reid didn't know if it was a sigh of welcome or a groan of protest. Either way, she was in his arms and she seemed willing enough to be there. He fully intended to follow through with this.

The instant their mouths connected, Reid swore he felt something explode inside him. Jenna must have felt it, too, because the next thing he knew, they were both sitting on the sofa again, their arms locked around each other. His fingers were in her hair, and hers were tugging at his shirt collar. It took him far longer than he wanted to collect his wits and move away.

Breathing hard, Jenna hung her head.

Reid was having a difficult time recovering his own breath. He thought she might want an apology, but it simply wasn't in him to find any regret.

"That shouldn't have happened," she said sternly.

Unable to speak, he simply nodded.

"That kind of…physical contact is asking for trouble."

"Right." Thankfully one of them was smart enough to recognize that. "Do you want me to apologize?" he asked warily.

She thought about it, then shook her head. "I was as much at fault as you."

Reid reached for his drink. He needed it, even more than he had the first one. As he'd told her, she'd taken ten years off his life, frightening him the way she had, and now he'd easily subtracted another ten by kissing her. If he spent much more time with Jenna Campbell, he'd be dead inside a week.

"I think the best thing I can do is go back to the bedroom. In the morning we'll both forget about this…indiscretion. Agreed?"

"Agreed." He was grateful, too, although he didn't say so.

She stood. "Um… I probably shouldn't tell you this—and my experience is pretty limited—but you're a very good kisser."

Reid didn't know if it would be proper etiquette to thank her, so again he said nothing.

She rubbed her finger across her upper lip and he realized his beard had probably grazed her tender skin. "I didn't hurt you, did I?"

"No, your mustache tickled me. That's all."

"Sorry."

"Good night, Reid."

"Good night. The storm probably won't be so bad in the morning and you can make that phone call to your mother."

"I'd appreciate it."

Just before she went into the bedroom, she stopped. "Is your artwork at the pump station?"

"Some of it."

"Would you mind showing me your pictures?"

He hesitated, then figured he might as well. "Sure."

"Thank you."

"I'll talk to you in the morning." He waited until she disappeared into the darkness of the bedroom before he lay down on the sofa. This time when he closed his eyes all he could see, feel and taste was Jenna.

Eight

Jenna woke at first light and memory came flooding back. Not only had she revealed her deepest fears to Reid Jamison, she'd welcomed his kisses. Even more damning, she'd *enjoyed* them. She'd read about people in instances such as this—instances in which captives fell in love with their captors. It was called the Stockholm syndrome. Except that Reid appeared to be as regretful over these unfortunate circumstances as she was.

She could hear him moving about the cabin and the smell of freshly brewed coffee wafted in from the other room. Jenna hurriedly dressed and combed her hair.

"Good morning," she said, entering the small kitchen.

"Morning." He kept his back to her. "Would you like a cup of coffee?"

"Please." Something wasn't right. Reid seemed to make a point of not facing her. "Reid?"

He turned then and she saw that he'd shaved off his beard. "When did you do that?" she asked, although the

real question was *why*. He was the one who'd stressed the importance of a beard for an Alaskan male.

"This morning," he barked.

"There's no need to snap at me." He was in a horrible mood, and she'd done nothing more than walk from one room to the next. "Why'd you do it?"

"Hell if I know. And it wasn't for you, if that's what you're thinking." He slapped a mug of coffee down on the table, half of it sloshing over the sides.

"Did someone get up on the wrong side of the bed this morning?" she asked in a singsong voice.

"I didn't sleep in a bed, as I might remind you."

"And why is that?" she asked sweetly. "Could it be because you offered your one and only bed to your kidnap victim?"

He scowled at her. "The storm's still raging, but we'll head out anyway."

"Can I drink my coffee first?"

"Fine," he said gruffly, stomping out of the room. He reached for his coat and shoved his arms into the sleeves. It took him another five minutes to lace up his boots and add the extra protective gear. "I'll be back in a few minutes. Be ready to go when I return."

"Yes, sir." She saluted him smartly.

He paused to glare at her. "Don't get cute with me, Jenna. I'm not in the mood for it."

"Now, just one minute." Jenna had endured enough of his temper tantrum. "I don't know what's wrong with you this morning, but I suggest you get over it. If anyone has the right to be annoyed, it's me. I'm not holding *you* hostage."

"You're not a hostage! Trust me, if I knew how to get you safely out of here, I'd do it."

"And I'd go, partying all the way."

He snorted loudly and threw open the door.

A blast of cold air enveloped her, sending a chill up her spine and spraying the room with fresh snow. Snuggling under her blankets, all warm in bed, she'd fantasized about Reid and their kisses. The charm of those few moments had been a fluke and any lingering pleasure had best be forgotten. He slammed the door, which only seemed to emphasize her decision.

Between tentative sips of hot coffee, she hurriedly dressed in her warmest clothes before Reid had any reason to change his mind about that phone call. No sooner was she finished than he came back into the cabin.

"You ready?"

"Ready," she said, echoing his clipped tone.

Reid hesitated. "Addy and Palmer saw me warming up the snowmobile." He glanced at her. "It seems Jake and Pete and the two of them plan to come over here for dinner tonight."

"I hope you don't expect me to do the cooking."

"No," he said, disgruntled. "I'll cook, but I wanted you to be aware of what they were planning."

"All right." Frankly she'd welcome the company. It would certainly be preferable to another evening trapped inside the cabin with Mr. Personality.

"Addy intends to bring his musical saw and Palmer plays the harmonica—and well, they're probably all going to want to dance with you. I just thought I should give you fair warning."

"I've been duly and properly warned."

"Good." He paused before opening the door. "You'd better take my arm. I know you'd rather not, but for safety reasons you should. Technically it isn't a blizzard

anymore, since the wind's down to thirty-one miles an hour, but it's still damn strong."

She slipped her arm through his and once outside, was grateful she had. Blizzard or not, the snow was thick and falling fast. The road was barely recognizable and drifts had formed against the sides of the house, stretching up toward the roofline.

"You okay?" Reid asked as they approached the snowmobile.

"I'm fine."

The pump station seemed to be half a world away. Driving slowly and carefully they made it, but Jenna could feel the tension in Reid. She didn't reveal her own apprehensions.

Inside the station, Reid led her into his office. The man was a constant source of contradictions. His house was an environmental disaster area, but his office couldn't be neater. It didn't stop there, either. He was unreasonable, demanding, bad-tempered and yet he'd kissed her with a gentleness that had practically melted her bones. He barked at her as if he was angry and then risked everything to get her to a phone so she could reassure her mother.

The telephone line was bad. Jenna heard heavy static as she waited anxiously for the number to connect to her mother's cell phone in California. When the first ring came, Jenna relaxed.

"Hello," the familiar voice said.

"Mom, it's Jenna."

"Jenna! Hello, honey! I was wondering when I'd hear from you. How's Alaska?"

"It's great, Mom." No need to worry her, Jenna decided.

"Why didn't you call earlier? Still, I'm glad you called now. I'm having a pedicure and you know how boring it is just to sit here." Jenna heard a little snuffling sound and realized her mother must be babysitting Bam-Bam, her neighbor's Pomeranian. Chloe found this the perfect way to have a pet—the benefits of companionship without the responsibilities of meals, vets or training.

"Well, honey," she said. "Tell me what's been going on."

Jenna hardly knew where to start.

"That Dalton friend of yours phoned," her mother announced before Jenna could tell her anything.

"Dalton called for me?" Her heart pounded crazily.

"He sounded worried."

"When was that?" Jenna pressed the phone hard against her ear, straining to make out every word.

"Oh, dear," her mother said, sighing. "I can't remember. You know how bad I am with details like that."

"Mom, I'm in Snowbound, Alaska. If Dalton phones again, tell him that right away." She glared at Reid, defying him to challenge her. She'd find her own way out of here, since she obviously couldn't depend on him.

"Snowbound, Alaska," her mother echoed. "Oh, that sounds romantic."

"Tell me everything Dalton said," Jenna insisted. He might be her only chance of escape.

"Let me think." Jenna could hear her mother tapping her fingernail against her teeth. "Well, I don't remember all of it, only that he was in Fairbanks and you weren't. We talked for a few minutes. He's very concerned about you."

"I'm with a man called Reid Jamison, Mom. If Dalton calls again, you tell him that, all right?" Reid stared at her, but he said nothing.

"Sure, honey. I'll do that. Are you having fun?"

"Yeah, Mom. Lots of fun. I just didn't want you to worry."

"Worry? Jenna, why would I do that? Well, okay, I was a *little* worried. But you're perfectly capable of taking care of yourself."

How Jenna wished that was true.

The line faded in and out. "Mom.... Mom?"

"I'm here. Oh, before I forget, Brad Fulton's new secretary called asking about you, too."

"Brad phoned?" Jenna was hardly able to take it all in. "What did he say?" she asked eagerly.

"Not Brad," her mother said. "His new secretary who, if you don't mind my saying so, isn't worth a hill of beans compared to you. She's the one who phoned."

"What did Ms. Spencer want?"

"Apparently Mr. Fulton's looking for you."

"Brad's looking for me?"

"According to Ms. Spencer, he wants you back."

Jenna bit her lower lip. She had no idea what to think—or say.

"Is there anything you want me to tell him?" her mother asked. "Because I'm sure he'll be contacting me himself."

"Oh, Mom, I don't know." Jenna had wasted years being infatuated with her boss. In all that time, Brad hadn't seen her as anything other than an efficient and capable assistant, and she suspected that wasn't going to change now. Brad viewed her the same way he would a comfortable pair of shoes. As soon as he broke in a

new pair, he'd forget about her. Besides, Brad was married to his job. He didn't need or want a wife.

The connection started to fade. "Mom?" she shouted. "Mom?"

"I can't hear you. Jenna? Jenna? You're fading out."

"Mom, I'm here."

"Oh, good, that's better," her mother said. "Okay, now what should I tell Dalton if he phones again? Oh, heavens, what was the name of that town?"

"Snowbound."

"And you're with some other man?"

"Yes, Reid Jamison."

"My goodness, Jenna, Alaska must be some kind of state. You haven't been there three days, and already you've got two men on the line. Maybe I should come up and check it out myself."

"Mom...no, don't do that."

The line went dead. Emotionally drained, Jenna replaced the receiver.

Reid stepped back and crossed his arms over his chest. "Who's Brad?"

Jenna frowned at him. "Although it's none of your business, Mr. Fulton is my former boss."

He let that information sink in. "Now I know why you hooked up with Dalton," he muttered.

She raised her eyes to meet his. "Why?"

"You're in love with your boss."

Nine

Chloe Lyman shook her cell phone in a desperate effort to hear her daughter. "Jenna. Jenna?"

Alas, there was nothing but static and then a droning sound that confirmed the connection had been severed. "Oh, drat!" Chloe pushed the button to turn off her cell. Tucking the Pomeranian more securely under her arm, she tossed the phone inside her huge purse and sat back, trying to relax. Bam-Bam snuggled close to her side.

"Everything all right?" Dolly, her nail tech, asked, coming into the spa room.

"That was Jenna."

"Oh, you heard from her?"

"I'm telling you, Dolly, I don't know what's come over that girl. It's like she hit thirty-one and decided to dive into the deep end of the pool without any swimming lessons."

"Jenna? I don't think you need to worry. She has a good head on her shoulders."

"Had," Chloe corrected.

Dolly lifted Chloe's foot out of the swirling water

and wrapped it in a fluffy white towel, propping it in her lap.

"She hasn't been in Alaska three days and already she's involved with two men."

Dolly looked up, astonished. "Jenna?"

"Not only that." Chloe dropped her voice, so none of the other women in the salon would overhear. "Brad Fulton wants her back. Apparently he's lost without her."

"He never appreciated everything she did."

"You're absolutely right!" Chloe had been saying as much for years. Jenna had refused to listen to her suggestions for luring her boss into a romantic liaison. Unlike Jenna, Chloe had never had a problem enticing men into her bed. But then again, Jenna hadn't gone through two husbands by age thirty.

"Did she meet up with the man she's been talking to on the internet?"

Chloe frowned as she mentally reviewed their all-too-short conversation. "No, she's with some other guy in a town with a funny name—something like Snow-drift. For the life of me, I can't remember what it was."

"Jenna's already got two men. Wow. Alaska must be something else."

Chloe's smile was slow and thoughtful. "Three men," she reminded Dolly. "Remember Brad Fulton."

Dolly dried Chloe's foot. "I think the competition will do him good."

Chloe nodded. "You're right. As soon as I'm done here, I'm going to visit Mr. Fulton."

"I thought you were banned from the building."

Chloe sighed gustily. "That was an unfortunate mis-understanding. Trust me," she said, leaning back in the

comfortable chair. "He'll be more than happy to see me—this time."

"Two men," Dolly said in a dreamy voice. "I wonder if Jenna knows what to do with two men."

Chloe giggled. "If she's anything like her mother, she'll figure it out."

An hour later, dressed in her skimpy high heels with cotton balls between her freshly painted red toenails and the Pomeranian under her arm, Chloe Lyman clip-clopped her way through the executive lobby on the seventy-seventh floor of the Fulton Industries building.

"I'm here to see Mr. Fulton," she announced to the receptionist.

"I'm sorry, we have a no-animal policy in this office building."

"Oh," Chloe said, hating the other woman's superior attitude. "Next time I'll leave Bam-Bam at home with his mommy. But I believe Mr. Fulton will make an exception this once, especially when he learns why I'm here."

The woman frowned. "And your name is?"

"Chloe Lyman." She paused for effect. "I'm Jenna Campbell's mother."

The woman's attitude change was instantaneous. "Oh, hello…"

"Hello," Chloe smiled sweetly, letting her know there were no hard feelings despite her lack of welcome earlier.

The receptionist looked around, then lowered her voice. "Everyone misses Jenna. I do hope she's coming back soon."

Chloe played dumb. "I wouldn't know about that. Do you think Mr. Fulton would be willing to see me?"

"I'll find out right away." She pushed a button and spoke to Brad Fulton's new executive assistant.

No more than a minute later, the large double oak doors opened and an older woman bustled through. "Ms. Lyman, I believe we spoke earlier."

"We did," Chloe confirmed.

"Mr. Fulton only has a couple of minutes, but he said he'd see you."

Chloe hadn't thought for an instant that he'd turn her away. "I knew he would." She trotted after Ms. Spencer. As soon as she entered the inner sanctum, Bam-Bam growled.

"Shh." Chloe hushed the dog, who'd apparently taken an immediate dislike to Jenna's former boss.

"Ms. Lyman." Brad stood up behind his massive desk as she entered his office. "It's, uh, good to see you."

"You, too," she responded although it was a lie. She'd never cared for this man, who appeared to be utterly blind when it came to her daughter.

"I understand you have some information regarding Jenna."

"I do." She sat down in the leather chair reserved for visitors and crossed her long legs. Bam-Bam settled nicely in her lap but kept his eyes on the evil man.

"Is she in Alaska?"

"Yes."

"Did she mention where?"

"Oh, yes. It's just a small town. I bought a map and looked it up before I stopped by." She'd checked all the places beginning with "snow," which made it easy to find. "Did you know Alaska has more than three million lakes?"

"No," he returned impatiently.

"Well, it's true," she said with a little nod.

As though he recognized that he wasn't going to extract the information easily, Brad Fulton sank into his chair. He steepled his fingers beneath his chin and waited.

This was more like it. Chloe enjoyed being the center of attention and she intended to take advantage of it.

"Why Alaska?" Fulton asked.

Chloe shrugged while she dug a dog cookie out of her purse and fed it to Bam-Bam. "It might have something to do with the men there."

"Men?"

"My daughter is like most women her age. She wants a husband and family. She chose a state where she'd have any number of eligible men vying for her affections."

Fulton frowned. "Are you saying she's involved with more than one?"

"Apparently that's the case. She's already mentioned two who are interested in her." It was gratifying to see him clench his jaw.

"I see."

Chloe sighed expressively. "I don't know if she's chosen one over the other. We only spoke briefly."

Fulton stood. "Are you going to tell me where Jenna is or not?"

Chloe fed Bam-Bam a second cookie. The Pomeranian gobbled it down, all the while keeping his gaze fixed on Fulton. "Ask and you shall receive."

"I'm asking."

Chloe smiled mysteriously…and let him wait.

"Jenna's in a little town called Snowbound," she finally said. "Isn't that something? Snowbound, Alaska."

Brad Fulton pressed the button for his secretary. "Ms. Spencer," he thundered. "Have my private jet readied for me."

"Right away, sir," the secretary's faint voice returned.

"You're going after her?" Chloe was too excited to hide her feelings.

"I need Jenna."

It was all she could do to keep from clapping with delight. "Bring her home, Mr. Fulton, bring my daughter home."

For the first time since she'd entered his office, Brad Fulton smiled. "I plan to do exactly that."

"Good." With her mission accomplished, Chloe got to her feet. "Then I'll leave you to your task." She cuddled Bam-Bam in her arms and headed out the doors. Suddenly remembering, she said. "Oh—I believe she's with a man named Reid Jamison."

Fulton wrote that down. "I'll have her home within a couple of days."

"Thank you." Chloe let him know how grateful she was. "You won't be sorry."

He had that determined look about him. The last time she'd seen it, he'd had her escorted from his office. That happened the week he'd hired Jenna, but Chloe recognized it even after all these years.

"You're aware of what Jenna wants?" She probably shouldn't force the issue, but Chloe wanted it understood that her daughter's demands had to be met. If he didn't accept Jenna's terms, then he'd be wasting his time. "My daughter is looking for a husband."

"Yes." He wasn't happy about it, but he seemed willing to comply.

Chloe smiled and petted Bam-Bam's head. "Don't worry. You don't need to call me Mom."

Fulton scowled. "I have no intention of calling you anything other than Ms. Lyman."

She didn't let this bother her. "Whatever makes you comfortable... Brad."

Judging by the way his lip rose in a snarl, it might be a good idea for Chloe to make her exit. "I'll see you soon."

He muttered something about anytime being much too soon, but Chloe let it pass. Fulton was going to bring Jenna home, and that was what mattered. By Christmas she'd be mother-in-law to one of the richest men in America.

"Have a good day," she said cordially to Gail Spencer as she tripped out of the office.

"Oh, yes. Thank you so much for stopping by."

In the elevator, Chloe realized she couldn't allow her daughter to make the most important decision of her life without her mother there to guide her. She toyed with the idea of asking Brad Fulton to take her with him. But common sense prevailed. The man had never been fond of her and he wouldn't agree to fly her to Alaska. Especially if it meant they'd be in the same plane.

No, Chloe was going to have to find her own way to Snowbound. Well, she could do that. She wasn't as helpless as her five husbands—and even her daughter—assumed.

Chloe was about to show them all.

Ten

Jenna kept her hand on the telephone receiver for a moment after the connection was broken. Away from her mother for three days, and already she missed her terribly.

"You okay?" Reid asked, sounding genuinely concerned. His bad temper had disappeared the same mysterious way it'd appeared that morning.

"I'm fine... It was just so good to speak to my mother." She turned away, fearing she might embarrass them both by bursting into tears. Alaska was nothing like she'd expected. The snow didn't bother her; in fact, there was a certain beauty in that. Even the blizzard hadn't disturbed her too much. Blackie had, but she'd lived to recount the tale of her encounter with the bear.

The isolation was a shock. Dalton hadn't prepared her for that aspect of life in the forty-ninth state—the isolation and the vastness.

All her dreams of Alaska had been wrapped up in her fantasies about Dalton. They'd exchanged messages every day, and she'd let herself believe he was everything he'd claimed to be. She was beginning to suspect

he wasn't, but she refused to admit that to Reid. This was what she got for being so desperate for—what? for *love*—that she was willing to risk her whole future, just like that. Could she have been any more naive?

"You ready to go back?" Reid asked.

Jenna nodded.

Reid gave her his arm and they headed into the storm. The wind and the snow stung her face. Jenna closed her eyes and allowed Reid to lead her to the hangar, where he'd parked the snowmobile. It wasn't until she was safely inside that Reid broached the subject of her former boss.

"When you said you had trouble attracting men, you were talking about your old boss, weren't you?"

She stared outside at the swirling snow and didn't answer.

"It's fairly obvious."

"Listen, Reid, it isn't the middle of the night and we aren't sitting in the dark, drinking Scotch and sharing secrets."

"Now look who's testy."

"I have a right," she flared.

"Okay, okay, sorry I asked."

He should be.

They rode in silence all the way back to Reid's cabin. As soon as they'd pulled into the enclosure, he got off and plugged the snowmobile into the heating element. As if by magic, Addy and Palmer appeared. They were both dressed in heavy coats and hats with earflaps hanging loose.

"'Morning, Jenna," Addy said as he helped her climb off the snowmobile.

Palmer stood directly behind him. "You cooking tonight or is Reid?"

"I am," Reid barked.

"Spaghetti for sure," Addy said with a disgruntled expression. "It's the only thing he knows how to cook."

"Are you makin' it with moose meat again?"

"I'll cook with whatever is in the freezer."

"Moose," Addy and Palmer said simultaneously.

Jenna wouldn't have minded cooking for the guys, but she didn't want Reid to assume she'd willingly take over all domestic tasks.

"I'll play you a game of cribbage," she told Reid. "Loser does the cooking."

"If I win, you cook?"

Jenna nodded.

He grinned, and without his mustache and beard blocking the view, she realized he had a very nice smile. "You're on."

Addy and Palmer instantly crowded around Reid, leaving Jenna to trudge to the house alone. Reid hurried around to meet her, Addy and Palmer close behind.

"There are ways to cheat so she won't know what you're doing," Addy murmured under his breath.

"Boys." Reid whirled around to face them. "Dinner's at six. We'll see you then. Understand?"

Addy's and Palmer's mouths gaped open. "You saying you don't want us around?" Palmer asked.

"You might need our help. We watched last month when Pete beat you at cribbage. This is too important, Reid! You can't lose this time."

"Yeah, Reid," Palmer said in a pleading voice. "This is important. You can't lose."

Reid slapped them each on the back in a good-na-

tured way. "I'm saying let Jenna and me work this out for ourselves. Whatever happens, you're going to be served a mighty fine dinner."

This seemed to appease the two men. "Can't ask for more than that," Addy told his friend.

"You want us to tell Pete and Jake to come here at six?"

"Good idea."

On a mission now, both men hightailed it over to the café.

Reid helped Jenna through the snowdrifts to the cabin door. "The guys don't mean any harm," he said as soon as they were inside.

"I know. They must be tired of their own cooking."

"I don't think either of them knows how. They eat everything out of tin cans," he explained.

The image that took shape in Jenna's mind produced an instant smile. She found Reid watching her, grinning, too. She *wanted* to be angry with him for ruining her plans, but she'd discovered it was impossible to maintain her irritation for very long.

Once they'd removed their coats, hats and gloves, Reid set up the cribbage board while Jenna made fresh coffee and poured it.

"Everything's ready," he said when she brought their coffee to the table.

Jenna pulled out a chair and sat down, sipping from her mug as she surveyed the board. "Are you planning to cheat?"

"Don't need to. I beat the socks off you the last time we played."

Jenna scoffed at him. "Nothing but a fluke, my friend."

Reid pushed the cards to her side of the table. "Deal 'em and weep."

She wasn't sure how Reid managed it, but she had one terrible hand after another. He was well on his way to winning before she'd rounded the last turn.

He didn't say anything as he triumphantly planted his peg over the finish line.

Jenna muttered under her breath. "Want to play two out of three?"

"That wasn't our bargain."

"What if I said I'm not all that great a cook?"

Reid leaned back in his chair and crossed his arms over his chest. "I wouldn't believe you."

"And why not?"

He didn't hesitate. "I may only have known you a short while, but in that time I've learned something about you."

This Jenna wanted to hear. "What's that?"

Reid wore a smug look, the same look that had annoyed her earlier but now amused her. "You'd never offer to do something you weren't qualified for."

He was right.

"Do you want to check out the freezer?" he asked.

"Looks like I don't have any choice." She pretended to be disgruntled about this turn of events, but she wasn't. In truth, cooking the evening meal for practically the entire Snowbound community gave her a genuine sense of purpose.

Reid settled down with his novel while she flipped through the only cookbook he had on the shelf. It must have belonged to his mother because it was nearly thirty years old. Sorting through the recipes, she found everal that looked appetizing.

The freezer had an abundant supply of seafood, and she took out clams, shrimp, crab and scallops, plus several loaves of frozen French bread. She laid everything out on the kitchen counter to thaw.

"What are you making, or is that another one of your secrets?" He lowered his book.

"Dinner," she said.

"Very funny."

"I'm glad you're amused."

He raised his book again. "You really do have to have the last word, don't you?" he muttered.

Jenna had never realized that about herself, but suspected he was right. From this point forward, she determined that she'd make an effort to respond to any unpleasant or teasing conversation with dignity.

That decided, she set to work. She tucked a dish towel into the waist of her jeans and rolled up her shirtsleeves. She collected the rest of the ingredients, impressed by Reid's well-stocked cupboards. Onions, chopped garlic in a jar, a choice of pastas, dried herbs… The next time she looked up, she found him napping.

What a complex person Reid Jamison was, Jenna mused, studying him. Rarely had any man made her so angry. Nor had anyone ever frustrated her more. He could be arrested for what he'd done, but she'd never press charges. Despite her frequent annoyance with him, she actually *liked* Reid and enjoyed his company.

Unfortunately, his companionship wasn't the only thing she enjoyed, but she absolutely refused to dwell on their kisses. They were both eager to admit it had been a mistake, something best ignored. And forgotten. Jenna, however, had been unable to put it out of

her mind. Try as she might, the memory resurfaced at the most inappropriate times.

Concentrating on dinner, Jenna had everything cut up and ready to go, plus she'd cleaned up the cabin a bit. Nothing major. As she'd explained to Reid, she wasn't about to become his maid, but his friends were arriving and pride demanded that there be a degree of order and cleanliness. When she'd finished, it was late afternoon.

Reid watched her bustle about, which unsettled Jenna when she noticed.

"Need anything?" he asked, slowly emerging from his chair.

"Cooking wine."

He shrugged. "Any wine I have is for drinking."

"That will do."

"How much do you need?"

Jenna checked the recipe. "Just a cup."

Reid rummaged in the room's one closet and came out with a bottle of white wine. "It seems a shame to open it, then let it go to waste. Would you like some?"

"Please." Jenna was far more accustomed to wine than whiskey.

Reid poured them each a glass of the chardonnay and gave her the rest of the bottle.

"I thought we'd have a salad," she said. "Do you think Pete would have lettuce at his store?"

"Not in the wintertime, unfortunately. Fresh fruit and vegetables are almost unheard of up here for most of the year. Supplies are shipped in once during the summer and other than that, we get everything either canned or frozen with a few exceptions."

"I found onions and potatoes in the pantry."

"Those are the exceptions."

"That's too bad." Their meal wouldn't be quite the same without a Caesar salad.

"Lucy makes a nice salad from frozen veggies. You could ask her when she returns."

Reid would be flying her back to Fairbanks at the first opportunity, but Jenna sincerely hoped there'd be a chance to meet Lucy.

"You're looking thoughtful," Reid commented.

"I was thinking about Lucy and how much I'd like to talk to her."

"The storm could be over as soon as tomorrow afternoon. Do you want to wait until Lucy and Jim get home before we take off?"

She nodded immediately. "I'd like that."

"Good, because Lucy would probably have my hide if you left before she got back."

Jenna sipped her wine and as she did, another thought came to her. "Do you have any rum?"

"Rum? Do you think I run a liquor store here?"

"Sorry, I should've asked for it when I requested the wine, but it just occurred to me. My third stepfather liked rum cake and Mom used to bake one or two a month. I thought it would be a real treat for Addy and Palmer. I know the recipe by heart, but it would help if I used real rum."

Shaking his head, he returned to the closet and ransacked it noisily. Eventually he pulled out a dusty bottle, handing it over.

"I don't know how old this is," he muttered. "But it's the good stuff."

"Thanks. I'm sure it will do nicely."

She set about mixing the cake batter, using his sup-

plies of flour, sugar and liquid eggs. Working efficiently, Jenna was surprised by how contented she felt. When she glanced up, she saw Reid watching her with a pad and pencil in his hand.

"What are you drawing?"

"You."

Jenna wasn't sure how she felt about that. "Can I see?"

He shook his head. "Not yet."

"You were supposed to show me your drawings when we were at the pump station," she reminded him.

"I forgot." He moved the pencil quickly across the page, then hesitated when he realized she'd stopped her work to stare at him. "Don't let me distract you."

"You're not," she said, but he had. She wasn't one who rushed to have her picture taken; in fact, she avoided it whenever possible. A lot of people felt the camera didn't do them justice, but in Jenna's case it was true. Photographs seemed to sharpen her features and make her skin look sallow. Every shot ever taken of her was unflattering.

"By the way, what are we having for dinner?" he asked.

"Spaghetti."

"Addy and Palmer won't be happy."

"Seafood spaghetti, with an olive oil and wine base. I use lots of garlic and basil."

"This is beginning to sound interesting."

"You're going to *love* it." She brought her fingertips to her lips and gave them a noisy kiss.

His gaze lingered on her lips for an embarrassingly long moment. As though both were aware that this

could lead to danger, they studiously ignored each other.

Ten minutes later, Reid said, "Are you ready to look at my drawing? Keep in mind it's just a quick sketch."

Jenna set the cake into the preheated oven and walked over to Reid's chair by the fireplace. She stood behind it and peered over his shoulder.

"Ready?"

"Ready."

Reid turned the tablet and there she was. Only it wasn't her. Not the way she saw herself in the mirror, or even the way cameras revealed her. The woman in his drawing was soft and gracious...and beautiful.

"Well?" he asked, watching her expectantly.

"It's very nice." She left abruptly and went into the bathroom and closed the door.

As soon as she was alone, she stared at herself in the mirror. Could that really be her in the drawing? She felt like weeping—and that was even more ridiculous than racing out of the room like a frightened rabbit.

Soaking a washcloth, she pressed it to her face and took a few moments to compose herself before she faced Reid again. Heaven only knew what excuse she was going to give him.

With her hand on the doorknob, she inhaled deeply in an effort to appear calm. She'd walk back into the living room, apologize and tell him how talented he was, and indeed that was true.

She didn't get the chance. Reid was waiting for her on the other side of the door.

"What did I do wrong?" he demanded.

"You didn't do anything wrong."

"Then why did you turn tail and run?"

"Because I'm an idiot."

Reid rejected that immediately, shaking his head with vehemence.

She had nothing left to tell him except the truth. "Okay, if you must know, when you sketched me, you made me look the way I've always wanted…the way I always *hoped* to look and never have."

"You are exactly the way I drew you. I didn't make this up, you know. I draw what I see."

Nothing she said would make him understand. She began to walk away.

Reid caught her hand and pulled her back, staring at her intently. "If you want to find fault with my technique, fine, but don't criticize my eye."

"You see me as…as soft and feminine?"

"You are soft and feminine," he countered.

"Oh, Reid." She only meant to hug him in thanks, and then, without another word on the subject, walk away. But their friendly embrace quickly became more.

Reid's mouth sought hers and she turned to him, trusting and open. Their exchange the night before was only a foretaste of what awaited them now. Their kisses deepened until Jenna's head swam and her heart pounded in her ears.

"I thought you said this was a bad idea," Reid said, dragging his mouth from hers and nibbling on her lower lip.

"It's a terrible idea," she moaned as she slipped her arms securely around his neck.

"It's only going to lead to trouble." He groaned between kisses.

"Big trouble," she agreed.

He lowered his head and kissed her jaw while Jenna

ran her hands along his back. This was so wonderful. She didn't want it to stop.

All at once, with an abruptness that left her reeling, Reid pulled away. He braced his hands against the wall on either side of her, and hung his head, his eyes closed. His breathing was ragged.

She reached up to touch her lips to his.

"Jenna, stop…"

"Okay," she said. "In a minute." She slid her moist lips across his and seconds later, their mouths and tongues became involved in an erotic foray that was gentle and slow and inexpressibly tender.

"You must enjoy tormenting me," he said, and his voice was unsteady.

"Do you trust me, Reid?" she whispered, outlining his lips with the tip of her tongue.

"Yes…yes."

"Then tell me about her."

Everything ceased. He instantly straightened and nearly lost his balance. "What?"

"You didn't isolate yourself on the tundra without a reason."

"Since when did you turn into Sigmund Freud?" His eyes narrowed.

"Come on, I'm not completely naive. There was a woman in your past. One who really hurt you. Otherwise you wouldn't be living such an isolated life."

"You're so far off-base, it's unbelievable." With that he marched into the living room.

"Really?" She followed him.

"This is what I don't understand about women," Reid said, throwing himself in the chair and grabbing

his novel. "One kiss, and you suddenly think you have access to my soul."

"So she did hurt you?"

"No, Jenna, she didn't. It was a mutual parting of the ways. And it wasn't exactly a life-changing relationship. Now that's all I'm going to say about it. You got that?"

"All right," she said mildly. "Don't—"

A knock sounded at the door, interrupting her. "Anyone home?"

Pete let himself in, followed by Addy and Palmer.

"We aren't too early, are we?" Pete asked anxiously. "I'm gettin' kind of hungry."

Jenna checked her watch. It was barely five, and she had yet to start the seafood spaghetti.

"We'll go ahead and set up our instruments," Palmer said, placing an antique washboard and wooden spoon alongside his harmonica on the sofa.

"What you got in the oven?" Addy asked. He leaned his saw against the wall.

"Smells like she's cooking rum to me," Palmer said. He looked at Jenna and added, "We've had liquor for dinner before, and we like food better."

"So, we too early or not?" Pete persisted.

"Don't worry about it," Reid said, glaring at Jenna. "I'd say you arrived in the nick of time."

Eleven

Addy slurped up the remains of his seafood spaghetti with a large piece of bread, then wiped the back of his hand across his mouth. He got up to look around the table, but the large bowl was empty and Palmer had already snatched the last slice of buttery French bread.

Sighing loudly, Addy sat down in his chair again, resting his hands on his stomach. They'd rearranged the living room and were seated in a circle. The table held the food, which they'd dished up buffet-style.

"Excellent dinner," Pete added. "Thanks to both of you."

"You ever decide to set up shop, you'd put me out of business," Jake told them. Unlike the others, he'd shown up at the appointed time.

Reid gestured in Jenna's direction. "The credit all goes to Ms. Campbell. The only thing you should thank me for is my cribbage skills. Otherwise, you'd be eating moose-meat sauce with your spaghetti."

The men stared at her with something akin to awe. Uncomfortable with their scrutiny, Jenna blushed. "You guys are easy to please."

Jake scoffed at that. "Well, maybe Addy and Palmer's tastes aren't as discerning as mine, but this meal would impress royalty."

"The company wasn't bad, either," Pete added, charming her with his smile. "Snowbound needs more women. Sure wish you'd stay until Christmas. We do it big up here—the whole community gets together. You'd be very welcome."

"I'll wash the dishes." Reid leapt to his feet.

"What's the matter, Reid? Don't you agree?" Jake pressed.

"We don't need any more women in town than the one we've already got."

"Who says?" Pete demanded.

"I do." Reid carried his plate to the sink.

"What would it take to convince you to stay?" Jake asked, looking at Jenna.

"She's leaving the minute this storm lets up," Reid insisted. He jerked Addy's plate from beneath his nose.

"Let's not be hasty about flying Jenna out of here," Pete said. "Let's listen to what the little lady has to say."

Jenna was enjoying the conversation. Imagine—four men eagerly seeking her company. If only her mother was there to see it. But Chloe was several thousand miles away in Los Angeles.

"Tell them how fast you want to get out of here," Reid said, crossing his arms. He seemed mighty confident that she'd set the record straight.

"Well, I was hoping to meet Lucy before I left."

"She wants to meet Lucy," Addy repeated, sounding righteous. "That could take a day or two, and there's no telling what might happen once the women get together. Jenna could be here for a month. Or longer."

"You think Lucy could convince Jenna to stay?" Palmer asked his friend in a whisper loud enough for everyone to hear.

"Can't say, but there's always hope."

"She's leaving," Reid said again, whipping Palmer's plate away before the older man had a chance to protest. "Remember, she's off to meet Lover Boy."

This remark about her meeting Dalton appeared to please Addy and Palmer. "You'll be back," Palmer said, nodding vigorously. Addy only grinned.

Jenna stood, prepared to take her wineglass to the kitchen. "What makes you think that?" she asked.

"Dalton's got a reputation with the ladies," Jake explained. "A *bad* reputation."

Pete looked over his shoulder at Reid and lowered his voice. "He's the love 'em and leave 'em type. If you do meet up with him, just remember that."

"I'm sure you've confused Dalton with some other man." She said that to get a rise out of Reid, and it did. He glowered at her and she sensed that he found it a struggle not to comment.

"I think it's time to start up the music," Jake said quickly to his friends.

"What about the cake?" Addy's attention had been on the rum cake from the moment Jenna took it out of the oven.

"I thought we'd save that for later," she said, still full from dinner.

"How much later?" Palmer asked.

"Soon," Jenna promised, which seemed to appease the two older men.

It wasn't long before the small band had assembled. Addy played the saw, with Palmer as backup on wash-

board with wooden spoon. Pete had a fiddle. Addy started alone, holding the saw between his legs and vibrating it over his knee, creating an eerie sound. He played "Amazing Grace" so hauntingly that it sent chills down Jenna's spine. Pete's fiddle joined in, followed by Palmer's rich melodic voice as he lifted his face toward the heavens, closing his eyes. If she hadn't seen and heard it for herself, Jenna would never have believed this unusual trio could put on such a stunning performance.

When the hymn was finished, she applauded enthusiastically. "That was lovely."

"Thank you." Addy nodded once. He set the saw aside. "Now it's time for real dancing music. You ready, Pete?"

"Ready." Pete lifted the fiddle to his chin and began a lively folk tune—music that made her think of hoedowns and barn dances, not that she'd ever been to any.

Addy stepped over to Jenna, and bowed low from the waist. "Might I have the pleasure of this dance?"

Jenna smiled and gave him her hand. Addy led her to the center of the room while Jake, Palmer and Reid pushed back the furniture. When the area was clear, Addy spun her around until she was so dizzy she could barely stand upright.

Palmer stood in one corner, rhythmically stamping his foot while playing his harmonica. Soon he was the one partnering her and then Addy was dancing with Jake. Reid clapped along with the old-time country music.

Jenna found herself passed from one man to the next, until their faces started to blur.

"Enough," she cried, laughing. Bending over, hands on her knees she labored to catch her breath.

"Are we wearing you out?" Jake asked.

"Only a little." She rested for a few minutes, and then she was back, kicking up her feet with the rest of them and loving it.

Pete went from one lively song to another with barely a pause in between. Jake and Palmer taught her a country two-step, an Irish jig and several other dances. Jenna picked them up quickly, grateful for her years in ballet class. She couldn't remember the last time she'd enjoyed herself this much.

"I'm exhausted," she finally said.

"Let her take a break." Reid held her gently by the shoulders and led her to a chair.

"We didn't overdo it, did we?" Addy asked, looking genuinely concerned.

"No...not at all." Sitting down, she stretched her legs in front of her.

"You're a fine dancer," Addy said.

"Mighty fine," Palmer agreed.

"How about that cake?" Jake asked. "I've worked up an appetite."

"You sit," Reid ordered Jenna when she started to get up. "I'll get it."

"You'll need help," Addy insisted and hurried after him, Jake on his heels.

"You did say that was rum cake, didn't you?" Palmer asked, and then with only the slightest hesitation, rushed after the other men. That left Jenna and Pete alone in the room.

"You play very well," Jenna told him.

Pete sat on the sofa across from her and set the

fiddle on his lap. "Music's good for the soul," he said simply.

Jenna nodded in agreement but her eyes followed Reid in the kitchen. When she looked away, she noticed Pete studying her.

"So you've taken a liking to Reid?" Pete didn't sound surprised by this.

Jenna wasn't sure how to respond. Reid had kidnapped her, claiming it was for her own good. And yet…maybe he'd done her a favor, strange as that was to admit. There was convincing evidence that Dalton wasn't what he'd seemed; not only that, she *liked* Reid. She longed to know more about him. "Reid is an interesting man."

"Yup," Pete said. "Sure is."

"What happened to him?"

"Happened?" Pete asked, frowning.

"Why isn't Reid married?" It wasn't any of her business, but she couldn't help thinking there was heartbreak in his past.

"I don't think there's any big reason, if that's what you mean. In fact, I think Reid has the same problem we all do. He hasn't met anyone who's willing to live up here."

That answer didn't satisfy her. Reid was a determined man; if he wanted to be married, he'd do whatever was necessary to bring a woman into his life.

"You're saying a woman *hasn't* hurt him?" she asked dubiously.

Pete scratched his beard. "I can't rightly say, but I doubt it. If any woman affected him negatively, I'd say it was his mother. She abandoned Reid and his dad

when Reid was ten and his sister was six. I gather she died quite a few years ago."

"Why did she abandon her family?"

"Apparently she hated it up here. Reid's dad never got over it. She was from somewhere in Texas, I think, and she couldn't handle the cold or the isolation. Reid's father always warned him about getting involved with women from the lower forty-eight." Pete sighed mournfully. "He died last year. Reid and Lucy took it hard."

"I'm sorry about his death," she murmured.

"I think he's got a girl," Pete announced in a sudden change of subject.

This was a shock to Jenna and information she didn't take kindly to hearing. "I beg your pardon?"

"Well, Reid flies into Fairbanks every few months and he's in real good spirits when he gets back. Reid's the kind of guy who keeps his cards close to his vest, if you know what I mean."

Jenna did indeed. So there was every likelihood that Reid had a girlfriend. And what about his trip to Seattle? Did he have a woman there, too?

"Want a piece of cake?" Reid asked, carrying two plates into the living room.

"Looks mighty good," Pete said, accepting one plate.

"I'll pass," she said, scowling at Reid, jealousy burning in her eyes.

Reid's head reared back as if he'd been slapped. He scowled at her in return.

Jenna purposely looked away.

"If you ain't interested, I could do with a second piece," Addy said, rushing across the room.

"You already had two pieces." Palmer elbowed his

friend out of the way. "I'll take Jenna's piece if she don't want it."

"She might change her mind later," Reid said, taking the plate back to the kitchen.

Pete rubbed his beard again and looked regretful. "I shouldn't have said anything. Besides, I could be misreading the situation entirely. I'd hate you being upset with him because of me."

Jenna ignored the comment. "Do you know her name?"

Pete hesitated. "No, can't say I do. Maybe you should ask him yourself."

She was overreacting and knew it. But being irritated with Reid helped her control the attraction that was beginning to gain momentum between them. She *wanted* to believe he had a girlfriend hidden away somewhere. It would make leaving him a whole lot easier if she could convince herself he wasn't trustworthy.

"I'm ready for more dancing," Addy said, leaping into the center of the room. Crossing his arms over his chest, he squatted down and kicked out his left foot.

Palmer grabbed for the washboard, and Pete his fiddle.

"Addy," Reid said, his voice low and full of warning. "The last time you tried this, your back went out."

"Play!" Addy instructed, thrusting his right arm into the air like a Russian folk dancer.

Pete set the fiddle beneath his chin and started slow and easy, the tempo gradually building as Jenna, Jake and Reid clapped to the music. Addy kicked out his legs one at a time.

When the song ended, Palmer and Jake helped Addy to his feet.

Jenna applauded loudly. "Addy, my goodness! That was incredible. Where did you learn how to dance like this?"

Addy blushed with pleasure at her praise. "When I worked on the Aleutians—lots of Russians there." He wobbled for a moment. "In the old days, I did this pretty often, but my knees ain't what they used to be."

"He only does it now when he wants to impress someone," Palmer said in a whisper.

"If I was staying longer, I'd bake you your very own rum cake." Jenna kissed Addy's cheek.

"Hey, what about me and my fiddle?" Pete said. "Don't we deserve a kiss?"

"Sure you do." She kissed his cheek, too. Then Palmer's and finally Jake's.

"Don't I get a kiss?" Reid asked.

She gave him her sweetest smile and took delight in refusing him. Reid Jamison had gotten all the kisses from her that he was going to get. "No," she said sweetly.

Addy and Palmer loved it, slapping their knees and laughing with glee.

"What's so funny?" Reid demanded.

"You," Addy told him.

Grumbling under his breath, Reid glanced at his watch. "Isn't it time for you to go home?"

"It's not even nine," Addy protested. He propped his hand against the small of his back. "Then again, maybe we should."

Palmer helped Addy on with his coat.

"You might have to take the top bunk tonight," Addy told his friend.

Palmer frowned in confusion. "I get the top bunk every night."

Addy chuckled. "Oh, yes, I guess you do."

"I think we should pack up and head out," Jake said. "Mighty fine dinner, Jenna."

"Best meal I've had in months," Pete muttered as he filed past, his fiddle back in its case. "If you change your mind about staying in Snowbound, you can always move in with me." He jiggled his eyebrows suggestively.

"Jenna's leaving as soon as the storm dies down," Reid said from behind her. His voice was as cold as the air that blew in through the open door.

"Can't blame a man for trying," Pete said with a shrug. "The winters are long and lonely in Alaska."

"Longer and lonelier for some than others," Jenna added with meaning.

"'Night," Jake said.

As soon as the last man was gone, Reid closed the door. He turned to look at Jenna. "What was *that* all about?" he asked.

"What?" she asked, putting on an air of innocence.

"That last comment, for one thing."

"Oh, you mean about long, lonely nights?"

"You know damn well what I mean." Reid stared at her as if he'd never seen her before. "What the hell is the matter with you?"

"I think the question should be reversed. *You're* the one who enjoys misleading people."

"I've never misled you."

She gave a short, mirthless laugh. "I'm going to bed."

"Go right ahead," he snapped. He pointed toward the bedroom with its cracked door. "Be my guest."

"I have been your guest for three miserable days."

"Well, you don't need to worry, because we're out of here the minute it stops snowing."

Angry now, Jenna stormed into the bedroom. Just so he'd know how upset she was, she slammed the door, which was a mistake. Reid had repaired it earlier, but it wasn't up to this kind of abuse. The instant the door hit the jamb, it came apart and fell inward in two pieces.

She gasped and leaped out of the way to avoid being hit.

Reid rushed in and stared at the door in horror. "You're a crazy woman."

"Then you'd do well to be rid of me."

"Yes, I would," he said, stepping over the broken wood and marching into the other room.

A sick feeling attacked her stomach. She was being ridiculous, and all because she was jealous of some unknown woman. Reid was right—there *was* something wrong with her!

Twelve

Dalton staggered into his hotel room and fumbled for the light switch. The storm had been raging for nearly two full days, and the only solace he'd found had been in the hotel's cocktail lounge. He was charging the booze to the company, although it wasn't official business. His bar tab was likely to be higher than the bill for his room, but he didn't care. It wasn't as if Larry was going to fire him, since Dalton was half owner, anyway.

The light came on with an irritating brightness. Dalton squinted and rubbed a hand down his face. He saw that the red light on his phone was flashing. Sitting on the edge of the bed, he searched for the message button and listened.

"Dalton, it's Larry. You're gonna want to call me back. I got news on that ladyfriend of yours. The one you've been looking for."

Dalton replaced the receiver. "Ladyfriend?" he said aloud and then remembered that all his troubles could be attributed to one Jenna Campbell. She was the rea-

son he was trapped in Fairbanks—although he'd been stuck in worse places.

Dalton had done his utmost to find her, to no avail. The airlines hadn't been any help, since he wasn't a relative. With security as tight as it was, even in Alaska, he hadn't gotten a word of information out of them. In his frustration he'd turned to alcohol, and that had seen him through the worst of the storm.

He squinted at the bedside clock and dialed Larry's home number. Larry answered, sounding groggy. "Hello."

"What did you find out?" Dalton asked.

"That's a fine way to greet me after dragging me out of bed."

"As you might've guessed, I'm anxious to find out what I can about Jenna."

"Worried, are you?" Larry pressed.

He wasn't—in fact, he was ready to forget the whole Jenna Campbell mess—but his partner didn't know that. "Of course I am."

"Her mother called."

"Her mother?" This wasn't news Dalton wanted to hear.

"Yes. Apparently she heard from Jenna."

"You mean Jenna phoned her mother and not me?" This could be a problem. Jenna was turning out to be way more of a headache than she was worth.

"Aren't you curious about what she had to say?"

He was more than curious and frankly a little concerned. He didn't like the mothers of his women friends having access to him. That might cause serious trouble later on. Mothers tended to protect their little darlings.

"Dalton, have you been drinking again?"

"What else is there to do in the middle of a blizzard?" Dalton demanded. "I'm stuck here, you know."

"All right, all right."

"Just tell me what mommy had to say."

"She's on her way up to Fairbanks."

"What?" This had to be a joke. "Jenna's mother?"

"Yes, like I said, she heard from her daughter and—"

"Where the hell is Jenna anyway?"

An uncomfortable pause followed. "You're not going to like this."

Nothing was working out the way he'd planned. Just how hard was it to figure out what to do when he was a few minutes late picking her up at the airport? Couldn't she wait? "Tell me," he growled.

"Remember how you suspected Jenna might've met up with someone on the plane?"

"Yeah." He'd done everything he could think of and hadn't managed to get that information.

"Well, she did."

"Who?" He breathed the question.

"Reid Jamison."

Dalton slammed his fist against the wall, shaking his fingers to lessen the pain. He couldn't believe that of all the people in the entire state of Alaska, Jenna would link up with the one man who'd do anything to thwart him.

"Where are they?"

"At his place in Snowbound."

"He took her *home* with him?"

"Yes, and damned if I know why."

Dalton knew. He'd have done the same thing had the situation been reversed. "So Reid was on her flight?"

"I don't know, but that's my guess. A friend of mine said he goes down to Seattle every so often."

Dalton released an expletive that was best not repeated.

"Either that or——"

"She hired Jamison to fly her into Beesley," Dalton said, finishing the thought. When he was late, Jenna had immediately taken matters into her own hands. Dammit, you just couldn't count on a woman.

"Why's her mother flying up?"

"I didn't get around to asking. The lady's something of a talker, if you catch my drift."

"From what Jenna said, her mother wasn't keen on the idea of her coming up here."

"Yes, well, she didn't sound all that upset when I spoke to her."

"Really?"

"No, in fact she sounded downright excited." Larry himself sounded puzzled. "I don't know what Jenna told her, but she said she's landing in Fairbanks in the morning."

"She's coming here?"

"Yes, and I told her she should connect with you."

"Why?"

"Well, because she needs someone to fly her into Snowbound."

So Jenna's mother wanted a ride to Snowbound. This might work out, after all. Jenna was with Reid, who had as much finesse with the ladies as a bull moose. Jenna was probably more than ready to leave the isolated town, and if he were to arrive with her mother, he wouldn't have any difficulty in getting her to leave with him.

"Did she give you her flight information?" Dalton asked.

"She did."

"Good," Dalton said, searching for a pen to write it down. Yes sir, this could be very interesting indeed, he thought, wincing as he clutched it with his sore fingers. He'd sweep Jenna off her feet, and if he was lucky, he could have a fling with her mother, too. That way, potential problems became a bonus instead.

Reid was too angry to sleep. He hadn't heard a sound from the bedroom since Jenna had destroyed the door for the second time. Okay, technically he was responsible for the original break, but she was the reason the door had gotten busted in the first place.

With nervous energy, he started picking up clutter in the house, making as much noise as possible. For the life of him, he didn't know what had gotten into her. They were all having fun and then, out of the blue, she'd turned on him. He couldn't understand it.

Filling the sink with hot water and soap, he washed the dishes and set them on the counter.

"You have a lot of nerve," Jenna said from behind him.

Reid glanced over his shoulder and was gratified to see her looking furious. Her hands were on her hips, her stance was aggressive and her eyes glittered dangerously.

"What's wrong now, Your Highness? Is there a pea under your mattress?"

"You kissed me!"

"Big mistake."

"You're telling me."

"No, actually you were telling me." He did his best to sound bored, when in reality he'd lost his sense of annoyance and was fast becoming amused. "Instead of throwing insults at me, why don't you just say what's wrong and be done with it?"

"I am not insulting you."

"Okay, you're not insulting me." He could tell his being agreeable irritated her even more.

"You're the one who's insulting *me*."

Reid reached for a kitchen towel and dried his hands. "Forgive me for being dense, but would you kindly explain how I managed that?"

"I already did. You kissed me like you really meant it."

The flicker of pain he saw in her eyes surprised him. "I did mean it, Jenna. It wasn't the right thing to do, but—"

Her only response was a groan of frustration.

"You're still upset about that kiss? You kissed me, too, remember?"

"Yes—but that was before I knew about your woman friend."

"What?" All at once everything was making sense. He sighed. "Who told you that?"

"Pete, but don't blame him. I asked."

"He tell you anything else?"

"He mentioned that your mother left your father when you were a child."

Reid frowned. "Pete's got a big mouth."

"He saved me from acting like more of an idiot than I already have. I…it mortifies me now to think of the way I confided in you."

"If it keeps you away from Dalton Gray, I can only be grateful."

"That's just fine and dandy. Go ahead and have your fun. You must find me a joke—a diversion between your sojourns in Fairbanks. And Seattle."

"Come on, Jenna."

"You keep telling me what a creep Dalton is, but you're no better." She marched back to the bedroom.

A knot formed in Reid's gut. He'd never viewed Jenna as vulnerable and insecure, but he realized she was. He hadn't meant to hurt her.

The room was dark when he strolled past. "Jenna," he called from the doorway. His eyes adjusted to the lack of light, and he found her sitting on the side of his bed. She ignored him.

"Listen," he said, "Susan's an old friend. Nothing more. We have dinner when I'm in town on business, but that's it, I swear."

A pause and then, "Does she know you're an artist?"

"Like I said earlier, no one knows about that—other than you."

"Oh."

She might as well hear it all. "I don't make a habit of kissing a lot of women, either, if that's what you're thinking."

"What about your trip to Seattle? Why did you go there if not to meet a woman?"

"If you must know, I took a weeklong art course."

"Oh," she said again, her expression rather sheepish.

A moment later, she said, "You didn't tell me about your mother."

He wasn't ready to delve into that. "You didn't tell me very much about yours, either, although you've

mentioned several stepfathers. If you want to know about mine, I don't really have all that much to tell you. She died when I was sixteen. A car accident in Houston."

"She left your father, though—and she left you and Lucy."

"Yes, but that has nothing to do with you and me."

"Oh…you're probably right," she whispered.

He waited a moment and then asked, "Friends?"

"Friends," she repeated. After a short hesitation, she said, "I feel like even more of an idiot, if that's possible."

"You're not. If I heard there was a man you were serious about, I'd wonder, too—considering the way you kissed me."

"I think I should just leave…. I'm not good with relationships. I mess them up every time. I apologize. You must think I'm insecure and silly and…worse. Good night, Reid."

He wasn't sure he wanted the conversation to end here, but if they continued, he was afraid they'd just end up kissing again. Which wouldn't be a good thing, since this was not a relationship with a future. "Good night, Jenna."

He made up his bed on the sofa and lay down with his head on the pillow. A half hour must have passed. He thought he heard Jenna tossing and turning, and called out in a husky whisper, "Are you awake?"

"Yeah."

"What are you thinking?"

"I'm so embarrassed."

Reid chuckled. "Actually I'm flattered. You were jealous and I loved it."

"I feel a whole lot better now," she muttered sarcastically.

He nestled his head against the sofa arm and closed his eyes. The attempt to sleep didn't last long. "Are you still set on meeting Dalton Gray?" He suspected he wasn't going to approve of the answer.

"Yes."

"I thought so." He closed his eyes again but the images that came to mind distressed him. His eyes flew open. "Is there anything I can do to persuade you not to?"

"Probably not."

At least she was honest. "Then I won't try."

A few more minutes passed.

"Reid, the picture you drew of me, can I have it?"

"I don't think so. I'd prefer to keep it myself."

"Why?"

He didn't have an answer, at least not one he was willing to share. All he knew was that he wasn't giving it up.

"I checked with the weather people," he told her. "The storm will be gone by morning."

"How early will you be flying me out?"

She didn't say anything about Lucy, and because of everything that had happened, he wasn't going to use his sister as an excuse to delay their departure. "Addy and Palmer will have the runway cleared by first light. We'll leave soon after that."

Thirteen

Jenna was up and dressed before dawn. She dreaded leaving Snowbound. Her short time here had been the best adventure of her life, which was exactly the reason she'd left Fulton Industries. In this brief period, she'd come to consider Addy, Palmer, Pete and Jake friends. Reid, too—only she'd made such a fool of herself with him, the only sensible option was to escape as quickly as possible.

She had coffee brewed by the time Reid woke. He sat up on the sofa and stared at her as if he couldn't remember who she was.

"Coffee's ready," she said.

"Thanks." He rubbed his eyes and made a growling sound that a few days earlier would have irritated her.

"How long have you been up?" he asked.

"Not long." She brought him a steaming mug.

Reid sipped the hot coffee. "Did you sleep well?"

She hadn't, but vanity insisted he not know that. "Fine. How about you?"

"All right, I guess."

"You can have your own bed tonight."

"Right." But he didn't sound too pleased and for that matter, she wasn't either.

"The snow's stopped," she informed him, making conversation and unable to think of anything else.

He nodded. "I figured it would."

Jenna set her empty mug in the sink and carried her suitcase out to the living room. "I'm ready anytime you are."

"Why the hurry?" he asked with a frown.

"I—no reason."

"Good. If you don't have any objections I'd like to linger over my morning coffee."

Jenna murmured a response, then returned to the kitchen and sat at the table. She felt Reid studying her, which made her self-conscious. Her emotions were more confused than they'd ever been in her life.

A knock at the door startled her. Reid answered it, his blanket draped around him. Addy stood on the other side, wearing a wide grin. "Jim and Lucy just landed."

Reid turned to ask Jenna, "Do you still want to meet my sister?"

"Sure." Jenna looked away. "I don't suppose an extra hour or so would matter."

Reid turned back to Addy. "Tell Lucy I'll be bringing Jenna by in about ten minutes."

"Okay," Addy said and leaned around Reid to find Jenna. "I already told Lucy all about you and how she should try to talk you into staying. We sure did enjoy having you."

"Thank you, Addy," she said and she meant it. "Thank you for everything."

"I'll go tell Lucy," Addy said and was off.

Reid disappeared into the bathroom and reappeared

a few minutes later, completely dressed. His expression was somber and cheerless as he reached for his coat. Jenna looked around the cabin one last time before Reid opened the door.

The world outside was a pristine, sparkling white and so lovely that Jenna paused for a moment to take it all in. The landscape stretched endlessly around them, punctuated by only a few stunted but sturdy trees now flocked with snow.

Addy and Palmer had been busy shoveling a pathway between the two houses, which touched Jenna's heart. No sooner were they out the door than Lucy stepped outside to meet them.

Reid's sister was short, with long dark hair and eyes that flashed with welcome and warmth. She held out both arms.

"You must be Jenna," she said, giving her a hug. "I couldn't believe it when Jim told me what Reid had done." She admonished Reid with a scolding look that grew into a smile. "Shame on you, big brother, but thank you for bringing me a friend."

"I'm afraid I'm flying Jenna out this morning," Reid informed her briskly.

"Not before we've had a chance to chat," Lucy insisted, ushering Jenna inside. Although the cabins were relatively similar in size, the difference between Jim's and Reid's was striking. Whereas Reid's place was utilitarian and almost stark, Lucy had turned hers into a real home, with feminine touches everywhere.

"I've already made tea," Lucy said, leading Jenna into the kitchen. "Now, tell me, are you completely disgusted with Alaska? I'm going to give Reid hell for

doing such a crazy thing—kidnapping you! Rest assured he's never done anything like this before."

"Lucy, honestly, it wasn't so bad. He was planning to have me stay with you, but then you were gone and there wasn't much he could do but take me home with him. Addy and Palmer did their best to make me feel welcome and last night Reid and I had everyone over for dinner."

"Those guys are such scoundrels! They manipulated you into cooking for them?"

"Yes, but I enjoyed it. I lost the cribbage game to Reid, so I agreed to do the cooking."

"That Reid. I don't suppose he told you he's a champion cribbage player?"

"Actually, it was fine. We had a wonderful evening."

"Knowing Addy and Palmer, they probably danced your feet off."

"I didn't mind," Jenna said. "We all had a great time."

"What about Reid? I certainly hope my brother was a gentleman."

Jenna looked down at the kitchen table with its colorful woven mats. "Reid was…wonderful."

Lucy sat across from her. "*How* wonderful?" she asked in a low voice.

Jenna didn't answer right away. "Well, you can imagine how I felt at first. I was furious."

"And rightly so."

"Then the storm hit, and there was nothing to do but make the best of it. He…wasn't so bad once I got to know him."

"My brother isn't someone who freely shares a lot about himself."

Jenna nodded. She barely knew Lucy, but she desperately needed a friend she could confide in. "Oh, Lucy, I'm afraid I made a complete fool of myself."

Her declaration was met with silence, a comforting pat on the hand and a question. "Do you want to tell me about it?"

"Oh…this is almost too embarrassing."

Lucy jumped to her feet, fists on her hips. "Reid didn't seduce you, did he?"

"No, no! It was nothing like that, but we did…kiss, and then later Pete told me that Reid flies down to Fairbanks to visit a woman and I assumed—"

"I can imagine what you assumed."

"Well, then I was jealous and silly and I confronted him as if it were my business, which it isn't. He could have six women stashed away, but it's none of my concern."

"He doesn't. If you're talking about Susan Webster, I can assure you she's just a friend of ours. There's no romantic relationship with her or anyone else. If there was, I'd know about it."

"If he's so private about his affairs, how would you?"

"He's my brother and if his heart was involved, he'd either leave to be with the woman in question or—more likely—find a way to convince her to join him here. Jim did. I would never have considered living in such an isolated location. Jim offered to move to Fairbanks, but I knew how much he cares about his job. Still, I didn't arrive with the best attitude." She paused, meeting Jenna's eyes. "Over the last year I've come to love it in Snowbound."

Jenna could understand that. In this brief time, she'd

grown to appreciate Reid and the tiny tundra community.

"Addy, Palmer and the rest treat me like a queen," Lucy continued. "Now that I'm pregnant, they're more protective than ever. I can only imagine how spoiled this baby's going to be with five honorary uncles."

Jenna smiled. "They want me to stay, too."

"I know. If I thought I could convince you, I'd certainly try."

It was now or never and Jenna had to ask. "Will you tell me about Dalton Gray?"

Lucy looked down, but not before Jenna saw the flash of pain in her eyes. "It's probably better if I don't."

"Why?"

Lucy sighed audibly. "You've got to form your own opinion of Dalton and you can't do that until you meet him for yourself."

Jenna had expected a scathing report on the other man. But Lucy refused to say one ugly word about him, despite her obvious distress. "You're right. I should at least meet him."

Lucy nodded. "You're an intelligent woman. You can come to your own conclusions—but be cautious. Dalton can seem very persuasive. That's all I'm going to say."

"Now," Jenna said, eager to learn more about Lucy, "How did you meet Jim?"

The sweetest smile lit her face. "Reid thinks he introduced us, but we actually met before that. I was living in Fairbanks and was at the library with a friend. Arlene caught sight of Jim and said he looked more interesting than any book we were likely to find."

Jenna smiled.

"He did, too, but when it came to meeting decent men, I didn't have much of a track record."

"I don't either," Jenna muttered.

"Well, anyway, I urged Arlene to go ahead and talk to him, but she'd just met this really wonderful guy and wasn't interested."

"So you went up and introduced yourself?" Jenna would never have had the courage, but she was sure that was what Lucy must've done.

"No," Lucy said, shaking her head. "I couldn't, although I wanted to in the worst way."

"Jim came up and introduced himself?"

"No." Lucy giggled. "I told Arlene that if I was supposed to meet him, then I would. I believe that things happen for a reason, I really do. Anyway, Arlene and I left the library. She had her bike and I drove, but when I went out to the car, the engine wouldn't start."

"And Jim rescued you?"

"I wish. No, some other guy did as Jim walked blindly past me. Of course, I imagined he was on his way to meet a girl. I could see it all in my mind, which made me feel like a fool after he was gone. I'd let a golden opportunity slip through my fingers and wanted to kick myself."

"But you did meet him eventually." That much was obvious.

"Yes, but it was weeks later. I kept thinking about him. I didn't know his name so I thought of him as 'the guy from the library.' I made countless trips back, hoping I'd run into him and of course I didn't, because I was trying to *make* it happen."

Jenna supposed she was doing something similar with this Alaskan adventure—trying to shape her fu-

ture…and perhaps trying too hard. But her seat on the flight from Seattle had been beside Reid's, so maybe things did happen for a reason, as Lucy said. Granted, she'd wasted all those years being infatuated with Brad Fulton, but that was behind her now.

"Then I got angry with myself for not having the courage to talk to Jim when I'd had the chance," Lucy went on. "Here I was, pining after a guy I'd never even met. But I'd had that glimpse of him and felt—I don't know how to explain what I felt."

"A sense of connection?" Jenna suggested.

"Yes. I did, Jenna, I really did, and then…nothing. I didn't see him anywhere. I didn't dare tell anyone, because it sounded like I'd lost my mind. I gave up. It seems crazy now when I think about it, but I sort of figured I was never going to find the right guy."

Jenna nodded, feeling much the same way. She was falling for Reid, although any hope of a relationship seemed unrealistic. And Dalton—well, she'd certainly learned enough about him, all of it bad.

"Go on," she told Lucy.

"Then one day," Lucy continued, "I was grocery shopping. I was outside in the parking lot when Jim drove past me in his car. I nearly dropped everything. He was in a vehicle that identified him as an Alaska Park Ranger. When he saw me, he stopped, put the truck in Reverse and drove back to where I stood. He rolled down his window and just looked at me."

"No!" Jenna burst out delightedly.

"I swear it's true. Then he grinned the biggest grin I'd ever seen and said he knew he'd eventually find me."

"Find you? You mean he'd been looking for you, too?"

"Yes! Oh, Jenna, it was the most magical, wonderful moment of my life."

"He remembered you from the library?"

"Yes, and he was furious with himself for not talking to me then. He had a second chance when he left the library and saw the other guy helping me with my car. He told me in the parking lot that he'd already let two chances go by and wasn't going to lose a third opportunity, which was why he stopped."

"You started dating then?"

"Yes, but we knew we were meant to be together. That was the scary part. Jim had just gotten stationed in Snowbound, and that was where Reid was. My brother had told me he wanted me to meet his friend, and I'd made all kinds of excuses. But Reid didn't pressure me, and besides, Jim hadn't been all that interested in meeting me, either."

"You mean to say that all along it was Jim he wanted you to meet?"

Lucy nodded. "It didn't take us long to figure that out, and then we decided we should just go along with Reid's plan to introduce us and let him think he was responsible for getting the two of us together."

"How long was it before you realized you were in love with Jim?"

Lucy blushed. "A month. I knew from the beginning that I could fall in love with him, but after one month together, I was sure of my feelings for him. Very sure."

"You left everything familiar and moved to a town where you'd be the only woman."

"Yes. At first, after Jim and I decided to marry, I didn't think about anything except being with him, but closer to the wedding I felt terrified. It isn't like I

can call and get an appointment for a haircut up here. Or run to the library." They both smiled. "The most mundane activities often require weeks of planning. Then there's the fact that I live twenty-four/seven with a group of burly men who don't have much appreciation for the niceties of life."

That would give Jenna pause, too. "But in the end you decided marrying Jim was worth it."

"Yes, and it has been. I got over my resentment—and my fear—about living so far from anywhere and now I absolutely love it. Snowbound's my home."

"Don't you get lonely?"

"Dreadfully. I miss my friends, but we made certain agreements before the wedding."

Addy and Palmer had explained that to Jenna. "Once a month you visit civilization."

"Yes, and I return a happy woman. Now that I'm expecting a baby, I'll probably make the trip every two weeks or so."

It was difficult to tell that Lucy was pregnant except for the happiness she sensed in the other woman. Given the opportunity, Jenna knew she could be good friends with Lucy. Unfortunately she was about to leave.

"Will you keep in touch?" Lucy asked. "No matter what happens with Dalton—or Reid?"

"Of course."

"If you need anything or just want to talk, you know where to find me."

"Oh, Lucy, what a warm, generous soul you are."

The other woman sighed. "I wish we had an entire day together. Are you *sure* you want to go? You'd be welcome to stay with Jim and me if you wanted. I'd love it, and it might give you time to clear your head."

Jenna was tempted, but she declined. Clearing her head was important, but she couldn't do that unless she got away from Reid.

"Do you want my advice?"

Jenna grinned. "You've already given me good advice—by example."

"What?"

"I'm going to take a hands-off approach the way you did."

"This could be very interesting," Lucy said, obviously satisfied at the prospect. "Very interesting indeed."

"I've decided that whatever *should* happen *will* happen," Jenna told her. "Just like it did for you."

Fourteen

Chloe stepped out of the jetway and into the interior of the Fairbanks airport. The trip had been long and gruelling, and she was badly in need of sleep and something edible, since airline food wasn't. She could only hope that Jenna appreciated the sacrifice she was making on her behalf.

The information she'd gotten from Brad Fulton's secretary assured Chloe that she could reach Jenna before Brad did, but she'd had to catch the red-eye out of LAX. It was imperative that she talk to her daughter before Jenna's former boss arrived.

Jenna needed motherly advice, and after five failed marriages, no one was better qualified to advise her than Chloe.

Slinging her purse over her shoulder, she looked around. She hadn't spoken directly to Dalton Gray, but his partner, Larry Forsyth, had promised her Dalton would be at the airport to pick her up. Since he'd already abandoned Jenna, Chloe didn't hold out much hope of Dalton's showing up.

"Are you Jenna's mother?" A tall, lean man with bloodshot, blue eyes approached her.

Well, speak of the devil. He must be over forty. This man would never do for her daughter; Chloe recognized that in a flash. "Chloe Lyman," she said sweetly, extending her hand, "and you must be Dalton Gray."

Dalton seized her fingers and raised them to his lips. "At your service."

"Exactly where is this place called Snowbound?" Chloe demanded, unimpressed by his hokey charm and fake gentility.

"About a ninety-minute flight from here."

"I need sustenance. Maybe, oh, a yogurt or a chai tea or something."

"I thought you wanted me to fly you into Snowbound?" Dalton said testily.

"I do, but first I *must* have food. They don't serve anything decent on planes these days."

"Okay, fine," Dalton agreed, muttering.

"Where's the closest restaurant?"

"Restaurant? You're joking, right? All we have open at this time of the morning is the cafeteria."

"A cafeteria?" Chloe shuddered at the thought

"That's the only place available, but from what I hear, the food's edible."

"You don't eat there yourself?"

"Not if I can help it," he said.

Chloe sighed. He led her to the baggage claim area, and she stood back and let him collect her five bags.

"Five suitcases," he whined. "Just how long were you intending to visit?" He tucked the smallest of the cases beneath his arm.

"Be careful with that," she snapped, "I've got my

yoga tapes in there." In an effort to be helpful, she took her cosmetics bag.

"You aren't going to find a yoga class in Snow-bound," he muttered.

"Don't talk down to me. I'm sure they have a VCR. After the trip I've had, I need peace and serenity."

He started to mutter something else, but Chloe wasn't interested. She was hungry, had gone without her morning chai and had taken an instant dislike to the man her daughter hoped to marry.

While Dalton took care of her luggage, Chloe followed the signs directing her to the cafeteria. It went without saying they wouldn't have soy milk, and, she soon discovered, no chai or yogurt either.

She slid the orange plastic tray along the steel bars and looked through the pitiful display, choosing a brownish banana, decaffeinated coffee and a bran muffin. The cashier added up her total, which came to a ridiculous amount, although Chloe didn't bother to complain. It wouldn't do any good.

"Have a nice day," the gentleman said pleasantly.

"Thank you." This was the first cordial greeting she'd received in Alaska.

She sat close to the entry, so Dalton would see her when he returned. No sooner had she found a table and added skim milk to her coffee than he was back.

"Dalton Gray," the cashier called. "Did you ever find your friend?"

Dalton turned to the other man. "How'd you know I was looking for someone?"

"Because she was in here asking about you."

"You spoke with my daughter?" Chloe was instantly on her feet. "When was that?"

The older man contemplated the question. "Oh, it must've been three or four days ago now. I hooked her up with Reid Jamison, who agreed to fly her into Beesley."

"My poor baby." Chloe scowled at Dalton. She felt like hitting that…that low-rent Romeo over the head with her purse. He had some nerve luring Jenna to Alaska and then abandoning her.

"You sure about this, Billy?" Dalton demanded.

"Positive. She came in here looking lost and asked me if I knew you. I told her I did, but that I hadn't seen you around in a while. I suggested she get a hotel room for the night and search for you in the morning, but she didn't want to do that."

"Why not?" Dalton cried. "It would've saved me a lot of grief if she had."

"Well, she was afraid she wouldn't know where to look, which is true. She had your address in Beesley and said if she could find a way north, you'd eventually show up there."

"Jenna is too smart for her own good," Chloe muttered. "That sounds just like her. My daughter wouldn't rest until she achieved her goal."

"So you're the one who hooked her up with Reid Jamison," Dalton said in a low growl. "Thanks a lot."

"Yes," the other man returned. "She seemed a little hesitant about going with him, but I convinced her she didn't have anything to worry about. Reid's a good guy."

"And I'm not?" Dalton protested.

"I wouldn't know about that," Billy fired back, "but I've heard plenty."

"Lies," Dalton insisted. "Are you ready, Ms. Lyman? I don't think we should delay. Jenna needs us."

"Jenna can take care of herself," Chloe assured him. "At least until I've finished my coffee." She could see this didn't please Dalton, but she really didn't care.

Fifteen minutes later, Dalton escorted Chloe to the tarmac where his plane was parked. Never in all her years would Chloe have believed she'd voluntarily fly in such a contraption. Somehow she managed to climb onto the wing and into the seat. This feat, she was convinced, could only be attributed to practicing yoga.

Once she was belted into place, she waited for Dalton to finish loading her suitcases. Chloe couldn't imagine what Jenna had been thinking when she flew up to meet this dreadful man.

As soon as Dalton was inside the plane, he put on a headset and handed her one, then began talking to the control tower.

Chloe waited until he was finished. "Can I speak to my daughter through this?" she asked him.

"No."

Well, fine.

"Not to worry, Ms. Lyman, we're going to rescue Jenna. If Reid Jamison has so much as touched a hair on her head, I'll personally beat the hell out of him."

It wasn't what Reid Jamison had done to Jenna that he needed to worry about, Chloe mused. It was what *she* intended to do to *him*—after he'd safely delivered her to her daughter, of course. She didn't know yet what punishment she could bestow but she'd think of something. One thing was certain; he had a snowball's chance in hell of getting within thirty feet of Jenna.

Reid glanced toward the house, where Lucy and Jenna had been sequestered for the last hour.

"What could two women who'd never met before today have to talk about?" he asked Jim.

"Don't have any idea," Jim muttered. He leaned back in his chair inside the park station office and Reid felt his friend's scrutiny. "So," Jim said, "how'd it go?"

Reid lowered his eyes. "All right, I guess. We didn't murder each other."

"No. In fact, since the last time I saw you, there seems to be a big change of attitude on both your parts."

Reid didn't confirm or deny his friend's assessment.

"The two of you were holed up together for how long?"

"Long enough," Reid said.

"Long enough for what? For you to start liking her—or more?"

Reid wasn't willing to discuss his feelings with Jim. The other man was a good friend, but Reid had yet to define what he felt for Jenna. That would take time he didn't have. In a little while, he was flying her back to Fairbanks, and what she did after that was none of his business. Or so he reminded himself.

"Addy said the two of you had the whole gang over for dinner."

"We didn't actually have much of a choice," Reid said with a grin.

"Invited themselves, did they?"

Reid nodded. "As I recall, you've had more than one of those impromptu parties yourself." He looked out over the runway where his Cessna 182 sat, fueled and ready for takeoff.

"It seems to me you don't want her to go," Jim said quietly.

Reid tensed. "Am I that transparent?"

"Not to everyone. I know because I felt the same way myself whenever I had to leave Lucy. The question is, what are you going to do about it?"

Reid had spent most of the night reflecting on his situation. "What *can* I do?"

"You could ask her to stay."

"Why would she stay?" Reid asked.

"Because of you," Jim said. "Give her the option, at least."

Slowly, Reid shook his head. "She came here to meet Dalton, and she's determined to do it."

"Then let her. We both know what he's like. It won't take Jenna long to get the lay of the land when it comes to Gray. You need to make sure you're around afterward, though."

This was something else Reid had thought about during the night. "In other words, I'm supposed to hang around Fairbanks or Beesley, and hope she'll come to me once she's recognized Dalton for the rat he is?"

Jim considered that, then shrugged. "More or less."

"But I work *here*."

"You're saying she has to come to you?"

Reid didn't like it, but that was the truth.

"In that case, she might just go back to California."

Reid didn't like that, either, but it could be the best solution all around. "She might."

Jim shook his head. "That doesn't bother you?"

"She's better off in California."

Jim's eyebrows shot up. "Really?"

"She'd be away from Dalton."

he'd finished the preflight check, he taxied away from the hangar.

Before he had a chance to change his mind, he removed his earphones and set them in his lap.

Jenna stared at him. "What's wrong?"

"Nothing," he said, "I have something to say and I'm not sure I can do this right. First, I'm sorry for bringing you here. Like I said a few days ago, it wasn't the most brilliant idea I've ever had, although I want you to know my intentions were good." He paused. "If you wanted, you could probably have me arrested and—well, that's up to you."

"I'm not pressing charges, Reid."

"Thank you," he said solemnly. "I have to tell you that it goes against everything in me to take you back to Fairbanks when I know you're going to link up with a no-account bastard like Dalton Gray."

"Reid—"

"I know, I shouldn't have said that, but it's how I feel." He replaced the earphones and was taxiing toward the end of the runway, when there was an unexpected transmission. Abruptly he cut the engine and returned to the hangar.

"What is it?" Jenna asked.

"I should just take off and be done with it," he muttered.

"Be done with me?" she challenged.

"No," he countered. "Another plane's about to land."

"Here?"

He nodded.

He watched as understanding dawned. "Dalton?"

He nodded again. "He's got a passenger."

"A passenger? Who?"

"Apparently, it's your mother."

Fifteen

"My mother!" Jenna repeated in shock. "What's she doing here?"

Reid expelled his breath. "How would I know?"

"There's no need to snap at me."

He didn't respond.

"Dalton's flying her in?" Jenna wanted to be sure she was clear on this.

"That was him on the radio," Reid said. "Apparently Lover Boy's coming to collect you."

"Stop calling him that."

"Yes, Your Highness."

"You're deliberately trying to irritate me and I refuse to let you."

Once again, he didn't respond, which was just as well. Although she claimed he hadn't upset her, it wasn't true. She was furious with him, and by all indications, the feeling was mutual—although she didn't know why. Reid didn't have a single thing to be angry about. Okay, he didn't like Dalton, but surely Dalton was more her problem than his? And in addition to

the Arctic gigolo, she had to deal with her lunatic if loving mother.

Reid taxied back to where the plane had originally been parked. Jim was outside to greet him, wearing a puzzled expression when Reid turned off the engine and climbed out.

Jenna didn't wait for him to come around to help her, knowing that in his present frame of mind he was just as likely to leave her sitting in the cockpit.

"What's wrong?" Jim asked.

"We've got company of the unwelcome variety," Reid told his friend.

"Dalton?"

Reid nodded.

"My mother's with him," Jenna inserted.

"Your mother!" Jim repeated and looked at Reid who shrugged.

The three of them stood there staring south as a speck appeared in the sky and slowly advanced toward them. Jenna's heart thundered. This was the moment she'd been waiting for all these weeks and months, but she experienced none of the anticipation she had when she'd first arrived in Alaska. Instead, a growing sense of dread filled her. And the fact that her mother was accompanying Dalton complicated everything.

The Cessna began its descent and attracted the attention of the others in town.

"Who's that?" Jake asked, coming out from his café.

"Any other women?" Pete demanded, stepping up next to Jenna.

"My mother," she whispered, and then she remembered how interested Pete had been in her when she'd landed in Snowbound. "Hands off, understand?" She

narrowed her eyes at him, letting it be known that she wouldn't approve of any flirting with Chloe.

Pete sighed forlornly. "Why is it," he muttered, "that there's a hands-off policy for every woman who comes here?"

"Depends on the hands," Palmer guffawed.

Jenna gave him a stern look. "Mom isn't staying long," she told Pete.

"Why not?" Addy asked, sidling up to Jenna. "We don't get much company in these parts."

"We could have another party," Palmer suggested.

"I think we've had all the partying we can take," Reid gruffly informed the pair, who grumbled something unintelligible.

The entire town had gathered at the airstrip by the time the Cessna landed. Jenna held her breath as the wheels touched down on the hard-packed snow. The two-seater plane came to a stop within eight feet of where Reid had parked his own Cessna.

Jenna's mother waved at her as though she were a beauty queen on parade.

Before anyone could stop him, Pete rushed toward the passenger side and held out his arm, offering her mother assistance as soon as she unlatched the door. With what appeared to be real delight, Chloe slid effortlessly into Pete's waiting embrace.

He released her with obvious reluctance.

"Jenna," her mother cried, hurrying toward her.

"Hello, Mom."

Her mother threw both arms around Jenna, clinging tight.

"What are you doing here?" Jenna asked. Show-

ing up in Alaska was the last thing she'd expected her mother to do.

"What does it look like? I've come to save you."

Save her? From what? "I don't need to be saved."

Her mother laughed. "Oh, Jenna, so much has happened. We must talk. I have lots to tell you."

"In a moment," she told her, looking over at Dalton Gray. Jenna broke away from her mother and steeled herself for the introduction. This man was the reason she'd traveled to Alaska. She'd longed to meet him, to know him and deep in her heart, she'd hoped to marry him. But that was before...

"Jenna," Dalton said reverently as he walked toward her. He held out both arms.

Jenna's stomach tensed and she watched Reid's face harden. It seemed for an instant that he was about to stop Dalton, but Jim placed his hand on Reid's shoulder, detaining him.

Before she could react, Dalton hugged her. "I have waited for this moment for three long months."

She returned his hug, but with little enthusiasm. There was no question that this man was not what he'd purported to be. She had that on good authority, and she suspected it wouldn't take him long to prove Reid and the others right.

"Tell me you're as glad to find me as I am to find you." He reached for her hand and raised it to his lips. "I've lived in horror of what might have happened to you in the last few days."

She snatched her gloved hand away. "I've been fine. Where were you?" He had to realize that if he'd been at the airport as he'd promised, none of this would've

happened. Yet he offered not a word of explanation or apology.

"I'll tell you everything later, when we can be alone." He slipped his arm around her waist, and then turned to face Reid as though flaunting her.

Jenna wrenched free from his grasp.

Dalton's face darkened with a frown. "What's wrong?"

"Nothing, but I think it's more important that I deal with my mother right now."

"Come on, everyone," Jake called. "Let's get out of the cold. I've got coffee brewing, and if anyone's hungry there's sourdough hotcakes."

While the others headed for Jake's Café, Pete unloaded Chloe's five suitcases from Dalton's plane and, with Addy's help, lugged them toward town. Out of the corner of her eye, Jenna saw him deposit the luggage at his store but didn't have the opportunity to ask why or to stop him.

Once inside Jake's place, sitting beside Palmer, Jenna realized that Reid hadn't joined them. He remained outside, talking to Jim, although Lucy was in the café, coffeepot in hand.

"It seems you're destined to stay in Snowbound," Lucy whispered as she slid past Jenna and set coffee mugs upright on the long counter. "I sometimes come over to help Jake out," she explained.

Before Jenna could respond, Dalton edged Palmer away from her. He grabbed hold of Jenna's hand with both of his. When he noticed Lucy, he hesitated, leaned close and then whispered, "I hope you didn't listen to anything Lucy had to say about me."

Jenna glared at him. "What makes you think she said anything?"

Dalton sighed as though burdened by his discomfort. "Reid and I have had troubles in the past. Lucy and I were once an item, but I broke it off, and big brother didn't take kindly to that. All I can do is hope you'll listen to my side of the story."

Out of fairness she would, but her sympathy inclined sharply toward Lucy instead of Dalton.

"Jenna," her mother whispered, sitting on the stool on her other side. "Tell me about that gorgeous man who helped me out of the plane."

"Mother," Jenna cried. "You don't want to get involved with Pete."

"Why not?" Chloe protested. "No man's been that sweet to me in years. Did you see the way he took my luggage directly to his store? I think he's attracted to me."

"Mom," Jenna said with a groan, "he's been stuck up here for months without seeing any women. He'd be attracted to—"

"Now don't insult me," her mother warned.

"I'm not insulting you, I'm worried about you."

"Don't be," Chloe said. "Besides I think he's cute in a caveman sort of way."

Jenna could see she was fast losing this argument. "I thought you wanted to talk to me."

"I do," her mother assured her, "but it doesn't have to be this very minute, does it?"

"I think we should speak privately," Dalton, who sat on the other stool, whispered. "Let's get out of here."

Jenna felt like a rubber band, being stretched and pulled from both sides. She looked out at the snowy

street, where Reid was still talking to Jim. If he cared about her at all, he'd do or say *something* to dissuade her from going with Dalton. Instead he was out there chatting with Jim as if he didn't have a concern in the world.

"Let me take you to my home," Dalton pressed. "Once we're there, I'll prove how much I love you. I want to take care of you, spoil you. But first we have to get away from all these people."

"I can't do that," she said. She longed for Reid to ask her to stay in Snowbound. Instead, he appeared willing to stand aside and allow Dalton to steal her away.

"Why can't you come?" Dalton asked, sounding hurt. "Let me make up for failing you earlier. I promise when we're through you won't have a thing to complain about. I know how to make a woman happy." What was presumably supposed to be a charming, sexy smile seemed more like a leer.

"I refuse to leave without my mother," Jenna insisted.

"Why not? She seems perfectly capable of looking after herself."

"She isn't, and I'm not deserting her for a…a rendezvous with you."

"You're angry," he said, his tone suggesting he was the injured party.

"Not angry—but you have to understand that none of this is turning out the way I anticipated."

Addy edged between their stools, and with several well-placed jabs against Dalton's ribs, managed to squeeze into the narrow space. "You want me to take Mr. Gray here outside and teach him a lesson or two?" he asked eagerly.

The thought of the older man tangling with Dalton wasn't an appealing one. "Thanks, but that won't be necessary," Jenna said, although she appreciated his eagerness to come to her defense. It was more than Reid seemed willing to do.

"You don't need to worry about me getting hurt," Addy said, dropping his voice to a whisper. "Palmer and I can handle him." He jiggled his eyebrows, as though to imply that they had their own methods of dealing with a tundra rat.

"I'm sure you can."

"Listen, old man," Dalton said, shoving Addy out of the way. "Isn't it time for your nap?"

"Dalton!" Jenna said, outraged at his treatment of Addy. "This is my *friend.*"

"Then I think you should analyze exactly who your friends are."

"Maybe I should," she said, disgusted by his selfish attitude toward her mother and now Addy.

Dalton exhaled sharply. "Jenna, please, I don't want to argue. We've barely had a chance to get to know each other. This isn't right! All I want is some time with you without a bunch of hangers-on. Surely you can appreciate that?"

"What I'd appreciate is the opportunity to deal with this situation as I see fit." Jenna didn't know what to do. Already her mother was deep in conversation with Pete. Their heads were close together and they were gazing into each other's eyes. This didn't bode well. Not only did she have to put up with Dalton, but she had to find a way to keep her mother and Pete apart.

"Leave with me now," Dalton urged, "and I'll fly back for your mother."

"I am not leaving my mother in Snowbound," Jenna said, a resolve strengthened when she viewed the lovelorn looks Chloe and Pete were exchanging.

She watched as Pete reached for her mother's hand.

"I need to get her out of here," Jenna muttered. Since Dalton only had room for two in his plane, she had no choice but to turn to Reid for help.

"Are you going to talk to her?" Jim asked Reid as they stood in the cold while Reid debated his next course of action.

"Talk to her about what?" Reid demanded impatiently. It'd taken every bit of self-control he possessed not to drag Dalton away from Jenna. For an intelligent woman, she sure seemed blind when it came to the other man. He hated the way Dalton had cozied up to her in the café, whispering in her ear. He didn't need much imagination to guess what that creep was saying, either. Apparently Addy had tried to step in, but nothing had come of it. Dalton seemed to be getting what he wanted.

If he'd left even ten minutes earlier, they would have missed Dalton entirely. Their planes would've passed each other in the skies. Now he was trapped here, watching Jenna get friendly with that…that sleazebag. Worse, Reid was forced to pretend he wasn't affected.

"Jenna's not stupid, you know," Jim said. "She'll see through him in no time."

Reid grunted noncommittally.

"Talk to her," Jim advised again.

"About what?" Reid asked, just as he had earlier.

A disgusted look came over his friend's face. "I can

tell you what to do but not what to say. That's got to come from you."

Great. What *could* he say to Jenna? He'd tried before takeoff, but it hadn't made any difference.

Reid wasn't going to beg Jenna to give him and Snowbound a second chance. He'd already said as much as he felt capable of saying. He'd told her how difficult it was to take her into Fairbanks, knowing he'd be delivering her to Dalton. What he *hadn't* said was how badly he wanted her to stay in town. He hadn't realized it himself until he taxied down the runway. The dread had built up inside him until he didn't know how he could stand to leave her in Fairbanks. With Dalton. But then Dalton had come here instead....

The café door opened and Jenna walked outside.

"Looks like the decision's been taken out of your hands," Jim said.

Reid wasn't amused.

"Can we talk a moment?" Jenna asked him.

"Sure." His heart felt as if it had lodged in his throat.

The café door slammed, and Reid glanced up to see Dalton Gray following in Jenna's wake.

Reid stepped forward to meet them both.

"I want to talk to you," Dalton shouted, pointing a thick finger at Reid's chest.

Reid wished he could shove the guy's teeth down his throat.

"Got a problem, Dalton?" he asked.

"No, I do," Jenna said, moving between them. "Dalton's plane will only take one passenger, and I can't leave my mother behind."

"So you're going with him?" Reid had hoped she'd

be sensible enough to recognize what kind of man Dalton was. Sadly, that didn't appear to be the case.

"Of course she's going with me," Dalton said, and slid his arm around Jenna's shoulder.

Jenna tried to shake it off, but Dalton's arm tightened.

"It seems to me Jenna would rather not have your arm around her," Reid said between gritted teeth.

"Are you afraid she prefers me to you?" Dalton smiled.

Reid bit down hard to keep from letting the other man know how much he'd enjoy seeing him in pain.

Jenna managed to shrug off Dalton's arm. "Would you two stop it? I'm ready to go, but I won't unless my mother's with me."

All right, if that was what she wanted, then Reid wasn't going to refuse her. But he had no intention of delivering Jenna to Beesley. He hadn't been willing to do it earlier and he wasn't willing now. Mother or no mother. "I'll fly you back to Fairbanks."

"Jenna's flying with me," Dalton insisted.

That was fine by him, but Reid wanted no part of it. "Then the deal's off."

"Reid," she pleaded. "I can't leave my mother here."

"Then don't go." There, he'd said it.

"You're being ridiculous. I can't stay here, and neither can my mother."

"If anyone flies Jenna out of here, it'll be me," Dalton said again.

Reid's gaze locked with Dalton's.

"She wouldn't be in this predicament if you hadn't dragged her here against her will." Dalton took one step closer to Reid.

"You want to make something of it?" he said, his voice low and menacing, fists clenched.

"You bet I would."

"For the last time, would you stop this nonsense?" Jenna shouted. Her right hand was planted against Reid's chest and her left against Dalton's as she strained to keep them apart. "This is idiotic! All I want is to get my mother back to Fairbanks."

Reid removed her hand. "I'll be more than happy to fly you both. I'm the one with the four-seater plane."

"The hell you will," Dalton shouted. He skirted around Jenna to take a wild swing at Reid.

It was sad to see Dalton's attempt go so far off the mark. Reid had been waiting for this moment too long to be denied, and immediately retaliated. His aim was far more direct and his fist made instant contact with Dalton's jaw. The other man reeled from the force of the impact and stumbled back several steps. Reid's hand hurt like hell, but that was a small sacrifice for the satisfaction of seeing Dalton Gray land on his ass in the snow.

"Now look what you've done," Jenna cried, dropping to her knees beside Dalton. Her eyes were full of tender concern. "Are you all right?"

"He's fine," Reid answered for him.

"That was despicable." Jenna focused her gaze on Reid with such intensity, he felt it burn straight through him.

All he'd done was defend himself. Dalton had thrown the first punch. It wasn't his fault the man was so inept.

"He sucker-punched me," Dalton accused, still in a sitting position and rubbing his jaw.

"No way. You swung first." Jim moved forward and offered Dalton his hand. "Seems to me you got what you deserved."

Standing, Dalton continued to massage his jaw, and his eyes narrowed on Reid. "You're going to pay for this. Come on, Jenna, let's get out of here."

Jenna stared at the sky, and when she spoke her voice was quiet and controlled. "Not without my mother."

"Unfortunately," Lucy said, joining them, "your mother is currently occupied."

"With Pete?" Jenna cried. She closed her eyes. "I had a feeling this was going to happen."

"Why don't you come back to the house with me," Lucy invited, "and leave the men to settle this among themselves."

Reid sincerely hoped she'd agree to that, and with his sister doing the talking, maybe they'd all listen to reason.

"All right," Jenna said, although she sounded reluctant. "But I've got to check on my mother first." She started walking backward, holding Reid's gaze. "Don't hurt Dalton, understand?"

Dalton took exception to that comment. "I can take care of myself," he snarled.

"Don't worry about Dalton," Reid said.

"This is something of a predicament," Jim murmured after the women had left.

"It wouldn't be if Reid hadn't kidnapped my woman."

Reid felt his temperature rise. "Jenna might be a lot of things, but 'your woman' isn't one of them. She doesn't belong to you."

"She will soon enough," Dalton said with confidence.

"I wouldn't count on it."

"She's a woman, isn't she?" His smile struck Reid as coldly reptilian. "Women like me. Lucy certainly did." Now it was Jim who advanced on him, and Dalton quickly got in a second dig. "She couldn't keep her hands to herself. Couldn't get enough of me."

"Keep Lucy out of this," Reid shouted.

"My turn," Jim said, and stepping forward, raised his fists. Dalton swung and Jim easily stepped aside. Apparently Dalton hadn't learned his lesson the first time and took a punch square in the stomach. Eyes wide with disbelief, he doubled over.

Jim shook the pain out of his hand. "Damn, that felt good."

"Jenna's mine," Dalton managed to choke out. "It'll give me even more pleasure to take her to bed, knowing you're sweet on her—and knowing she chose me over you."

Reid wasn't going to respond to his taunts. The man seemed to be looking for a fight; given his experience of the past few minutes, Reid couldn't figure out why.

"I suggest you drop this now," Jim said to Dalton, coming between the two of them.

"Don't worry," Reid assured his friend. "If he wants Jenna so badly, he's welcome to her."

"You lose!" Dalton's voice was smug. "Because Jenna wants me. Why else would she uproot her entire life to come to Alaska? Do you think she'd do anything so drastic if she wasn't serious about me? It's me she came to meet and it's me she'll fly out of here with." His face showed his contempt. "Get used

to it, Jamison. You're a loser. You always have been and you always will be." With that he sauntered away.

Jim waited until Dalton was out of earshot, staring at Reid as though he couldn't believe what he'd heard. "You don't mean that about Dalton being welcome to Jenna."

"I do," Reid said. "If she can't see the truth by now, then she never will. Or at least not until it's too late."

"Have faith in her," Jim urged.

Reid wished he could.

Sixteen

"Are you comfortable?" Pete asked Chloe as he brought her a fresh cup of tea.

"Oh, yes." Chloe sank into the large chair, resting her feet on the ottoman. He'd placed a blanket over her lap and seemed intent on pampering her. They'd come here, to his residence at the back of his quaint little store, to talk privately, which was impossible at the café with everyone pestering them.

"I don't understand why my daughter's in such a hurry to leave," Chloe complained. "I just got here."

"Exactly." Pete lowered himself into the chair across from her. "Tell me about yourself."

Chloe believed in getting the bad news over with first. "I've been married five times," she said abruptly.

"*Five* times?"

"I just can't seem to get it right."

"Perhaps you haven't found a man who'll love you the way you deserve to be loved," Pete suggested.

She could have kissed him for that remark alone. "No, it's my own fault. I keep marrying the wrong man."

"Maybe it's time you found the right one."

Good idea, but Chloe seemed to have difficulty making the distinction. "They're not as easy to find as you might think."

Pete got up and perched on the ottoman, gazing up at her. "Perhaps you've been looking in the wrong places," he said.

Seeing him there, his face so full of adoration and concern, Chloe was beginning to think he might have a point. "Tell me about you," she said, sorry now that she'd brought up the subject of her five failed marriages. "How did you end up in Alaska?"

"I was working on the pipeline, same as Addy and Palmer."

"But that was finished twenty years ago."

"Even longer now, but I liked Alaska and I drifted around from town to town, seeking a little corner of my own. A friend of mine had this store and wanted out. He made me an offer I couldn't refuse and I'm happy here—except for one thing."

"Yes?" she breathed softly.

"I need someone to share it with."

"Oh?"

Pete leaned closer to her. "Now, I realize we haven't known each other long...."

Chloe checked her watch. "We've been together all of forty minutes."

"That's long enough for me. I'm positive you and I could make each other happy. *Very* happy."

"Oh, Pete." Chloe's hand fluttered to her throat. "You don't even know me."

"I know you're a good mother."

"I try, but Jenna's actually the capable one."

"Reid's in love with her."

Her daughter had more men than she could handle, it seemed. "Reid, that big burly man who stood outside and ignored her?"

"That's him."

"Oh, dear, and how does Jenna feel about him?"

Pete shrugged. "Can't say. I don't know her nearly as well as I do Reid, but they spent three days together and…well, she seems smitten."

"This could be a problem."

"Why? It seems to me you'd be more inclined to stay in Snowbound if your daughter was here."

"Stay in Snowbound?" Chloe repeated, shocked by what he was saying.

"I can't let you go, Chloe. Not yet."

Her heart melted. "You're very sweet, and I have to admit that after my divorce from Greg, I'm feeling low and unloved. But you can't *possibly* expect me to live so far from civilization."

"You have to stay, because I think I'd shrivel up and die if you left me now."

That was one of the most romantic things anyone had ever said to her. Chloe smiled softly. She was flattered…and tempted…but she needed more than such a tiny town had to offer. And how could she cope with all this snow and cold? She was a California girl!

"You don't believe me, do you?"

"It isn't that. Let me be honest, Pete. This isn't the right place for me. And you and I…" She shook her head. "After a while we'd get on each other's nerves. I'm speaking from experience here."

"If you stay with me, I'd make it worth your while," he said eagerly.

Chloe couldn't help being curious. "Exactly how do you intend to do that?"

He gave her a smile that warmed her from the inside out. "Let me show you," he murmured in a sexy voice.

Whew. Chloe sipped her tea, and thought it best to change the subject before she succumbed to his undeniable charms. "I'm worried about Jenna. You don't really think she'll leave with that Dalton idiot, do you?"

"I doubt it."

"Good." But Chloe did have doubts. Over the years she'd experienced more than one lapse in good judgment. Until now, Jenna had been sane and sensible, but this flight to Alaska was completely out of character. She seemed to be following in Chloe's footsteps, which was a frightening prospect. Especially for Chloe.

"More tea?" Pete asked.

"No, thanks. I've had enough."

"I haven't." Pete knelt and once more stared up at her with adoring eyes. Slowly, sadly, he shook his head. "You *must* stay. I don't think I can bear it if you leave now."

Chloe giggled with sheer delight. It'd been so long since a man had given her this much attention. And oh, how she needed it.

"You think I'm just flirting."

"Of course you are."

"Don't be so sure…my love."

Chloe blushed. "I should go and see what's happening with Jenna."

"Now? Do you have to?"

"I'm afraid so. My daughter might need me."

"What about *my* need for you?" Pete asked.

Chloe smiled and on impulse leaned forward and kissed his cheek.

Pete's hand went instantly to his jaw. "I won't wash my face for a week."

Chloe smiled again. She'd been doing a lot of smiling in the last hour.

"Allow me to escort you to your daughter, then," Pete said. He offered her his hand and helped her up from the chair.

Arm in arm, they left the store and walked into what remained of the daylight. "It'll be dark in a couple of hours," he told her.

"That soon?"

"In Alaska we have very long nights."

"That would bother me," Chloe interjected.

"Not if you had someone to cuddle with. Then you'd barely notice."

This man made her feel sexy again—sexy and alluring. She dared not listen to his flattery, though; otherwise she'd fall into his bed and, worse, his life. That was a mistake she'd already made five times.

"I wonder where Jenna went," she muttered, glancing around.

"I'll check the café." Pete bounded next door, returning a few minutes later. "She's not there."

"Is Dalton?"

"Yes, and he doesn't seem to be in the best frame of mind."

That was good news, anyway.

"Could anyone tell you about Jenna?"

"Not to worry, she can't be far." Pete guided Chloe toward the ranger station.

Jim stepped out from his office. "We've got another plane coming in."

"Another?" Pete asked. "Who?"

"I can answer that," Chloe said confidently. This was the moment she'd been waiting for since her arrival.

"You know who's coming?" The question came from Reid, who'd joined Jim.

"Brad Fulton," Chloe announced joyfully.

"The business tycoon?" Jim looked as if he had trouble believing this.

"Her former boss?" Reid asked.

Chloe nodded, resisting the urge to crow in triumph. "It's Brad, all right. He's going to ask Jenna to marry him."

Seventeen

"Did you *see* that?" Jenna cried as she followed Lucy into the cabin. "Reid actually punched out Dalton. Of all the stupid things to do!"

Lucy giggled. "I wasn't there for the full show, but it did seem to me that Dalton swung first."

"He did." Jenna blew out an exasperated breath. "But Reid should've ignored him. Dalton wasn't even close. In fact, his swing was downright pitiful."

"Dalton got what he deserved," Lucy said, grinning, hands on her hips.

"I suspect you're right," Jenna muttered. "Do you, by any chance, still have feelings for Dalton?"

"No way." Lucy shook her head. "I'm so over him you wouldn't believe it. I learned a harsh lesson because of him. I can honestly tell you that when I look at Dalton Gray I don't feel anything but contempt." She chewed on her bottom lip for a moment. "I've said more than I intended. You need to make up your own mind about him."

Jenna mulled over what she'd seen. "Reid was looking for an excuse to fight."

"Yes, I know and I apologize for that," Lucy said.

"The animosity between them has nothing to do with me. Or rather, I'm just the latest…object of contention."

Lucy turned around to face her, leaning back against the kitchen counter. "True, but it doesn't discount the fact that my brother and Dalton both want you."

"Sure they do—as a trophy." Jenna was under no illusions about this.

"It's much more than that," Lucy said with quiet certainty. "At least for Reid."

Suddenly exhausted, Jenna sat down. This hostility between Reid and Dalton was bad enough, but she had other problems. "Do you happen to know where my mother is?"

"She's with Pete at his store."

Jenna groaned. "That's not good news."

"What are you worried about? Pete's an old darling."

"That, my friend, doesn't reassure me," Jenna said. Her mother had a weakness for men. In fact, she seemed to be addicted to them—addicted to male attention and to that first, giddy flush of being "in love." Which meant she and Pete were both craving what they thought the other could provide. "I'd better find her," she said grimly.

"Let them be," Lucy advised. "You've got enough on your plate without worrying about your mother."

"*Someone* has to," Jenna insisted. "And who other than me."

"Find her then, and bring her here for tea."

Jenna was halfway to the door when she hesitated. "No, you're right. If Mom hasn't figured out men and marriage by this point in her life, nothing I do is going

to save her." For far too long, Jenna had been in the business of rescuing her mother, only this time, she had troubles of her own.

Lucy carried the teapot over to the table and Jenna sat down.

"So," Lucy said, pouring them each a cup. "This hasn't turned out the way you planned, has it?"

Jenna sagged against the back of her chair. "Not at all." Even now, this was a little difficult to admit. "The fact is, I don't like Dalton. I thought I knew him. When I agreed to meet him, I thought we shared something special. But I can see that we don't." So much for her illusions. She gave a resigned shrug. "I believed he was sensitive and artistic and—" She was interrupted by an indelicate snort from Lucy.

There was a brief silence.

"How long did you and Dalton email each other?" Lucy asked.

"Four months."

"And on that basis you decided to quit your job and come to Alaska?"

Jenna lowered her eyes. "It sounds ridiculous, doesn't it?" As she looked back on the decision, she realized this was something her mother might have done. In fact, Chloe had said so in no uncertain terms. Jenna had always viewed herself as different from Chloe—more practical, anyway—but she was forced to acknowledge that they were more alike than she would've believed possible.

"Not ridiculous exactly," Lucy said thoughtfully. "I don't know you very well yet, but this doesn't seem typical of you."

"It was—it *is* crazy. I knew it even when I made the decision to move."

"So why *did* you? Aside from Dalton, I mean."

"I felt like I had to get away from Los Angeles and—" She paused to stare down at her tea. "I was turning into a frump."

"A frump?" Lucy repeated as though she'd never heard the word before.

"My entire life revolved around my job with Fulton Industries and Brad Fulton. I was his executive assistant, and for a long time I was in love with him. Naturally I would've died rather than let him know that."

"Was he married?" Lucy sounded worried.

"In a manner of speaking. Brad's married to Fulton Industries. I finally figured out that if he hadn't noticed me in all those years, he probably never would. I was afraid I'd end up dedicating my entire life to him, and later I'd be some pathetic spinster who's always carried a torch for her boss. I want a husband and children. A family. It seemed I was constantly taking care of Brad and my mother, and there just wasn't anything left for me."

"But if you're looking for a husband, why choose to meet a man over the internet?"

"I didn't. That just sort of happened."

Lucy frowned.

"I met Dalton in a poetry chat room."

"Dalton reads poetry?" Lucy's eyes widened with disbelief.

"Somehow, I doubt it. That was all part of his deception." In retrospect, Jenna could see that he'd been lurking at the site, seeking someone naive and trust-

ing. Like a true predator, Dalton had recognized her weakness and gone in for the kill.

Heaven only knew what might have happened if she hadn't run into Reid.

"What are you going to do now?" Lucy asked.

"I…don't know."

Lucy leapt up, throwing both arms around her. "I do. Stay here! Make Snowbound a two-woman town."

"But what kind of work could I do?"

"Oh, I think we can come up with something. If you're as valuable an employee as I suspect, Fulton will keep you on. You could work for him via the internet."

The idea appealed to Jenna, although she wasn't sure she could ask Brad Fulton for any favors. "There aren't any jobs here?"

"Sure there are. Jake would like to take a day off now and then, and you could work for him. I help him out occasionally. No reason you shouldn't do that, too."

Jenna would need more income than part-time work could provide; still, she was tempted. "Where would I live?"

"At first you could stay here with Jim and me."

Jenna dismissed that out of hand. Jim and Lucy were recently married and expecting a baby, and Jenna refused to intrude on their lives.

"Just for a few days," Lucy said. "You'd be our houseguest, and once everything died down, we'd wait for Reid."

"*Wait* for your brother?"

Lucy grinned. "You'll see what I mean soon enough."

Jenna had a fairly good idea of what Lucy was talking about. She wanted Jenna to hang around town

until Reid made up his mind about her. Forget it. Jenna wasn't about to put herself in a situation where she'd be dependent on the whim of a man. Any man. Especially after years of watching her mother do exactly that.

"No," Jenna said, "I'm returning to California."

"But you can't!" Lucy told her. "You just can't."

"I don't see any other alternative. Dalton's a waste of time and Reid—" What could she say about Reid? She felt weak and disoriented just thinking about him. They'd only met a few days ago; they were essentially strangers. No, she couldn't stay in Snowbound and she had nowhere to go except back to the life she'd always known.

"Reid isn't the type to chase after a woman," Lucy warned her.

Jenna had already guessed that. "No, I don't suppose he is."

Lucy began to pace in agitation. "This isn't right! It just isn't right. You and Reid should have a chance to see if you want to be together. And I need a friend. I'm not letting you go, and that's all there is to it."

Jenna loved the determination she saw in Lucy's eyes, but it didn't solve her problems. Her bags were packed and once she retrieved her mother, she'd send Dalton on his way. As soon as he was gone, Jenna would ask Reid to fly her and Chloe back to Fairbanks. From there, the two of them could book the earliest flight home.

Home, she repeated. The word echoed in her mind, hollow and meaningless. Home to her boring, mundane life. Back to being a spectator on the sidelines of life when she so desperately yearned for love and adventure.

"Where are you going?" Lucy asked when Jenna started toward the door.

"To talk to Dalton." She offered her friend a brave smile. "It's time I told him to get out of here."

"Good riddance," Lucy said, giving her a thumbs-up.

Jenna returned the gesture.

"After that, you're going to talk to Reid?" Her look was hopeful.

Jenna nodded, but the subject of her talk with Reid wouldn't be what Lucy assumed. She opened the door and stepped outside. A buzzing noise attracted her attention, and she shaded her eyes against the sunlight as she stared into the skies. She wasn't the only one watching the approaching plane.

"I wonder who that is?" Lucy said, joining her. She, too, shaded her eyes. "Good grief, I can't remember the last time we had this much traffic."

As the plane drew near, Jenna recognized the logo and gasped. Her legs nearly went out from under her. In an effort to keep her balance, she grabbed hold of Lucy's arm. "No," she breathed, hardly able to trust her eyes.

"You know who it is?" Lucy asked.

Incapable of speaking, Jenna merely nodded.

"Am I supposed to guess?"

"It's Brad Fulton."

"Your former boss? The one you said you were in love with?"

Again Jenna nodded.

"Oh, boy," Lucy muttered, sounding depressed. "I guess I'd better get used to the idea that you're leaving Snowbound."

* * *

"Who's that?" Palmer asked Addy.

Both men stood outside Jake's Café and studied the plane. "No idea," Addy said. Life in this town had turned mighty interesting ever since Reid brought Jenna here. For many years, Addy hadn't had much use for women. Snowbound had done just fine without 'em. Then Jim had to go and get married; Addy had figured that would ruin everything. He'd been against it and tried, with Palmer's backing, to talk the park ranger out of getting hitched. Jim, however, wouldn't hear of it. Reid wasn't any help, either, seeing that the intended bride was his sister.

The day Jim brought Lucy to live in Snowbound, Addy was convinced their way of life was over, but he'd been wrong. It took a big man to admit he'd made a mistake, but Addy was willing to own up to his. Unfortunately, that was a weakness of Palmer's, who'd jump into a lake full of ice before he'd confess he'd been wrong.

But even Palmer had to admit that Lucy's arrival had been a boon to them all. She didn't say a word about how often they bathed. Nor had she asked questions that were none of her business. Women he'd been with in the past—the distant past—were notorious for wanting to know everything about him. Lucy hadn't pried into his private affairs and he appreciated that.

What she did was invite him and Palmer to dinner, and he appreciated that even more. She was a mighty fine cook, too.

"There's something written on the plane," Palmer commented, squinting up at the sky. "Can you read it?"

"You know I don't see good without my glasses."

"Then why don't you wear them?"

"Why don't you wear yours?"

"'Cause I don't."

"Well, I don't either." Palmer could be real irritating at times.

"If you wore your glasses, you could read Jake's menu." Palmer went on, refusing to drop the matter.

"Now why would I need to do that?" Addy demanded. It was a good thing he was a patient man, because there weren't many who could tolerate Palmer's annoying questions. Darn it, he was worse than the women Addy used to know. "Jake hasn't changed the menu in ten years. We both have it memorized."

"That's true," Palmer muttered. He continued to squint. "Fulton Industries," he cried triumphantly. "That's what it says on the plane."

"Fulton Industries," Addy repeated, then asked, "When was the last time we had two planes land here within an hour of each other?"

Palmer shrugged. "Never."

"That's what I thought." A promising idea was beginning to take shape in Addy's mind. Excitement coursed through him and he raised his arms in the air and shouted, "We've been discovered!"

Palmer stared at him. "What?"

"All of a sudden, Snowbound is on the map. It's turning into a tourist destination."

Frowning, Palmer scratched the side of his head.

"Don't you see?" Addy said urgently. "People are coming here in *droves*."

"We got two planes, Addy."

"Still, that's two planes more than we had a week

ago. It wouldn't surprise me if people started flying in here off of those cruise ships."

Palmer looked confused. "We're a long ways from any cruise ships."

"It's what they call an excursion. The cruise ship sends 'em to Fairbanks by train."

"Yeah," Palmer agreed readily enough. "But we're a long ways from Fairbanks, too."

"Don't you get it?" he said. He didn't know how Palmer could deny the evidence when it was right before his eyes.

"Get what?"

"That people have a hankering to visit the tundra."

"Maybe," Palmer said slowly. "But what's that got to do with us?"

"You and I are going to start a tour business. That's what."

"Touring where, Addy?"

"Here. The tundra." Sometimes his friend could be downright obtuse. "People want to see it."

Palmer scratched his head again. "There isn't anything to see out there."

"Yeah, but the tourists don't know that."

Palmer agreed with him but still seemed puzzled.

Addy was getting tired of explaining the obvious. "Do you want to be my partner or not?"

Palmer hesitated. "I think we should talk to Reid first."

Addy shook his head. Reid had a habit of squelching their ideas. The last time he'd thought of a way to make their fortunes, Reid had talked him out of it. Okay, so maybe selling genuine tundra snow wasn't

his most brilliant plan, but he kept thinking about the guy who came up with pet rocks.

"Reid's smart about these things."

"I don't have time to wait on Reid," Addy insisted, marching into the cabin he shared with his best friend.

"What are you doing?"

Addy found a piece of cardboard, then got a black felt-tip pen from the kitchen drawer. "What does it look like I'm doing?"

"Making a sign," Palmer suggested tentatively.

"Yup."

"What's it gonna say?"

Addy groaned in despair. "Just find me a two-by-four, would ya?"

"Sure, Addy."

A few moments later he could hear his partner rummaging about in the cabin's one closet. Palmer returned just about the time Addy had finished with the sign.

"Can't find one," Palmer said. "What about one of the pickets off that old fence down by the airfield?"

"Now you're thinking."

"You won't tell Jim I was the one who took it, will you?"

"Nah," Addy promised, although it wouldn't take Jim long to realize where that missing picket had gone.

Addy found a hammer and nail and attached his sign to the weathered picket. When he finished, he decided his effort looked surprisingly good.

"Where you gonna put it?" Palmer asked.

"Right outside our office," Addy told him.

"We've got an office?"

"We sure do, and it's right here." He walked outside and set up the picket directly in front of the cabin.

Anyone who happened by would read the sign that said: TOURIST INFORMATION. TUNDRA TOURS ARANGED. WELLCOME TO ALASKA!

Palmer joined him and they stood straight and tall with their sign between them. Now all they had to do was wait for the tourists to start arriving.

Eighteen

Reid viewed the approaching plane with a feeling of unease. Brad Fulton had come for Jenna. He couldn't prove that—yet—but why else would a powerful industrialist fly into Snowbound? He obviously wanted Jenna, and from what Reid could tell, she wanted him, too. So much for any romantic notions *he'd* entertained.

The Learjet landed, its wide body taking up every inch of the airstrip. The entire town had come out in the fading light of the short November afternoon to see what was happening. Everyone lined up along the edge of the strip, including Addy and Palmer, who carried some kind of ridiculous sign. Everyone except Pete. Reid frowned suddenly. Correction, everyone except Pete and Jenna's mother.

The plane door opened, and a set of stairs appeared. The business tycoon stepped forward, his face peering out. He looked around, and when his gaze landed on Jenna, he smiled.

He climbed down the stairs.

Addy and Palmer rushed toward him and planted themselves directly in his path, holding up their sign.

Fulton ignored them and walked over to Jenna. Reid wanted to groan out loud when Dalton slipped into place beside her and put his arm possessively around her shoulders.

Reid would have turned and walked away then, but he wanted to know what Jenna was going to do. Jenna had confessed that she was in love with her boss and now Fulton had arrived to claim her. He felt an immediate sense of loss.

"What are you doing here?" Jenna asked. To her credit, she'd skillfully removed Dalton's arm from her shoulders.

"I came for you," Fulton said, as though that was a foregone conclusion.

No surprise there, Reid thought.

Addy and Palmer stood a respectable two feet behind Brad Fulton, holding their sign as high as they could manage.

"Is there someplace we can go to talk?" Fulton asked. "Someplace private?"

"The café," Jenna suggested.

Fulton glanced past her to the café and sighed. "Perhaps we could talk in the jet?"

"I don't think so," Dalton said.

"Stay out of this, Dalton," Jenna snapped.

Fulton regarded Dalton with a look of disgust, and asked, "Who is this man?"

Jenna waved her hand between them. "Brad Fulton, meet Dalton Gray."

The two eyed each other suspiciously.

"We need to talk," Fulton said again, leveling his gaze on Jenna.

"Before you do, I have something to say," Dalton

insisted. He reached for Jenna's hand, got down on one knee and stared longingly into her eyes.

It was all Reid could do not to gag.

"You're the midnight sun to me," Dalton began. "You're the mysterious moon and the stars in the night sky." He waited, apparently gauging the effect of his words. When she stared at him openmouthed, he brought in the pièce de résistance. "Marry me," he declaimed.

"I beg your pardon?" Jenna said, leaning closer.

Reid held his breath. If she accepted Dalton's proposal, he wasn't sure what he'd do. It wasn't a prospect he wanted to consider.

"Marry me," Dalton repeated. "I've loved you from the moment we first shared our thoughts on the internet. I know why Mr. Big Shot is here, and that's to steal you away from me. I'm not going to let that happen."

"I don't believe you have a lot of say in the matter," Fulton said coldly. "The choice is hers."

"I'm not interested in marrying you, Dalton." Jenna didn't hesitate, and Reid had to restrain himself from cheering out loud. She did have the common sense he'd credited her with. Relief filled him, quickly followed by despair. If Jenna rejected Dalton, that was one thing, but if she left with Fulton that was another.

Fulton sent Gray a victorious smile. "You have your answer."

Dalton glared back at the other man, then turned to Jenna, his face suffused with sincerity as he got to his feet. "I refuse to take no for an answer. At least hear me out."

"There's nothing to hear," Jenna told him. "I don't mean to be cruel, but I'm not interested in any kind of

relationship with you. I came to Alaska to meet you, I have, and that's all there is to it."

Like a bad actor, Dalton struck his forehead, obviously intending to signify his grief and shock at her heartlessness.

No one appeared to notice.

"If Jenna marries anyone, it'll be me," Fulton announced.

Reid knew that was coming, but he hadn't expected the other man to propose in front of the entire community.

"Marry you?" Jenna said.

"Surely this can't be a surprise," Fulton said with a good-natured chuckle.

"I was your assistant for six years. Why are you asking me to marry you *now?*"

"I need you, Jenna," Fulton murmured. "Nothing's right without you. I want you back."

"As your assistant?"

"Yes...no. I want you, period. I didn't realize how empty my life would be without you. You've been with me nearly every day for the last six years and all of a sudden, you weren't there anymore. That was when I realized what I should always have known. I need you in my life." He looked a bit embarrassed to be declaring his feelings in front of all these strangers.

Jenna seemed on the verge of tears, and Reid strained to hear her response.

"I was in love with you for years," she whispered.

Dalton shook his head angrily. "You might've said something to me," he spat. "Take her," he muttered as if this were his decision alone. "I'm getting out of

this pathetic little burg." With that, he stalked toward the airfield.

Addy and Palmer followed him, holding up their sign. As soon as Dalton got in his plane, the two old men returned to stand behind Fulton, patiently waiting for the tycoon to acknowledge them.

"Then it's settled," Fulton said. "You'll marry me."

Reid could no longer remain silent. "Congratulations, Jenna," he said, approaching the couple.

"Congratulations?" She looked at him in a daze.

"Who's *this?*" Fulton asked.

Reid offered the other man his hand. "Reid Jamison."

Jenna gestured toward him. "Reid...flew me into Snowbound."

Fulton nodded as though that explained everything. "I see."

"For a woman who claims to have trouble with relationships, you seem to be doing all right for yourself," Reid said. "I doubt many women can claim to have received two marriage proposals within five minutes. That's quite a feat, isn't it?"

"Yes... I suppose it is," she replied distractedly.

"Congratulations, Fulton," Reid said, shaking the other man's hand.

Fulton shook his head. "She hasn't accepted my proposal yet."

Everyone looked at Jenna, anticipating, no doubt, a resounding *yes*. When she did speak, she hardly sounded like herself at all. "Where's my mother?"

"She's still at Pete's," Jim told her.

For reasons Reid couldn't explain, she turned to face him. "I need to talk to my mother."

Fulton frowned heavily. "You're asking your *mother* for marital advice?"

Jenna nodded, although, in fact, she had other compelling reasons for finding Chloe. Like getting her away from Pete—and onto a plane home.

"Do they serve anything stronger than coffee over at that café?" he asked Reid.

"Sure do," Jake said, steering the other man toward his establishment. "We got beer and wine."

Fulton marched off to the café, with Addy and Palmer directly behind him, still holding up their sign.

"I'll help you find your mother," Reid volunteered.

Jenna nodded. "Did you hear?" she said, her voice awed. "Brad asked me to marry him."

"I heard." It was difficult to conceal his antagonism, but he managed. "You'd be a fool to turn him down."

"Why?"

"Why?" Reid echoed in disbelief. "You're in love with him. You said so yourself. This is your dream come true."

"I used to think it was," Jenna said slowly. "What if I said I wasn't sure I wanted to marry Brad?"

Reid shook his head. "Why wouldn't you? He's perfect. The two of you have worked together for years. He knows you, and you know him. Besides, he's so rich you could have whatever you want."

"Money isn't everything," Jenna informed him primly.

"Maybe not everything," he agreed, "but it's a good ninety percent."

She dismissed his comment with a shake of her head. "So you think I should marry him."

"I didn't say that," he was quick to tell her.

Her face turned red, which Reid recognized as barely controlled anger. He'd seen this same look a dozen times in the last three days.

"Let me see if I've got this straight..." she began.

"You don't want to talk to me about this," Reid interrupted. "Let's find your mother."

"Right," she agreed with a sigh. "My mother's been married five times. I'm sure she'll have a simple solution to this."

In his opinion, there weren't any simple solutions, but he wasn't going to tell her that. He led the way to Pete's store, which had a closed sign in the front window. He ignored that and walked inside. "Pete?" he shouted.

Almost immediately he heard a rustling sound from Pete's living quarters in the rear of the shop. "Are you in the back?" Reid called.

"Out in a minute," Pete returned gruffly.

His words were followed by the distinct sound of a female giggle.

"Mother!" Jenna charged ahead and tore open the curtain that separated the store from Pete's private quarters.

Reid charged after her and stopped abruptly at the sight before him. Pete, wearing the most incredulously happy grin, sat up in the sofa bed. Jenna's mother sat next to him. She was clearly naked, clutching a sheet against her breasts.

"You *slept* with him?" Jenna was aghast.

"Now, sweetheart, it isn't what it looks like," her mother protested.

"The two of you are naked in bed together!" Jenna shouted. "What else could you possibly be doing?"

"Pete was just demonstrating why I should stay in Snowbound."

"He took you to bed for that? If you'd been smart enough to ask, I would've told you all he wanted was sex."

"Well, yes, I realize that, but it's really wonderful sex." Her mother blushed as she said it. "I mean…well, sweetheart, if you were more experienced, you'd know what I'm talking about. There are men and there are *men,* and well, I don't suppose there's a genteel way of saying this—but Pete is one hell of a man." She sighed expressively and rested her head against his bare shoulder.

Pete beamed with pride.

"This might not be the best time for a heart-to-heart with your mother," Reid suggested. Taking Jenna by the hand, he steered her out of the room.

Jenna pointed back at the closed curtain. "My mother went to bed with a total stranger."

"Pete's a good guy."

"He just slept with my mother!"

"I didn't say he was perfect."

Nineteen

Life had certainly taken an unexpected turn. Jenna had left Los Angeles, hoping for love and adventure in Alaska, and she'd found them—but not with the man she'd intended to meet. Now she was about to return to California. When she boarded Brad's Learjet, she would leave both her mother and her heart behind.

"You're sure this is what you want?" Lucy asked, walking out to the airstrip with her.

It wasn't, but Jenna didn't feel she had any choice. "It's what has to happen."

"I'll keep an eye on your mother," Lucy promised and hugged her, looking forlorn.

Jim slipped his arm around Lucy's shoulders.

"You're really leaving?" Palmer asked. He removed his hat with the dangling earflaps and stared down at the frozen snow as solemnly as if he were attending a funeral.

"I have to," Jenna said. She couldn't stay in Snow-bound, much as she wanted to. She needed a reason and the one person who had the power to give her that had remained silent.

"I'm going to miss you," Addy said in a low voice. He, too, had removed his hat and stared down at his muddy boots. "It isn't going to be the same without you here."

Palmer agreed with a nod of his head. "Never had seafood spaghetti that tasted better than what you cooked for us that one night."

"Me, neither," Addy said.

"Thank you." Jenna kissed Addy's forehead.

"Doesn't feel right having you leave like this... We were just getting to know you," Palmer whispered.

"I know," Jenna said and kissed the other man's stubbled cheek.

"Are you ready?" Brad asked.

Jenna gave the town a final look before she boarded the plane. She hadn't said goodbye to Reid, who'd mysteriously disappeared. The moment she'd announced she was returning to California with Brad Fulton, he'd vanished. She'd hoped he'd ask her to stay, but he hadn't. That hope refused to die, though, and she'd held out until the last possible moment.

She'd just started up the steps when Reid shouted her name. She turned to see him, her heart pounding with a mixture of dread and excitement. Hurrying toward him, she didn't bother to disguise how pleased she was.

He took both her hands in his. "I can't let you go without saying goodbye." He glanced at the plane. "Fulton will be a good husband."

"Perhaps." Jenna wasn't convinced she would marry Brad. He didn't truly love her. He was accustomed to working with her, to seeing her five or six days a week. He enjoyed the ease she brought to his professional and

private lives. That wasn't a firm enough foundation on which to establish her future.

"You *aren't* going to marry him?" Reid asked, frowning.

She hesitated, then explained. "I've agreed to come back to work for him."

His frown deepened. "But eventually you'll marry him." He made it sound like an immutable law of nature—like something that couldn't possibly *not* happen.

"I don't know." She hesitated, hoping Reid would say the words she longed to hear. When he didn't, she hung her head, defeated.

"Right," he said abruptly. "Well…"

"Jenna," Brad called impatiently from the plane's opening.

"I have to leave. Thank you," she said, putting on a brave front. "You know, when we first met, I thought you were horrible."

His grin was sheepish. "I *was* pretty detestable."

"No," she whispered and ran her index finger tenderly along his shaved upper lip. "You were wonderful. I might have made the biggest mistake of my life if not for you."

Reid dismissed that, shaking his head. "You would've seen through Dalton in five minutes. You're a lot more savvy than you realize. I should never have brought you here," he said and then with meaning added, "but I'm glad I did."

"I'm glad you did, too." Impulsively she hugged him and, for just a moment, closed her eyes and savored the feel of Reid's arms around her. It broke her heart that she might never experience this again. She

waited, her heart in her throat, for some sign that he wanted her to stay.

"Goodbye, Jenna." He stepped away from her.

"Watch out for my mother?"

He nodded, grinning. "She seems a little preoccupied."

Jenna rolled her eyes and he laughed. She took in the dear, sweet faces of her friends, then walked purposefully toward the plane.

"Jenna! Jenna!" Her mother shouted from the distance as she raced toward the plane. Pete was with her. Judging by their open coats and flapping scarves, the two had dressed quickly in an effort to catch the plane.

"Mom..." Jenna narrowed her eyes at Pete. She began to warn her mother about staying with such a man, but then changed her mind. As she'd told Lucy, Chloe was old enough to make her own decisions and live with the consequences. Jenna was through rescuing her.

"You're really leaving?" Her mother apparently hadn't believed her earlier.

"I told you I was."

Pete stood next to her, his hand at the back of her neck and his gaze, as always, adoring.

"I'm staying." They exchanged a long glance, obviously drunk on love. The only thing wrong with that, Jenna thought wryly, was the nasty hangover that came later.

"All right, Mother, stay," she said in an even voice.

"I *can't* leave," Chloe whispered, her gaze not wavering from Pete's. "I've never known this kind of happiness."

"Yes, Mother."

Chloe looked away. "I mean it, Jenna."

Jenna was sure she did. "I don't doubt you, Mom. It's just that I've heard this all before." Still, she wasn't going to list her mother's failed marriages now. More than likely, Pete didn't know a thing about any of the previous men. That was her mother's habit. She didn't see any reason to compromise a new relationship with a small thing like the truth.

"I've discovered my soul mate," her mother said dreamily.

"Of course you have."

"I mean it," she insisted. "When you fall in love, you won't be so skeptical."

That was true enough, she supposed. "You'll call me, won't you?" Jenna urged.

"She can use the phone in the office," Reid assured her.

"Thank you." Jenna offered him a grateful smile. She'd give her mother a week, two at the outside, and then Chloe would return to California, disillusioned, miserable—and cold. For two or three weeks afterward, she'd be an emotional wreck, waking Jenna at all hours of the day or night. Then, miraculously, Chloe would snap out of it and everything would go back to normal until the next man. And the next, and the man after that.

"Jenna," Brad called to her a second time. "We need to leave."

She nodded and gave each of her friends one final hug before racing up the stairs, blinded by tears.

Pete's store was closed for an entire week. Everyone in town was ready to complain, but on the seventh

day after Jenna flew out of Snowbound, the sign stated OPEN. Apparently Pete was back in business.

Reid had to admit he was curious. Who wouldn't be? No more than half an hour after the sign appeared, everyone in Snowbound found an excuse to visit. Reid wasn't the first customer of the day. Jake had beaten him by a good ten minutes. Pete was totaling up the other man's purchases when Reid entered the store.

"'Morning," Pete said, sounding more jovial than Reid had ever heard him.

Reid acknowledged the greeting with a nod.

"Anything I can help you find?" Jenna's mother asked, stepping out from behind the curtain. She looked mighty chipper herself, Reid mused.

"I was thinking of making myself a pot of chili," he said, taken aback by her bright smile.

"He'll want kidney beans and a packet of spices," Pete told her. "And add a package of toilet paper. I figure he must be nearly out." Pete had an uncanny ability to keep track of all his customers' household supplies.

"Right away." Chloe scurried behind the counter and assembled Reid's groceries.

"Chloe's agreed to be my partner," Pete explained.

"Do you want me to put this on your tab?" she asked Reid before he could ask what Pete meant. Business partner? Marriage? Or the living-together kind of partner? He wondered what Jenna would think of *that*.

"Please."

She nodded, and Pete smiled benevolently in her direction.

"So," Reid said, hoping the "partners" might give him a few more details. "How's it going with you two?"

"Fabulous," Chloe assured him.

Pete pulled her into an embrace. "Life couldn't be better."

Reid could only hope it lasted. "Do you want to phone Jenna this afternoon?" It was an innocent enough question, but he wasn't just being neighborly. He hadn't been able to get the woman out of his mind. At the end of the day, his cabin felt empty. *He* felt empty. He didn't know what he could've said or done to persuade her to remain in Snowbound. He had nothing to give her, nothing except his heart, and that wasn't enough. He couldn't compete with everything Brad Fulton had to offer.

"I probably should call Jenna," Chloe said. "She worries, you know."

"I'll drive you out to the station on the snowmobile," Pete murmured.

"See you both later, then," Reid said, and taking his purchases with him, he left. He returned to the cabin long enough to put the ingredients for his dinner in the crock pot, then hopped on his snowmobile and drove out to the pump station.

Chloe and Pete showed up early in the afternoon. He found it difficult to be around them, constantly reminded as he was of their overwhelming happiness. Reid hadn't considered his own existence bleak or dull until he saw Pete with Chloe. He felt like a man who didn't realize he was hungry until he stumbled upon a table sumptuously set for dinner.

"Would you dial for me?" Chloe asked, handing him a scrap of paper with the number.

Reid dialed and waited for the connection, then passed the phone to Jenna's mother.

"Don't you want to talk to her?" Chloe asked, not taking the receiver.

Reid did, more than he cared to admit.

"Hello?"

Her voice made him weak with longing. "Jenna?"

"Reid? Oh, Reid, it's so good to hear from you! Is everything all right with my mother?"

"Everything's fine. She's here now. Do you want to talk to her?"

"Of course, but… I'd like to talk to you, too."

"Okay. I'll give you to your mother first." He passed the phone to Chloe. It occurred to him that from the moment she'd left Snowbound, he'd been waiting for the sound of her voice. He just hadn't known it.…

Absorbed by his thoughts, Reid didn't hear anything Chloe was saying. When he did start paying attention, Jenna's mother was making plans to collect her things in California and move to Alaska permanently. Apparently Jenna was objecting and the conversation wasn't going well.

"Here," Chloe muttered, handing him back the receiver. "*You* reason with her."

Reid preferred not to be caught between mother and daughter, but he was so anxious to talk to Jenna, he disregarded his better judgment. "What's going on?" he asked.

"Mom and Pete want to get married."

"I see." Pete was holding Chloe and she'd buried her head in his shoulder, weeping quietly.

"This would be her sixth marriage," Jenna said.

"I guess practice makes perfect," he said frivolously, immediately sorry when his remark was greeted by disapproving silence.

"They've barely known each other a week." Jenna was definitely aghast. "A week! Reid, you've got to *do* something."

Reid felt at a complete loss. "I don't see how I can. They're both adults and they certainly seem compatible."

"That's an understatement if I've ever heard one," Jenna agreed with heavy sarcasm. "Besides, when my mother gets like this, it's impossible to reason with her. I'll do my best to talk her out of it when she flies down to get her things."

"Worth a try if you feel that strongly about it."

"It's the best I can do for now," Jenna muttered. "How are you?"

"Fine," he told her heartily. "What about you?"

"Good," she said after a moment.

"Are you working for Fulton Industries?"

"Yes."

She didn't sound happy or excited, and selfish as it was, Reid felt downright glad.

"How's Lucy?" she asked, changing the subject.

"Doing well." Reid hadn't talked to his sister much. Lucy and Jim were in love, and their relationship, like Pete and Chloe's, emphasized how alone he was. At this point, Reid didn't want to think about that.

"Addy and Palmer? Have they come up with any more business ventures lately?"

"Not yet."

"Oh."

"Give them time, it's only been a week."

"A week? That's all?" she asked.

"It seems longer to me, too."

The line went quiet, and Reid discovered that he'd

admitted more than he wanted to. "I guess I'd better go," he said briskly, as though he had a dozen other things he needed to be doing, when all he really cared about was talking to Jenna.

"Yeah, me, too. You'll call again?"

"If you'd like." He didn't want to appear too eager.

"Only if it's convenient," she said.

"Okay."

"Bye."

"Bye." Reid replaced the receiver and kept his hand on it for an extra moment before he realized that Chloe and Pete were watching. He cleared his throat and straightened. "It was good to talk to Jenna," he said.

Pete and Chloe exchanged glances. "So it seems," Chloe said with a knowing smile.

Twenty

Jenna received three letters from Snowbound on the same day. The first was from her mother, the second from Lucy and the third, the shortest of the three, from Reid. Jenna opened her mother's letter first.

My Darling Jenna,
I know you're upset with me, but please don't be. I'm insanely, deliriously happy. Pete is a wonderful, wonderful man. For the first time in my life, a man sincerely and utterly loves me. Because of your objections, we've decided to wait a month before applying for a wedding license. That should please you.

You assumed I'd be home by now, I know you did. I thought I'd miss California, but I don't. This is *love,* my darling daughter. Love as I've never known it with five previous husbands. I don't expect you to understand, although I'd appreciate it if you'd try. You didn't expect me to last a week in Alaska, knowing how I thrive in

the sun, but I've discovered I could be happy living in a desert as long as Pete and I were together.

I can hear all your arguments. I agree with you, it *is* too soon. You think Pete and I don't know that? You see, my sensible daughter, I've wasted almost forty years on men who were wrong for me. I knew the first time Pete took me in his arms that we were meant to be together. Scoff if you want. I can't say I'd do anything different if the situation were reversed. But in my heart I know Pete's the one and only man for me.

Everyone asks about you. Addy and Palmer are such dears, aren't they? When they heard Pete and I wanted to get married, they decided to turn their cabin into a wedding chapel. They're still trying to get a minister, though.

I'm planning on making a trip back to Los Angeles in the near future. I need to pack my things and put the house on the market. I know you're living there right now, which I appreciate, but I hope you won't mind finding a new place. With your salary increase from Brad Fulton, it shouldn't be hard.

Write me soon, and please, Jenna, try to understand. For the first time in my life, I'm truly happy.
Mom

Jenna went through the letter a second time, attempting to read between the lines to be sure Chloe hadn't backed herself into a corner and was afraid to admit she'd made a mistake. Her decision to sell the house was a shock. Throughout her five marriages,

she'd maintained her own home, a gift from her parents, refusing to give it up. Now she wanted to put it on the market. If anything, this convinced Jenna that her mother was telling the truth—she was in love.

Lucy's letter confirmed it. Her friend wrote about Christmas preparations in the town, about Addy and Palmer's wedding chapel and how everyone was amazed at the changes in Pete since Chloe's arrival. Most days the store didn't open until noon and the two of them seemed passionately involved with each other. She concluded with a discussion of the names she and Jim were considering for the baby.

Jenna purposely saved Reid's letter for last. His was a single page, written in his slanted scrawl. He, too, mentioned her mother and Pete. They appeared to be the main attraction in Snowbound. He asked about her job and told her the cribbage board was gathering dust. In the end, he said he'd be happy to hear from her. Very little of what he'd written was personal, but he added a series of comical pencil sketches in the letter's margins, depicting Addy and Palmer holding up their Tourist Information sign and decorating their wedding chapel.

Jenna searched for any hint that he missed her or was thinking about her. Well, perhaps the comment about the cribbage board. If she wanted, she could attach a lot of significance to that—which was something she couldn't afford to do.

She wrote everyone back the same day.

The next week, she wrote again and included small gifts. A shop apron for her mother, a baby blanket for Jim and Lucy and for Reid, she enclosed a new deck of cards.

Almost right away, she got two letters from Reid and

learned that mail was delivered only twice a week in Snowbound. Her mother sent word that she was coming home on December tenth to make arrangements for the house. Jenna was dying to talk to Chloe, dying to learn about her friends, but mostly she wanted to ask about Reid. She treasured his letters and read them often, sharing bits with her friend Kim, seeking her advice. Even when she knew she wasn't likely to receive a letter, she hurried home to check her mailbox.

Her mother was due to land early in the afternoon, and Jenna had agreed to meet her at the house directly after work.

"Is something bothering you?" Brad asked her at the end of the day.

They'd quickly fallen into their old routine. He hadn't brought up the subject of marriage again, and really, why should he? She was in his office the way she'd been for the past six years. Nothing had changed, except that she had a substantial raise.

"Sit down, Jenna," Brad said, motioning to the chair across from his desk.

She didn't want to get home late, not today, when she was so eager to see her mother.

"This will only take a moment," he assured her.

"All right." Pen and pad in hand, she positioned herself in the comfortable leather chair across from his massive desk.

His eyes grew serious. "You're not happy, are you?"

She opened her mouth to deny it, and then decided that would be a lie. "I miss Alaska."

"Alaska?" he repeated. "Or Reid Jamison?"

She dropped her gaze. "Both."

Brad didn't say anything for a long moment. "I thought so. You're in love with him, aren't you?"

She nodded, not trusting herself to speak.

"You haven't been the same person since you returned."

"I hope my work's still satisfactory." She hadn't been as scrupulous about details and sincerely hoped she hadn't disappointed her employer.

Brad dismissed her worries with a shake of his head. "I could see it when I flew into Snowbound. I assumed if I brought you back here you'd eventually forget him. That hasn't happened, has it?"

"I tried to put him out of my mind," she admitted. She'd tried to convince herself that her feelings for him had dwindled, but then the letters had started coming and her heart had refused to maintain the pretense.

"What are you planning to do about it?" Brad asked next.

Jenna knew the answer, although she'd delayed facing the truth. "I'm going back with my mother. I'm sorry, Brad. I'm letting you down, but this isn't working."

To her amazement, he grinned. "I know, Jenna. Don't feel guilty about it. Go, with my blessing."

Jenna leaped to her feet. Dropping the pad and pen, she blinked back tears. Until he'd pressured her for an answer, she hadn't realized how lonely she was for her friends, her mother and—above all—for Reid.

She understood now what her mother had tried so hard to tell her in letters and phone calls. Chloe had indeed found her soul mate in the unlikeliest of places, and so had Jenna. But Jenna didn't have the courage or the faith in her own judgment to follow the dictates

of her heart, to believe in her feelings. Not anymore. She knew she loved Reid and as soon as she could, was telling him exactly that.

"Go," Brad said again. "I know you're in a hurry to leave. Don't worry about giving me your two weeks' notice. And wish your mother much happiness, all right?"

"My *mother?* You want me to give my mother your best wishes?"

"Sure do." Brad chuckled. "I've let bygones be bygones." He gave her a quick, affectionate glance. "Keep in touch, Jenna. And send me an invite to your wedding."

Jenna hurriedly, joyfully, gathered up her personal effects and was out the door. She drove to her mother's house, which was in a friendly neighborhood of row houses constructed in the early 1950s. Signs of Christmas were everywhere. Lights glittered from rooftops and brightly colored bulbs dangled from trees and bushes. A Santa and reindeer were propped on the roof across the street. She saw that the front door to the house was open.

Jenna parked in the driveway and hurried inside. "Mom?"

But it wasn't her mother who came to greet her. Instead, Reid walked out of the kitchen.

"Reid?" She felt as if someone had knocked the breath from her lungs. "What are *you* doing here? Where's my mother?" Then it occurred to her that none of those answers mattered. What did matter was seeing him. She tossed her purse aside and ran into his outstretched arms.

Reid lifted her from the ground, and their mouths

met in an urgent, hungry kiss. A kiss that held back nothing, gave everything.

Jenna was weak and breathless when they finished. Her legs would barely hold her upright. Reid's large hands framed her face as his eyes devoured her in the same way his mouth had.

"Your mother's with Pete," he murmured, his voice husky.

"In Snowbound?"

"No, here. They went out to get boxes."

"Pete came with her?"

He nodded. "They couldn't bear to be apart, so he left Addy and Palmer to run the store."

"You came, too?"

He smiled, and Jenna swore it was the most beautiful smile she'd ever seen. Then he kissed her again, and finally, reluctantly, eased his mouth from hers. With what appeared to be a huge effort, he clasped her shoulders and stepped back. "Let's talk, all right?"

"Sure." There wasn't a chance in hell that she'd object.

Reid led the way into the kitchen, where they sat side by side at the small table. "I got a phone call from Brad Fulton last week."

"Brad phoned you?" This was a shock. "Why?"

"Frankly, I wondered the same thing."

"What did he want?"

Reid held her gaze. "He asked me if I was in love with you."

Her heart stopped, then started again at an accelerated pace. "What…what did you tell him?"

Reid shook his head. "It irritated me, if you want to know the truth."

Jenna bit her lower lip and looked down, trying to hide her disappointment.

"I asked if he'd called to gloat," Reid said with a humorless chuckle. "But Fulton said I'd won. You're in love with me."

"He told you that?" Jenna cried.

"Is it true?"

When she hesitated, he added, "Your mother said it, too."

"And if I am?"

"Then I think Addy and Palmer might be on to something."

"What do Addy and Palmer have to do with this?"

"Well, you know they've opened a wedding chapel. I'd like to give them some business."

Jenna stared at Reid. Unlike her mother, Jenna intended to marry only once in her life—and she wanted it all. She wanted the romance *and* the companionship, the laughter *and* the heartfelt declaration of love. She needed the sure knowledge that this man would move heaven and earth to make her his.

"Are you asking me to marry you, Reid?"

"Yes." Then he quickly said, "You came to Alaska for adventure and romance. I want to give you both, but I want our marriage to last longer than a vacation. What I need is forever." He took her hand in his and gazed into her eyes. "I love you, Jenna. I don't have anything to offer you but my heart—and an entire community that loves you and wants you back. Please say you'll marry me. Be my snow bride."

With tears blurring her eyes, she nodded.

Reid kissed the inside of her palm. "I hope you don't believe in long engagements."

"No."

"Good. Because I propose a Christmas wedding."

She was in his arms then, and Jenna knew that was exactly where she was meant to be.

Epilogue

Jenna and Reid were getting married in Snowbound on Christmas Eve. The ceremony would take place in Jake's Café, with Addy and Palmer serving as wedding consultants. Their own cabin was far too small for the expected number of guests, so they'd agreed to the restaurant instead. Thankfully Lucy and Chloe offered the two entrepreneurs lots of assistance with all the arrangements. In fact, the entire community was caught up in the wedding plans.

A couple of hours before the ceremony, Jenna stepped into the brightly lit café to look around. She was astonished by the transformation the rather mundane café had undergone. The tables had been set against the wall, covered with white tablecloths. Orderly rows of chairs had been arranged in a churchlike setting, with an aisle wide enough for Pete to escort her down. Poinsettias lined the front of the room, where a square table held a large candle, as yet unlit, and a Bible.

"I wondered if I'd find you here," Reid said from behind her.

Everyone in town was preparing for the wedding. The only two who seemed to be at loose ends were Jenna and Reid.

"It all looks so beautiful," she whispered, glancing around the room, feeling the love of her friends in every detail. Even Brad Fulton, who wasn't able to attend, had sent two cases of the best champagne and his very good wishes.

"Who's there?" Jake called, sticking his head out from the kitchen. "Hey," he muttered, wearing a cantankerous frown, "the groom isn't supposed to see the bride before the wedding."

Reid was having none of that as he gave Jenna a quick hug. "I didn't know you were so conversant with wedding etiquette."

Jake shook his head. "If I wasn't so busy, I'd chase you out of here, but I'm rolling meatballs for the reception and I don't have time for you."

"Good." Reid shared a sexy grin with Jenna.

Still mumbling under his breath, Jake returned to the kitchen.

"How are you holding up?" she asked, sliding her arm around his middle. She'd been in town a week, and was living with her mother and Pete—who'd been married, much to Addy's and Palmer's consternation, while visiting California.

"I'm doing okay," he muttered, which told Jenna he wasn't.

"Honestly?"

"No," he confessed, and leaned down to kiss the bridge of her nose. "I want you with me. Every minute we're apart is torture."

Although Jenna loved hearing it, she had to point

out that her situation these past few days hadn't been any easier. "I don't think I've ever seen my mother this much...in love. Those two—I can't believe it." She shook her head. "Oh, Reid, they're just crazy about each other."

"I'm crazy about you," Reid whispered. "My snow bride."

Jenna basked in his words. "I love you, too." She giggled, adding, "My snow man."

"I can't believe you're actually willing to marry me."

"It took you long enough to ask," she said sternly, reminding him that he'd made no effort to stop her from leaving Snowbound.

"You flew out of here and it was as if my whole world went dark."

"It *is* dark in Alaska," Jenna said, "especially in winter." In December there was barely an hour of daylight before night descended on them again.

"That's not what I mean and you know it," Reid said. "I let you leave, thinking I was better off without you, but I was wrong."

Reid couldn't come up with poetic lines the way Dalton could, but he possessed so many more of the qualities she considered important. "I felt pretty dreadful, too."

"The only reason I let you go was that I assumed you'd marry Fulton, and really, why shouldn't I think that? One of the richest men in the country came chasing after you."

"Why shouldn't you think that?" Jenna echoed. "Because, my soon-to-be husband, I'm in love with *you*."

Reid pulled her into his arms and held her close.

"Do you mind saying that again? I can't seem to hear it often enough."

The door opened, and Kim and Lucy entered. Both came far enough into the café to notice Reid and Jenna with their arms entwined and stopped cold.

"What are you two doing here?" Lucy cried.

"Together?" Kim added.

Jenna exchanged a look of longing with Reid, a look that reminded him that within a few hours they'd be together. Forever.

"Everyone was hustling and bustling about," Reid confessed. "I was only in the way."

"Me, too," Jenna told her friends.

The café door opened a second time, and Addy and Palmer hurried in, each carrying a small wicker basket filled with what Jenna assumed were wedding favors. She didn't think it would be a good idea to examine those too closely.

"You're early," Addy commented, and rubbed the side of his neatly trimmed beard. He wore his heavy boots and hat with dangling earflaps; his nose was red from the cold.

"You aren't dressed proper, either," Palmer complained, glaring at Reid. "If I'm going to wear a suit, *you* should have to."

"You're wearing a suit?" This Jenna had to see.

"He looks good, too," Addy said, nodding proudly in his friend's direction.

"It's a bit tight." Palmer reluctantly removed his heavy winter jacket. "I can't remember the last time I tried it on, but I think it'll do. As soon as the preacher finishes, I'll take off the jacket."

The suit, a bold green-and-blue plaid, looked like

something out of a fifties clown catalog. Jenna managed to squelch a laugh when she realized how hard her friends had tried to make her wedding as beautiful as possible.

"Oh, Palmer," Lucy whispered.

"He looks dapper, doesn't he?" Addy said, as if to claim credit.

"Quit talking about me," Palmer insisted. "I don't want to grab any attention away from the bride. Jenna's the one people should admire, you know." He sent Jenna an apologetic glance. "Sorry, Jenna, I didn't mean to steal your thunder. This is your big day, yours and Reid's. If you want me to change, I will," he said hopefully.

"Oh, no, Palmer, you wear your suit. I'll take my chances."

Reid reached for her hand and squeezed her fingers, letting her know he appreciated her patience with his friends.

"You're going to be a beautiful bride," Kim whispered.

"She is," Lucy agreed.

Despite herself, Jenna blushed.

"Now scoot," Lucy said, ushering Jenna out the door. "The wedding's in a couple of hours and we want to have everything ready."

"I think we have our marching orders," Reid said.

"It seems that way."

Before Jenna had a chance to object, Kim and Lucy whisked her out the door and away from Reid. She shrugged and cast him a resigned smile before the door closed.

Two hours later, with the entire population of Snow-

bound in attendance, Pete escorted Jenna down the aisle to the makeshift altar, where Reid waited. She wore a white dress that was elegant and traditional at the same time—the perfect garb for a snow bride. Chloe stood off to the right, in the front row, weeping decorously. Loud sniffling came from Palmer and Addy, who sat on the other side. Kim and Lucy were serving as maids of honor, while Reid had asked Jim to be his best man.

The flame on the candle danced and cheered as "Silent Night" played softly in the background.

Reid held out his hand. With tears of happiness blurring her eyes, Jenna stepped toward him, ready to link her life with his.

* * * * *

#1 *New York Times* bestselling author

DEBBIE MACOMBER

delivers a heartwarming story about one woman's determination to find the perfect husband this Christmas!

At thirty-three, Cassie Beaumont wants a husband and kids, and so far nothing's worked. Not blind dates, not the internet and certainly not leaving love to chance.

What other options are there? Well…she could hire a professional matchmaker. Simon Dodson has quite a reputation, but he's very choosy about the clients he takes on. Cassie's astonished when he accepts her as a client.

Claiming he has her perfect mate in mind, Simon assigns her three tasks to complete before she meets this paragon: being a charity bell ringer, dressing up as Santa's elf at a mall and preparing a turkey dinner for her neighbors—most of whom she happens to dislike. Despite a number of comical mishaps, Cassie does it all—and then she's finally ready to meet her match. But just like the perfect Christmas gift, he turns out to be a wonderful surprise!

Available now, wherever books are sold!